Also in the Dynasty Series:

THE DARK ROSE

THE MORLAND DYNASTY SERIES

BOOK 2

CYNTHIA HARROD-EAGLES

sourcebooks
landmark

Published by Sourcebooks Landmark, an imprint of Sourcebooks, Inc.
P.O. Box 4410, Naperville, Illinois 60567-4410
(630) 961-3900
Fax: (630) 961-2168
www.sourcebooks.com

Originally published in Great Britain in 1981 by Macdonald and Co (Publishers) Ltd.

Library of Congress Cataloging-in-Publication Data

Harrod-Eagles, Cynthia.
  The dark rose / Cynthia Harrod-Eagles.
    p. cm. — (Morland Dynasty ; 2)
  1. Morland family (Fictitious characters)—Fiction. 2. Great Britain—History—Henry VIII, 1509-1547—Fiction. I. Title.
  PR6058.A6945D27 2010
  823'.914—dc22
                              2010017232

Printed and bound in the United States of America.
    VP 10 9 8 7 6 5 4 3 2 1

Noises at dawn will bring
Freedom for some, but not this peace
No bird can contradict; passing but here, sufficient now
For something fulfilled this hour, loved or endured.

W.H. Auden
'Taller Today'

Then, Love, standing
At legend's ending,
Claim your reward;
Submit your neck
To the ungrateful stroke
Of his reluctant sword,
That, starting back,
His eyes may look
Amazed on you,
Find what he wanted
Is faithful too.

W.H. Auden
'Legend'

For George Reynolds, gratefully, for all the years of friendship, advice, and encouragement.

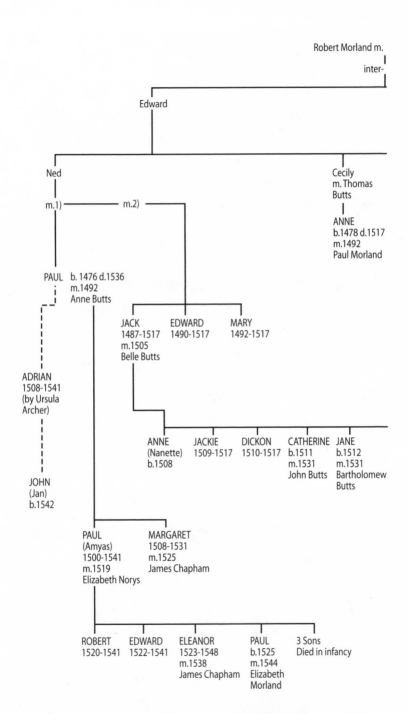

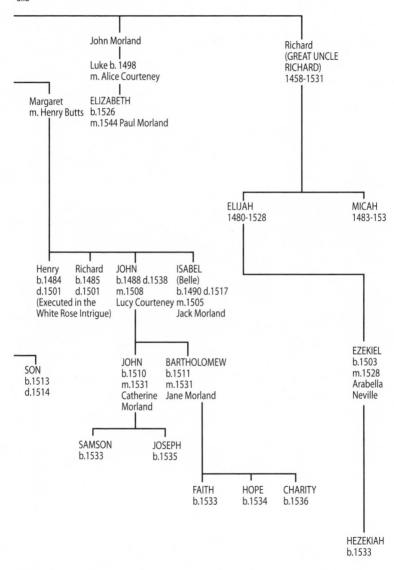

Eleanor Courteney

alia

John Morland

Richard
(GREAT UNCLE
RICHARD)
1458-1531

Luke b. 1498
m. Alice Courteney

Margaret
m. Henry Butts

ELIZABETH
b.1526
m.1544 Paul Morland

ELIJAH
1480-1528

MICAH
1483-153

Henry
b.1484
d.1501
(Executed in the
White Rose Intrigue)

Richard
b.1485
d.1501

JOHN
b.1488 d.1538
m.1508
Lucy Courteney

ISABEL
(Belle)
b.1490 d.1517
m.1505
Jack Morland

EZEKIEL
b.1503
m.1528
Arabella
Neville

SON
b.1513
d.1514

JOHN
b.1510
m.1531
Catherine
Morland

BARTHOLOMEW
b.1511
m.1531
Jane Morland

SAMSON
b.1533

JOSEPH
b.1535

FAITH
b.1533

HOPE
b.1534

CHARITY
b.1536

HEZEKIAH
b.1533

FOREWORD

*O*F ALL OUR KINGS, HENRY VIII IS PROBABLY THE MOST instantly recognisable, and probably also, with the exception of Richard III, the subject of the most popular misconceptions. The myth of the bloodthirsty lecher, at least, has been exploded—in all his life, Henry had only two mistresses, a very moderate score for his time; and to judge the political executions of his reign by present-day standards would certainly be to misunderstand the man and his times. Removing the myth, however, does not seem to leave us much nearer the real Henry. Probably we shall never know very much about this subtle, enigmatic man; but without a doubt he was possessed of very great personal magnetism, and was loved as well as feared by those who were close to him.

For the interpretation of his relationship with Anne Boleyn I am indebted to Hester Chapman's sensitive and scholarly work *Anne Boleyn*. The main works in addition which I have found useful are as follows:

Bindoff S T	*Tudor England*
Bowle John	*Henry VIII*
*Cavendish George	*Life and Death of Cardinal Wolsey*
Dickens A G	*The English Reformation*

Elton G R	*England Under the Tudors*
Fletcher Anthony	*Tudor Rebellions*
Laver James	*A History of Costume*
*Leland W	*Itineraries*
Quennell M & C	*A History of Everyday Things in England*
Richardson W C	*History of the Court of Augmentations*
*Roper W	*Life of Sir Thomas More*
Savine A	*English Monasteries on the Eve of Dissolution*
Scarisbrick J	*Henry VIII*
Stow J	*Annales*
Strickland Agnes	*Lives of the Queens of England*
Williams Neville	*Henry VIII and His Court*
Winchester Barbara	*Tudor Family Portrait*
*Wyatt G	*Life of Queen Anne Boleyn*
Trevelyan G M	*English Social History*

*Contemporary material

BOOK ONE

THE FOX AND THE BEAR

Right shall the foxes chare,
The wolves, the beares also,
That wrought have muche care,
And brought Engeland in woe.

John Skelton
'A Laud and Praise'

One

When the old king, Henry VII, died, his mother—the ancient Margaret Beaufort—was so grieved that she survived him by no more than a few weeks, dying in the middle of the new king's revels and being bundled off unceremoniously so as not to spoil the fun. It would have been hard, however, to find anyone else in the kingdom who regretted the passing of Henry Tidr, and impossible to find any such person in Yorkshire.

In Yorkshire dwelt the old York families with their illustrious names—Neville, Fitzalan, Percy, Mortimer, Clifford, Holland, Talbot, Bourchier, Strickland—and their long memories of personal rule by successive York lords—Richard of Warwick; Richard of York; and Richard of Gloucester, their sweet King Richard who died at the hands of this same unloved and unregretted Henry Tidr.

In Yorkshire also dwelt the Morland family, with their history of lives spent in the cause of the House of York. The founder of the Morland house, Eleanor Courteney, had been a personal friend of the Plantagenets, and King Richard himself had been a frequent visitor at Morland Place before he became king; and her youngest son Richard had served under that king in France. Richard Morland, now universally known as Great

Uncle Richard, was the elder and guiding spirit of Morland Place, though Eleanor's great-grandson Paul was the nominal head of the family. Great Uncle Richard had always been a gentle man and averse to killing or hurting anyone, but even he had had his moment of blood-letting for the cause, and in his case it was purely for revenge.

The battle of Bosworth Field had lost King Richard his life, partly owing to the treachery of Lord Stanley, but even more owing to the treachery of Lord Percy of Northumberland. 'Proud Percy' had delayed in his duty of calling out the men of the north to the King's aid, with the result that the huge Yorkshire army—Morland men amongst them—was still on the road when the battle was lost and over.

Richard Morland and Paul's father Ned had felt the shame and anguish deeply, and when a fugitive from the battle had told them that Percy, after holding back from the fighting, had been one of the first to do homage to Henry Tidr, they knew that come what may they must be revenged on proud Percy. There were many who felt thus; their chance came not quite four years later.

It was Lord Percy's task, among others, to collect the taxes imposed by his new sovereign lord upon the people of the north, and in 1489 in April a tax was imposed to raise funds for an invasion of France. Word flickered through Yorkshire like flames through dry bracken; messages passed to and fro between certain members of Percy's own household, and certain other men whose hearts burned with revenge. When Richard Morland heard of the plot from Ned, he was at first shocked.

'His own henchmen?' he queried. 'He is their lord, their special lord, to whom they owe the firmest duty. It is shame to them not to protect him.'

Ned, normally cheerful and light, looked grim. 'They are already shamed,' he said, 'and by their own lord. Percy failed in *his* duty to the King, betrayed and abandoned him to his death. His henchmen want to wipe out that shame—it can only be paid for by his blood.'

'And who is to strike the blow?'

'We shall draw lots.' Ned's candid gaze met Richard's. 'Are you with us, or against us?' he asked simply. Richard's heart was torn; murder was prohibited by every tenet of Christianity and by every impulse of his gentle soul; yet something older and more primitive was stirring in him, the acknowledgement of duty to one's feudal lord. He had served under King Richard, had sworn that same oath to him. His eyes fell on the blazoning of the Morland arms over the fireplace, and the motto underneath, the single word *Fidelitas*. Faithfulness, the Morland creed.

'I'm with you,' he said.

It was not hard to raise a mob—northern men never liked paying taxes to a southern king, and Henry VII was particularly unpopular. Last year and the year before, tax collectors had been attacked, and goods constrained had been forcibly rescued by their seething owners. Percy with his household men and retainers marched south to meet the mob and put down what appeared to be a rebellion against the Tudor king and his taxation policy. The two armies met at Topcliffe, near Thirsk.

It was a strange scene. At first there was yelling, brandishing of weapons, threats and insults, but when Percy rode forward into the small space between the groups, a silence fell. Perhaps he thought it was the power of his personality that created the silence; if so, it was his last earthly gratification. There was no man there, from the greatest to the least, who by now did not know what was coming. Two smaller groups detached themselves, one from the Yorkshire mob, one—his closest henchman—from the Northumberland army, and gently, almost tenderly, closed round the mounted lord. A brown hand took the horse's bridle and the horse fidgeted and shivered, smelling the atmosphere. Percy smelled it too, and looked round, suddenly wary, at the ring of faces, and the cold eyes.

The old fox, they called him—he was thin and red-haired and scar-faced; he had never been lacking in courage—you don't stay long in the high chair of a Border lord if you're a coward—but there was something in the quiet, hard purpose of the men who surrounded him that chilled his blood.

'What's this?' he demanded. 'What's going on?'

'Better dismount, my lord,' said a voice beside him. It was his steward, a man who had grown up in his service from boyhood. Percy stared into his eyes, and read his death there. There was no appealing against that look. Trembling now, he dismounted. The soft wind, blowing the smell of spring from the south, fluttered across the high field, stirring the men's hair and the horses' manes. The two great armies stood silent, like a vast congregation, and between them stood the small circle of men surrounding the white horse and the great lord. Now that the moment had come there was no anger, no glee, no delight in revenge—there was only a kind of sober sadness, almost a pity. At the last moment Percy begged his men to remember their vows, their oath of loyalty to protect him, but silence was the only reply, and that silence bid him remember his own broken oath. Pride stiffened him again.

'Strike from before, then,' he commanded. 'I never took a wound in the back.' His eyes went round the circle coldly, to meet in each face that same pity, and came to rest on a man bearing a naked sword. Others held swords at the ready, but in this face was his death. It was a man in his thirties, fair and handsome, with a great spreading beard, dressed in a simple long gown of good cloth. 'It is you, then?' Percy asked. The man nodded. 'Let me know your name, at least.' The man opened his mouth to answer, but Percy's steward prevented him.

'No,' he said. 'This is not an execution. We are despatching a sick animal. Strike now.' But the fair man shook his head.

'I bore this sword in the King's service, though I never killed with it,' he said. 'Blood calls for blood.' His eyes left Percy's and met, over his shoulder, those of the two men standing behind their lord. Percy made a movement to turn and look too, but rough hands seized him from behind, pulling his arms back and stretching his chest taut, and the sword went home up to the hilt.

The white horse screamed and reared back at the smell of blood, and the quiet men turned away from the scene, the twitching body bleeding slowly into the bracken, its astonished eyes regarding the pale-grey, windy northern sky. The henchmen lifted the body on to the horse to take it away, and the man with the sword wiped it slowly and thoughtfully on a handful of dry grass. Ned put his arm across Richard's shoulder and turned him away from the scene.

'The horses are down there. Let's go home,' he said. Richard was still staring at the blood on his hands and the smears of it on the sword blade.

'I never killed a man before,' he said slowly.

'It was the luck of the draw,' Ned comforted him. 'Besides, Hal was right. It was putting down a beast, not a man. An old fox.' Richard looked back at the trampled patch of bracken where the blood was soaking into the earth. He shook his head.

'It wasn't that,' he said. 'It was a sacrifice. A sacrificial beast. Offered up for all of us who have ever broken faith.' He walked on a little, and then said even more quietly, but with a little of a smile, 'No, it wasn't even that. It was done for love of our lord, that's all.'

For Richard, that closed the matter, and for Ned too—they had seen too much, were perhaps too worldly-wise, to think anything more could be gained. Others in the family were not so resigned, and continued to struggle for the cause that was dead, running to each new standard raised against the Tudor on behalf of the young sons of Edward IV, who had been smuggled out of the country in the first year after Bosworth.

Ned's young nephews, Henry and Dickon Butts, the sons of his sister Margaret, were both killed in the so-called 'White Rose Intrigue' in 1501, and Ned himself might have been drawn into plots on more than one occasion had not Richard been so firmly convinced that each new pretender was an imposter.

'But how do you *know* they aren't the princes?' Ned would ask him, and Richard would merely shake his head.

'You can ask that, you who knew the boys personally? You were in the Household itself.'

'I do ask it. How do you *know*?' Ned would persist, and Richard would tap his big Morland nose.

'This tells me. I think those children are dead; died in some obscure lodging in Antwerp of some childish disease. It's foolishness to go on hoping and struggling. It's all over. Now there's just the family and the estate to think about.'

And so Richard went back to his occupations about the estate, and Ned went back to his pursuits of drinking and gambling and chasing women, and Henry Tidr went back to his activities of governing, and eliminating Plantagenets, and making the throne safe for his son to inherit. And in 1509 when the old King died, his son succeeded to the throne without even a murmur of opposition, proof indeed if proof were needed that the cause was dead; and that sweet spring day twenty years back when Richard had killed Lord Percy amid the bracken always marked for him the true end of the struggle. The world was Tudor now for ever.

Paul Morland, whom the villagers called French Paul because his mother had been a Frenchwoman, was a tall, well-built, and exceptionally handsome man. His lustrous, curling hair was dark brown, almost black, his skin smooth and brown. His features were sensitive, his mouth beautifully sculptured, and his large dark eyes a woman would have been glad to own. He rode superlatively, played many games, danced with grace, and was a fine musician. He was also head of the household, the master of the entire Morland fortune, and he took himself very seriously.

It was perhaps inevitable that he should do so. He was only ten when his great-grandmother Eleanor Courteney died, but he remembered her perfectly, a woman of such stature and power she had seemed to him to stand in rank somewhere between the King and God. She had treated Paul even as a child with the respect due to the eventual heir to Morland Place. Paul's tutor had been a serious-minded young man and a firm disciplinarian; and Paul had had before him constantly the bad example of his frivolous father who spent money like water, was drunk more often than not, frequented low places and low women in the city, and finally met his death by a knife between the ribs during a tavern brawl in the back yard of the Starre Inn.

Paul was twenty-five when Ned's death gave him control of the estate, but he was already virtually in charge, and had been running the farm and the business with Great Uncle Richard's help for some years, for Ned never did anything that even approximated to work or worry. Yet in spite of intending to be everything his father wasn't, Paul still loved Ned, and was stricken when he died. Paul's mother had died when he was an infant, and his father's second wife was a common, ignorant girl from the city whom Ned had married because he believed her pregnant. Paul had hated her all his life, from the belief that she was cuckolding his father with his cousin Edmund Brazen.

Well, she was dead now, and so was Edmund Brazen; so was everyone of that generation except Great Uncle Richard; but Morland Place was shared by Paul's half-kin, his stepmother's children, Jack, Mary and Edward, and Paul hated them from the depths of his heart, because he believed that they had been fathered not by Ned, but by Edmund. He could tell no-one of this, no-one but the family chaplain, Philip Dodds. Week after week Paul confessed his hatred, and was shriven, and swore to cast the hatred from his heart, but nothing could change it, and after a while Master Dodds stopped lecturing him and merely gave the penance with a sigh and a shake of the head.

One of the ways in which Paul took himself seriously was as lord of the manor, and so the family dined in the great hall almost every day, though most gentry folk nowadays dined privately and left the steward to preside in the hall. On feast days Great Uncle Richard also dined at Morland Place, though he had his own manor close by, about a mile away at Shawes, which had been given to him and his heirs on Eleanor Courteney's death; and it did not necessarily need to be a feast day for his big, bearded form to be seen seated at the high table. Richard had been born and brought up at Morland Place, and he felt more comfortable there. His eldest son Elijah ruled at Shawes along with his wife Madge and his young son Ezekiel, and Richard always felt a little superfluous to their small happy circle. Richard's own wife had died many years ago, and he had never remarried. He had always felt drawn to the life of celibacy, and had thought at one time of being a monk. His second son, Micah, had in fact been ordained in 1501 and was now attached to the household of the Earl of Surrey.

The state of the Church was a subject that often came up at dinner, and was eagerly canvassed at this table as it was at almost every gathering of educated people, for the argumentative English were all reformist by nature.

'How can you justify the existence of the monasteries in this day and age?' Paul asked Richard at dinner one day. 'It's fifteen-twelve, Uncle, and we have a more vigorous approach to religion than we did a hundred years ago. The truly devout man wants to go out and *do* something for his faith, not just a sit back in luxury and think about it.'

'There is a value in the contemplative life as well as the active life,' Richard countered mildly. 'God receives both offerings gladly. Remember the story of Esau.'

'Come now, Uncle,' Paul said genially, 'you don't believe that. Why, you yourself, as you've often told me, gave up the idea of being a monk because you wanted to walk round the country and meet God's people and work with them.'

'That was my way. It is not every man's. Some men prefer to contemplate the holy mysteries from a retreat. It is not for me—or for you—to say that way is wrong.'

Philip Dodds joined in. 'But even if the contemplative life itself has value, the monasteries no longer provide it. Look at the abuses that they contain—idleness and luxury and vice. I doubt if you would find anyone in the country today leading a true life of contemplation within a monastery.'

Richard waved the goblet he had lifted for a page to fill with wine. 'My dear Philip,' he said, 'you cannot condemn the practice because of the imperfection of the practitioners.'

'I don't see why not,' Philip said. 'If there are no perfect practitioners, perhaps it is because the practice itself is at fault.'

'Precisely my point,' Paul broke in triumphantly. 'In this year of Grace fifteen hundred and twelve there is no place for that kind of life. There is no-one to follow it. Most of the houses now contain no more than a bare handful of inmates, and most of *them* took orders when they were children too young to know what they were doing. Ask them now and I dare swear they would be as glad to come out as to stay in.'

Paul's wife Anne Butts joined the argument against him, not because she had strong views about it—she had strong views on almost nothing in life—but because she loved to oppose him. They were cousins and had been betrothed as children and married as soon as they reached good age—when Anne was fourteen and Paul sixteen—and their marriage might have been as content as such marriages usually were, except that Anne had fallen in love with him, only to find that he did not love her. He rather despised her, finding her colourless and uninteresting. Anne suspected he had a mistress, or maybe more than one, and she hated him almost as much as she once loved him.

'There *is* a place for them,' she said in flat contradiction, and then, because all eyes were on her, she hastened to justify herself. 'Who would look after the poor and sick if there were no kindly monks to take them in and feed them and give them alms?'

Paul glared at her. 'Don't talk about things you know nothing of,' he snapped, and Philip said more gently, 'We give more alms at our gates here than they do at most abbeys. Perhaps in the Border country the monks may still do good work of that kind, but here and further south it is not so. The poor could be better helped by application of the wealth locked up and useless in the closed houses.'

'I'm a little surprised at you, Philip, I must confess,' Richard said. 'I thought that being a priest yourself—'

'We clerics are not so prejudiced we cannot see that Holy Mother Church has her faults—isn't that right, Edward?' Philip said, turning to Paul's half-brother who, at twenty-two, had just returned home after taking orders and was looking for a position. Edward smiled. He had inherited his mother's good looks if not her poor brains. Whoever his father was, he was a credit to him.

'Indeed, sir,' he said. 'Hate the sin, but love the sinner, that's the way we proceed. There are many, many areas in which the practice of the Church could and should be improved. Pluralism, simony—'

'Spare us the list, dear child,' Richard said, putting his head in his hands in mock despair. 'I have heard it over and over again from your brother Paul—I think I know it by heart.'

Edward laughed and turned to attend to something his younger sister Mary said, but Richard's eyes were on Paul. He hated to be called 'brother' to his stepmother's children, and he was stabbing furiously at a piece of meat on his plate with the point of his knife, his fine lips set in a hard line.

'What troubles you, Paul?' Richard asked softly. Paul looked up and his eyes met Richard's with a plea for silence. Richard knew the boy was troubled about something—there had always been a vein of deep-seated unhappiness beneath Paul's quietness—but he had no idea what it was. Well, perhaps he would tell him one day. If not—he must possess his soul in patience. In any case, a change of subject was called for.

'What do you think of the progress of the war?' he asked.

After dinner, since the hall was warm from the fires, the family remained there instead of withdrawing, and the children were brought down from the nurseries for their daily visit to their parents. The governess, whom the children called Mother Kat, brought them, with Paul's eldest son leading the way and trying to look as though he had nothing to do with the younger children. His name was Paul too, but he was usually called Amyas, which name he had been given at his christening in honour of his godfather Amyas Neville. Amyas was twelve, and older by far than any of the others, a tall, well-made, fair boy, pink-complexioned and golden-haired like his mother. He was in the care of Philip Dodds, who acted as tutor to Amyas as well as chaplain to the household, and as he walked into the hall he kept as far as possible from Mother Kat's side, to emphasise how many years ago he had left petticoat government.

He walked straight to his father, and bowed, and then reached up for a kiss. To his mother he merely bowed. Paul adored him, and he adored Paul, and it was another source of resentment to Anne that the child had so readily learned his father's contempt of her. In fact, this was not entirely true. In his anxiety to show that he was a man of full years, Amyas slighted his mother along with his ex-governess without realising the hurt he was giving; but to Anne the slight seemed intentional. She glowered, and the child was glad to return to his father's side.

After Amyas was born, Anne had gone through a long, unhappy succession of stillbirths and miscarriages, a misfortune which should have brought her and Paul closer together but in fact only drove them farther apart, for Paul felt she was failing in her duty to provide him with children, and she blamed him for her continued suffering. The chain of disaster had been broken in the end by the birth of a healthy girl, and after that there were no more pregnancies. The girl, Margaret, was now a plump, golden-haired toddler of four, and her mother's pet as much as Amyas was his father's. To have given birth to her after so many failures made her very precious to Anne, who fretted at the slightest sign of an ailment, for she was dogged with the dread of losing her. But Margaret was not only healthy, but of a sunny, equable disposition, and no amount of cosseting seemed to spoil her. She curtseyed formally to her father as she had been taught, and then ran to her mother to curtsey sketchily and then climb into the silken lap to be cuddled and cooed over.

The other children who were brought in from the nursery caused, in their innocence, only pain to Paul Morland, for he could never see them without the knowledge gnawing him like a tooth that they were not his brood, but his half-brother Jack's. Jack had married, as was becoming customary with the Morlands, his cousin, Isabel—or Belle—Butts, the younger sister of those two Butts cousins who had died in the White Rose Intrigue. It was a source of displeasure to Paul that the Butts cousin Jack had married not only made him happy but gave him a brood of healthy children.

Belle, who accompanied the younger children into the hall, had lost their first child, but had soon repaired the breach with a girl, born within a month of Margaret. She had been named Anne, but was always called Nanette, because she was so diminutive, like a fairy child. 'My little changeling' Belle called her sometimes, for she was tiny and dark and delicately made, pretty and sweet and graceful and sharp as a needle, the perfect foil to plump golden Margaret. The two little girls were constant companions, which also galled Paul, who would have been happier if the children had all hated each other.

After Nanette had come two sons, Jackie and Dickon, now three and two years old, and another girl, Catherine, not yet a year old, and brought in in Mother Kat's arms in her long robes; and Belle was pregnant again, large with child, which was why she had not been at dinner—she had been resting upstairs. Paul shut his mind to the rest of the children, and concentrated on Amyas, asking him about his lessons and his sports, and sending him to fetch a book so that he might read aloud to his father and have his progress judged. Paul was a hard critic when it came to his son, but Amyas was a good scholar, and managed this time to wring some praise from his father, which pleased both of them.

'Well done, child,' Paul cried when the boy came to the end of the passage. 'Thou hast learnt that lesson well. I am very pleased.'

Amyas looked up from under his eyelashes, quick to follow up an advantage.

'Then, sir, would it please you to give me permission to go into the city and visit my Uncle John? Aunt Belle says his boar-bitch has whelped, and you said that I might have a puppy if I learnt my Greek.'

'A puppy?' Paul caught Belle's eye across the hall, and saw the sharp amusement there. John was her brother, the heir to the Butts fortune, which was closely bound up with the Morlands, for the Butts family were merchants, and they dealt with the selling and shipping of the cloth that the Morlands made from the wool they grew. John Butts, too, had married a cousin, Lucy Courteney, another great-granddaughter of Eleanor Courteney, and had two fine baby boys. It sometimes seemed to Paul that everyone was happy but him.

Amyas was looking up at him with expectation and hope. 'You cannot go into the city alone,' Paul said, and saw for a fraction of a second the disappointment shadow that loved face, before he added, 'But I have business there—I will take you, and you may stay the night at your Uncle John's house, and I will send a servant to fetch you tomorrow.'

'Can't I come back with you tonight, sir?' Amyas asked, liking the thought of being seen riding in company with his father. Being fetched by a servant was not half so splendid. Paul's eyes slid away.

'I shall be too late for you,' he said. 'I cannot say what time I shall have finished my business.' Now Anne's eyes were on him, and questions trembling on her lips. She wanted to ask what the business was, and he must prevent any further discussion. He got to his feet abruptly and said, 'But I must go immediately. Get your cloak, child, and say goodbye to your mother. I will meet you in the stable-yard. Don't be more than five minutes.' And he strode from the room, aware of two sets of eyes in particular—Anne's hostile and resentful, and Belle's, no whit less amused. She was a very disconcerting young woman.

Amyas bid his mother and his tutor goodbye, bowed to Great Uncle Richard, and hustled Mother Kat as fast as her bulky skirts would allow her to the cope chest to get him out his riding cloak, and while the little bustle of his going was still disturbing the air, there began a larger bustle as Elijah and Madge arrived with their nine-year-old son Ezekiel to spend the evening.

'What a pity Paul didn't know you were coming,' Richard said as he greeted them in Paul's place. 'He has gone into the city on business and won't be back until late.'

Elijah cocked an expressive eye at his father. 'But he did know we were coming,' he said. 'Jack is coming home tonight, and we were all to take supper together.' Richard looked thoughtful, and then glanced over his shoulder at the other occupants of the hall, who were talking and admiring the children round the fire. Elijah had spoken low, and no-one had heard.

'Best not say anything, then,' Richard said at last. 'He has something on his mind. I dare say he forgot.'

'I dare say he did,' Elijah said, then, more loudly, 'Now you must come and admire your grandson, who has been practising a song for you this entire week and hasn't seen you for long enough to sing it. You aren't at home enough; is he, Madge?'

'Indeed he is not,' Madge said, putting an affectionate hand on his arm. 'You are almost a stranger to us, Father.'

'I assure you it's for the good of my soul. I'm too much beloved at your house—it makes me vain. Now then, Ezekiel, come and stand by my knee and sing me this song. Stand square, now, child, and keep your head up, as you've been taught. That's right—' The family settled down again.

The stir caused by Jack's arrival was much more prolonged, and it was as well for Paul's peace of mind that he was not there to see it: there was a great deal of kissing and hugging and exclaiming, for all that Jack had only been gone four days, for he was much beloved by everyone. He had been away in Westmorland, to Kentdale for the christening of one of the numerous Neville family connections. Jack's responsibility in the family business was on the merchanting side, as Paul's was on the farming side, and that, together with his frank and easy manners and cheerful humour, meant that he had a great many friends and connections, not only in Yorkshire amongst the numerous old Yorkist families, but also throughout the country. All the great merchant families were known to him, and there could scarcely have been a gentleman's household in all the country where Jack Morland could not have called to take his dinner.

That Jack should be so well liked was yet another thorn in Paul's side, and though he too had been invited to the christening at Kentdale Castle, he had refused, knowing he was only included out of courtesy and that it was Jack who was really wanted. Now, when the greetings had been exchanged, Jack took his seat by the fire with Nanette on one knee, and Jackie on the other, and Belle on a stool at his feet, and the rest of the family gathered round to hear his story; a casual observer might have been forgiven for thinking *he* was the lord of this manor after all.

'Tell us, then,' Elijah said. 'Was it a boy or a girl?'

'Oh, I forgot, you don't even know that much, do you?' Jack began. 'Well, it was a girl, but to tell the truth I don't think the Parrs minded in the least. I've never seen a prouder father than Sir Thomas, walking up and down with the babe in his arms like the most dedicated of nurses and talking of her beauty and intelligence, though to any spectator the child was no different from any other. And he was wearing, of course, the chain that the lord King gave him—'

'—of one hundred and forty pounds value,' Belle chimed in, and everyone laughed. Sir Thomas was the Comptroller of the Household, and the King had given him the great gold chain as a token of favour and respect, but Sir Thomas could never mention it without also mentioning its price—not because he was an avaricious man, but because he was delighted with the extent of the King's regard.

'Yes, the very same,' Jack said, smiling. 'And when the babe took hold of the chain, as wee babies will, he was delighted and said this betokened the child's good sense in knowing who was her lord and benefactor.'

'Did the King send a christening gift?' Richard wanted to know.

'He did—a handsome silver cup. Maud Parr, with her usual good sense, was far more impressed with that than she was with the babe's supposed wisdom. She's the most remarkable woman, you know—tiny as a child, and barely seventeen, but she orders that household like a matron of forty, and has her husband as well controlled as a jessed hawk. She said to Boleyn—'

'Boleyn was there?' Elijah asked.

'He brought the King's gift. *Everyone* was there—the Latimers, the Boroughs, the Greens, more Nevilles than you could shake a stick at, the Fitzhughs, old St Maur, looking worn out as well he might with all *his* children. Boleyn is just in the process of moving house—they're going to live in Kent for his lady's health I believe—and he said he was glad to get away from the dust and noise and trouble. And Lady Boleyn is pregnant again—what a beautiful woman she is!'

'Even great with child?' Belle asked innocently. Jack smiled down at her and stroked the plush curve of her cheek.

'Women are most beautiful when they are great with child. She has had bad luck, of course—seven pregnancies and only three living children—but she remains both serene and vivacious—she is all loveliness! Such a wit! And as beautiful as—as—'

'As my mother?' Nanette asked innocently. Jack laughed and kissed his daughter.

'Almost as beautiful as thy mother, poppet. And she never forgets she's a Howard. Even little Maud Parr treats her with reverence, and she's the kind of woman who bows to no man. Just think of her choosing to lie-in at Kentdale when there's an invasion likely from over the border at any moment and she might find herself besieged by mad yelling Scots!'

'From what you say of her,' Elijah said, 'she'd probably give them a terrible trouncing, single-handed.'

'She'd tell them to go home and wash themselves,' Madge added, and everyone laughed again. Jack was one of those rare spirits who really liked and admired women, and he was often lavish in his praise of women like Maud Parr and Lady Elizabeth Boleyn. It might, perhaps, account for Belle's strong spirit and unabashed behaviour in company.

'What did they call the baby—you haven't told us that, yet?' Belle said now.

'Oh, Katherine, of course, in honour of the Queen. They could hardly do otherwise, considering Parr's position in the Household. Well, we wet her head with a great deal of good wine, and we had some fine hunting the following day, and exchanged all the news. The war is going badly—but I expect you know that. Never was there such an ill-fated venture! The army is ill and hungry. Boleyn was telling me that more men desert every day, and those that are left are scarcely fit to fight.'

'I said from the beginning a young, warlike king would lead us into trouble,' Richard said. 'However much I disliked his father, at least *he* kept the peace.'

'It isn't the King,' Jack said carelessly, 'it's that almoner of his, Wolsey. He advises, the King disposes. The King wouldn't mind which side he fought on, as long as he could dress up and have banners and trumpets and horses to ride up and down. But Wolsey wants us to protect His Holiness against the French so that the Pope will make him Archbishop. And while we keep the French occupied, the Queen's father can carry on over-running the lands he wants without opposition. But of course neither Wolsey nor the King can see that they're being used.'

'And you can, I suppose,' Richard said drily. 'Tell me, what makes you so much more clear-sighted than either the King or any of his ministers?'

Jack laughed. 'It's not just me, Uncle Richard. All we merchants know which way the wind is blowing—ask John Butts. We aren't blinded by self-interest, that's what makes the difference.'

'Aren't you?'

'No,' Jack said firmly. 'We are self-interested, of course, but not blinded by it. The ministers of the crown, on the whole, are children playing with toys. Diplomacy is a game to them. To us it's shillings and groats.'

'I'm not sure you should talk like that,' Richard said, still uneasy.

'Don't worry, Uncle,' Belle said, holding out a hand to him. 'We're all family and friends here. We are quite safe—no-one would repeat anything.'

'Yes, and talking of family,' Jack said, looking round, 'where is my illustrious brother? And his son-and-heir is missing too, I notice. Sister, what have you done with them? Come, tell, I can keep a secret as well as the next man.'

'Paul has gone into the city on business,' Anne said flatly, daring anyone to ask any further questions, 'and my son is to John Butts's house to choose a puppy. He will be brought back tomorrow.'

Jack's quick sympathy went out to Anne. 'What a pity business should have dragged him away tonight. I'm sure he would have much rather been here with us all. Well, perhaps he will be able to join us for supper. Talking of which, when is that to be?'

'Soon, now, dearest,' Belle said. 'It's almost the hour for mass, and we shall eat at once afterwards. Perhaps we should go and prepare ourselves. So many of the village people will come in to mass to see you. Anyone would think you had been away a year instead of a week. I don't know what it is you do to make them love you—' Unwittingly, she was rubbing salt into Anne's wounds, Jack could see. He pressed her arm in warning and said lightly, 'Why, I bribe them, of course. I distribute pennies as I ride through. Come then, let us go and wash and change.'

Richard, as the senior member of the family, led the way into the chapel a while later, but it was to Jack that all eyes turned. Mass was sung twice a day in the chapel at Morland Place, and more frequently on the greater feast-days, and many of the village people preferred to go there to hear mass than to go to their local church. Everyone was always welcome, and today the beautiful chapel with its family memorials was especially full, for Jack did a great deal of good amongst the ordinary folk, and he was much loved.

The family took their places, and all knelt in private prayer, but Philip Dodds, looking round covertly, saw two faces not absorbed in their devotions. Belle, distracted by her physical discomfort, for she was too large with child to find kneeling easy, was watching Anne; and Anne was wondering where Paul was. Philip frowned. He must speak to her afterwards, and give her penance to do, for such secular thoughts when she should be adoring the host, but he was a very human man, and his heart moved with sympathy for her and for her husband, so needlessly unhappy. And he, too, wondered where Paul was.

And then the altar-boy rang the bell, and the congregation prepared to open their hearts to the beautiful words of the mass, and to share in the sacred mystery of the sacrifice of the precious Body and Blood of our Blessed Lord.

Two

THE HOUSE IN THE SHAMBLES WAS NARROW AND THREE
storeys tall, the uppermost one hanging over the street
and clearing by a bare eighteen inches the gable of the house
opposite. It had no glass or even horn in its windows, and the
gleams of light that shewed through the closed shutters revealed
how leaky and imperfectly fitting even those shutters were.

The room behind the shutters in the topmost gable was tiny
and bare. There was no furniture but a small clothes chest and a
crude wooden frame to hold the washing-basin. The bed was a
mere pallet on the floor, and there were no hangings nor even
a scrap of paint on the walls. Yet for all that, there were unexpected touches of fineness about the little room. The rushes
on the floor were fresh, and were sprinkled with fleabane,
and sweet camomile that gave up its fragrance when crushed
underfoot. There were pillows on the mattress-bed instead of
the usual block of wood. And the room was lit not by a wick
dipped in animal tallow to give off a stinking, smoky glow, but
by the straight clear flames of several beeswax candles.

It was the candles that occupied the attention of the woman
lying on the pallet that spring evening of 1513. She was resting
on one elbow, clothed in nothing but her magnificent hair
which, had she stood up, would have reached almost to her

knees. It was of a gold so moony-pale it seemed to reflect and magnify the candlelight and fill the room with its glow.

'Candles,' she said. Her voice was low and clear, and when she spoke it seemed that laughter lay so close to the surface that it might break through her words at any moment. 'Such luxury! Such extravagance! But they are so beautiful, and they fill the room with the smell of honey. Thank you for bringing them.'

She turned to look at him, her dark eyes warm in her pale face, and he smiled and reached out to cup her cheek with one hand.

'I thought they were appropriate, with their fine straight bodies and their pale hair,' he said. Her eyes accepted the compliment. He never had to explain things to her—her mind was as subtle as his own, which was one of the reasons that he loved her. 'I wish you would let me bring you more things, and richer things—presents worthy of you.'

She shook her head. 'Do I have to say it again?'

'No,' he said. She always said that she did not want presents from him, that she wanted only himself. 'But you deserve so much more than you have, and Anne deserves so much less than she has.'

'Hush,' she said. 'Don't talk of her in that way. Don't talk at all just now—' And she rolled over in one swift movement and pressed her naked body against his, lifting her arms round his neck and kissing him. His reaction was immediate, though they had already made love; he grew hard for her, folded his arms round her and twisted her under him, and entered her again in an agony of relief. For a little while there was an end to thought, there was only their physical delight and their feelings for each other, rising to an exquisite crescendo; the act of making life, that seems each time like a little death.

She pressed her nose against his skin here and there, at cheek, neck and chest, like an animal snuffling.

'You smell so lovely,' she said. 'So different from everyone else. You smell rich, of wool and leather and perfumes.'

'And you,' he said, 'smell of apples and honey, little bear.'

She laughed and thrust herself up on both arms to hang over him, looking down through a cloud of silver-gold hair.

'How should I not? Those are the things bears love, are they not?'

'They are,' he said, reaching up his hands to wind them in the golden glory as a man might take up handfuls of corn in sheer wonder at its abundance and goodness, 'but I hope also that they like venison pasties and wine, because that is what I brought with me today.'

'Oh lovely,' she cried, 'and some of those little cakes?' He nodded, amused at her childlike enthusiasm. 'Lovely,' she said again. 'Lovely lovely Paul. Let's eat now. I'm so hungry.'

'You are such a little animal,' he said a while later as they ate and drank the things he had brought for their refreshment. 'Snuff and growl, make love and eat and sleep, with no thought for anything. Well are you called little bear.' Her name was Ursula.

She looked at him sharply over the pasty she held in both hands. 'You like me for that. So why do you sound—discontent?'

Paul laughed uneasily. 'Your ears are too sharp. I don't mean to bring my discontent here to trouble you.'

'It clings to you like fog clinging to your clothes,' she said. 'You come here to be easy—then tell me what is wrong. You may speak of anything to me without fear.'

He touched her wonderingly. 'You never ask for anything for yourself,' he said. 'For you, all is to give.'

'I am a woman,' she said with simple dignity. 'Even your wife would give, if you would let her. Women grow that way, as trees grow upwards, until the cold wind warps them.' He turned his head a little away, not wanting to speak about Anne now. She saw the gesture, and understood it, and said, 'What is it, then, that makes you discontent? What has happened?' She regarded him for a moment, and then said, 'It is something about your brother.' It was not a question. Paul met her eyes.

'Sometimes I think you must be a witch, for you seem to know things you have no right to know.' She did not like that, he saw, and so he said, 'I don't mean that, Ursula, forgive me.'

'It is bad to talk about those things,' she said. 'To give them their names gives them power.' She lay down on her back, staring into the darkness of the ceiling, and the candlelight flowed like water across her white skin. Paul bent his head and kissed her throat and her breasts and her belly in pure love and she reached out and touched his head lightly in forgiveness. 'Tell me,' she said.

Paul lay down beside her and took her into his arms. This was the way they usually talked. 'Yes, it is Jack,' he said. 'His influence seems to grow and grow. Anyone looking in from outside would think that he is master, and not I. He got his sister Mary a place at Court, as waiting-woman to the Spanish Queen and arranged it all without even consulting me.'

'It is a good thing, is it not, to have a sister at Court?' Ursula asked without emphasis.

'I do not want to have to be grateful to *him*. And at every turn my gratitude is demanded. You know that I applied for the grant of a crest for the family?' She nodded. 'And I had hoped the grant would come through in time for the midsummer tournaments, and it seemed unlikely that the business would go through in time. Then my *brother*—' Paul filled the sound of the word with scorn—'used his influence, his considerable influence at court, and had the business pushed through, and the grant was made yesterday.'

There was a silence during which Paul wondered if Ursula was going to tell him what Anne and Philip Dodds and his own conscience had already told him, that he should be grateful to have such a kind and thoughtful brother; but when she did speak, it was rather sadly.

'Perhaps,' she said, 'he also longs to give things to you. Why are you so hard to give to, Paul? Why do you shut yourself away? Do you think he does things for you out of spite?'

Paul longed to say yes, but there was a simplicity in Ursula that demanded the truth from him. At last he said, 'No, he doesn't, but that only makes it worse.'

'Why do you hate him?' The quiet voice was relentless. He struggled with himself, and the words that came seemed wrenched out of him.

'Because he is so good, so beloved of everyone. He can laugh and talk to the common people, and they love him. Me they salute respectfully; but they don't love me. He is welcomed everywhere. The sun shines on him. His wife adores him, and he her, and they have five healthy children. He will take everything from me in the end, I know it. He will take the hearts of the people who ought to love me, and he will take Morland Place too.' His voice became a cry of anguish. 'I have such a fear that it will be his children's children who inherit, and not mine. And he has no right, no right! He is a bastard! He is not my father's son! Morland Place is mine!'

He was gripping Ursula so tightly that he must have hurt her, and yet she made no cry, and kept still, as if afraid of giving him more pain. Slowly he relaxed enough for her to breathe, and then she spoke.

'Dear heart,' she said, 'Morland Place *is* yours, and no-one denies it. Why do you feel you have it not? Why are you so afraid?'

Paul did not answer at once. His mind was roving over the place that he loved, the beautiful house with its tall chimneys, the pleasure gardens, the dovecotes and fish ponds and orchards; the great demesne lands, the forests, the rolling purple moors where the sheep grazed; the river and the mill and the tenter-fields; the great fields divided into strips which his tenants farmed, tenants who owed him allegiance, whose lives and fortunes and interests he ruled through the manorial court. He loved them all, the land that was his and the people that were his, and yet—and yet he could not possess them. He was the great lord, he was the master, and yet it was Jack they loved. In some way he could not understand, it all belonged to Jack, son of Rebecca. Paul was French Paul, the outsider, the unloved, unable to possess that which was his.

'I have nothing,' he said at last.

'You have me,' Ursula said. He looked down at her in the cradle of his arm. His own skin was dark, its natural sallowness made darker by the sun where he stripped off in the summer to help with the sheep, and by the sleek black hairs that grew everywhere on his body. He was big and hard and dark; against his skin hers looked almost unnaturally white—she was small and white and curvy, soft and tender-skinned. It was borne in upon him at that moment how utterly different they were; not like the male and female of the same species at all, but like two different kinds of animal. Here, with her, naked in her tiny garret, he felt safe, he felt loved, for a little while he could put off with his garments the troubles he bore that no-one could understand. 'You have me,' she said again.

'No,' he said, and his voice was dark with defeat.

'I love you,' she said. Their eyes met, dark eyes looking into dark eyes, like to like, in the hope of understanding.

'I know,' he said at last, 'but it isn't the same thing.'

The family was gathered in the winter-parlour when he returned to Morland Place, for having dined in the hall they had supped in private. It was a pleasant room, with panelled walls and plaited rushes on the floor, and a great table which, when not in use, was covered by a rich Turkey carpet. It was warm even in winter, for one of the walls was the back of the great hall chimney, and the room had a fireplace of its own, too. Over the fireplace was a panel painted with the black-and-white Morland arms—the white running hare on a black fesse—and the motto, *Fidelitas*. Paul looked at it as he came in and his expression soured. To it soon would be added the crest, a black leopard sejant with its paws on a broken chain: for this, Paul had to be grateful to Jack.

Anne, seated on a stool by the fire, turned to look at him. Her eyes were hidden in the shadow of her tall gable head-dress, but Paul knew they were burning with hatred in that pale, tallowy face.

'So, you have come,' she said bitterly. 'You could not finish your "business" in time to be here for supper, I suppose.'

'I could not,' Paul agreed abruptly.

'And what, pray, was so important that it kept you from your table?' Anne went on.

'You dare to question me?' Paul said, enraged. 'Be silent, woman, and mind your place.'

'My place—' Anne began—

'Is to be meek and serviceable and obedient,' Paul finished for her in a hard voice. 'If you have any doubts about that you had better seek counsel of your confessor.'

Anne might have argued, even then, but Jack threw her a look of warning, and she retired, smouldering, to her embroidery. Paul saw the look. He knew whom to thank for a disrespectful wife: the man who loved bold women, whose own wife sat on a stool at a little distance and watched with unabashed eyes which held a little mocking gleam that was never absent.

'And what was the talk at supper, brother,' Paul said to Jack now, his voice rich with irony. 'What news of Court, eh? There must be something to tell.'

Jack, in the interests of peace, took the question unambiguously. 'It is said that the King is going himself to lead the war in France, because it has been going so badly.'

'No doubt someone has told him that it will make all the difference,' Belle said irrepressibly, but Jack silenced her with a swift glance.

'So it will be a Court without a King to which my sister goes—when?' Paul asked. It was Edward who answered.

'In August. I ride with her, and Jack. I am hoping to see my lord of Surrey and ask for his patronage. Micah says—'

'You do not need to rely on Micah's influence to ask for my lord's help,' Paul said smoothly. 'The house of Morland has always been close to the house of Norfolk.'

Edward, realising his tactlessness, bowed his head graciously and said, 'I was indeed relying on your friendliness with my lord, sir.'

Paul, undeceived, turned back to Jack. 'And who rules while the King is abroad?'

'The Queen, as Regent,' Jack said shortly. Paul laughed.

'The Queen! I wonder how long the King will remain infatuated with her? Not long, I suspect. With the King away we shall have trouble with the Scots, I don't doubt.'

'His Grace won't stay long away,' Mary said quickly. 'The Queen is with child again.'

'God send she has better luck this time,' Paul said in a voice which said he had no hopes of it. 'In four years, what is it? Two stillbirths and a son who lived six weeks only?' He turned his eyes on Anne. 'A bitter thing to have a wife who does her duty no better than that.'

A dull flush crept across Anne's face at the accusation. 'There is time yet,' she said. 'She is still young.'

'Not so young,' Paul said viciously. 'Perhaps it would have been better for all concerned if she had died in childbirth. Then he could have taken a better wife—a more virtuous wife.'

'Perhaps the fault may not lie with her,' Anne said, raising her angry eyes to her husband's. He has been lying with another woman, she was thinking; all this long day, in another woman's bed, wasting his manhood on her. 'Perhaps he may be at fault, and God is punishing him.'

It was clear now even to the others that Anne and Paul were no longer talking about the King and Queen. Jack said, 'There is no reason to suppose there will not be a happy outcome this time. When Mary and I saw the Queen last week she was looking very well and happy.'

Boasting, Paul thought, that he is more intimate at Court than I am. 'Even women who look healthy may die in childbed. The childbed fever is no respecter of nobility, or beauty, or wit, or even virtue. As you know, Jack, as you know.'

'You refer to Lady Boleyn,' Jack said. 'Poor lady, she was so young.' He took the bitterness out of Paul's barb by his own simple kindness. Jack's idolised Lady Boleyn had died in childbed the year before, only weeks after Belle had been brought to bed of her last daughter, Jane. Jack had been very upset, and even more so when Sir Thomas, left with three young children, had married a local farmer's daughter of no education, birth or wealth, a choice that seemed an insult to Elizabeth Howard's memory. But he refused to let Paul use that as a weapon against him. 'You are right, the childbed fever may take anyone; but the King would not wish it so, I assure you. He loves Queen Catharine as dearly as on the day he married her—else he would not have made her Regent.'

'And if he did not love her he would not have stayed faithful to her,' Anne said sharply. Paul rounded on her and was drawing breath for an onslaught when Jack intervened with quiet firmness.

'Paul, may I speak to you for a moment in private?' Paul looked at him in surprise. 'Now. It's important.'

'Very well,' Paul said at last. 'We had better go into the steward's room.'

'No,' Mary said, getting to her feet. 'Stay here. Anne and I were going up to bed anyway, and I'm sure Edward is tired too, aren't you Edward? Perhaps you would call for the dips.'

In a moment a servant had brought the slender rushlights to light them up to bed, and Jack and Paul were left alone in the winter-parlour with no sound to disturb them but the ticking and settling of the last of the logs in the fireplace. Paul leaned on the chimney piece and kicked a spurt of flame out of the charred remains with the side of his foot.

'Well,' he said. 'What is this well-rehearsed scene for?' Jack looked a little uncomfortable.

'I do not know quite how to go about this. Paul, where were you this evening at the supper-hour?'

Paul raised one dark eyebrow, and his black eyes gleamed with a kind of vicious amusement.

'And why should I tell you that?' he asked. Jack shrugged.

'Because I know already.'

Paul straightened slowly, removing his weight from his elbow and drawing himself up to his full, dangerous size. His nostrils flared with anger, and a white line etched itself round his beautiful mouth.

'What did you say?' he said menacingly. Jack stood his ground.

'I know where you were. I followed you. I saw you go into the house on the Shambles, and a few enquiries and a handful of coins soon disclosed to me the name of the woman, and the fact that you have been a frequent visitor there for the past five years.'

'How dare you?' Paul's voice was a whisper of rage. 'How dare you follow me and spy on me? How dare you interfere?'

'How dare I?' Jack's matter-of-fact briskness was a horrible contrast to Paul's barely-leashed rage. 'Because your wife is unhappy, and suspects—more than suspects. Because the reputation of the family is involved. The honours of both our families—the Morlands and the Butts. Belle and Anne were brought up together. We are all cousins. And, finally, because what you are doing is wrong, and you know it. Otherwise you wouldn't be so angry at being found out.'

Paul crossed the room in a stride, and took Jack by the throat, lifting him, in his rage, clear off the ground. His body vibrated with anger, with frustration that even now he wanted to kill him and could not.

'You upstart, you foundling, you bastard slip, how dare you follow me? How dare you criticise me? I've kept you here out of charity, and this is how you repay me. You have no right to be here at all, you misbegotten son of a slut. Your mother came from the gutter, your mother cuckolded my father with his own cousin. That's the sort of stock you come from, yet you think you can steal my inheritance. You want to usurp my kingdom, disinherit my son, put your own children in his place, disaffect my wife, subvert my servants. Don't think I haven't noticed the way you bribe their loyalty away from me. I've seen you smiling and sweeting them. But you won't have it, do you hear? I won't let you have Morland Place. I'll kill you first. I'll burn it to the ground, and slaughter every living thing in it, and salt every inch of soil before I let you have any part of my inheritance.'

He stopped for sheer lack of breath, and for a moment remained glaring into Jack's face, his teeth bared, his body shaking with emotion; and then very slowly he released Jack, letting him back down to the ground and removing his cramped, trembling hands from his brother's throat. Jack stared at him with a terrible pity.

'So that's it,' he said at last. 'So that's what you think. But you're wrong.' Paul didn't answer. He was staring into the fire with dark unseeing eyes, and Jack didn't even know if he had heard. But he went on anyway. 'I am my father's child, as are Mary and Edward. We share the same father, you and I. We are half-kin. My mother didn't—do what you said.'

Paul's head turned painfully, like that of some beast goaded half to death.

'My father loved you. He thought you were his own. She deceived him. She cuckolded him, but he loved you, you devil-spawn.'

'Yes, he loved me. He loved us all. *Our* father, Paul, *our* father. He loved us all, but you were his first-born. The inheritance is yours. I don't want it. I couldn't have it if I did want it, and I don't. You are the eldest son. It's yours.'

He put all his emphasis into his words, not knowing how much Paul heard or understood in his anguish. Paul shook his head slowly as if trying to clear it.

'He loved you,' he said. 'He loved you *best*.' His eyes, full of pain, met Jack's. 'I hate you,' he whispered.

Jack reached out a hand, and then drew it back, knowing there was no way that he could give anything to this tormented man.

'No,' he said, 'you don't.' Paul's eyes filled suddenly with tears. 'You don't hate me.'

Paul turned away. 'Just go,' he said. 'Leave me.' Jack hesitated. 'Just go.'

For a long time after the soft sound of the door closing behind Jack, Paul remained motionless, his head bent, his eyes staring unseeing before him. No, he didn't hate him. Acknowledgement of the truth was no comfort. He didn't hate him. He loved him. He loved Jack, and he loved Amyas, and he loved Ursula, and he loved Morland Place, and every love instead of enriching him seemed only to drive him further and further into the darkness that filled his soul. He reached out, but could never quite touch those bright things for ever beyond his grasp.

For a long time he remained motionless, and then with a sigh he left the room and walked the few steps down the passage to the chapel. It was lit only by the faint glow of the altar lamp and it was as dark and red and peaceful as a womb. He knelt at the altar rail and tried to pray, but all that came from his mind and heart was an inarticulate crying. He was still there at dawn when the servants rose and the boy came in to light the candles for the first celebration.

The trouble with the Scots which Paul had foreseen came promptly that summer, in August. While the King was in France enjoying mild success, capturing Thérouanne and Tournai, and tasting the pleasures of a soldier abroad, an army of Scots under their King, James IV, crossed the Tweed and began to march south. For once Paul heard about it other than through Jack, for Jack was on the road to London with his brother and sister, taking Mary to Court to join the Queen's Household.

The Queen and the Council despatched the Earl of Surrey—son of that Jack of Norfolk who had died beside King Richard at the battle of Bosworth—with an army northwards to defend the Borders. Micah came with Surrey's household, and when the army halted at York he was able to visit home for the first time in many years, pay his respects to his father Richard, see his nephew Ezekiel for the first time, and bring the news fresh and hot to his cousin Paul at Morland Place.

'I have to bring you my lord Earl's compliments and best wishes,' Micah told Paul. 'He wishes me to say he knows that he has always been able to count on the support of the Morlands, and that he hopes you will be able to spare him some men now.'

'At harvest time,' Paul said drily. 'Well, there are worse causes, I suppose, than keeping the Scots at bay.'

'We are not so near the border as to feel the wind rising,' said Great Uncle Richard, who had come to Morland Place with his younger son, 'but still there is threat enough.'

'Jack's friend Parr I suppose is holding Westmorland?' Paul said.

'Aye,' said Richard, 'and though I hate to say it, this is a time when that traitor Percy is almost missed. They would not have got so far south if Percy had still been holding the border. His son is not the man *he* was.'

'Never mind,' Micah said. 'My lord of Surrey is twice the man even Percy was, as the Scots will discover.'

'Their King must be mad,' Richard said, 'to march against his own brother. If marriage alliances are not to prevent that, I can't imagine what they are for.'

The Scottish King has married King Henry's sister Margaret as part of a peace treaty between the two countries.

'It does seem a strange thing to do,' Micah said, 'especially since his son is at present heir apparent to both England and Scotland—'

'Unless the Queen bears a son,' Richard said. This was a subject better avoided in this house, and Paul broke in with, 'Well, you may tell my lord that of course I shall furnish him with men and arms, even though it is harvest time. For two pins I would march with them myself.'

'You cannot be spared, Paul,' Great Uncle Richard said. 'However, I am completely expendable—'

'Father, you can't go!' Micah said, half aghast, half amused. 'At your age!'

'I'm fifty-five, that's all,' Richard said, outraged. 'Don't tell me Surrey's not older than that, and he's commanding the forces!'

'In any case,' Micah went on, 'you were never one to take lives, not even Scots' lives.' Micah didn't know about the Percy incident. 'The very idea of you with a bloody sword in your hand is absurd and unpleasant.'

'And you are not expendable,' Paul finished the argument. 'I rely on you far too much to spare you, and with Jack away—'

Richard grunted, appeased. 'You're all just trying to flatter me out of what I want to do,' he grumbled. 'You think I'm too old. Too old at fifty-five! Wait until you're my age, then you'll realize.'

'You're not even fifty-five until September,' Paul interrupted him, smiling, 'so you needn't pretend *you* don't think it a great age.'

The army marched on, gathering men from the different musters as it made its way north, and on the ninth of September it met the Scots army near Flodden. The news came back a few days later of a massive defeat for the Scots, a defeat bordering on a massacre, for a third of the Scots army was killed, including King James, who died of his wounds within hours of the battle. He left an infant of two as King after him, and a Queen to be Regent who was only twenty-four and who had never been renowned for her good sense. It looked as though the Scots would not be giving much trouble for some years to come.

In October the army dispersed again, and Surrey's household went home, and King Henry, tired of soldiering, slipped home from France with a handful of men to join his rather too successful Queen-Regent at Richmond. Edward and Jack came home to Yorkshire, having missed Surrey both ways, and Edward's future was no nearer to being settled than before.

Then in November the news came that the Queen had miscarried, and Paul was gloomily triumphant to have been proved right again.

Christmas at Court was very quiet that year, and some of the newer and younger maids were allowed to come home, Mary amongst them. She brought the story of the miscarriage, the poor Queen's grief and fear, and how the King, to cheer her and let her know he still loved and valued her, had confirmed the plan to marry his other sister, the Princess Mary, to Charles of Castile, the Queen's kinsman.

'So you see, he doesn't blame her, as some people have been saying,' Mary finished. Paul looked at her questioningly.

'Have people been saying he blames her? The people of London, you mean?'

Mary blushed at her mistake. 'It's only rumours—gutter gossip. Everyone in the Court knows how he loves and respects her. He always asks her opinion on matters of state, and he couldn't praise her enough for the way she managed the Regency while he was in France.'

'The King's a good man,' Anne said significantly. Paul only gave one of his sarcastic smiles, and turned away.

On Christmas Day itself the family went to the mass at the church of the Holy Trinity within the Mickle Gate of York, as was traditional. The Parish Church of Saint Nicholas was nearer to Morland Place, and it was to that church they went each Sunday, but on the great feasts they went into the city to Holy Trinity, and to the great Minster itself at Easter.

After the mass the congregation gathered before the doors in the churchyard and spilled over into Priory Street to talk and wish their neighbours well and exchange news and gossip. All the Morlands had new clothes for the festival and like many others wanted to shew them off. Anne had a new gown of watchet-blue velvet, slashed and lined with bear's-ear silk in which she felt herself to be very splendid, and she was in no hurry to leave the gathering and return to Morland Place where there would be no polite neighbour to comment on its glory. She stood at the church gate nodding and smiling and occasionally patting the ornament at her throat to draw attention to it—a cross of gold set with tourmalines.

'Oh yes, my season's gift from my husband,' she would say when her companion obligingly noticed it. 'Or rather, one of his gifts. He's very generous. These gloves—yes, they are lovely, aren't they? Scented with civet. From Venice, of course—'

And gradually she became aware that she was being watched. First she shivered; and then she turned, cautiously so as not to appear to be looking, this way and that to seek out the eyes that were making her uncomfortable. Yes! There, over there, by the porch itself, a woman, plainly and neatly dressed, a yeoman's wife perhaps, poor but not indigent. The woman was dressed in a grey woollen gown with a stomacher laced over a white linen chemise; neatly-starched white cap framing a pale face and shewing a little hair at the front. Dark eyes watching her without expression, shifting away as Anne turned towards her.

Anne stared, sickness creeping into her stomach. The hair that shewed above the mild forehead was silver-gold, so fair it made Anne's seem coarse and yellow by comparison. The woman was at some distance, and her gaze had been removed at the same instant as Anne's found her: Anne had no evidence but a woman's instinct—a wife's instinct that she had been watched. And then a movement caught the corner of Anne's eye, and she turned her head to see Paul, his head towering above the crowd as always. He was looking towards the church porch, his eyes burning in his face like black fire.

Anne's hands were cold and wet inside her new gloves and she clasped them together. No, please no, she thought, though she hardly knew what she was protesting about. Perhaps begging that it should not be as important as her heart already knew it was. She glanced back towards the woman in the grey gown, but she had already turned away and was threading her way through the crowd towards the east gate. As she reached it and passed through, the crowd parted a little, and Anne could see what before had been hidden from her—that the woman held by the hand a sturdy little boy of four or five years old. The child had black curly hair.

$\mathcal{T}$HE WINTER WAS HARD, AND SPRING CAME SO LATE IN 1514 that many of the poorer people simply starved to death as their winter supplies of food ran out. There was a grant of food every day at the gate of Morland Place, but it was little enough, for there was not much to spare. The dire weather had brought the wolves much further south than they normally ran, and the Morlands lost some sheep and even more lambs, to add to the losses caused by the weather. Ploughing and sowing would be late, which would mean that, if next winter set in early, some of the crops would be lost and others would simply never ripen.

Added to that, the household normally eked out the winter salt-meat by fresh game, mainly venison, but the bitter cold and the prowling wolves had driven the herds from their normal runs, so that even that source of relief was lost. The Morlands grew gaunt, but only the weakest suffered: Belle's newest baby, a boy born in the autumn, shrank away and died; and in the city Ursula dropped a dead baby well before its time. In the magnitude of the white death that gripped the land, these little deaths went as unnoticed as a sparrow that falls frozen from the branch.

When at last the weather softened and the roads became passable again, the King's former almoner and present chief advisor, Thomas Wolsey, came north to be invested as the new

Archbishop of York. The appointment came as a surprise to many of the northerners, who had had no opportunity to keep up with developments in the distant and inaccessible south since Christmas.

'It was said at Court,' Jack said, 'that he was an up-and-coming man, but I had no idea how fast he was rising.'

'No doubt starting from so far down he feels he needs to move fast to make up the ground,' Belle replied with a smile. 'It's said his father was only a butcher.'

'What of that?' Paul said. 'The Church is a great leveller of men. If a man has the right qualities, the Church will not ask who his father was.'

'It remains to be seen whether this Wolsey has the right qualities,' Jack said. 'It can certainly be said, though, that he has the successful ones.'

'It's all very well to talk about the Church advancing a man,' Edward said rather peevishly, 'but one still has to make a start somewhere. I'm twenty-four and I still haven't begun a career. I've a mind to see Master Wolsey and ask him how I had better go about it.'

Jack grinned. 'More to the point, brother, why don't you ask him for a position?'

Paul looked thoughtful. 'You echo my thoughts,' he said. 'I was intending to seek an audience with the new Archbishop to ask if Mary might travel down with his household when he goes south again. While I'm there, I think I'll ask if he has an opening for you, Edward.'

Edward stared at him, amazed at such generosity. 'Would you? That would be kind of you. To be in Wolsey's household seems to me to be a very good way of advancement. But hadn't I better come with you? He may want to see me.'

Paul hid a gleam of amusement. 'Not so eager! If he is interested in you, he will no doubt wish to see you before making up his mind, but it is best for me alone to make the first approach. He's a busy man, he won't want to be surrounded by supplicants.'

'Well, if you think that's the best way,' Edward said hesitantly.

'I am sure of it. Leave it to me.'

Paul had no difficulty in securing an audience, for he was one of the leading men of those parts, with considerable local influence, and he set off for the city very early on the day in question, for he wanted to visit Ursula while he was in York. He had been worried about her during the winter. It had been hard, during the worst weather, to get to her, and since she had had her miscarriage at a time when Morland Place had been cut off by snow, she had gone through that terrible time quite alone and unaided. He had managed from time to time to send food to her, but he had had to be very circumspect since Jack had discovered her existence.

So on this day he set off before dawn, and reached the house in the Shambles while Ursula was still dressing. He shed his attendants outside the Minster, bidding them wait for him, and went on attended only by his most discreet and faithful man, who kept watch outside the house. Paul climbed the dark, narrow spiral stair, the padded shoulders of his doublet brushing the walls on either side.

He knocked at the low door and entered at once, and Ursula turned in surprise which melted quickly into a welcoming smile as Paul crossed the room and took her in his arms. She was dressed in chemise and underkirtle, and was brushing her hair preparatory to hiding it under one of her linen caps.

'Dearest,' she murmured, lifting her lips for his kisses. 'I had not expected you.' Paul smiled.

'If you had, would you have hastened or delayed your dressing?'

'Which do you think?' she laughed. 'How long can you stay?'

'A moment only. I wanted to see if you were well. Let me

look at you.' He put her back to arm's length and frowned critically. 'You are too thin. And pale.'

'Everyone is thin, my heart, after such a winter. *You* are thin—see how this doublet hangs on you.'

'You know what I mean, little bear. I'm afraid your miscarriage has affected your health. Tell me truly, how is it with you?'

'It is always hard to lose a child,' she said, 'but, truly, I think I am well enough—or shall be when the warmth comes back into the world.'

He took her close to him again, and she pressed her face against the fur of his collar and rubbed it like a cat.

'Perhaps it may be as well that you lost the child,' he said gently. 'It could only have been an added burden.'

Ursula's face was hidden, but he knew the expression on it. 'Only a man could talk about it being as well to lose a child.'

'I'm sorry, but you know what I mean. God knows I wish—'

She pulled her face back and freed a hand to lay her fingers on his lips.

'Shh, don't say it,' she said. 'We are what we are.' She moved away from him and resumed brushing her hair, and he watched, fascinated as always by the pale fire of it. 'Isn't it strange to you, Paul, that what you blame in your wife you are glad of in me. That *I* have only one child seems a blessing to you, but in her it is a grave fault.'

He shifted uncomfortably. She rarely used his name, and when she did it always seemed to preface some awkward truth such as this. 'You know that it is different.'

'Yes, I know. But the difference is your difference, and not ours.'

Now her strong fingers were flying amongst the golden threads, drawing the mass into neat braids which she would pin up and cover for the day. He hated that women had to cover their hair, just as he would have hated it if his flower-garden had been covered over with blankets. He became aware suddenly of the silence and asked a little awkwardly, 'Where is the boy?'

She looked up under her brows. Often the child slept in the tiny windowless room next door while they were making love in that bed that otherwise she shared with his son. 'It's all right, he has gone.'

'Gone?'

'To school. You had forgotten he was going to school at St Sampson's now?'

'I hadn't realised he had started already. I forget how time passes. It seems he has only just stopped being a babe in arms. And talking of how time passes—'

'I know—you have to go. Ah, don't look so guilty, my dearest heart, I am used to it now. I know that you come when you can. What brings you to the city today?'

He told her of his audience, and his plan to ask for a place for Edward.

'So generous,' she said, and the laughter was close under the surface. He stepped nearer and put his arms round her waist.

'You are laughing at me,' he said, mock-threateningly. 'You know I won't be laughed at.'

'You are so transparent. Do your half-kin realise too that you are doing it to be rid of them? Mary at Court, and Edward away with the Archbishop; if you could find Jack a place in Calais you would be happy.'

'You know too much and see too much. One day you will be—' He was about to say 'burned as a witch' when he managed to stop himself; but she had divined his thought and turned a little paler even than before. Her eyes widened.

'Don't,' she whispered in terror. 'Don't, don't, don't ever say it. Don't think it.'

He kissed her forehead contritely. 'Little bear,' he said, 'it's all right. It means nothing.'

She controlled herself with an effort, and the little colour she had crept back. She forced her mind to his business. 'While you are speaking to the Archbishop, why don't you ask him if he has a place for your son? It could be a very good advancement for him.'

'My son?' he said puzzled. 'You mean—'

'No, not my Adrian,' she said with a wry smile. 'I meant your acknowledged son, your Paul Amyas.' Paul frowned. 'Yes, I know what you would say, that you don't want him out of your sight. And being your only son,' there was no irony in her voice, 'you would be afraid of losing him. But he needs experience. One day he will inherit everything. He needs to see how a great house is ordered.'

'I suppose you may be right,' he said doubtfully.

'The poor child has no friends,' Ursula went on. 'Look at Jack and all the people he knows, through being out in the world. Contacts and patronage go with wealth and success and happiness. Would you want your Amyas to grow up alone and knowing no-one?'

'Like me, you mean.'

'I didn't say that.'

'No, you didn't. I did. You are right, my hinny. I have been selfish in wanting him at home with me. He is almost fourteen. Two or three years in and around the Court would be wonderful experience for him. I shall do as you suggest.'

'Good. And now, dearest love, though I hate to see you go—'

'Jesu, yes, I must go. Kiss me once more. I will try to come and see you again soon—this week or perhaps next—'

'Go on, go on. I know you will come when you can. God have you in His keeping.'

'And you, little bear.'

The business was quickly concluded. All three of Paul's requests were acceded to; a sum of money was suggested by Paul and indicated to be acceptable to the Archbishop; Amyas was to enter Wolsey's service as a gentleman groom of the bedchamber, Edward as junior chaplain; and Mary was to travel down with her brother and nephew and be delivered by them to Court. Paul was not surprised that the business had been so smoothly completed—he had understood that Wolsey was a businessman. What had surprised him was the state the man kept, more like a king than an archbishop.

The room where the audience was held was richly, lavishly furnished and decorated. Priceless tapestries—real Arras tapestries—lined the walls; there was a carpet on the floor as well as on the table; Wolsey's chair was huge, gilded and filled with velvet cushions; pages, grooms, clerks and secretaries stood around as if it were the King's presence chamber.

And then there was the man himself—a man of Paul's own age, between thirty-five and forty, and yet in his hauteur and arrogance and splendour seeming much older. He was a fair-skinned, ruddy-faced, broad man, already running to fat, his wide face softening into a loose chin like something melting downwards. His scanty hair was mouse-coloured, his eyes a faded blue, hidden for the most part under heavy white lids. His clothes were sumptuous and crusted with embroidery and jewels; his white, fastidious hands were loaded with rings, and played constantly with an orange stuck with cloves which he lifted from time to time to his nostrils as if the gross air that ordinary human beings breathed needed some palliative for him.

Paul's instant feeling was of dislike for this wide, white man. He seemed to Paul to epitomise the south and all it stood for—soft, sluggish life, corruption, foul air. Against Wolsey,

Paul knew that he must seem hard and rough and brown, like something hewn out of rock or roughly carved from native oak. Yet, as he waited to be dismissed, he studied the man with a kind of fascination, and suddenly the heavy lids lifted, the pale eyes flashed, and the fair ruddy face wreathed itself in smiles, and Paul was forced to admit that the Archbishop could be charming, if he wished.

'Have you no questions before you go?' Wolsey asked him. 'Nothing you wish to know?' Paul hesitated, not knowing where the question tended, and Wolsey added 'I never knew a man of the north who was not eager for news of the Court, and of the war.'

'Yes indeed, Your Grace,' Paul answered quickly. 'I should be glad of news—it has been a long winter.'

Wolsey sniffed at the orange, and lowered his eyelids slowly, like a cat. 'We have abandoned the Spanish alliance, and are negotiating with the French. What think you of that, Master Morland?' He replaced the orange on the desk and steepled his long white fingers, resting them against his mouth; but behind the relaxed mask the small eyes were alert, and Paul knew he was being tested: for what reason he did not know.

'The Spanish alliance did not seem to bring us much gain, Your Grace,' he said carefully. 'King Ferdinand changed his mind and his side so often. A French alliance—against him—?' He allowed a faint questioning note to creep in. The hands came down from the mouth and rested flat on the table. The wide face was hard.

'The King would like to press the Queen's claim to Castile, with French help against Ferdinand.'

Still being tested. Paul was not *au fait* with international questions as was Jack, but he thought it unlikely anything could come of the Queen's claim on Castile. He avoided the implied question.

'The French are strong. It is well to have strong allies. And with their traditional interest in Scotland, it might be well to have them at our side instead of at our back.'

He breathed cautiously, and then relaxed—not too visibly—as he saw Wolsey smile again. Apparently he had passed the test.

'We think alike, Master Morland. Tell me, you have been to Court before, I believe?'

How on earth did he know that? 'Yes, Your Grace. Once, when the King and Queen were receiving, not long after the coronation.'

'Perhaps it is time you were presented again. It is well to make one's face familiar. The Princess Mary is to be married to the King of France in the summer. Your sister would perhaps be a suitable addition to Her Grace's entourage. You will come to Court for the proxy marriage, and it shall be discussed. You have our leave to retire now.' There was no requirement for any comment, not even thanks, and in silence Paul knelt to kiss the proffered ring, and then bowed himself out as from a king, his mind a whirl of conflicting thoughts. So Wolsey, apparently seeing some value in him, was making his patronage obvious; but was there a veiled threat in the words that had passed? Paul longed suddenly for Ursula and the simplicity of her speech and desires. If only life could be that simple! But it would be pleasant to have influence at Court which did not depend on Jack, even if that influence stemmed from a one-time butcher's son.

When he reached home, Paul found he could not even now be first with the momentous news, for Great Uncle Richard had ridden over from Shawes with Elijah to dinner, bringing the news of the French alliance which they had heard in a letter from Micah.

'And the messenger who brought the letter had other news that could not be committed to paper,' Elijah said.

'More in fact was said than was written,' Uncle Richard put in, somewhat sourly.

'Now, Father, don't sound like that. You know you like gossip as well as the next man.'

'Do I? Well, perhaps, when it hurts no-one.' Richard helped himself from a dish as if dissociating himself from the conversation, and Elijah looked at him affectionately.

'It hurts no-one, Father. It is only passing on information. But if it offends you—'

'Come, come, cousin, you can't stop there. You must tell us this mysterious news now, having whetted our appetites,' Jack interrupted.

'Yes, for heaven's sake tell,' Anne added. 'We have been starved for news these long months.'

Elijah looked apologetically at his father and Richard shrugged moodily.

'Very well then,' Elijah said. 'After Christmas, when the Court moved up from Greenwich, the King took a mistress.'

Silence greeted the revelation. Anne looked away, a dull flush colouring her face. Jack stared in astonishment.

'What is the lady's name?' Paul asked, the only one to speak.

'It is one of the Queen's ladies, a mistress Blunt, Elizabeth Blunt. She has been at Court for some years, the King has known her from childhood.'

'Is it sure?' Jack asked.

'Quite sure,' Elijah said. 'These things cannot be concealed at Court. The Queen takes it very philosophically, it seems. After all, for a king, one mistress after all these years is not so very terrible. Kings are not like ordinary men, they cannot be judged by ordinary standards. The King of France—'

'Let us not take France for an example, my son,' Richard

said. 'And as to kings being unlike ordinary mortals—they ought to be better, if they are different, and set an example to their people.'

'Oh Father, you know that's not the case. Besides, the King, it seems, did not take a mistress purely for his own pleasure but for reasons of State.'

'Reasons of State!' Richard said explosively, but Paul broke in more quietly, 'What reasons, cousin? Is it something to do with the French alliance?'

Elijah turned to him, nodding. 'The Queen's inability to bear a child, and her father's duplicity during the French war, were the combined reasons for repudiating the Spanish alliance. The King, it seems, spoke to the Council about the possibility of putting the Queen aside and marrying again.'

'Putting her aside? But he can't!' Anne cried. Paul turned his eyes on her, about to say something bitter and hurtful; but in his mind he heard Ursula's voice—*The difference is yours, not ours*—and he held his tongue. Elijah went on, 'It seems he has doubts of the validity of the marriage on account of his consanguinity with the Queen. She was married to his brother, which is a forbidden degree of relationship. When the old King first suggested he marry her, it seems he spoke then against the idea, but was persuaded afterwards for it. But her inability to bear a child seems to support the view that the marriage was not a true marriage.'

There was a long silence while these ideas were absorbed. Finally Jack said in a rather distant voice, 'Whether or not these things be true, what can this have to do with the King's taking a mistress?'

'I believe,' Elijah said unhappily, 'that the idea is to prove that it is no fault of his that the Queen has no child, so as to make it certain.'

'That's enough! This is shocking talk, and we shall have no

more of it at the table,' Great Uncle Richard said, bringing his large fist down with a bang that made the plates jump. It was not his place to say such a thing, but Paul agreed with him, though for political rather than moral reasons, so he broke in smoothly, 'You are right, Uncle. Should we not instead talk of my sister's great good fortune? How should you like to go to France, Mary?'

Princess Mary was married by proxy on the thirteenth of August, at Greenwich. At the end of a long and exhausting day, Paul and Richard retired to their quarters, a tiny room in a remote part of the huge and rambling palace, and prepared for bed. They undressed in silence, unlacing each other since their servants had long since disappeared in the general drinking and merrymaking, but at last Richard paused, stretched, and said, 'Well?'

'Well what?'

'What are your impressions? What do you think of the principal characters in the play we have just seen?'

Paul was rather fuddled with wine, and he too paused in taking off his hose to consider.

'The Queen didn't look well,' he said at last. 'Perhaps the heat, and her pregnancy—but she looked tired, and—old.'

'She is past thirty,' Richard mused. 'She conceives easily enough, it seems, but—'

'Perhaps that supports the King's idea—' Paul began. Richard crossed to him quickly.

'Shh! Not here. I think that has all been forgotten, anyway, now that the Queen is with child again. The King, tell me what you thought of the King.'

Paul cast his mind back to the brief moment when it had

been his turn to approach the dais, kneel, kiss the King's hand, and rise again. There could never have been any doubt in anyone's mind, not even a stranger from the other end of the world, which person in the room was the King, for he towered above the rest, taller even than Paul, and altogether bigger-built: a giant of a man, well-built, powerful and athletic, his sheer physical presence enhanced by the jewelled splendour of his clothes, white and deep blue sewn with pearls and sapphires and diamonds, trimmed with fur, lined with silk.

A young man, Paul remembered, twenty-four or five; a fair, clean-shaven face, broad at the cheekbones and as pretty as a girl's, clear-skinned and pink-cheeked; bright blue eyes, long-lashed; smooth reddish-blond hair hanging to the shoulders from under a velvet cap. It was a face, he thought, innocent of guile, innocent, perhaps, even of power. He thought of Wolsey, remembered the King's arm flung affectionately across 'Our dear Tom's' shoulder. Yes, innocent of power, perhaps. The blue eyes had smiled at Paul, the melodious voice greeted him. And yet—and yet—there was something ugly, wasn't there, about his mouth? Paul, drink-dazed, didn't know.

'An improvement on his father,' he said at last, making a joke of it. Richard looked thoughtful.

'I wonder. He reminded me of King Edward. He looks a lot like him, tall and golden. The same broad, long-chinned face. But King Edward was—subtle. A king brought up to know his king-ship and what it entailed. King Henry has never had to wonder what gives him his power. Perhaps that's the difference.'

'You were disappointed?' Paul asked, puzzled. He had heard the tone rather than the words.

'Not disappointed, really. I hadn't expected much more. Paul, do you remember my mother?'

Paul rubbed his eyes sleepily. 'What a question, at this time of night! Yes, I remember her. I remember dancing with her on her last birthday. She smelled of roses. I was afraid of her.'

'She once said to me that King Edward and King Richard had made kingship different—that they had shewn that a king serves the people rather than the people the king.'

'What an extraordinary idea,' Paul yawned. Richard stared into the darkness sadly.

'I think King Henry would agree with you. I don't think he'll ever have any doubts as to who serves whom while he reigns.' He thought for a moment, and Paul, down to his shirt at last, flung himself onto the mattress and tugged at the blanket, ineffectually since he was lying half on it. 'I think it is not a step forward,' Richard said at last. There was no reply. Paul, giving up on the blanket, had fallen asleep.

All princesses are automatically beautiful, but the Princess Mary would have been considered beautiful even had she not been a princess. She had a delicate, heart-shaped face, brilliant violet eyes, hair like burnished copper, an exquisite, dainty figure. Everyone in the Court was in love with her, and there was no doubt that she would lead the King of France a merry dance, provided he remained alive for long enough: it was said he was very, very old and also frail. A sad waste, it seemed, to be marrying such a vivacious young girl to such a grey old stick.

Such, at least, was Mary Morland's opinion, and she found it was shared by many of the girls who were gathered at Court to be looked over by the new Queen of France with a view to being included in the entourage. Mary felt a little out of things, for she was older than the other unmarried maids, and too young to be included with the more senior matrons.

Having not been at Court for long, she did not know many people, and although she was not the only young woman from distant parts, it made her feel isolated. She did have one friend, however—Mary Boleyn, the daughter of Jack's friend, and also a recently-joined member of the Queen's Household. Mary Boleyn was sixteen, six years younger than Mary Morland, but she was quite bright and forward for her age, and so the two girls got on reasonably well.

Mary Boleyn did not share Mary Morland's views on the Princess's plight.

'I shouldn't mind at all. Being so old, he won't trouble her much. She only has to lie with him until she gets with child, and then she needn't trouble any more. Once she has given him an heir, she may do as she pleases, and take a lover. Better to marry an old man you don't like than a young one.'

'That's shocking talk,' Mary Morland said. 'The Princess, take a lover?'

'Haven't you noticed,' Mary Boleyn said, 'the way a *certain person* looks at her, and she at him?'

'Who do you mean?' asked Mary Morland, who hadn't.

'Why the King's friend, of course—Charles Brandon. Didn't you know they were in love? It's all over the Court.'

'You're making it up,' Mary Morland said. Mary Boleyn looked indignant.

'Indeed I am not—ask anyone. Ask Anne Grey or Anne Dacre if you don't believe me. They say,' she drew closer and lowered her voice, 'they say that the Princess only agreed to marry the King of France on condition that when he dies she'll be allowed to choose her own next husband. And that's why the King made Master Brandon Duke of Suffolk, because the Princess couldn't marry anyone less than a Duke.' Mary Morland's astonishment was very satisfactory. Mary Boleyn felt worldly-wise beside her.

'Choose her own husband? Who ever heard of such a thing,' Mary Morland said at last. Mary Boleyn smiled knowingly.

'The Princess believes it will be so, but it's my belief the King only said that to keep her sweet. When the time comes, he will make her marry the person he chooses. She is too valuable to him.' She had heard her father and his friends talk like this, and it was good to be able to be knowing, especially with someone older than herself. 'I hope we *are* chosen to go to France,' she said next. 'It will be so much more fun than here.'

'Will you stay here, then, if you aren't chosen?'

Boleyn made a face. 'I don't think so. My father will send me to Burgundy I expect, if I don't go to France, and that will be even worse. Still, I think we'll be chosen. The Princess is to have a very big retinue. The Grey girls are bound to be chosen, but after all, *we* are relatives of the King, through our mother.'

'We?' Mary Morland queried. Boleyn nodded vaguely.

'My sister Anne is under consideration as well. But she's only twelve—she won't get in our way. Our mother, you see, was sister-in-law to the King's aunt, so that makes us cousins, of a sort. We're almost sure to be chosen.'

'Yes, my brother knew your mother quite well,' Mary Morland said, not to be left out. Boleyn gave a glance of slight surprise, and shrugged it off.

'What's your connection with the Court? I mean, what influence have you to get you chosen?'

'Archbishop Wolsey,' Mary Morland said shortly. Mary Boleyn looked taken aback. Even she knew of Wolsey's influence.

'Oh well,' she said, 'you should be all right then. If we are both chosen, shall we ask Lady Guilford if we can share a bed? It's as well to arrange these things if you can, otherwise you might find yourself sharing with someone you don't like.'

In the event, both girls were chosen, and along with the rest of the retinue they finally set sail at the beginning of October in one of a fleet of fourteen ships collected at Dover for the purpose. They were delayed for over two weeks at Dover by terrible weather conditions, and were at last packed off hastily during a slight lull in the storms. There followed a nightmare five days when the ships were blown and tossed in a tempest which scattered the fleet up and down the Channel, but miraculously no-one was killed, though everyone suffered so terribly from sea-sickness that death would have seemed a kindly alternative to them.

And all, in the event, for so little. A month later the entire retinue was on its way home again, the old French King having dismissed all his new bride's English attendants since, he said, she would be better, as Queen of France, to be served by French people. He allowed her to choose four girls to remain with her, and without much hesitation she chose her young kinswomen, Anne and Elizabeth Grey, and her two favourite attendants, Anne Dacre, and Mary Boleyn's younger sister Anne.

By the end of November Mary Morland was back in the Queen's Household in Greenwich where she had started from. She did not even keep her new-found friend since, as she had prophesied, Mary Boleyn was sent off to the Court at Burgundy for her further education; and little as she had liked the brash young woman, Mary Morland missed her, having no-one else with whom she was intimate.

She began to think longingly, and rather hopelessly, of marriage. She was twenty-two, and ought to have been married before this. Even an old man, like Princess Mary's, would be better than nothing, she thought, better than being left a maid all her life, and unprovided-for. Yet her brother Jack and her half-brother Paul did not seem to have her fate at all on their minds, and there was no-one else to look to her interests.

The southern winter set in gloomily; and in early December Queen Catharine was brought to bed of a boy-child who lived only a few minutes, and Mary Morland had the terrible feeling that nothing would ever change, but that the same pattern would go on repeating itself for ever, until she was an old woman.

*I*N THE AUTUMN OF 1515 ARCHBISHOP WOLSEY, CHANCELLOR of England, was made a cardinal. It was, of course, a compliment to England and to England's king, but most of all it was a tribute to Wolsey's untiring effort, his devotion to the Pope's interests, and his skill in maintaining the international balance of power so as to defend the Pope from threatening alliances. The King chose to view it as a compliment to himself. Whether or not he appreciated the other aspects of the appointment could not be known, but at any rate he did not absent himself from the party Wolsey gave in celebration at his London home, York House, that September.

Jack, who had been in London for some weeks on business, was there. Wolsey kept in close contact with members of the merchant class, and invited several of them to the feast; and for Jack it became something of a Morland family reunion. The first person he met after paying his respects to his host was his younger brother.

'Well, Edward, and how are you?' he cried. 'You are looking very prosperous and happy. How are you liking your new life?'

Edward smiled and stroked the velvet facings of his long black gown. He had put on weight, and had quite lost, Jack noticed, that discontented expression. He looked altogether like the cat who was locked in the dairy.

'Well, I thank you,' Edward said. 'It has opened my eyes, I can tell you. We thought we did things well back at Morland Place, but we had no idea, no idea at all, how things are done in a great household. Our ideas of luxury are very poor and small, you know. Why, here at York House, there are over five hundred in the household. Think of that!'

Jack's amusement was just apparent. 'Five hundred! Then I take it *your* duties are not too onerous?'

Edward frowned slightly. 'Everything is done properly, in the chapel as elsewhere. I have enough to do. My duties are mostly secretarial. The Cardinal gets through an enormous amount of business every day. Why, the supplicants from amongst the common people alone—'

'You must be pleased,' Jack broke in to forestall a list, 'with Wolsey's good fortune in getting his cardinal's hat at last.'

'We are all delighted with His Grace's good fortune, which he so amply deserves,' Edward said, and his tone was a rebuke for Jack for his levity. Jack grew impatient.

'Come, Edward, you needn't be overawed. A man's a man, however high he climbs!'

'Not so,' Edward shook his head. 'When a man climbs so high, he is more than other men. You are too independent.'

'And you are too easily impressed. But let us not quarrel. I am glad to see you looking so well. You will have flesh on your bones at the end, and that's more than can be said of me. Now, tell me, where is our nephew?'

'Amyas? He should be—ah, yes, over there. In the green livery.'

'Is that him? He has grown this last year! He might make his father's height after all. And who is the red-haired lad with him?'

Edward screwed up his eyes short-sightedly to make out Amyas's companion. 'Oh, that must be young Harry Percy, Northumberland's son. He has only recently joined the household—I did hear that he and Amyas had struck up a friendship, both being from the north. Percy's rather rough and uncouth, I believe, but that will wear off. Meantime, I dare say Amyas is looking after him. He does not get on well with the other young men, so perhaps he is glad to have someone who is even more an outsider to condescend to.'

'Northumberland's son, an outsider?' Jack was surprised. 'I would have thought an Earl's son—'

'These border-raiders,' Edward said with infinite scorn. 'Cattle lords, always covered in mud and smelling of horses. No idea of gentle manners. I'm sorry in a way Amyas should take up with him. He's awkward enough as it is, without rubbing shoulders with stable-boys.'

'Pride goeth before a fall, Edward,' Jack said seriously. 'I'm sorry to hear you speak so contemptuously of ordinary folk. What's in a man's heart is more important than his appearance or his manners.'

Edward raised an eyebrow. 'What nonsense, brother. The Lord advances those in His special favour. How can a man God blesses with good fortune be less admirable than one He condemns to obscurity? God judges us on our merits—do you wish to tell me that God is wrong, or makes mistakes?'

This interesting theological point had to be abandoned because at that moment fanfares of trumpets announced the arrival of the King, and shortly afterwards of the French Queen and the Duke of Suffolk.

'She is still called the French Queen, then?' Jack whispered to Edward as the former Princess Mary made her curtseys to the King. The King raised his sister and kissed her coolly, and then greeted his old friend Brandon with rather more warmth.

'I think the King encourages it,' Edward whispered back. 'He cannot love Suffolk any less, but he still cannot bring himself to approve of the marriage.'

Princess Mary had been married only three months when the King of France died on New Year's Day 1515, and King Henry had begun negotiations to marry her to the new French King, Francis, in spite of his promise to her that she might choose her second husband herself. In desperation she had done an almost criminally rash thing—she married Brandon, whom she loved, secretly while she was locked away in royal mourning at the dower house at Cluny. During the royal mourning period the Queen was not supposed to leave her room or meet anyone but her close female servants—an obvious precaution to ensure that any child born to the widowed Queen within a certain period could name its father with confidence.

King Henry had been furious in the extreme and for a time it had appeared that the couple might have to spend the rest of their lives in exile. But using Wolsey as an intermediary they had begged the King's pardon and stripped themselves of all their wealth as guilt-money, and had at last been allowed home in May, to be married at Greenwich and to retire immediately to the obscurity of Suffolk.

'She does not look any the less beautiful,' Jack said. 'Pregnancy suits her, it seems, and it really was a love-match after all. Look how Brandon follows her with his eyes.'

'It is lucky for her that she did not conceive earlier,' Edward said. 'It could have cost her her life. King Francis is not like King Louis, my master tells me.'

'It is never a happy thing to be too closely related to a king,' Jack said. 'I must go and talk to Amyas and that young friend of his. I'd be interested to meet the Old Fox's grandson. He's inherited the hair, if nothing else.'

'And the temper too, I believe,' Edward said. 'Who's this looking for you—?'

Jack turned, and his face broke into a spontaneous grin. 'Tom! Well met, my friend, well met! You came with the King, I suppose? How are you? And how is your wife?'

'God's day to you, Morland. Well, I thank you, we are both well,' Boleyn said. 'And you too, I hope. God's day, master Edward. The Cardinal's house is becoming quite a meeting place for the Morland family. Isn't that your brother's son over there?'

'It is,' Jack said. 'We were just talking about him, and his new friend, Northumberland's son. We northerners find we have to stick together, you see, Tom. You southerners think us uncouth.'

Thomas Boleyn grinned back, an unaccustomed exercise for his dark face, and one which Jack as few others could occasion. 'And so you are Jack. Why, I remember that time in Antwerp—'

'Then you should be ashamed of yourself. I have forgotten it, as a good son of the Church should. How are your children, tell me? What a brilliant brood you sired! They take after their mother,' he concluded rather wistfully. Boleyn's face closed too as he remembered his enchanting first wife. But his second match had been a love-match, and he probably thought rather less often of Elizabeth Boleyn than Jack did. Jack went on, 'Wasn't one of your girls with the French Queen's household? What became of her? Did she come back with the Queen?'

Boleyn shook his head. 'That was an awkward business,' he said, lowering his voice, 'but we came well enough out of it. Anne and the three other maids who stayed on with Queen Mary were all transferred into the household of Queen Claude, and there they stay. They will get a good education there. Queen Claude is a virtuous and religious woman, and the

French Court is the most brilliant in the world. I hope Anne will acquire a good deal of polish while she is there. She will need it if I am to get her a good match.'

'Why, surely you will not have any difficulty? I remember her as a charming child,' Jack said.

'Charming, yes, but not pretty. Still, I have my plans for her. For them all. Ah, this must be the Queen arriving,' as another fanfare sounded. 'She agreed to call in for a short while.' Boleyn lowered his voice. 'She is pregnant again, you know, and did not wish to stir out, but His Grace wished the Cardinal to be honoured, and so she must agree. And there, if I mistake not, is another of your brood, Jack. Is that not your sister?'

'Yes, it is. See, Edward, our sister Mary? We must try to speak to her too. How ill the Queen looks, poor lady. What hopes, I wonder, of a happy outcome this time?'

Boleyn glanced around him. 'That is a subject better not spoken of, Morland. But now I must go and pay my respects to some other acquaintances. When will you dine with us again, Jack? It has been over-long since we had you under our roof. Will you come next week? I shall be at home again by Saturday, at Hever. Will you come and hunt with me?'

'I will, right gladly Tom,' Jack said. 'Will we take out that lad of yours and shew him how men hunt?'

'A good idea. Perhaps you could bring along your young nephew, too,' Boleyn nodded towards Amyas, 'for company. It would be a pleasant thing if they could be friends. George is over-fond of poetry for my liking. An interest in hunting and wrestling would help him find favour with the King when the time comes, and competing with a boy his own age might sharpen him up.'

'I will see if it can be arranged. Till Saturday, then.'

The uneasy political situation abroad kept Jack a good deal in London that winter, and so it was that he was in the capital in February 1516 when the Queen was brought to bed, at Greenwich, of a live baby. The joy in the city was intense, for though the child was only a girl, it was large and healthy and gave every appearance of intending to survive, and everyone who loved the Queen was glad that she should have had this joyful outcome after all the sad miscarriages.

The child was named Mary, and was christened with great pomp and celebration, and the good news spread so rapidly and joyfully through the country that as Jack rode home on the day after the feast he was besieged at every halt by demands for the most detailed descriptions of the new baby and everything surrounding her.

'Yes, yes, a very pretty child,' he said a dozen times on the journey home. 'In faith, the Princess is the prettiest baby I have ever seen, and I have five of my own to judge by. She looks very like the King, as far as I can judge. And, yes, she is the image of her mother. The King and Queen dote on her. I have never seen such happy, loving parents. The King took the little Princess in his arms and carried her round all the ambassadors of Europe so that they could admit she was the most beautiful baby they had ever seen.'

It was a hyperbolical journey altogether, for it took him longer than ever before and he drank more wine and ale and spent less money in doing so than he had ever done between London and York; and when he finally reached home it had all to be said again.

'Well,' said Belle with satisfaction, giving a complacent glance at her own children gathered round her, Catherine and Jane sitting at her feet and Jackie and Dickon lolling against her knees, one either side, their round young eyes fixed on the glamorous figure of their father, 'I am so very, very happy for them both, and particularly for the Queen, poor lady. God is good.'

'And it disproves those stories about the Queen's former marriage,' Anne said with a satisfaction of her own, and a covert glance towards Paul. Paul, standing alone by the fireplace and once more aware of the size of Jack's brood compared with his own, turned his morose gaze from his sole representative, seven-year-old Margaret, sitting next to Belle and sewing, to his wife and said, 'Not at all, Madam. Why should you think so?'

Anne compressed her lips a little in anger. 'Because, sir, it was thought that the Queen was cursed with childlessness, and that has proved untrue.'

'You misunderstood, if you understood that,' Paul said with a bitter satisfaction. 'The Bible states that marriage within the prohibited degree of consanguinity will be cursed with a lack of sons; daughters are not mentioned.'

Uncle Richard stirred restlessly. 'The problem is not solved yet,' he said. 'I fear that we shall have a repetition of the troubles of my youth. Nothing drains a country's strength like wars of that sort, quarrels over the crown. Better for England, in good faith, if the King did put aside the Queen, virtuous lady though she may be.'

'How can he put her aside now that she has a child?' Belle said indignantly. Jack sighed.

'A child she may have, but I'm afraid Uncle Richard is right. It is only a daughter.' His arm was at that moment about the waist of his own first-born daughter, seven-year-old Nanette who was standing by his chair and leaning against him, her smooth cheek close to his own and her dark curling hair falling over his shoulder. Nanette had always been his favourite, and she adored her father in return, and now, despite his comforting arm round her little waist she looked at him in some consternation.

'Papa,' she said anxiously, 'why do you say *only* a daughter? Is a daughter no use at all?'

'My dear little girl,' Jack said gently, 'a daughter is a wonderful thing for a man to have, like a soft little pet bird to nestle in his palm and sing to him and make him happy. But a king is not like other men—he must have a son to be king after him, or there will be no-one to rule the country, and then there will be troubles and wars.'

Nanette's brilliant eyes, blue as the sapphires on the king's cap Jack always said, regarded her father with puzzlement. 'But Papa, cannot the new Princess rule the kingdom after the King?'

'No dearest—a girl cannot rule; only a boy.'

'Why not, Papa?'

Jack rolled his eyes heavenward, and Paul laughed abruptly.

'If you will educate them, Jack,' he said, 'you must expect trouble.' Jack grinned. 'I'll take the trouble along with the sweets,' he said, and drew his daughter on to his lap. 'It's a complicated thing, sweeting. Do you really want to know?' Nanette nodded. 'Well then,' Jack said slowly and carefully, 'if a girl should become queen, she would have to leave a son to be king after her; so she would have to get married. And if she married, her husband would be king. Do you follow?'

Nanette nodded.

'Well now, who should she marry? If she marries a foreign prince, that would mean a foreign prince would be King of England, and the people wouldn't like that.'

'Then she should marry an Englishman,' Nanette said decisively. Jack was pleased with her for following him thus far, and kissed her round childish cheek.

'Quite so. But every man would want to be chosen, and the man she did choose would have enemies in all the men she rejected, and so there would be strife and quarrels and troubles. And sooner or later—'

'Sooner or later,' Uncle Richard took over, 'one man would emerge with some vestige of a claim to the throne and there would be a war and the queen would be queen no more. There was only ever once a Queen of England, and the country was torn apart with civil strife because of it.'

'Queen Maud,' Jack nodded.

'So there will be no more Queens of England, other than king's wives. It won't do, Nanette. Depend upon it, a girl can't take the throne.'

Nanette looked so disappointed that Jack decided to tell her there and then the news he had intended to keep from her until he had spoken to Belle about it.

'Never mind, sweetheart,' he said. 'A girl may not be Queen, but there are lots of things she can do, and there is no reason why she can't have as good an education as a boy. That is why I have made arrangements for you to go away to a place where you can get an education that will fit you for any station in life you care to choose.'

'Jack! You've spoken to him!' Belle exclaimed in delight.

'Yes, my dear, and I meant to tell you first but—' he shrugged meaningfully.

'Papa, do you mean I am to go away from here? To go away from you?' Nanette asked anxiously.

'Yes, my darling. You remember my friend Sir Thomas Parr? You have heard me speak of him, at least?' Nanette nodded. She was afraid to speak because the tears were too close to the surface and she knew it would displease her father if she wept. 'Well, Sir Thomas and his wife have a little girl named Katherine, and she is a little younger than you, but a very intelligent child. Lady Parr will supervise her education herself, and she will be taught Latin and Greek and French and Italian and

Spanish and mathematics and theology just like a boy. When I spoke to Sir Thomas he told me that he had just taken another little girl, a cousin of Katherine's called Elizabeth Bellingham, to live with them and be educated with Katherine, and he said that you could go too, and make a third.'

He paused and surveyed his eldest child solemnly, to impress upon her her own good luck. Nanette knew enough of the ways of the world to know that this was, in grown-up terms, a good thing to happen to her, but her own natural feelings were fighting with her understanding.

'Where shall I be living, then, Papa?' she said at last.

'In Kentdale, at the castle there. It is a beautiful place, and very healthy for young girls growing up.'

'Unless the Scots invade again,' Paul added, sotto voce.

'It's wonderful news, Jack,' Belle said, and, to Nanette, 'I hope you realise how lucky you are, child, and how kind your father is in taking this trouble for you?'

'Yes, Mama. Thank you, Papa,' Nanette said dutifully. Her eye travelled round the group and met that of Margaret, her friend since infancy, sharer of all her plays, and a lump grew in her throat of almost intolerable size. She turned back to her father who, seeing her eyes perilously bright, drew her against him in a hug so that she could hide her face. Nanette pressed her face against the soft velvet of her father's doublet and smelled the familiar smell of him, of leather and clean linen and the fresh open-air scent of his skin, and felt his hard, comforting arms around her, and she knew that she must not let him down, must let him be proud of her. Yet to do that she must shew herself willing to leave him, and how could she give the lie to her heart? She wanted only to stay here in Papa's arms for ever and ever, and she didn't in her heart care about getting educated or being married or any of those things. She gave one convulsive sob, and then, with supreme effort, drew herself upright. Her father's darling face was very close to hers, and his eyes looked huge. She heard her voice say, as if from very far away, 'I shall try to work hard and make you proud of me, Papa.'

And she heard his voice answer, 'That's my good, clever girl.'

But the touch of his hands on her body told her that though her heart was breaking, his was too. It was the way of the world, she knew, that the mind and the heart went different ways about things, and she did not understand it. She accepted it, because she had to, but she did not understand it.

Popple Height was a favourite place of Paul's. It was a hill at the edge of the moors, where great lumps of granite thrust up through the sward like rocks from water at low tide, and the rough heather and bitter grass gave way to dark green moss and patches of golden lichen. From one side you could look down on the white-walled city; from the other the faint line of the Roman Road could be discerned; one of its chief attractions for Paul was that from here you could spot anyone approaching when they were still a mile off, for it was here he came with Ursula.

The moss was still a little damp, so they sat on Paul's spread cloak with their backs to the sun-warmed granite. Paul's horse dozed a little way off, his hind foot cocked and his lower lip pendulous, quivering with his peaceful breathing. In the sun at the foot of a rock beyond him Adrian slept with a very grubby cheek on the flank of Paul's dog Jasper, both of them worn out with running and wrestling. Paul had stripped down to his shirt, which was open to the waist, and Ursula had taken off her starched linen cap and let her hair loose, and as she leaned back against him with her head on his shoulder, it flowed over his brown skin like water. They had been still for so long that a lizard had ventured out from its hole in the rocks near them and was spread out absorbing the afternoon heat. Paul watched it idly, noticing the irridescent shimmer of its scales and the blank remoteness of its little dark eyes. He was sleepy with the heat, but was too happy to want to be asleep, for that would be to waste the precious time. To rouse himself he said, 'Are you asleep?' He spoke quietly in case she was, and the lizard didn't stir.

'No,' she said in the same quiet tone. 'Thinking.'

'What about?'

'I was wondering what it would be like if we were married to each other.' This was almost a forbidden topic, and to soften the words she added, 'Probably if we were we shouldn't enjoy just sitting here together like this.'

He turned his head and kissed her white brow, and the lizard ran in one flicker of movement to the top of the rock and paused, its tongue sipping the air.

'Who can tell,' he said. 'Perhaps we should.'

'I should have liked it, risk or not, for the boy's sake. I wonder sometimes what will come of him,' Ursula said. She stirred and sat up, leaning forward to clasp her hands round her updrawn knees, and as the disturbed air reached the lizard's enquiring tongue it twitched itself neatly down a crack in the rock and was gone.

'You should not worry about that,' Paul said. 'I have told you I will see that he is all right. He will be apprenticed to some decent trade. Do you think I would let my son come to any harm?' Ursula smiled apologetically over her shoulder. Paul marvelled at the colour of her hair where the sun touched it; it seemed almost a miracle, surely more lovely than any human agency could make it, sun and moon together, a God-given glory. 'You should be glad, at any rate, to have him at home with you. If we were married, I should have had to send him away.'

'Like Amyas?' Ursula said. 'You miss him, don't you?'

'He is doing well,' Paul said, avoiding the question.

'Is that why you didn't send Margaret away? Like Nanette?'

'Nanette is a different child altogether,' Paul said regretfully. 'An irony, really—that child is very clever, and will benefit by being sent to Parr's household, but she also cared very much, was very unhappy to be leaving home. While Margaret—Margaret is dull, and would not have minded in the least being sent away, but she is too dull for it to be worthwhile. I wish Nanette was mine and Margaret his.'

Ursula reached out for his hand and pressed it. She did not need to ask who 'he' was. Paul went on with a trace of bitterness, 'And now I even have to be grateful to him for Amyas's betrothal. Oh, didn't I tell you that?' he responded to her start of surprise.

'No, you didn't. Who is the lucky girl?'

'Elizabeth Norys, one of Boleyn's numerous attachments. Another Howard niece, you see, so a Boleyn cousin. Amyas met her on one of his hunting trips to Hever with George Boleyn. Boleyn had a word with her father and he had a word with me, and the whole thing was arranged in no time.'

'But it's a good match? One you approve of?'

'Oh yes, it's a good match. The Noryses are a numerous clan and well connected at Court.'

'So—?' Ursula prompted. Paul stirred restlessly. She said for him, 'It's just that you don't like to owe your brother favours? But, Paul, how is this his favour? The Howard connection is as much yours as his, or more so. The boy seems to have met her without Jack's intervention, and her father evidently thinks you a worthy family to be allied to. So where is the obligation, the debt?'

Paul laughed and put his arms round her. 'Little bear, you are too clear-sighted for me. You are like a clear stream, running over rock, and I am a turbulent, muddy whirlpool. It's fortunate that God is more merciful than just, for I could not have deserved you.' He hugged her and then, looking into her eyes only inches from his own, felt the power of her all over again, and grew serious, and placed his lips tenderly on hers. The warmth of her lips, the taste of her mouth, the scent of her skin! He closed his eyes and let himself slip down into his familiar passion as a man slides down into a rock pool on a hot day. It was she who broke the dream, for she heard the child stirring. She withdrew her mouth from under his and pushed him gently away.

'It grows late,' she said squinting up at the sun. 'We had better gather ourselves together. I have still to look for herbs on the way home, or I shall have no reason to shew for having been here. Besides I am genuinely in need of some things—marsh-mallow and wild thyme and gentian and some others. Come, help me with my hair, dear heart. I mustn't shock the good citizens of York. I am Mistress Archer, the herbalist's widow, who is known never to have a hair out of place.'

Paul carried her and the child, one before the saddle and one behind, as far as the woods above Akcham, which was as near the city as he dared take them. There he put them down, helped her gather her herbs, and rode off to enter the city through one gate, leaving her to walk the rest of the way and enter through another gate.

He thought afterwards that it must have been some divine intervention that put into his mind to ride the long way round and make a diversion along Petergate so that he would pass the end of the Shambles. It was not his route home, but he suddenly had a fancy to pass close to her home, and as he turned the horse into Petergate, he came up against the tail of a huge crowd of common folk in a state of great excitement, all pressing down towards the narrow mouth of the Shambles.

His horse snorted and half-reared and he pulled it to a halt and called out to the nearest members of the crowd, 'What is it? What's going on?' Various answers came, most of them incomprehensible, but one man, a decent-looking fellow in a carpenter's apron, called up to him, 'Best go another way, Master. You won't get through here.'

'What's happening?' Paul asked him. 'Why is there such a crowd? Is something happening in the Shambles?' A faint apprehension was beginning to touch his mind. The carpenter said, 'The Church Council are going to arrest a witch and take her for trial.' Thank God! thought Paul, that that's all it is. But Ursula should avoid the crowd, especially with the child. They could get trampled or crushed. He hoped she was already safe in her house, or else had seen the crowd in time to withdraw to safety. What was the carpenter saying now? 'By the look of some of these women, she'll never get to be tried. They'll tear her apart with their bare hands. Go round another way, Master—it won't be a pleasant sight.'

'Thanks, fellow, I'll take your advice,' Paul said. The man nodded and touched his forehead respectfully, and added, 'It's a bad business. It's always the women, the old screech-owls. Even an accused witch has a right to be properly tried. But the old ones will burn her without a trial if they can get her alive as far as Thursday Market. And the younger and prettier they are, the worse the old 'uns hate them.'

Paul had already turned away, but the last words caught his ear and he swung round in the saddle, his mouth opening in soundless horror. Young? Pretty? He shouted after the carpenter, but the man had been swept on by the crowd and did not hear. Paul grabbed at the nearest man and yelled at him, asking the name of the witch, but the man shook off his hand and passed on, his face a bawling mask, probably never even noticing that he had been stopped. In a nightmare Paul stared round frantically at the contorted, yelling faces, lusting for blood and excitement. A mobbing or a burning, it didn't matter which—it was exciting, it was thrilling, it was the entertainment they craved.

Sickness rose like bile in him. It couldn't be, it *couldn't* be! There were other young women in the Shambles, other pretty young women. But all the same he must be there, he must get to her to make sure. He must skirt the crowd, he could get in from the Fossgate end, or make his way through the back alleys. He drove his horse on, lashing it unmercifully so that it thrust against the outskirters of the crowd, knocking them down if they were not nimble on their feet. The yelling of the crowd solidified and clotted into a rhythmic chant, gathering weight and power with each repetition: 'Burn the witch! *Burn* the witch! *Burn* the witch!' *Christ help me*, Paul prayed in his mind.

He was so blind and deaf with anguish that he did not hear himself called as he crossed the corner of Saviourgate and Fossgate, nor see the waving arm, and it was only when the horse's bridle was seized that he looked down and saw the face of his cousin, John Butts, staring up at him whitely, the mouth open and yelling like every mouth in every face in that city. Almost he raised his hand to smash his fist down into that bawling horror; but sanity returned to him in time.

'Get down!' John was shouting. 'Get down! You'll never get through on horseback. They've got your mistress. If you want to save her for God's sake come with me.'

Paul slithered from his horse's back and grabbed John's arm. 'What's happened?' John grabbed him and pulled him along with him, heading for the narrow alleyway that ran behind St Crux and talking rapidly as he went.

'An accusation was put before the Church Council that Mistress Archer was a witch, and the Council set off to arrest her, gathering the usual crowd as they went. Then some other elements joined in—the old Shambles wives—and the crowd turned into a mob. If they get her she'll be torn to pieces. They've already started dragging faggots together in the market for a burning.'

'Jesus Christ preserve us,' Paul moaned. 'Why? Oh why? What has she ever done?'

'She's not liked,' John said grimly. 'She's too beautiful to be a widow. They say her hair is a gift from the Devil to lure men to damnation, and that her herbal remedies and simples are witches spells. But that's only the old women. The rest of them don't care who she is, they just want sport. All it needed was an accusation.'

'But who would accuse her? She has no enemies,' Paul groaned. He stumbled on the uneven cobbles, and John snatched at him roughly.

'Hurry, man, hurry. Jack is rounding up some men to try and break up the crowd. If we can get to the house and hold the door we may be able to save her. Even a mob will think twice before it attacks two such well-known gentlemen.'

They burst out into the Shambles a few yards from the house, and here the struggling yelling crowd was at its densest. Even though Paul was taller than most men he could not see what was happening. He and John thrust forward, their own yells lost in the roar of the crowd. Their feet slipped in the heaps of ordure on the street and its stink mingled with that of the crowd. An elbow caught John painfully in the face and a backwards surge of the crowd thrust him against Paul so that they both almost lost their footing.

And then, clearly through even the din of the crowd, there was a scream, a woman's anguished shriek.

'Too late, they've got her,' John muttered, his hand clapped to his bleeding nose. Paul was driven to a frenzy, and struggled forward like a man possessed, seeing now, over the heads of the last of the crowd that separated him from her, Ursula's terrified face turning this way and that as the cruel hands bit into her. He saw her lifted above the crowd, saw her held, struggling wildly, across the shoulders of three strong men while the hooked fingers of the old women ripped at her clothes, lusting to tear her flesh as if they were jackals and she some stricken deer. Her cap was snatched off, and her head, tilted backwards, trailed her glorious silvery hair towards the filth of the gutter. The crowd's yelling redoubled at the sight of it—the Devil's mark, that enticing, platignum shower!

'Ursula!' Paul yelled, and dragging John with him he forced his way by the sheer weight of his frenzy through the last of the crowd. Hands grabbed at him too, but he scarcely felt them. His sword was in his hand now, shortened for close work, and he slashed about him, to left and right, hearing with savage delight the shrieks of those whose flesh he felt it bite. The old women fell back, and he cut down the nearest of the men who held Ursula, and as the man fell, cursing, clutching at his wounded arm, the others let her go, and only a swift leap from Paul prevented her from falling.

She was in his arms now, half-fainting with terror. With one arm round her body, holding her up and against him, he fell back towards the house, his sword busy in his other hand. John was there beside him now, sword out, his bloody face a terrifying mask. With relief Paul felt the wall of the house against his back, and as he shifted his balance he felt that Ursula was struggling to take her weight on her own feet, already recovered enough to try to help herself.

'Back, get back, or I'll make corpses enough to satisfy you all!' he shouted. Those in the front of the crowd were pushing backwards, unwilling to be the martyrs for those behind who were still pushing forward. Yet the sheer weight of the crowd might have precipitated a tragedy, had not at that moment Jack's reinforcements arrived at the other end of the street and begun cutting their way through from the back of the crowd. It was quickly over. The mob's blood-lust did not extend to their own blood. The noise changed tone, and then died down, and the fringes of the crowd began slipping away.

Now at last the representatives of the Church Council pushed their way through to the group in front of the house.

'What is the meaning of this, sir?' said the leader. 'Why have you interfered with the processes of justice?'

'Justice? What justice?' Paul snarled at them. 'Is it justice to allow an innocent woman to be torn apart by a mob?'

'This woman is an accused witch. We have come to arrest her and try her. The Church court will give her justice.'

'You would not have given her a trial, unless you give the dead justice,' Paul said. 'You had not the power to arrest her against the wishes of these *good citizens.*' He spat the words contemptuously.

'Nevertheless, the woman must stand trial,' the leader said. 'And you, sir, have interfered with the due processes and wounded several good citizens in the process. That will have to be taken into account.' Jack now joined the group, breathless and dishevelled, along with several of the Butts serving-men, and the Council looked distinctly nervous. Their leader wavered visibly, but stuck to his guns. 'I must ask you to hand over that woman so that justice can take its course.'

Paul felt Ursula shiver with fright, and he pulled her harder against him. He towered above them, his dark face hard with anger, his white teeth bared like an animal's. 'This woman is innocent of the accusations. She is known to be an honest herbalist's widow, who carries on her husband's business just as she should. There is no substance in the accusations.'

'Nevertheless there must be a trial—'

'I will answer for her,' Paul said.

'I repeat, sir—'

'*I will answer for her!*' He turned on the watching crowd. 'And anyone who harms a hair of her head will answer to me. You all know me—and my brothers here. This woman is innocent, by Christ's Holy Blood I swear it, and I swear I will kill anyone who so much as spits at her. And now, go home, all of you. There will be no sport for you here today, nor any day. *Go home!*'

There was no-one there who could outface him. Sullenly, the crowd dispersed, and reluctantly the Council went on its way too, leaving the little group of men and the fainting woman suddenly exhausted and silent. John Butts spoke first.

'Come, we must seek shelter. My house is not far. Bring her there. She is bleeding, she must be attended to.'

'Ursula?' Paul whispered in sudden fear, and lifting his hand from her body saw that it was smeared with blood. She turned her face to look at him, and then with a little cry flung herself against him, sobbing. She was bleeding from a dozen bloody rents, the work of dirty scrabbling nails. His own strength was flagging, but still he was a giant of a man, and he picked her up in his arms and walked with scarcely a stagger towards the Butts house on the Lendal. At the corner of the road he remembered the child. 'Where's Adrian?'

'Within, unharmed,' John Butts told him. 'Jack is bringing him. Go on, go on or you'll fall. Shall I take her from you?'

'No,' he cried fiercely. 'No-one shall touch her but me.' In a daze he staggered on, guided by John, stared at by passers-by who ducked their heads in shame at the sight of the wounded woman, until he reached the great Butts mansion; there John's wife Lucy received them, crying in pity and astonishment, and she and her women persuaded Paul at last to give up his precious burden, and they took Ursula away to attend to her. Moments later Jack arrived carrying Adrian, who was in a state of such deep shock he neither spoke nor cried at all, and the child too was taken away by the women.

And then Paul collapsed, shaking and weeping helplessly, hunched on the floor by the fire, holding his bloody hands to his breast as if they were themselves wounded. John and Jack exchanged a glance, and let him cry until he seemed to be easier, and then they gave him wine to sip, and helped him on to a chair, and soothed him. It was a long time later that he asked, lifting dull, shocked eyes to their concerned faces, 'Who was it who made the accusation?' The question had been forming itself in his mind for some minutes past, and his brothers had dreaded the moment when he would ask it. They looked at each other, and then Jack shrugged slightly and said, 'You know already. You have guessed it.'

'It was Anne.' Paul whispered the words, not quite a question, and yet hardly credible. 'That's how you knew about it.'

'Yes. She was distraught. I don't think she knew what she was doing. As soon as she found out what the woman's name was, she went to the Council, and then she came here. She was crying—'

'She's here?' Paul interrupted, half starting up from his seat, his fists clenched. Jack looked at him gravely.

'Sit down, calm yourself,' he said. 'No, she's not here. Belle took her home.' Paul sank down again, and stared into the heart of the fire, his face dark. 'You will do nothing,' Jack told him firmly. 'Nothing, do you understand?'

Slowly Paul looked up, and there was such pain in his face, and such desolation that Jack's heart cried out for him. 'I have to thank you,' Paul said unwillingly, 'for what you did. Both of you. I don't understand why you did it, but you saved her life.

I do thank you, from my heart. But I don't understand why you should have done it.'

'No,' Jack said sadly, 'I don't suppose you do. Poor Paul, life is so difficult for you, isn't it?'

'I don't want your pity,' Paul said.

'No, you don't,' Jack answered. 'But you won't accept my love.'

Five

$\mathcal{U}$RSULA'S WOUNDS WERE WASHED AND BOUND, AND SHE WAS given a strong draught of wine laced with poppy and put to bed along with Adrian, already sleeping. A servant was ordered to watch over her and not to leave her for a moment, and when Paul went to look in on her she was sleeping heavily, her face shadowed and wan.

'Don't worry about her,' John Butts told him. 'I'll keep her here for a few days until she's recovered, and then—'

'She had better not go back to the Shambles,' Jack said. John nodded.

'Just what I thought. I'll find somewhere for her. I can place her with one of the weavers' families, and she can earn her keep with spinning or carding or something of the sort. I'd give her work in the house but the situation is rather delicate. Anne is my cousin—'

'I understand,' Paul said harshly. 'If it is a question of money—'

'Don't worry about her. I'll take care of her,' John said.

In spite of Jack's warning, Paul went home to Morland Place fully intending to kill Anne for what she had done. The house was strangely silent when he arrived, the servants, it seemed, having gone to bed. All was quiet in the hall, but in the winter-parlour he found Belle apparently waiting up for him, perhaps to remonstrate with him. But the waiting had proved too much of a strain and she slept where she sat on a stool, her back supported by the wall, her head fallen forward and her embroidery frame slipping from her fingers. Hushing Jasper with a gesture, he walked quietly out. Anne was upstairs somewhere.

He went up the dark spiral staircase, his feet making no sound on the stone steps, and he could hear the silence above listening. She was not asleep. She knew he was coming for her. His hands flexed. He would put them about her throat and squeeze and squeeze until the life was out of her. He opened the bedroom door, hearing, he thought, a soft rush of movement, and found it empty, the bedclothes flung back as if hurriedly. He walked across to the garderobe and flung back the curtain—and there she was, in her nightgown, her arms folded round her, shivering with fright.

She gave a little muted cry when she saw him, and as he grabbed her with one hand he put the other over her mouth and pulled her roughly out from her pathetic hiding place into the middle of the room. She struggled, whimpering behind his hand, and he twisted her about so that he could hold her against him with one arm while he drew his sword with the other. At the sight of the blade she began to shriek, jerking her head from side to side, her hands scrabbling before her. Jasper, who had followed him into the bedroom whined and came towards them and Paul spurned him with a foot and ordered him sharply away. The dog retreated unwillingly.

'And you,' he said to Anne, shaking her roughly, 'shut up. I'm not going to kill you with a sword. A sword is for men's deaths—and you aren't even a woman.' He flung it from him and it landed on the bed—an omen, he wondered vaguely. 'I'm just getting it out of the way, so that you won't be tempted. And now—what have you to say for yourself?'

He turned her about again and held her at arm's length, both his hands on her upper arms, his fingers biting in cruelly. Her mouth, freed at last, poured out a stream of rebuke, pleading, justification, and almost incoherent babble. Paul did not try to understand it. He looked at her, but he saw Ursula, Ursula ashen and bleeding, but still trying to stand. This, this creature was just a bundle of clothes, an empty sack of fat, air and water.

Holding her with one hand he hit her across the face with the other, first one way, then the other, smack, smack; and he went on doing it, hitting her rhythmically, her head jerking like a puppet's from side to side with each blow. At first she shrieked, and then she moaned, pleading through bubbling spit for him to stop, her face soaked in tears, sweat and blood. Servants came to the door, and Jasper snarled, not knowing whether to attack them or his master. Paul snatched up his sword from the bed, still holding Anne, and turned on them.

'Back, all of you. Get out, shut the door. This is none of your concern. Take the dog with you. And shut the door.'

They could only obey. Discipline of a wife was a husband's prerogative. Unwillingly they shuffled back, and the door was closed slowly. Anne was sagging now in his hands, hardly able to take her weight. Her face was swollen with his blows, bleeding from mouth and nose, and one eye was closing under a bruise with a cut at its centre from his signet ring. Blood and saliva ran over her chin and soaked the front of her nightgown. His anger was gone, he was only disgusted now, and he let her go so that she sank to the floor like a heap of washing.

'I should kill you,' he said coldly, 'but you aren't worth it. Besides, I owe John Butts a debt, and I don't want a blood feud.' The heap of washing stirred and grew hands, imploring hands, and then began to crawl towards him, the hands feeling ahead. Unseeing, the swollen face turned up to him, and it gibbered. He tried not to hear the words, but they were repeated, brokenly, but unmistakably.

'It was only because I loved you, I loved you, I loved you—'

Sickened, Paul took up his sword and walked out of the room, closing the door behind him.

Ursula was never mentioned in the house. No comment was passed, either, on the state of Anne's face the next day, or any of the days afterwards until she healed, minus a tooth. Paul slept apart from her after that, and scarcely ever spoke to her. In fact, he was more silent and morose than ever, and scarcely spoke to anyone except the tenants and servants, to whom he was as courteous as ever.

What was worse for him was that he could no longer see Ursula as he did before, which was ironic, since now that her existence was public it ought to have been easier. But he could not visit her at the weaver's house, and where else could he meet her? It was only now that he realised how much he had depended on his infrequent times with her, how much he needed her to talk to. Remembering his debt, he tried once or twice to talk to Jack, shyly and awkwardly, but it was too much of a strain. The habits of reticence proved too strong to break. He had only ever confided in Ursula, and now it seemed he had even lost her. There was nothing to do but plunge himself into the work of the estate and try to find release in that.

Kentdale Castle stood at the height of a green hill overlooking the town of Kendal and the sweet valley of the River Kent. It was a pleasant place to be, the massive grey keep being surrounded, within the curtain walls, by gardens as well as all the usual offices. It was healthy, too, dry and cool with clean winds blowing all the time from the hills over which they rode sometimes, hawking and hunting.

It was not home, but apart from that, Nanette was content. There were four of the little girls altogether, Katherine Parr, Nanette, Elizabeth Bellingham who was six, and another cousin, Kate Neville, who was eight like Nanette. The little Parr was the youngest, being only five, but she was very bright for her age, and had had the advantage of the rest of them in education.

The four little girls shared a bed in the nursery in the south-west corner of the keep. It was a very comfortable bed, with feather-filled pillows, an indulgence Nanette had not known before, and a great fur covering for the cold winter nights when the icy air blew in through the arrow-slit windows and fingered its way past the bedcurtains. On those days one had to break the ice off the water in the bowl to wash, but all four of the girls were northerners, born and bred, and the cold troubled them less for being familiar.

Nanette got on well with her companions, and quickly became the leader of their plays, perhaps because she had all her life had to organise her cousin Margaret. Kate Neville was one of a numerous family, and knew more games even than Nanette. Kate was a jolly, lively girl, not very good at her lessons, and often in trouble because she was untidy or dirty or made too much noise. Bess Bellingham was pale and fair and very quiet, a mouselike child who asked nothing better than to follow where she was led; and Katherine Parr was clever and imaginative and Nanette's co-conspirator, although she some-times felt the need to restrain them all, which she did from her authority as daughter of the house.

The four girls rose at six for mass, which was held in the chapel except on Sundays and major feasts when they rode with the grown-ups to the town, an arrangement with which Nanette was quite familiar from Morland Place. Breakfast followed at seven, and was generally ale, beef and bread, and was eaten in silence. 'Just like monks,' Kate whispered once to Nanette, and was severely reprimanded. Then followed lessons until twelve. They studied Greek and Latin and French and Italian, Katherine and Nanette well, Elizabeth adequately, Kate very badly indeed.

At twelve came dinner, generally of fifteen to twenty dishes, and afterwards lessons in music, playing on lute, harp, viol and virginals, and singing. In the afternoon sometimes they rode out or hunted, at other times there were more lessons, this time in the womanly arts of sewing and embroidery, or in composition and poetry. Supper was at five in winter and at six in summer, a meal of less elaboration than dinner, and after it there would be dancing, games, and recreation, until bedtime at nine o'clock.

Over all their lives, their lessons, their games, their meals and their devotions, was the watchful eye of Maud, Lady Parr. Nanette found her terrifying, a tiny, slender woman of immense energy and powerful character. She was at that time only twenty-one, but that seemed an inaccessible height of adulthood to Nanette. Lady Parr had very strict standards and a quick temper and a tongue as sharp as the icy winter wind. She seemed to be everywhere at once, and the child who thought Lady Parr safely in the hall chivvying the servants and thought on that account to relax in the safety of the school-room was likely to receive an unpleasant shock.

Katherine was as much in awe of her mother as the other children, and Lady Parr made no difference between her four charges on account of their relationship with her. Nanette found Sir Thomas Parr less frightening, but also less interesting. He seemed to her to be immensely aged, hovering on the brink of the grave. He was often absent on business, and spent much of his time in London, and when he was at home the girls saw little of him—he did not move in their sphere. But when they did see him, he was kindly, vague, bumbling and a little ponderous. He would sometimes pinch their cheeks and ask them how they did, and sometimes bring them presents from London, and that seemed to them his chief value in life.

There was also Katherine's brother, William, but they did not see much of him, for he had his own establishment apart from theirs. Nanette did not care for him much. When they did see him, he was very lordly and condescending to them, and sometimes did cruel things to their kitten and laughed about it.

There was a pleasant rivalry between Katherine and Nanette that brought them closer together as they got to know each other. Katherine was very good at Latin and Greek, while Nanette far excelled her in music and composition. Both hated needlework, and both had lively imaginations, and loved telling stories and playing games of make-believe.

But the times Nanette liked best were the times when she wrote her letter home, and even more, when she got the reply from her darling, darling Papa. At the arrival of these precious letters Nanette liked to go away on her own and read them in private, and her favourite place was a sheltered corner of the battlements, the south-east corner, where she could stare at the blue distance and imagine she could see her home. Katherine found her here one day in May 1517, when she had been at Kentdale just over a year.

'Nanette, there you are—I was looking for you—why, what's the matter?' Katherine asked as Nanette looked up to reveal that her eyes were full of tears. She looked at the letter in her friend's hand and dropped to her knees beside her. 'It isn't trouble at home, is it, Nan? Oh I do hope not.'

'No, not trouble,' Nanette said, and then laughed and flung her arms round Katherine, even while her cheeks were wet with tears. 'Not trouble at all. I don't know why I'm crying—I'm so happy. Katherine, I am to go home!'

'Go home?' Katherine said in dismay, which, being a kind girl, she tried to hide. 'I thought you said you had come here for longer, but I'm glad for you, though I shall miss you sore—'

'Oh no,' Nanette said, 'not for good—just for a visit. I'm glad you said you would miss me, for I think I'd miss you too, if I were to be sent home for good. But this is to be just a visit for a few months. My aunt is to be married, and all the family is coming home for the occasion.'

'Your aunt? Is that the one who is in service to the Queen?'

'That's right—my aunt Mary. She's terribly old—older than your mother, you know—and I think she is surprised to be getting married at all. Papa says she is contracted to a gentleman of the Court, a widower of wealth. He is older than Aunt Mary, so he must be really *ancient*.'

'I should not like to marry an old man,' Katherine said with a delicate shudder. 'It would be like—marrying my father.'

'I should not mind marrying Papa,' Nanette said judiciously, 'but then, he is different from other old people. I should not care to marry Master Nicholas Carew.'

'Is that your aunt's gentleman's name?'

'Yes. He met her at Court, of course. He was waiting on the King, and fell in love with her, so Papa says, though what old folk can know about falling in love I can't imagine. The King and Queen gave their consent, and Aunt Mary is to come home in July to be wed from Morland Place. And I,' she said, jumping to her feet and carolling the words like a bird, 'I am to go home! Go home! Go Home! Oh Katherine, I wish you could come too—it's such a lovely, lovely place! And you'd meet Papa and Mama, and my brothers and sisters, darling Jackie and Dickon, and dear little Catherine and Jane who are as pretty as rosebuds. You'd love them all, and they'd love you, too.'

'I'd like to see your home,' Katherine said wistfully. 'Perhaps I will some day, when I'm grown up.'

Nanette sobered and looked at her friend with sudden realisation. 'But when we are grown up, you will be married and I will be married and unless our husbands are friends, we shall never see each other.'

Katherine looked concerned. 'That would be dreadful indeed. Perhaps our husbands will be friends—after all, our fathers are. Perhaps,' brightening at the thought, 'perhaps we shall marry two brothers, and live together under the same roof.'

'Or perhaps we shan't marry at all,' Nanette said. 'We could be nuns then.'

'I don't think I should care to be a nun,' Katherine said thoughtfully. 'I think I shall certainly be married—my mother will arrange it.' And thinking of Lady Parr, both girls knew that there was no chance of Katherine being left unmarried. 'But if I marry and you don't, Nan, shall you come and live with me as my friend?'

'Oh yes, of course I shall. But I think I'll be married too. My father knows so many people, he's bound to marry me to one of them.'

'Well, anyway,' Katherine said, linking her arm through Nanette's and walking with her towards the stair-hole, 'we shall be able to write to each other, whatever happens. And that will be something. Tell me some more about your home. And about your brothers and sisters.' And talking, the friends went down the steps.

Paul was out in the fields supervising the shearing one hot, perfect day about a month later when a message was brought to him. He did not need to supervise the shearing, or any other of the farm tasks, but he liked to do it. He liked to strip off and work beside his tenants and servants, for with them he felt sure of the relationship, sure of their respect for him and his for them. There was something peaceful, too, in purely manual labour. He found a release in it.

The message was brought by one of the children who fetched and carried amongst the workers, bringing them water or buttermilk to assuage their thirst, and gleaning wool from the bushes and hurdles and thickets. The child was very young, only just old enough to perform its task, and still too young to be shy of talking to the master, to French Paul, the great owner of the Morland inheritance.

'A lady wants to see you,' the child piped, tugging at Paul's arm. Paul looked down and wiped the sweat from his brow with the back of his arm—his hands were oily with sheep-yolk.

'A lady? What lady? Where?' he asked. The child merely pointed towards a thicket of trees nearby. 'What does she look like? What does she want?' But the child stared in blank incomprehension, and realising that it was too young to tell him more he released the sheep he had been holding and watched it bound away on its unlikely slender legs, its great fleece bouncing with the movement. That would be another that would have to be caught all over again, he thought, as he strode towards the trees. He was glad to get in under their shade, for it was burning hot out there in the field.

A slender shadow detached itself from the cool gloom and came towards him, and he opened his arms, dirty and sweaty as he was, and took her in.

'Ursula, it's been so long since I saw you,' he murmured, kissing her again and again with rising passion, while trying to remember to keep his filthy hands from her white linen. She kissed him avidly in return, leaning her body against him and feeling his desire rising to meet her own. She gave a little half-humorous groan and pushed him back from her.

'Not here, Master, nor now. Not the time or place,' she said softly.

'But what are you doing here?' he asked. 'Is something wrong?' He saw in that moment, as his eyes became accustomed to the gloom, the slight figure of Adrian waiting in the shadows behind her. At nine the lad had grown tall, and his small face had filled out, his features now more closely resembling Paul's own. He would be a handsome man when he was full-grown, Paul thought.

'Nothing that hasn't been wrong for a long time,' Ursula said.

'Why, little bear, what is it?'

She paused for a moment to gather her thoughts, and he let his arms drop from her, seeing that this was some kind of formal interview. His heart misgave. There was bad news coming.

'I can't live like this, Paul,' she said at last. 'I was a respectable wife, and then a respectable widow. Enough money, some independence. I did not see you as often as I wanted, but often enough. The boy was going to school. Then—all that trouble.' She shuddered even at the memory of it. 'It wasn't your fault, I know, but look what it has brought me to. I live now like a servant, with no independence, no money of my own, no freedom—and now I don't even see you.'

'My dearest—'

'I know, that isn't your fault either. It is the way things are. But I can't live like that.' She paused, and he knew that she had reached the heart of the matter. 'There is a man—a decent man, an artisan, a leatherworker from Wakefield. He wants to marry me.'

'But—' Paul could think of nothing adequate to say. Why was she telling him this? Surely she could not be thinking of accepting the man?

'He wants to marry me, and to bring up Adrian as his own child. He is a widower, and childless. He will make me respectable, he will be kind to me. We'll live in Wakefield where no-one knows me or my history. And I'll be free again.' She turned her face away from him, looking out through the trees to the wide sky and the open country. Free was a relative term. She would never be free again as she once was; but we must all make the best bargain we can.

'You want to do this?' Paul asked, still unable to take it in. She answered without looking at him.

'I can go and stay with his sister until the wedding-day. She is a decent woman.'

'When?'

'I can go tomorrow, and we can be married by Lammas.' Now she turned to look at him, and her eyes were pleading, desperate—but what did she want of him? He was too dazed to think. He only knew what he needed, what he must have to survive.

'Ursula, don't go. Please don't go. Little bear, you can't really mean this? You can't really mean you would leave me and marry this—*leatherworker?*'

'I can't live this way, Paul,' she said stonily, and then, breaking through, 'You must let me go. *Let me go*, Paul!'

He stepped towards her and took her in his arms, careless of his oily hands now. He held her, pressed her close, feeling the shape of her under his hands, her light bones and graceful carriage. Unfairly, he pressed his lips to her brow, her eyes, her mouth, feeling her unwilling, helpless response.

'No, Ursula. No. I can't. I have to have you. I can't live without you. You know that. You know it. You can't go—I can't let you.'

'Paul—'

'Things will be better. I swear it. I'll find some way. Perhaps I can get rid of Anne. Or she may die. If necessary I'll poison her—'

'No!'

'Yes. Even that. You must not, must not go, little bear. You see what you will drive me to if you say you will go.'

She pulled herself partly free of him, though he kept hold of her shoulders. She stared at him, her face set. 'What can you do?' she asked hopelessly.

'I can at least set you up in place of your own. The danger you were in is past. And if all else fails, I can come and live with you.'

'And give up your inheritance? No, you can't do that. You won't do that.'

He was silent. It was true, and they both knew it. She went on,

'So this is what you say: unless your wife dies—which heaven forfend—' and she crossed herself—'the best you can offer me is to live alone in obscurity and be visited by you, in secret, whenever you can manage it, which will not be often. And for that, you want me to give up my only chance of respectability, and happiness, and freedom.'

Put like that, he could see clearly what it was he was asking of her. And yet—and yet it was so. He *did* ask it. His need knew no other way.

'I can't let you go,' he said quietly. For a moment longer she stared at him, and then glanced, just once and swiftly, behind her at the boy. He was watching with dark, smouldering eyes, though how much he understood Paul could not guess. Ursula turned again to Paul, her expression unfathomable. 'I love you,' she said. He took it as her answer, and gathered her into his arms in relief.

'My darling, my darling,' he said. 'You couldn't have left me. You'll never leave me, will you?'

'God help me,' she said, her face against his shoulder, 'I never will.'

That summer was hot, and wet, and the Sweat—that dreaded disease brought to England by the mercenary soldiers of Henry VII and never since eradicated—struck London and spread outwards to the provinces. The Court moved to Richmond and thence to Windsor, and it was from there that Mary Morland travelled home to York in July for her wedding. She was twenty-five, and though still pretty had given up any hopes of ever marrying when Master Nicholas Carew asked for her hand. She had never had any idea of refusing, and had waited with bated breath and crossed fingers for the varying permissions to be forthcoming, for, though she was not in love with him, she admired and respected him, and was very glad indeed to be rescued from her ignominious state amongst the Queen's waiting ladies.

Carew was tall and thin and balding, but a kindly man, scholarly and respectable, wealthy and obviously very much in love with Mary. At forty-five he was still young enough to give her children, while old enough to think her years few. Altogether it was a very good match. Neither Paul nor Jack had had any objections, and Edward, with whom she travelled home, thought it excellent. He had come from York House to collect her and form her escort. Amyas, who was also being allowed home for the occasion, was travelling separately and would meet them at Hatfield.

Mary had not been home for eighteen months, and was eagerly looking forward to it.

'You'll find things somewhat changed,' Edward warned her. He had been home more recently. 'You heard, I suppose, about the trouble over Paul's mistress.'

Mary nodded. 'A little. A shocking business.' She did not feel it necessary to clarify which aspect of the affair she found shocking.

'It made a difference,' Edward said. 'You will find Anne much changed. She is not well, her health seems much impaired. And Paul is hardly ever home. He spends most of the time out on the estate, and when he is home he never speaks unless he has to. Jack and Belle run the house, and it seems more like their house than Paul's. Uncle Richard never comes now—he disapproved of Paul's behaviour. And now, of course, there has been a breach between Paul and John Butts, because he has taken the woman away from John's protection and set her up in a house in the city, just as if she were a king's mistress.'

Mary made a face. 'You don't make it sound very attractive,' she said.

'Believe me, we were lucky to be away from it,' Edward told her. 'But everything will be merry enough for your wedding, I doubt not. Amyas will be glad to be home, and Nanette too. It will be the first wedding at Morland Place for ten—no, twelve years. There will be nothing to cloud it.'

He proved right. The welcome at Morland Place was rapturous, and even Paul did not darken the pleasure, and smiled as if he were really glad to see Mary. He did not need to pretend to be glad to see his son. The time away from home had done Amyas good—he was more self-confident, had grown taller and filled out, and though he would never make his father's size or height he was a well-looking young man now. His fair hair had darkened to a barley-gold, and he had his mother's bland prettiness of features, but there was a manliness about his bearing that pleased Paul and made him feel that perhaps Morland Place might find in this boy a defender against the encroachments of Jack's progeny.

Paul was also glad to welcome back Jack's firstborn, for whom he had always had a curious fondness. She reminded him, in her intelligence and innocent integrity, of Ursula, and he sometimes thought that if he and Ursula had had a daughter, she would have been like Nanette. Nanette was rapturously glad to be home, and ran wild like a dog as soon as the restraint of strangeness and a year of hard schooling had worn off. She soon gathered her brothers and sisters and her erstwhile companion to her and ran off with them to investigate all their old haunts and to tell them of life in Westmorland.

And then, two days after the arrival of Edward and Mary, another, silent, and uninvited guest arrived, creeping in unnoticed on the warm damp air and slipping into the crowded bedchambers. The Sweat had followed them up from London. Reports of cases of the sickness in York coincided with the first symptoms at Morland Place, and, as was its nature, it spread like wildfire. There was some evidence that women were less susceptible than men, and certainly the first to go down with the sickness were three male servants, and Jack's two sons, Jackie and Dickon. Plans were made at once to send the female children out of harm's way, and Nanette was woken early on the fourth day, most unexpectedly, by her father.

'What is it, Papa?' she asked, shocked into wakefulness by his grave face. 'What has happened?'

'Nothing yet, my sweeting. Get up quickly and get dressed, and help your sisters to dress themselves. You are going to Shawes to stay with Elijah and your cousin Ezekiel.'

'Because of the sickness, Papa?' Nanette asked.

'Yes, that's right. You will be safer there, away from the city and away from—Jackie and Dickon. Now, no more questions, that's my good girl.'

But she had to ask. 'Where's Mother Kat?' She got out of bed as she spoke in obedience to her father's harassed gesture. 'Can't she help the girls?'

'She's with your brothers, she's busy. Hurry now, child.' He turned towards the door, and as he reached it, he shivered violently, and swayed slightly. Nanette's heart lurched with fear.

'Papa! Are you all right?'

He turned to her, his face reassuring, the old familiar smile on his lips. 'Of course I am, little one. Just tired. I've been up all night. Many of the servants are sick.'

Nanette accepted that, because he had never lied to her, he was always right, her omnipotent Papa. But outside in the corridor, as soon as he had closed the chamber door, he collapsed against the wall, shivering violently and streaming sweat. *Dear lord God*, he thought to himself, *I've got it too.* Cold fear clutched at his heart, and he felt so terrified and alone that he longed to go back into the room he had just left and put his arms around his eldest daughter for comfort. But he knew he must not, and as soon as the shivering was sufficiently under control, he made his way carefully towards the room where Mother Kat was tending his sons. *My sons*, he thought, *not my sons*. But even his thoughts were rapidly becoming incoherent as the fever gripped him.

Nanette woke Margaret and between them they dressed themselves and Catherine and Jane, and, since no-one had come for them, they made their way down, through the hall and into the courtyard. The sun shone through a milky, hazy cloud, and perspiration started up under their armpits at its damp heat. There was no-one in the yard. Leaving Margaret with the little girls, Nanette went inside to look for a grown-up. She found, at last, not quite a grown-up, but her cousin Amyas.

'Where is everybody?' she asked him. 'Papa says we are to go to Shawes, but there is no-one to take us.'

'I am to take you,' Amyas said. His face was white, and he was trembling, but he had himself in control. 'My father has told me I am to take you to Uncle Richard and stay there with you.'

'Where is your father?'

'In the chapel, praying. He says that since Master Philip is sick, someone must do it.'

'Master Philip sick too?' Nanette said, vaguely shocked that a priest could catch the Sweat like any normal man.

'Everyone is sick,' Amyas said, fighting back the tears of fear and resentment that filled his eyes.

'Not Papa,' Nanette said firmly. Fear made Amyas cruel. He wanted to see someone else hurt besides himself.

'Your father *and* your mother,' he said. 'And Uncle Edward and Aunt Mary and nearly all the servants. Only my mother and father are not sick.'

'Not Papa,' Nanette said again, and she remembered his sudden shiver. Her voice rose a pitch. 'Not Papa! I must go to him.'

'You can't,' Amyas said, grabbing her as she tried to dash past him. 'Don't be a fool.' He was sorry now that he had spoken so cruelly, now he saw the effect he had had. Tears were running down her face and she struggled against him.

'Papa! Mama! Let me go, I must go to them,' she wailed. She was tall and strong for her nine years, but Amyas had no difficulty in holding her. He began to drag her towards the door.

'You can't, you wouldn't be allowed,' he said. 'Come on, we have to go to Shawes. There's nothing you can do. We must go and take the others. Listen, maybe they won't die. People do recover sometimes. Maybe they'll get better. Don't cry.'

Nanette stared at him aghast, her tears stopped in mid-flow. Then they began again on a hiccough, but more quietly. Papa had said she must go, and so she must go. She walked with her cousin towards the door obediently, but he kept a hand on her arm just in case.

'We'll have to saddle the horses ourselves,' he said. 'I don't suppose there's a servant to be found.' And his voice was more cheerful, for an adventure of any sort is always exhilarating.

Paul rose from his knees and swayed dizzily, but it was from exhaustion and not from sickness. He did not remember when he had last slept. With Anne and the remaining servants he had attended the sick, and when he was not doing that, he was praying in the chapel for the sick and for the dead. Women from the village had come—unwillingly and for much coin only—to lay out the dead. So many dead. The candles in the chapel burned for them: Jackie and Dickon and their mother and Edward and six of the servants. And Mary, hopeful bride, was very sick, near to death. And Jack—he did not like to think about Jack. Jack must not die, or how could he live with his guilt? He had prayed until his mind was numb and his knees raw with kneeling, and now, unable to pray any more, he staggered to his feet supporting himself with a hand against the wall. His fingers rested on a marble effigy, a memorial. He glanced down at it. 'Isabella Morland 1437-1469. In God's Hand' were the words. So many dead.

There was a movement by the house door, and he turned and saw a slight dark figure there in the shadows.

'Who's there?' he said wearily. Some servant come to fetch him to yet another victim, he supposed. This was a child, though. 'Who is it?'

He moved a step forward, and the shadow did the same, and the burning dark eyes of his son Adrian came towards him out of the darkness.

'My mother is sick,' he said. 'You must come.'

His mind fumbled with the words, but his body acted more promptly, and he was walking, fast, to the door before he had properly comprehended what had been said.

'How did you get here?' he asked.

'I ran,' the boy replied.

'I'll get a horse. You'll ride behind me. Is someone with her? Did you get a doctor?'

'No,' he said, and he glanced up at his father with contempt for the question. 'In the city, at this time?'

'I had better bring something. How bad is she? No, never mind that. Can you tack up a horse?' The boy nodded. 'Go you and do it while I get what I can. I'll be with you in the yard in a moment.' ,

The boy ran, and Paul went the other way to gather up the various bits and pieces of herbal remedies that were tried against the Sweat. Tried, and failed, his mind reminded him. There was no cure known but a man's own strength. Still, women were less susceptible. Yet Belle had died. God, God, not Ursula, please. He ran.

Intelligent child, he had chosen the best horse, and had saddled and bridled it most swiftly. Paul wasted no words but mounted while Adrian held the bridle and then put a hand down to the boy. Adrian put a foot on Paul's boot-toe, seized the hand, and was up behind him in a second, and then they were out of the yard and galloping along the road to the city. The house he had found for her was in Priory Street, just beyond Holy Trinity Church; downstairs a potter lived and had his shop—Ursula lived above.

'Could not the potter's wife have gone to her?' Paul asked as he flung himself from his horse and hitched the reins over a bush—not that the animal would stray far, lathered and gasping as it was.

'The potter and his wife are gone, fled the city when the sickness came,' the boy said, at his heels as he climbed the stairs. At the top Paul paused a second to look at him, and the child's remarkable self-possession wavered at last.

'Sir—my mother—?'

Paul could not say anything to comfort him, but he put a hand out to the boy's shoulder and gripped it, and saw the child grow stronger with the contact. And then he went in.

It was only then that it struck him—before it had been just words. But Ursula was there, in her bed, her nightgown and the bedclothes soaked in sweat, her face yellow and shiny with it; a reality, the real person. Paul flung himself on his knees beside her and took her head in his hands. She had been rolling restlessly from side to side, but at his touch she stopped for a second and her eyes flickered open.

'Ursula! I'm here, I'm here,' he said. The eyes closed again, and she resumed her rolling, groaning quietly in rhythm with her movements. He did what could be done—bathed her and mopped her, forced some herbal remedies down her resisting throat, and then simply sat beside her, watching. He knew—one part of him knew—that it was no use, but the other part, the inner part that clung fiercely to life and would not admit defeat, not for him or for her, would not believe it. He saw that she grew weaker, but told himself that she was growing calmer, that the restlessness of fever was leaving her. Across her body his eyes met those of their son—eyes like his own and like hers, their expression unfathomable.

It grew full dark, and then it seemed the fever left her. A cooler breath came in at the window, but neither Paul nor the child noticed it, for if they had they would have jumped up to block it out—night air was well-known to kill. But its coolness seemed to revive her. She stopped moving and rolled on to her back, and opened her eyes. They wandered over the ceiling, and then found Paul, and her face curved weakly into a smile of recognition.

'I dreamed you were here,' she whispered. Her lips were parched and cracked and she licked at them feebly. Paul hastened to give her wine, but she could not drink, so he wet her lips with the tip of his finger.

'No dream,' he said. 'I am here.'

'I wanted to see you again, just once more,' she said. She closed her eyes for a moment, gathering her strength. Even to talk was an effort. Her breathing dragged like a tired ox-team. 'Take care of the child,' she whispered. She opened her eyes again to meet his, to emphasise the importance of what she was saying. Paul took her hands in his and pressed them to his chest.

'You won't die,' he said. 'You're better—the fever has left you. See, you'll be better.'

She saw that he didn't believe it. Tears began to roll helplessly from his eyes.

'Don't leave me,' he said. 'Please don't leave me.'

'I said—I never would,' she said. Another long pause. 'Dearest—'

'Ursula.' What was there to say now that was important? 'I love you.'

Yes. That was important. Her eyes were straining to see him now in a darkness that was overcoming the light of the candle he had lit. Her hands were in his but it was not enough. She tried to lift herself towards him, and he understood the movement, and carefully put his arms under her and lifted her against his breast. Her head rested heavily on his shoulder. Her long hair was sticky and smelled of sweat. But she was as she had always been. He strained her against him as if it might stop her from leaving him. Her cheek was against his, and he felt her smiling.

'So cool, your cheek,' she whispered. 'I've been—happy.' His tears were wetting her face, falling on her neck. He did not hear the next word, only felt the shape of it with something more than the sense of touch, something love gave him. 'Paul.'

She grew heavier, relaxing against him, and then he felt her life go out in a small shudder. He had felt it before, once when a newborn lamb had died in his hands one bitter lambing-time; he knew what it was. He put her back from him, looking anxiously into her face. She could not go from him like that! Her face was still hers, was the place she had last been, the place she had only just left. He drew her close again and held her, rocked her, as if she would come back.

The moments moved on, drawing him farther and farther from that instant when she had been there. She stayed behind, and the world and he moved onwards, and the body he held no longer felt as if she might return to it. The candle was guttering, needed trimming. He snuffed it, and laid her gently back on the bed, and got stiffly to his feet. In the darkness there was only the sound of the child's breathing. Paul moved clumsily round the bed and felt around until he found the shoulder, arm, hand.

'Come on,' he said. With only a small resistance, the child got up and walked with him.

Six

ECAUSE OF THE NATURE OF THE DISEASE, AND THE TIME OF the year, the bodies had to be buried at once, without ceremony, but when the epidemic had died away there was a joint funeral mass held for all the victims of that foul disease. Morland Place seemed very silent and empty, and of the family there seemed few indeed to mourn the many dead: Jack and Belle, Edward and Mary, Jackie and Dickon, Master Philip and the many servants—oh yes, and Anne. Anne had not succumbed to the Sweat, but she had died all the same, of a stroke, probably brought on by the strain and the lack of sleep. She had not been well since the beating Paul had given her, and had Philip been alive he would have said that death was a merciful release for her.

But there were mourners enough, though they were not of the family—Jack's friends from all over the county came to the mass to pay their respects to that much-loved man. Paul grieved deeply and silently for him, and welcomed for him all the guests, amongst whom were some very eminent men—Sir Thomas Boleyn and his son George; Sir John St Maur, the west-country merchant-gentleman: Lord Dacre; Lord Borough; the Earl of Essex, who was the descendant of Richard Duke of York's sister; and of course Sir Thomas Parr, who rode up from

London and would take Nanette back to Kentdale with him after the service.

Nanette had accepted the news of her parents' deaths with outward calm, but she grieved inside, the more desperately because she hid it away. Paul, watching her, was glad for her sake that she would be going back to Kentdale and to her friends and her stern occupations—better that she should leave these scenes of misery behind.

Nanette, too, was glad. Home would be home no longer for her, and she looked towards Kentdale as a prisoner looks to the open hills. She felt the loss of a kind of innocence. Her beloved Papa was dead, had taken love with him out of the world. She was no longer a child, and love, if it ever came again, would not be easy or innocent. All happiness from now on would bear a shadow.

On the eve of Nanette's departure the whole family was gathered together in the great hall, along with Sir Thomas Parr and the Butts family—John and Lucy and their sons, John, aged seven, and Bartholomew, six. Adrian was there too—Paul had taken him back to the Lendal after leaving Ursula, and he was to live in the Butts household and attend school as before until Paul found a place for him, an apprenticeship, or a place in a household, or whatever seemed most suitable. The child had a quick intelligence and might do well in the law, Paul thought. Adrian held back from the group, as his equivocal status demanded, keeping to the shadows when he could. But wherever he was, his eyes, burning like live coals, never left his father.

'Well, you are going back to Kentdale tomorrow, Nanette,' Paul said to the pale-faced little girl in black. She was a figure all black-and-white—her hair tumbling down her back was not less black than her gown, her face not less white than the little round cap of starched linen she wore. 'You must work hard and be dutiful and obedient and grow up a good young woman.' Nanette bowed her head submissively, and he went on in a softer tone, 'In a few years you will be old enough to be wed. Your father would have found a match for you, I know, at the first opportunity. But you need not be afraid—I will take over that duty from your father.' He looked round the group, gathering all eyes to him. 'I swear here, before you all, that I will be as a father to Jack's children, and they shall not want for anything. I will provide them with dowry when the time comes, and find them suitable husbands. I take this upon me as a most holy trust.'

His eyes went back to Nanette, who had lifted her head and was looking at him searchingly. He smiled at her, and a small troubled smile touched the corners of her lips. 'Trust me,' he said quietly. 'Look on me as your father now. Jack was my brother—I will take care of you and your sisters.' She nodded, and then, in a jerky movement born of pure impulse, she flung her arms round him, and he held her against him for a moment tightly. There was in each of them a grief that could not be tapped, and in that moment they recognised it in each other.

The next day the guests departed and Nanette and Sir Thomas Parr and his attendants rode out into the milky morning on their way to Kentdale. There was one more thing to be done before Paul resumed his normal life and learned to be alone. Ursula had not been buried at Morland Place—not even for his love of her could he have so offended against the family. She had been buried in the grounds of Holy Trinity Church, and Paul had chosen a corner of the churchyard where the creamy, pink-tipped bindweed grew and poured its mass of flowers over the churchyard wall, for that was the flower that the common folk called bear-bind.

But she should not be forgotten in the house which, had things been otherwise, she might have graced as mistress.

Paul called in the stone-mason, and gave him instructions; the mason, puzzled, did as he was told. He did not understand, but it was not for him to question, and if that was what Master French Paul Morland wanted—why, he was the man to do it. And so in the stone of the wall next to the place where Paul sat or knelt at his devotions in the chapel of Morland Place, there was carved the outline of a small bear. Nothing more—more would have been a betrayal of a different loyalty. But when Paul sat to listen to the holy words or contemplate his Saviour's suffering, his fingers would reach out and trace the shape of it beside him, as once they had searched out the essential shape of a woman. There was nothing else to put into the emptiness inside him.

The great hall of Morland Place was crowded and hot and suffused with the multitudinous smells of unwashed humanity, for the manorial court was being held, and all the tenants and servants were there. Paul took his duties as lord of the manor seriously. In the south, it was said, the old ways were dying out, and there were more and more freeholders and lease-holding tenants and less and less of the manorial system. But up here in the north folk liked the old ways, and had pride in maintaining them, and were glad to boast of the relationship of master and peasant.

True, almost all the peasants on the Morland estate were free men—there were in fact only two bondmen left, the old men, brothers, who lived in a hovel on the edge of the common and had done all their lives. They had never married, and it was thought they were a little simple—'naturals' the other peasants called them. Nobody knew how old they were, or remembered their father or mother. They had become part of the scenery.

Most of the tenants were tenants-at-will and copyholders, but there were some leaseholders, mainly men who had farmed strips on the Shawes estate and the new Watermill estate that had been taken in recently, both of which estates had been run on more modern lines. These leaseholders were somewhat resented by the other tenants, for their rents were fixed and could not be raised, and they were felt to be over-privileged, somehow foreign, subject to the southern influence, effete, modern men, outsiders. The hostility made them keep together in a group to one side, and this grouping reinforced the idea that they were separate from the others.

Paul dealt first with financial business, for he always felt it was as well to get that out of the way before anything more contentious was brought up and fired the sturdy independence of these Yorkshiremen. Fines and rents were collected, fees for the use of the corn-mill, fees for commuting work-days when Paul allowed it, which was not often, merchets and death-dues, and the fees for the sale of strips that had fallen vacant. There was also generally a brisk trade between the tenants themselves in strips, for the growing fashion was for having several strips in one block so that it could all be ploughed and sowed at once without having to walk sometimes a mile or more between them. Paul had no objection if one tenant wanted to sell a strip to another, and a fine was always payable on the transaction to the master. However many strips in one block a man owned, they still had to be planted and cropped in accordance with the common policy that was decided at the midwinter court, so it made no difference to him.

These things being done and the money gathered in and locked away by the steward, it was time for the quarrels and complaints and requests to be heard, but before beginning, Paul had something pleasing to announce. He put his arm round the shoulders of Amyas, who had been seated beside him on the dais watching and listening, aware that one day he would have to preside over this same court, and said, 'My friends, you all know my son, Amyas.' There was a murmuring of agreement and approval. The master's son, recently returned from the court of the great Cardinal Wolsey, was indeed known to them, and was a source of pride to them. A well-set-up lad with a handsome face and dark gold hair and clothes that marked him out as a gentleman of both means and fashion. 'I am very happy to tell you that my son, who has been betrothed these two years past is to be married next week to the young gentlewoman in question—Mistress Elizabeth Norys, who is a niece of the Duke of Norfolk and therefore distantly related to our Sovereign Lord the King himself.'

Loud cheers and cries of congratulation and well-wishing.

'And so it is my pleasure to invite all of you, my loyal tenants, and your wives and families to come up here to the house for the wedding feast, and there will be ale and beef and all manner of dainties for you all, and dancing on the lawn, and other entertainments. You will all be most welcome.'

'God bless you, Master,' called out one old man near the front. 'And the young master too.'

Amyas smiled, enjoying the attention, and Paul nodded in satisfaction at the renewed cheers. He would never have Jack's common touch, but in the last two years, since the death of Jack, his relationship with his tenants had improved. He would never be a demonstrative man, but those who had always respected him as a fair master now thought they detected a softening of his manner, a leaning towards friendship, man with man, which he had never been able to manage before. Many of them thought that he would remarry, and looked forward to the day, for, fine though Master Amyas was, it is not good for a man's inheritance to depend on so slender a thread as one son (and of course the daughter, pretty little Mistress Margaret, and the love-child hidden away at Master Butts's house that no-one was supposed to know about). It put them in mind of the lord King, who had but the one daughter, and the poor Queen having, since the Princess was born, only another miscarriage and a stillborn baby.

But the master did not shew any signs of intending to marry again, and the nurseries at Morland Place contained only the three little girls, Margaret, Catherine and Jane.

The announcement made, Paul carried on with the business of the court, hearing requests, recording births and deaths, approving marriages, and settling disputes—always a great number of the latter, for the Yorkshire men were contentious folk. Here one man disputed with another the responsibility for a repair; here a woman accused another of stealing her hens; there a family blamed another for fouling a stream used for drinking-water. A man was punished for poaching; a woman fined for not going to church one Sunday (a matter for the church courts, really, but these things were often dealt with by the lord of the manor where he took a close interest in his tenants' lives); and a family punished for throwing their litter into a next-door garden.

Paul listened carefully and with patience to the confused and rancorous narratives, and on the whole the people were satisfied with his judgements. Amyas found this part of the proceedings rather boring, and moved restlessly, staring about him, and afterwards, when the court had been closed and the tenants had all gone Paul spoke to him sharply about it.

'You cannot take too close an interest in their quarrels, my son,' he said. 'If they will not come to you for justice, they will give you only half their loyalty and half their service. And they will not come to you if they think you are careless, or do not listen, or give arbitrary judgements. Remember, these are your people, and you owe them service as much as they owe it to you.' He was remembering Richard's words about the duties of kingship as he spoke, and he was pleased when Amyas said, 'My people? You talk as if I will be king over them.'

'You will be, in a way,' Paul said. 'A lord and his tenants is like a king and his people in miniature. It is out of such relationships that the whole world of men is built up. If it fails in the small way, it damages the whole, and one day it may then fail in the larger sense. Be a just king and servant to your people, Amyas.'

'Yes, Father,' the boy said, but he was thinking, if I were King, I should make sure the people served me, and obeyed me, or they'd feel the weight of my hand.

They were about to go out from the hall to seek the steward when there was a sound of horses' hooves in the courtyard, and a moment later John Butts was announced.

'God's greeting, cousin,' he called cheerfully, striding into the hall and pulling off his leather riding gloves. His dogs ran in ahead of him and growled at the Morland dogs round the hearth, and walked stiff-legged around Jasper, who stood his ground haughtily as king-dog should.

'Welcome, John,' Paul said, going forward to clasp his hand. 'I didn't know you were back from London.'

'I had just this minute come up the road from the south. I haven't been home yet—thought I'd call in here first since I was passing. How is everyone? Amyas, you are looking well. How are the little girls?'

'We are all well, I thank you. Amyas, do you go and fetch wine for your cousin and tell them in the kitchen to prepare food.'

'A draught of ale, only, thank you, to wash the dust from my throat. I must go home shortly.'

Paul nodded to Amyas, who went through the screen door to the buttery to find the butler to draw ale for John. He performed the task with overt willingness, but privately he thought that as heir to Morland Place his social position was higher than that of John Butts, and that therefore he shouldn't have to wait on him. Amyas liked always to be the centre of attention.

'Well, cousin, what's the news from London?' Paul asked when Amyas had gone. The two men moved over to the hearth and leaned against the chimney-piece, looking each other over. They made enough of a contrast. John Butts was a small, thin man with pale hair and a narrow, beaky face, and was dressed in leather boots, moleskin britches and a leather jerkin over a shirt streaked with sweat and dust from his journey. Paul, on the other hand, tall and handsome and dark and full-fleshed, was richly clad in a doublet of scarlet velvet whose sleeves were slashed and the fine linen shirt puffed through. His jacket was of scarlet silk, and his gown was charcoal grey, long and trimmed with wolf-fur. His hose and britches were of fine white wool, and his ornamented codpiece of white silk, and on his long dark hair he wore a bonnet of scarlet trimmed with grey feathers.

John Butts was dressed for riding, and when the occasion demanded he dressed as finely as Paul now was—but even then, he would always, beside his tall cousin, look like an ill-favoured weed beside a flourishing rose-bush.

'News of great import,' John said abruptly. 'The King has a son.'

'What?' Paul was astounded for a second, but realised what it must mean at the same moment as John explained.

'By his mistress, of course. Elizabeth Blunt has a son, and the King has named him Henry Fitzroy. The boy is a fine, healthy child, apparently very beautiful and the image of his royal father. The King is almost beside himself with joy.'

The two men exchanged a glance. Though it was not to be said aloud, they each knew the import of this event. It was proof at last that the fault that caused the Queen's barrenness was not with the King. The fault must lie with the Queen—or with the marriage itself, which came to the same thing. The King had now proved that he could generate a healthy son, that he was capable of supplying the kingdom with heirs. What would happen to the wife who now quite clearly was not fulfilling her duty?

'Poor lady,' Paul said at last. John Butts raised an eyebrow—such sympathy came oddly from Paul, who had hounded his own wife almost to the grave for the same fault.

'Poor lady?' John said. 'In what respect, poor?'

'All those miscarriages and lost children,' Paul said. He thought of Ursula's distress. All women were faulted images of that one woman for him.

'Save your sympathy for the King,' John advised shortly.

'He doesn't need sympathy,' Paul said. 'He is still young. At twenty-eight he has much of his life before him. He can have more children.'

John Butts shrugged. 'The Queen is well past thirty, and not strong. There is some doubt whether she will be able to conceive again. That is not a happy situation. And the King, it is said, has turned from his old mistress to a new one, perhaps hoping to prove himself again.'

'A new mistress? The Blunt is out of favour, then?'

'She has served her purpose. The new one is very pretty, fresh back from the court at Burgundy, ripe and ready for pleasure. Who can blame His Grace?'

'Is the girl's name known?' Paul asked with mild interest. John smiled a tight little smile.

'Certainly it is—these things are never secret for long, especially when the father is anxious for advancement at court. And Boleyn is not the man to miss an opportunity.'

'It is Boleyn's daughter?' Paul asked in surprise.

'The elder girl, Mary—a pretty little baggage, and a dutiful daughter.'

'Wasn't she at court with our Mary? I seem to remember her talking of it.'

'That's right. Well, there will be sweets for all now, a place at court for young George, and revenues for Thomas, if the girl knows her business. Perhaps some advantage may come your way, too, cousin. Amyas and George are intimates, after all, and you and Thomas are well acquaint.'

Paul laughed suddenly. 'No, John, he is much more your friend than mine. Let the advantage come to you—you have two sons to get on in the world. I have given Amyas his taste of court—now I want him at home with me. I can't part with him again.'

'But you have another son to advance,' John said seriously. 'Or had you forgotten? Adrian is eleven—in a year he will be old enough to place in a household—why not the King's?'

'I don't look that high for the boy,' Paul said. 'Let him be apprenticed to some decent trade, and that will suffice for him.'

John looked at him curiously. 'I should have thought you'd be more ambitious for him,' he said. 'He is a handsome and intelligent boy. He could go far. And seeing the way you felt about his mother—'

A look from Paul warned him that here was a subject not to be continued. Instead John said, 'At any rate, you ought to take more interest in the boy. Take him hunting with you, talk to him. You hardly know him.' Paul shrugged and turned away, and John saw that there was no point in pressing this now. Instead he changed the subject. 'But, now, cousin, let us get on to more serious matters.'

'What matters are they?' Paul said sullenly.

'Ships,' John said, and watched, amused, as Paul turned back with renewed interest. Amyas came back accompanied by the butler bearing the ale for John Butts, and he too pricked up his ears. Father and son loved ships; Amyas in particular, for in his childhood when he had spent so much time at the Butts house in the city, he had often slipped away to spend the whole day on the wharves at the King's Staith to watch the great ships come in and out.

'What of ships, cousin? Now there's a subject I will discuss with all my heart. Will you not stay to dinner then we can talk at our leisure? If you are not expected at home—?'

With a sigh and a smile, John Butts consented. Once they began to talk he knew, in any case, that they would not leave off for hours.

'I feel the time has come for us to buy a ship, rather than pay carriage for our goods to another shipowner,' he said when they were settled at the hearth with cups of ale. 'We have some gold in surplus, and it would free our goods from lying in bond waiting for the ships to come in. I have heard of a suitable vessel which is for sale, and if the price is right, I don't see why we shouldn't buy it.'

'What is this ship?' Paul asked eagerly.

'There are two, actually, belonging to a merchant of the Levant who died last year. His heir does not wish to continue the trade—he has bought land with his inheritance and had sooner keep his feet on the solid earth than venture out with nothing but three boards between him and the salt water—so he wishes to sell them. They lie at Hull, where they were built.'

'What ships are they?' Amyas asked.

'The *Mary Eleanor* and the *Mary Flower*. Fine ships, both of them, built only two years ago, sound and sweet and as weatherly as any in the world. I would favour buying the *Mary Flower*—she's a little bigger, and better adapted to our purposes. The *Mary Eleanor* was a spice-ship—she's already well-known about the Mediterranean where she collected luxury cargoes.'

Paul looked thoughtful. '*Mary Eleanor* would be a lucky name for us—named after our great-grandmother. Cousin, why should we not buy both ships?'

'Both?'

'Yes—I have a great deal of gold put aside, enough I am sure for this venture. And then, with the *Mary Flower* we could ship our own goods, and with the *Mary Eleanor*—continue this Mediterranean trade she knows so well.'

John Butts thought about it. Amyas looked from one to the other in a ferment of excitement.

'It would need thinking about,' John said at last, 'but there seems no reason why we should not expand into other trades. Elijah, I know, would be interested.'

'Elijah could be the captain,' Paul said with a smile. 'Ever since he went to sea with Master Chetwynd, he has had salt-water fever. He would welcome the chance to go again—I don't think he's really happy on dry land.'

'Oh father, couldn't I go too?' Amyas asked, unable to contain himself longer. 'I would make a good captain, and my years with the Cardinal taught me a lot about silks and spices and dealing with merchants.'

'My son—' Paul began, and then thought better of a direct denial. 'Perhaps you might be able to make one trip—but don't forget your place is here. You are the heir to Morland Place, and you must be ready with your hand at the rein whenever the time comes.'

It was a good compromise—the possibility of at least one trip, and the reminder that better things were assured. Amyas knew when he was well off, and held his peace, but in his eyes were the misty dreams of all men who have ever loved the ocean.

Seven

$\mathscr{I}$N THE WINTER OF THE YEAR 1521 ENGLAND WAS ONCE more at war with France—and this only a year after the enormously ostentatious meeting of friendship between Henry of England and Francis of France, which had since been nick-named 'The Field of Cloth-of-Gold' owing to the prevalence of that material on that occasion—even the tents had been made of it! One consequence of the declaration of war was the return home, early in 1522, of the last four English girls at the Court of Queen Claude: Anne, sister to the King's mistress Mary Boleyn; Lord Dacre's daughter Anne; and the two Grey girls, the King's kinswomen, Anne and Elizabeth. All four were quickly found places in the Queen's household, and Lord Dacre, of his friendship, used his influence to secure a place as maid of honour for Paul's daughter Margaret, now fourteen.

Margaret was delighted with her good fortune. She found it dull at home, although it was pleasant to be looked up to by her two young cousins, and she enjoyed riding and hawking; but going to Court meant new clothes, new experiences, new friends, all the glory and prestige of being a maid of honour to the Queen of England, and the hopes of a good marriage. At fourteen she had begun to be much occupied with the thought of marriage.

The maids of honour were divided into messes, and because of the friendship of their fathers, Margaret was put in a mess with Anne Dacre and Anne Boleyn. The maids slept together in a long dormitory, three to a bed, and, unless duties called them elsewhere, they took their meals together at a long trestle in the great chamber. Each maid was allowed one female servant and one small dog, and, if she was of noble rank, stabling for one horse. The allowance of food was plentiful though, on the whole, plain—for breakfast a chine of beef, a chet loaf and a gallon of ale; for dinner beef and mutton, ale and wine; and on fast days salted eels, plaice and flounders. Sometimes, however, additional meats would find their way to the maids' tables—coneys and pigeons and game. The young men of the Court were always pleased to purchase the maids' favours by such 'anonymous' gifts if hunting had been good. And, of course, there were the banquets and entertainments they might be called upon to attend.

A maid's duties were light, and consisted mostly of attending the Queen. She might be sent to fetch a book or some embroidery silk, or be required to take a dog for a walk, or feed the Queen's pet monkey; if she had a pleasant voice, she might be asked to sing, or read aloud from a devotional book; if she had musical skill she might be asked to play on the virginals; but otherwise, there was little to do but simply be there. This meant a great deal of sitting and sewing—the Queen was very particular about her Christian duty to provide shirts for the poor people—and a great deal of attendance in chapel, for the Queen was very devout, so her entire household heard mass twice a day every day, and as much as four or five times on saints' days and holy days.

To Margaret the Queen, in her rich black gowns, her glittering jewels and her great head-dresses, was a glamorous figure, and even when she grew accustomed enough to the glamour to perceive that the woman within the clothes was elderly, plain and sickly, she still felt a respect bordering on awe for her. The Queen was so very, very good and so very, very stately. She never forgot etiquette at any time. Everything had to be done according to the ceremonial procedure, and woe betide the maid who forgot the correct order or the correct form. Queen Catharine was a great lady, and it was felt by everyone, even the King himself.

The King was much seen about the Queen's rooms, and to the inexperienced new maid of honour, if the Queen was grand, the King was godlike. His sheer physical size was overwhelming—hugely tall, hugely broad—and the effect of his presence was enhanced by his magnificent clothes—great padded shoulders, massive furred mantles, great protuberant codpiece, jewels everywhere, on fingers, round the neck, sewn into the rich, sumptuous materials of every article of clothing from cap to shoes. He was surrounded, too, with the courtly ceremony of a King who was God's anointed representative: one might not speak, or sit down, or turn one's back in the King's presence, and if one came across him by accident—in the corridor, say—one sank to the ground in a low, low curtsey, and did not raise one's eyes from the floor until one was quite sure he had passed and was gone.

Margaret was terrified of the King, but she found it very pleasant to see the great affection there was between him and the Queen. He called her Kate, and she called him Henry (which seemed almost suicidal daring—to call the King by his name!). The Queen was always much more cheerful when the King was there, and she would laugh and be gay in a manner that would astonish anyone who had only seen her before alone with her maids. The King liked to behave informally with her, and would sit on a stool with his beringed hands on his great spread knees talking to her, asking her advice and discussing the business of the realm with her.

When the King visited the Queen's apartments, the Princess was generally sent for, and there was a pleasant time while father and mother talked to six-year-old Mary, and listened to her playing on the virginals and singing. The King liked to talk in Latin to her, and to see her dance. Both the King and the Queen adored Princess Mary and were intensely proud of her, and indeed any parents would have been, for as well as being very pretty, the auburn-haired, grey-eyed little girl was very intelligent, quick-witted, and good at her lessons. She was a merry child, and she loved to dance and play, and when the King sent for her, the Queen's rooms would ring with his booming laugh and the Princess's happy chuckling.

But, on the whole, the young maids were glad when the King had gone, for it was so terrifying to be continually on guard in his presence against offending in some point of etiquette. Even Anne Boleyn, who had served at royal courts for eight years and was (to Margaret) an old woman of twenty, and whose sister, to boot, had been the King's mistress, was dumb and nervous like the rest of them when the massive glittering figure of the King came by, while Anne Dacre, who likewise had eight years' experience, almost fainted with fear one day when the King spoke to her, though it was only to ask her to fetch a book from a table across the room.

Much more interesting to them was the presence in the ante-rooms of the young men of the King's Household. They were often there, even when the King wasn't visiting the Queen, for, like the maids, they had not much in the way of real work to do. A bevy of pretty, high-spirited girls attracts young men like wasps to plums, and the older ladies-in-waiting kept a watchful eye on behaviour and reported anything unseemly to the Queen, whose reprimand it was counted great shame to earn. Almost as numerous as the youths of the King's Household were those of the Cardinal's, and since the Cardinal was in almost daily attendance on the King, it was often hard to tell of the young men in the Queen's rooms which belonged to the King and which to his minister.

Margaret had only been in the Queen's service for a week when she was approached in the anteroom by a very attractive, well-dressed young man who bowed and pronounced her name. Margaret curtseyed automatically, but her eyes were wide with surprise as she surveyed the red-haired, freckled, muscular young man.

'Well, Mistress Margaret, don't you know me?' he asked with a pleasant smile. Aware that she was being closely watched, not only by the older ladies, but by her envious peers, Margaret could only blush foolishly and shake her head. 'It is a long time since we met, I admit, but I claim acquaintance with confidence, since you are the sister of my one-time best friend.'

Then she knew him. 'Sir—my lord—' she stammered. 'Master Percy, is it not? Your father—my lord of Northumberland—'

'Harry Percy, at your service, your most humble service,' he said, sweeping another bow, and Margaret knew she was being teased, but in a pleasant way. To be claimed as an acquaintance by the son of the Earl of Northumberland, a young man who would himself be an Earl one day, was a great thing. Aware that her two mess-mates, the two Annes, were watching with their eyes on stalks, Margaret preened herself a little, and tried to edge herself and her attendant further away so that their talk might be private.

'It is a long time since we met, sir,' she said, regaining her composure, 'but it was uncivil of me to have been so slow to remember you.'

Harry Percy looked a little surprised. 'Why, Mistress Margaret, you have already learned to talk with a courtier's tongue. Tell me, how is your brother, my good friend? Many a happy time we had together when he was in service with me.

And many a time he protected me from the teasing of the other boys, for which I owe him much gratitude.'

'Amyas is well—and his family too,' Margaret said.

'I had heard he was married—to Mistress Norys, was it not? Her cousin Hal is at court here, in the King's Household—have you seen him?'

Margaret shook her head. 'I am so recently come to court, sir, I hardly know one face from another.'

Percy laughed. 'You will soon know Hal's, I promise you. He is the prettiest, wittiest young gentleman about the King, and all the ladies are madly in love with him. I promise you shall be in love with him too inside a month. But tell me about Amyas. Is he happy now he is wed?'

'I believe so,' Margaret said, not really understanding the import of the question. What had happiness to do with it? 'He has two sons now, Robert, who is nearly two, and Edward who was born in March.'

'My friend Amyas, a father of two sons!' Harry Percy laughed. 'It hardly seems possible.' He sobered suddenly. 'I am to be wed, too.'

'When is that to be?' Margaret asked with interest—marriage was an all-absorbing topic to her.

'There is no date set,' he said. 'But there has been an understanding for many years between my lord father and my lord of Shrewsbury that I should be wed to his daughter Mary. Mary Talbot,' he finished, and his tone was cold with disgust. Margaret was about to probe further into this, to discover why he was not overjoyed at such an, apparently, good marriage, when they were interrupted by a dark, slightly husky voice with a hint of a foreign accent which had already become familiar to Margaret.

'You are being watched,' said Anne Boleyn. 'Mistress Ratcliffe has her eye on you, and will not be best pleased if you continue to talk to each other alone in this corner. You had better let me rescue you.'

Harry Percy had bowed to the newcomer, and, straightening up, was now looking her over with unmistakable interest. She was certainly worth looking at; even Margaret, who, obedient follower of fashion that she was, did not care for dark looks and preferred auburn hair and fair skin, conceded that. Though not conventionally beautiful, Anne had enormous, lustrous dark eyes which were so magnetic they prevented you noticing anything else about her face. Her hair was long and thick and black and hung down her back from under the French halo cap which she wore. At the front of the cap, from under the gold gauze binding, a little neatly parted hair also shewed. It was an entirely new fashion, and all the young women were wild to copy it, while the older women, who had never shewn their hair to anyone, thought it likely to breed immorality. However, the Queen had permitted the fashion to be worn, so there was nothing they could do about it.

But the long hair and the large eyes, the long slender neck like a flower stem, the slight foreign accent that made her husky voice liltingly beautiful, the elegant French fashions, and her graceful carriage made Anne very much worth looking at. And it was plain to Margaret, as she introduced her brother's friend, that Anne found Harry Percy worth looking at too. It also became plain that the warning about Mistress Ratcliffe had been nothing but a ruse, for that lady was nowhere to be seen when Margaret glanced cautiously round, and when she returned her attention to her companions they were deep in conversation which seemed not to take any account of discretion. It was lucky, thought Margaret later, that they were all called a few moments afterwards to go in to the Queen's chamber, and she said so that night to Anne as they were preparing for bed.

'Otherwise you might have got into trouble. The way you were looking at him—'

'And why shouldn't I look at him?' Anne said dreamily, brushing her thick curling hair which had reached almost to her knees. 'He is beautiful, the most beautiful man I have ever seen—and,' her eyes turned to Margaret and grew sharper, 'let me tell you I have seen many, many beautiful men in my years at Court. But Harry Percy! Harry Percy—' She lingered over the name as if the very syllables tasted sweet on her tongue.

Margaret sniffed. 'He is well enough, I suppose, though he is not as handsome as my brother. But in any case, there's no good in falling in love with him, for he's to wed Mary Talbot, he told me so himself.'

'Tush, child, what do you know of these things?' Anne said crossly. Anne Dacre, who was already in bed, sitting up and listening to them, added gently, 'But it's true, Nan—I heard my father mentioning it once. It's all been arranged for years. And you,' she added shrewdly, 'are also betrothed, so where's the use in talking like that?'

'I'm not betrothed,' Anne said hotly. 'If you're referring to James Butler, his father and my father cannot agree on the terms, for which I call God's blessing on both of them for I swear I will not marry him, not if he's the only man—'

She stopped abruptly and turned her head away, biting her lip. She had been about to say, 'not if he's the only man I'm ever offered,' and it brought home to her the unpleasant truth that she was twenty and still unwed, while her sister Mary had been wed nine months and had been the King's mistress into the bargain. Mary was fair and pretty. Anne knew that her father was having difficulty placing her because she was not pretty and, moreover—she folded her right hand over her left in a gesture which had become automatic.

Anne Dacre watched all this, and with a sigh she climbed out from between the sheets and crawled over the bed to the end where Anne was sitting and put her arms round the thin shoulders. Margaret, realizing they meant to be private, looked away, but she heard what was said all the same.

'Don't cry, Nan,' Anne Dacre said gently. 'Nobody who knows you minds in the least about your finger. We all love you, and you will have a husband who loves you too, never fear.'

'I've heard servants say sometimes it's the mark of the Devil,' Anne said in a low voice.

'But God sees into your heart, and he knows you are pure. Everyone who knows you loves you. Don't be unhappy. Why, it's such a little thing, a stranger wouldn't notice it.'

And Anne allowed herself to be comforted. Later that night when they were all in bed, Margaret reflected and wondered. Anne wore long sleeves which fell in a point over her hands, covering them—a fashion she had brought from France, like her halo head-dresses. Margaret didn't remember seeing her hands, ever. The other two occupants of the bed were breathing quietly, evenly. Cautiously, Margaret sat up. There was a little moonlight in the room, and by it she could see Anne Boleyn sleeping on her side with her hand under the pillow. Then, as she watched, the sleeper sighed and turned on to her back, and her hand came to rest on her breast, just above the cover. Margaret stared, and then, just in case, crossed herself. The little finger of the left hand looked crooked, wrong somehow. Half way along it was a strange horny growth, as if the bone were sticking through the skin, or as if a sixth finger were beginning to grow.

During that summer, while Margaret, out of a confused sense of loyalty, was finding herself time and again covering up for Anne and Harry Percy, whose love affair was growing more and more blatant, tension was growing at home between her father and her brother. The roots of the quarrel lay in Amyas's enforced idleness. Paul had never relinquished any of his responsibilities in his son's favour although he insisted that Amyas accompany him to learn how to run the estate and the businesses, never ceasing to remind him that one day it would all be his. So Amyas had not enough to do and, in his own opinion, not enough importance, and he blamed his father for it.

At first Amyas occupied himself with the house. He had begun to be interested in architecture and the design of houses while he was in the Cardinal's service, and, since the actual running of the house was his wife's business, and the running of everything else was his father's, he began on a plan to improve the structure itself. The house built in 1450 was easily capable of expansion, and the first thing that Amyas did was to have bedrooms built in the attics under the roof for the servants. At present the upper servants slept with the family, and the lower servants slept in the great hall, but it was becoming acceptable nowadays for them to be accommodated separately and Amyas desired to make his mark on Morland Place.

It led to the first quarrel between Paul and Amyas. 'You want to shut the servants away from us like beasts?' Paul said. 'Are they not people like us?'

'They are people and deserve accommodation like people,' was Amyas's argument. 'They sleep more like beasts in the straw in the hall than they will in proper bedrooms in my attics.'

'It is separating them from us, as if they were not worthy to live with us,' Paul said, but Amyas laughed.

'Nonsense. They will have rooms like our own. If they are worthy, then they are worthy of their own apartments, are they not? It is you who separate them, making them sleep on the floor.'

Paul had eventually to agree, for on the surface Amyas's argument was sound; but he felt, though he couldn't explain it adequately, that he was right, and Amyas wrong, and when he spoke to Uncle Richard about it, the latter agreed.

'Servant and man have always slept together, side by side, within reach and call of each other. Once the master slept in the great hall with all the household, and then there was true fellowship. The further we go from that ideal, the more we separate men into two categories, the servants and the served. You are in the right, Paul.'

But the building went ahead anyway, and Paul repeated Richard's views often enough to Amyas to worsen the relationship between them, and to mend the breach between himself and Richard. Richard was running Shawes again with his daughter-in-law's help, since both Elijah and Ezekiel were away at sea much of the time, and returning to being master of Shawes had given him a new lease of life.

The tension between Paul and Amyas arose again early in 1522 when Paul, in response to much nudging from John Butts, brought Adrian to live at Morland Place.

'You hardly know the boy,' John had said. 'It's time you took an interest in him—he's your responsibility, not mine. Get to know him and decide on his future.'

And unwillingly Paul had agreed, and Adrian had entered once more under his father's roof. He was fourteen now, already taller than Amyas, and possessing his father's dark curling hair and something of his handsome features, blended subtly, and for Paul painfully, with a certain delicacy that was his mother's. Paul was very reserved with him, almost afraid of him, but was glad in a way that he was being forced to get to know him. Adrian, after all, was all that was left in the world of the one women he had loved, flesh of her flesh. He had not allowed for the hostility of Amyas.

'It's an insult to bring that boy under this roof,' he said to his father, having secured an interview with him alone in the steward's room. 'The bastard child of your mistress, to live here as if he had some right—it's an insult to the memory of my mother.'

'Your mother is not remembered,' Paul countered coldly. 'Not by me, and not by you either.'

'It's an insult to me,' Amyas went on.

'It is no insult to you, my son. Adrian is my child, and my responsibility. I am master of Morland Place, and if I choose to bring my bastard son to live here, no-one can blame you for that. It does not reflect on you at all. There is no threat to your position.' Paul remembered as he spoke the terrible wasted years of his own jealousy of Jack, which was grounded on such a fear. 'I would like you to be friends.'

'Friends!' Amyas ejaculated.

'Why not friends? You are both my sons. Had things been different you might have been brothers by law. The accident of his birth is not your shame, nor his, nor his mother's, but mine alone. Don't hate him. I have only two sons—'

'You have only one son,' Amyas said fiercely.

'Then all the more need,' Paul replied quietly. Amyas stopped and thought, casting around for a new argument.

'Father,' he said, taking a step nearer and looking wheedling, playing on the affection Paul had had for him as a child, 'you have me—what want do you have of another? Wasn't I always enough for you before? Why have you changed now? And as for need—I have provided you with two grandsons, and will get you more by and by. Morland Place is safe for generations to come. You don't need the boy. Send him away, father.'

Paul swayed, hearing the child's appeal from the lips of the man, but when he looked at Amyas he saw not the child he had loved, nor the young man to whom everything that he had would pass, but the selfish child of a selfish mother. In the fair hair he saw suddenly Anne Butts, weak, sly and greedy, and his heart hardened. Ursula, he thought, why could it not have been you and I who were wed, our son to inherit, and this boy to be taken care of, given second-best always, according to his merits.

'No,' Paul said. But it was not so easy, alone, to resist Amyas's righteous anger. Every day the complaints and the quarrelling went on, and every day it grew harder to present the eccentric case for the love-child's rights. And Adrian himself did not help matters. At first he was silent and withdrawn, but as he saw himself championed by the master against the master's son, he grew insolent, to Amyas and to the servants. No-one seemed to like him. The servants grumbled and Amyas cursed and even the little girls in the nursery shrank away from him when the family was gathered at the fire.

In the end it was Great Uncle Richard who suggested the solution. 'Let him come to me at Shawes,' he said. 'Madge will mother him, and I will discipline him, and my servants, being a surly lot, will not be bullied by him. He can learn from me the ways of running an estate, without getting the wrong ideas about his station, and when he has learnt how to conduct himself he can be usefully employed in the running of the family businesses.'

'It sounds like a good idea,' Paul began doubtfully.

'Then let it be done,' Richard said. 'I need another man about the place, with my son and grandson gone, and you are not good for him, Paul. Your own feelings blind you to both his faults and his virtues and to the impropriety of his position.'

So it was settled, and Adrian went to live at Shawes, and Amyas felt he had won a battle even while he felt, resentfully, that no battle should have been necessary. Occupied with these matters, Amyas heard with only distant interest the news from Court of his old friend Harry Percy's disgrace. Margaret mentioned it in her letters home: Percy and Anne had declared themselves engaged to each other, and the Queen had complained to the King about their behaviour. It was, of course, forbidden for anyone in the Royal service to contract themselves without the King's permission, and so young Anne Boleyn had been packed off home to Hever Castle in disgrace, while Harry Percy had been brought before his master, the Cardinal, for a severe reprimand. When he protested that he was engaged in honour to marry Anne Boleyn, his father was called in, and between them, with threats and harryings, they had broken the boy's spirit and he too had been sent home, to await the fulfilment of his engagement to Mary Talbot.

The disgrace of the two lovers, her friends, had touched Margaret less than the marriage of her other bedfellow, Anne Dacre. Margaret, nearing fifteen, was more anxious than ever to be married, and urged her brother to speak to their father about it if he could. Amyas pushed the question aside. He avoided talking to Paul at all if it could be helped, and longed for the time when his father would die and leave him sole control of his inheritance. His father was nearing fifty, Amyas thought, and evidently did not mean to marry again. What use was his life to him? Once Paul was out of the way, he, Amyas, would change things, put things on a more modern footing, shew the tenants who was master! Paul, in clinging on to his useless life, was being inconsiderate. Amyas told these things to his wife in the privacy of their curtained bed, and Elizabeth, pregnant and placid, only half listening and less than half understanding, murmured her agreement.

The time for the winter killing came, and in the middle of it, when everyone was as busy as they might be, Uncle Richard came down to Morland Place on horseback—proof indeed of urgency!—and took Paul aside to talk to him.

'It's about Adrian,' he said. Paul looked at him anxiously. It was evidently bad news.

'What's the matter? Is he ill?'

'No, not ill. In fact, that child has the strength of the D—of ten men,' Richard corrected himself unsmilingly. 'Paul, you must send him away.'

'Not you too, Uncle Richard,' Paul groaned. 'Why does everyone hate that poor child?'

'I don't hate him, and he's not a poor child. Paul, I don't want to have to explain—I don't know if I could explain—but you must send him away, for your own good, and for his good, and for everyone's good in any way concerned with us. For the family, Paul, think of it that way. You know that I wouldn't ask this if I didn't think it was entirely necessary.'

Richard gazed levelly into Paul's troubled eyes, thinking with a shudder how like Adrian's they were, and, more essentially, how unlike.

'Why?' Paul said at last.

'Don't ask me,' Richard pleaded. Paul shook his head.

'I must ask. Don't you see, I owe that child a debt. I can't dismiss him without knowing why.'

'Don't look on it as a dismissal.' It was an evasion.

'Why,' Paul persisted. Richard shrugged helplessly.

'He has a shadow about him. He carries it like a scar. It will spread from him like a blight over the whole family if he is not removed to a climate where it cannot grow. Paul, trust me. I don't hate the child. You know my heart. *Trust me.*'

'I do trust you,' Paul said at last.

'Then send him away,' Richard said simply. Paul's shoulders slumped as he gave in, and he was aware of a strange, perfidious feeling of relief.

'Where to?' he asked.

'I have thought about it, and I think it would be best if it could be arranged for him to be taken in by Micah,' Richard said.

'In Norfolk's household? Do you look so high?' Paul said in surprise.

'I think it could be arranged. He is a likely enough boy, and Micah could then keep an eye on him. Micah is strong, and wise beyond his years. The boy would not deceive him for a moment. I think your connections and credit are enough to get the child a place.'

Paul shrugged. 'Well then, let it be done. It is not dishonour-able, and perhaps it may serve everyone for the best.'

Richard clasped his hand in glad relief. 'Let it be done as quickly as possible,' he said. 'I should have liked him to be gone before winter, but as it is—' He shrugged. 'As soon as possible.'

The matter was arranged without much difficulty, and the boy was to leave by Candlemas to take up a position under Micah in the Norfolk household. Morland Place seemed to breathe more easily, and even Amyas became expansive with his father at the news. On Candlemas eve Paul was in the chapel at vigil, but his mind had drifted from his devotions to more profane channels. He knelt, and his eyes were fixed on the banks of candles and the flower-wreathed statue of the Blessed Virgin, but his left hand rested against the wall beside him, and his fingers moved over and over again around the outline of the little bear. The candle names were still, but the shadows in the corners seemed invested with life, and it was as if the air was filled with the sound of wings, a fluttering and whirling and rushing sound around his head. The darkness was the dark depths of eyes, depths into which once he could sink; now they rejected him, they watched him resentfully from the other side of the grave, and the wings beat at his head like angry birds. Was it a betrayal? *Was it?*

'What can I do?' he cried aloud. 'For pity, what can I do?' And the shadows drew back, the wings fell away from him, the eyes sank again into the darkness, and he was alone again, bereft and alone.

No, not alone—there was someone in the chapel, someone in the dark corner behind him: he felt the presence with his spine, with the stiffening of the hair at the back of his neck. He turned to look, and as he turned he crossed himself without knowing why he did it. It was Adrian, standing by the door, looking at him with burning eyes as he had done once before, on the day Ursula died. Paul sighed, and his fingers, dug into the outline carving, relaxed. He stood up.

'Did you want to speak to me?' he asked softly. The boy stood tall and erect, a handsome, strong, intelligent boy of whom any father would be proud; in his carriage was something of that upright dignity that had marked out Ursula from amongst other folk.

'You are sending me away,' Adrian said. 'I leave tomorrow.' It was not a question, yet Paul felt as it was said that here was one last chance to—to what? Elusive, the feeling was gone before he could grasp it. Everything was already arranged.

'Yes,' he said. 'It will be a good position for you. You will have the chance to prove yourself, to make your mark in the world.' Why did it sound like an excuse? It was true, all true! 'Better than that you should be a servant all your life.' Adrian took a step closer, and the candlelight flickered in the shining darkness of his eyes like angry flames within them.

'You killed my mother,' he said quietly. The silence in the chapel deepened, as if the stones were listening.

'No,' Paul said. 'That's not true. I loved her.'

'You killed her. I was there that day, don't forget, the day she came and begged you to let her go. If she had gone, she would not have died of the Sweating Sickness—but you wouldn't let her go. You had her, and you wouldn't let her be free, and so she died. *That* is on your soul.'

'Adrian,' Paul pleaded.

'And now you wish to be rid of me, too. You send me away from you, but one day I will come back. When I am a man, I will come back, and then I will kill you if I can.'

'If you can,' Paul repeated, dazed.

'Look for me,' Adrian said. 'Every day of your life. I will be your death, or you will be mine.'

And he turned away and went to the door, but there he stopped, and his shoulders looked strangely brittle, as if he were a child trying not to cry. He turned again, very slowly and looked towards the man. His face came out of the shadows, young and clear-cut, filled with longing.

'Father,' he said, and there was an appeal in it that Paul recognised. He was only a child, a child no-one had ever wanted. He had seen his mother abused, threatened, attacked, reviled, he had seen her die, he had been shunned and scorned and given evil names. Where was the love without which, like a weed in the darkness, his soul would grow crooked? Paul saw that this was the last chance he had almost recognised—the last chance to give the child the love that was his right, the love that would save him. Don't make me hate you, said that pleading face. Don't force me back into this darkness my soul has become. I don't want to hate. Give me love, and sunlight. 'Father!'

Paul shuddered at the pitiful cry, and the old paralysis came over him. He could not love, he did not know how it was done, how to reach out, how to open himself for the giving. If the love could be taken—but how was *that* child, of all others, to know how to take? He heard the appeal, and in torment he could not answer it. The eyes tortured him. In desperation he turned away; and as the tears flooded his eyes, washing the bright halo of candlelight into a blur, he heard the chapel door click closed, a soft, final sound.

Eight

*I*N THE AUTUMN OF 1525 NANETTE CAME HOME TO MORLAND
Place, leaving Lady Parr's establishment. Her education
was at an end, for Lady Parr's daughter Katherine was to be
married, at the age of fourteen. It was not the first foray Lady
Parr had made into the marriage market: two years earlier she
had entered negotiations with Lord Dacre's son, Lord Scrope,
for a marriage between Katherine, then not yet twelve, and
Lord Scrope's son and heir. Nanette had been prepared to be
dismissed and sent home, but nothing had come of the negotiations, since Lady Parr and Lord Scrope each wanted more in
cash terms than the other had been prepared to give.

The man who was to marry Katherine in the new year was
a widower of fifty, Edward, Lord Borough, and in the tangled
web of interrelationships that prevailed in the north, he was a
cousin of some sort of his young bride. His grandmother Alice
Beauchamp was the daughter of Richard Beauchamp, Earl of
Warwick, and she had afterwards married Edmund Beaufort,
the patron of the Morland family a hundred years ago. Lord
Borough had several grown-up children, all of them older than
their prospective stepmother, but when Nanette asked her
friend if the idea troubled her, Katherine said only, 'No, not at
all, though it will seem strange when they address me as "my

lady mother". Edward is very proper, and says that he will make sure they do so.'

'And you shan't mind that your husband is so much older than you?' Nanette asked next. Katherine didn't answer directly.

'He is very kind,' she said. 'I respect him, and I enjoy conversing with him.' Her eyes met Nanette's, and they both thought of the other aspect of marriage. Katherine seemed to shrink a little. What would it be like to be wife to an old man?

'I suppose—' Nanette began, but Katherine had regained her composure, and straightened a little, proudly.

'It must be a little alarming the first time, whoever one marries. I should think it would be better to be marrying an older man, who will be kind and patient, than a young man who is all fire and carelessness,' she said. Nanette agreed for the sake of her friend's peace of mind. Katherine had no choice in the matter, so it was as well that she was resigned to it—and she was really an amazingly sensible child for her age. But Nanette, who was seventeen, felt a stirring of revolt at the thought of wedding an old man, and a firing of her blood at the thought of a passionate and careless young bridegroom. Well, at least perhaps Katherine would find herself a widow before she was too much older, and then be able to choose a husband more to her liking.

'The thing I really regret,' Katherine was saying now, 'is that I cannot have you with me. I shall miss you, Nan, very much.'

'And I you, Katherine,' Nanette said seriously. 'Do you remember how we talked about marriage? We knew even then that it would mean separating from each other—but we agreed that we would write, didn't we?'

'Oh yes, and we shall, shan't we? Do, sweet Nan, do promise me you will write to me!'

'But of course I will, chuck!' Nanette said, flinging her arms round small Katherine and hugging her. The hug was returned, hard, and with a little of a tremble in it, and Nanette almost wished that she could marry this old man for Katherine to save her the anxiety.

'I expect you will be married soon,' Katherine said, her voice muffled by Nanette's shoulder. 'You are so very beautiful that if you hadn't been hidden away here at Kentdale you would have been married long before this.'

'I think perhaps my uncle has tended to forget me, thinking me safely disposed of here with you,' Nanette agreed thoughtfully. 'But I don't mind. I don't know that I really want to be married.'

Katherine pulled back from the embrace and stared at her in surprise. 'But Nan, you must! You are so pretty! Now, if you were plain, like me—'

'Oh Katherine, what have looks to do with it?' Nanette laughed. 'Still, when the time comes I suppose I shall have no more choice in the matter than you have, and perhaps that's as well. I dare say we should all make unwise marriages if it were left to us, and not arranged by those wiser than ourselves.'

Margaret also came home to Morland Place that autumn, at about the same time, for she was to be married at last, on St Nicholas's day, to a gentleman of York. The man concerned was a merchant who lived on the Lendal, almost next door to John Butts, and he was a childless widower of thirty. Margaret was delighted to be getting married—at seventeen she had been growing worried about her virgin state—but she was not best pleased at the choice of husband her father had made for her, as she told Nanette when the girls were settling down to sleep on their first night together for so many years.

'It isn't his age I mind,' she said. 'Thirty is nothing really, for a man. He is still in his prime at thirty. But he is only a merchant, and he has no connections at Court, and never goes to London—well, not above three or four times a year,' she corrected herself at Nanette's murmur of enquiry.

'Why, what would you have, Margaret? It seems a reasonable match to me—and your father surely would get you the best he could.'

'Well, I would have thought so,' Margaret said peevishly, 'but after I have been at Court, and been maid of honour to the Queen, I would have thought—and then, father has so many connections. Really high people. My lord of Norfolk, and Lord Dacre, and the Boleyns—well, look how high they have risen recently. Sir Thomas has been made Lord Treasurer of the Household, and his son a gentleman of the bedchamber, and they say the King visits Hever Castle all the time in the grease season.'

'Yes, I have heard that the hunting is good in Kent,' Nanette said with quiet amusement.

'Well then,' Margaret went on, growing more and more indignant, 'since father knows Sir Thomas, and goes to dine with him—'

'Very rarely,' Nanette reminded her.

'And your father was Sir Thomas's intimate friend,' she went on undeterred, 'and Amyas is George's friend—'

'Was, before he married.'

'—and I was a close friend of his daughter's—at least before she was sent away in disgrace, though if he's been given such an important appointment that can't be being held against him—well,' she drew breath, 'what I say is, why shouldn't I have been got a gentleman of the Court for a husband?'

How different, Nanette reflected, was Margaret's reception of the news from Katherine's calm acceptance. 'Perhaps,' she said soothingly, 'your father's friendship with these people does not extend as far as being able to influence marriage negotiations. They are very complicated things, you know. In fact, it is a wonder to me that anyone ever manages to get married at all.'

Margaret, unconvinced, continued to grumble. Before her father, however, she was all acquiescence, for she had always been a little afraid of him, and had heard rumours about his violence that had filtered through from the servants, rumours she was not supposed to have heard. And when she saw her bridegroom, she was instantly reconciled, for he was a tall and handsome man of enormous charm. James Chapham was slender and elegant, and dressed in the best and richest of styles; his oval face was smoothly olive-skinned, his features pronounced but finely-drawn. Under level black brows his olive eyes shone with intelligence and humour; his brow was high under thick, swept-back dark hair just lightly touched with grey. His mouth was subtle and humorous, his white teeth showed often in a charming smile, and his voice—for Nanette his voice was the best thing about him, melodious and of a beautiful timbre, and tucked and ruckled with laughter as if he found pleasure and humour in everything.

He is too good for Margaret, was Nanette's instant, guilty thought as she made her curtsey, her eyes immodestly fixed on his face, for she could not bring herself to lower them as she should. She saw what she thought was recognition and under-standing in his eyes as he bowed over her hand and, likewise, did not look away from her face for one moment. In those few seconds Nanette was glad, thoroughly glad for the first time in her life, that she was beautiful, for she wanted to impress herself upon him, she wanted him not to be able to forget her. And the expression of his eyes, which was for her only, told her that he would not.

Nanette rose from her curtsey, withdrew her hand from his, and instantly remembered herself and blushed for shame. This was her cousin's husband, how could she so forget herself as to want to attract him? Now, belatedly, she dropped her eyes as became a modest maiden, and drew back a step, and, to make amends for her shamelessness, she would not allow herself more than one or two glances at the handsome stranger all evening. Margaret, licensed by her position, stared at him with open admiration, only withdrawing her gaze, blushing furiously, if he looked at her.

Paul watched her in amusement. When his daughter had come home, he had been struck at once by her airs, her fashionable gestures and langours, her Court chatter, her evident high opinion of herself. She was plumply pretty it was true, and her fair hair and skin were fashionably admired, but she was not outstanding in any way, and he could not imagine what had convinced her she was so out of the ordinary. It was, perhaps, the inevitable reaction of one coming home from the centre of the universe to an out-of-the-way country residence; it might also have been the effect of the open admiration bestowed on her by little Catherine and Jane, to whom she seemed like a creature from another world.

Now he saw this self-regarding young woman turned into a gawping ninny by the elegant charm of James Chapham, and he was amused, as well as pleased. He liked Chapham, finding him conversable and undemanding, easy to like, which was important for someone like Paul; but more than that he needed him, for Chapham was very rich, and had no relatives. Wolsey, Paul's one-time patron, had been flaying the country with forced loans to pay for the wars he so eagerly waged on his master's behalf. There was one in 1522 and one in '23, and then in '24 there had been three tax commissions out at once, sucking the life-blood from landowners in what was called 'The Amicable Grant'.

The men of the north, traditional non-payers of tax, whose remoteness from the centre of administration increased their natural dislike of parting with their money, threatened a rebellion, and the King had been forced to step in and cancel the tax; but not before much of it had been gathered in—and of course, what was gathered was never given back. Taxes were always unwelcome, but things had been particularly bad recently. For the past twenty years prices had been rising faster and faster, and the landowners, depending on rents which did not rise as fast as prices, were finding themselves growing poorer.

Paul Morland was better off than many, for part of his income came from wool and cloth, where prices were rising along with all other prices. In addition to that he was cushioned by the fact that he ran the estate along the old lines of work-service by the tenants. Those landlords who had commuted feudal service for cash payments had found more and more that the money they took in in that way was not enough to pay for the hire of labourers to perform the necessary work.

Added to those problems, the capital outlay he had made on the two ships had not answered as well as he had expected, for the *Mary Eleanor* had had two disastrous trips which had lost him money, and the difference to costs made by the *Mary Flower* was much less than they had hoped. They really needed another two ships at least to make a profit by them. So, all in all, Paul was more than grateful that James Chapham wished to be allied to the Morland family, and was willing to take his daughter Margaret to wife. Paul's next duty, of course, would be to arrange marriages for Jack's daughters, and the thought worried him, for he had sworn to do as well for them as Jack would have done, but in the present circumstances he was unable to give them large enough dowries to attract the kind of men Jack would have approved of.

The following day he decided that he must at least interview Nanette, who, at seventeen, had a right to expect to be married—more especially now that Margaret's wedding day was approaching. A little before dinner-time he came back to the house from his duties and found the girls—Margaret and Nanette, and fourteen-year-old Catherine and thirteen-year-old Jane—sitting together in the solar sewing, and talking over the elder girls' experiences away from home. As he entered the room all four rose at once to their feet and curtseyed, and all eyed him with some curiosity. He was rarely in the solar—it reminded him too much of Anne—and chose rather to sit in the evenings in the great hall, or the winter parlour if it was very cold. His young hound, Alexander—a son of Jasper, who had died some years ago—thrust forward to push his muzzle up at each of the girls in turn, and Margaret pushed him away with a little shriek, afraid he might dirty her dress.

Paul called the dog off, and said, 'Girls, I have a particular wish to speak to Nanette in private.' He paused, but Margaret was not quick enough on the uptake to offer to withdraw, so he had to go on, 'Margaret, why don't you take Catherine and Jane and pay a visit to the nursery? Your nephews will like to see you.'

Amyas now had four children in the nursery, Robert and Edward, aged five and three respectively, a two-year-old daughter called Eleanor after the founder of the line, and a new baby, a son Paul who was born in the summer. Elizabeth was already pregnant again, doing her duty with the wordless patience of a ewe.

'Yes father,' Margaret murmured dutifully, and made a show of bustling the younger girls out to shew her authority, pausing at the door to cast a glance at Nanette that expressed the desire to know exactly what was said at the first possible opportunity.

When the girls had gone, closing the door behind them, Paul went to the fireside and sat on one stool and gestured

Nanette to sit on another opposite him. Alexander lay down between them with a sigh, stretching his belly to the heat, and Nanette, while she waited without obvious curiosity for Paul to begin, put down a hand and rubbed the dog's ears. Paul liked her for the gesture—there was something of uncalculated kindness in it.

He did not at once enter into the topic, for he hardly knew what he wanted to say. Instead he studied her. She had not been home since the death of her father eight years ago, and in those years she had changed from a child to a woman—and a very beautiful woman. She was of less than middle height, and slender, but shapely as a woman should be. Her skin was very white and fair, surprisingly so, since her hair was as thick and black as it might be, darker even than Jack's had been—darker even than her grandmother Rebecca's, whom she somewhat resembled. Her features were fine and delicate, like an alabaster carving one might have thought, had it not been that no alabaster statue ever had such a disturbingly alive, red, sensual mouth, or such brilliant, sapphire-blue, intelligent eyes—strangest contrast to that black hair!

Paul felt himself stirred by her, and was instantly ashamed. Yet how could he help himself, when she was so very much a woman, and when he had been celibate for so long? He drew his mind away from that thought, and considered her from another viewpoint. He knew that she had had an excellent education, that she was learned and accomplished. Her manners, too were polished, and she had a natural grace and poise. She wore her clothes well, and chose them to compliment her looks. Her gown today was of a very dark blue that did not challenge her vivid eyes, the skirt divided at the front to show a kirtle of deep crimson whose contrast was subtle and satisfying. She wore a low French hood of the same blue, edged with tourmalines, from under which, unveiled, her lustrous hair tumbled curling to her waist. The neckline of her gown was filled in with her chemise, of the finest white linen which was almost transparent, the neck pulled into a ruff round her throat by the silken draw-string. She was quite lovely, he thought, and shifted uncomfortably, too much aware of her and of the penetrating glance of her blue eyes.

'Well, uncle, you wished to speak to me?' Nanette said at last, divining that he was having trouble in beginning.

'Yes, I did,' he said, clearing his throat awkwardly. 'You are now seventeen. You have perhaps thought that I had forgotten you, since you had been so long away.'

'I was well provided for, sir,' she said. 'How could I think myself forgotten?'

'I did not mean to suggest you had not a grateful heart, child,' Paul said, unprepared for the subtlety of her reply. 'But you must at least now be wondering what provisions I intend to make for your marriage. You know that I promised to take care of you—promised it for your father's memory.'

'I remember,' she said. She remembered too that strange moment of sympathy that had passed between her and her uncle when last she had left this house. 'I have always supposed that you will tell me what is planned for me when the time seems right to you.'

'You are a good girl, Nanette,' Paul said, leaving off formality. 'You are like your father, I believe, and so I will be frank with you.' There was a slight question in his tone that he was not aware of until she answered it by saying, 'I shall be honoured by your confidence, uncle.'

'Well, then: you know, of course, that your father was a well-loved, well-connected man, and that if he had lived he would have found good matches for you and your sisters.' She nodded. 'I do not want to do less for you than he would have done, but I have not so many friends. So I would have to rely on generous dowries to do for me what favour would have done for your father. The times have not been favourable recently, what with taxes for the war, and the ships doing badly, and the husband I have got for your cousin my daughter has cost me all the money I have at present. In short, at present I have not enough gold to provide you with a dowry sufficient to your position.' He paused, more to think what to say next than because he expected an answer, but Nanette made a small gesture as if she would touch him in sympathy, and said, 'I understand, uncle. I am content.'

'Content?' he said, a little puzzled. 'But you must wish—you must expect to be married.'

'I don't care about it,' she said. He looked at her still in surprise, and she saw that she must explain a little more. 'If it pleases you to arrange a marriage for me, I am content in your will, but truly, for myself, I don't desire to marry. Since—since my father died—' her voice faltered and stopped, and, meeting her eyes, Paul was suddenly moved, and stood up abruptly and walked about the room to hide his face. This girl—no, this woman— affected him deeply. If only—if only she were not related to him. He had never wanted a second wife—never wanted anyone but Ursula—and yet now, sitting here with her—. He drew deep breaths to calm his pulse, aware of a strange, deep longing that he had not expected ever to feel again. He remembered too, now, that moment of their last parting, when she had flung her arms round him. He turned to her abruptly, and said, 'Love comes in many forms, not always as we expect it. For me it was already too late when I learned, but for you—I can only say, don't turn it away, when it comes, from whatever source. There is not enough love in the world to turn any away.'

Nanette's eyes shone as she gazed at him, and he saw why a moment later when two tears broke free of her dark lashes, reflecting the firelight a moment as they touched her cheeks.

He went to her and knelt clumsily before her and took her hands in his, and stared at her in a troubled way.

'Nanette,' he began hopelessly, 'Nanette—I—' He had no words for what he wanted to say, and she knew it. She freed her hands from his and put them to his cheeks, cupping his face between them, and suddenly his restraint broke, he put his arms round her and kissed her savagely, knotting his hands in her silken curling hair. Passion surged through his body like a flood-tide, and as her soft lips parted under his, inviting him in, he found his passion answered by her own, knew her body was trembling for want of him as his was for want of her. The blood pounded madly about his body and he drew her tighter against him, his tongue seeking out hers in the sweetness of her mouth.

Then the dog whined, and he was suddenly, horribly sane again. This was forbidden! She was his niece—what was he doing? He wrenched himself away, so abruptly that Nanette almost fell, lurched to his feet and took a blind step away from her, finding the chimney wall with his groping hands. Nanette, dizzy and bruised, stared at him with anguish as he leaned against the chimney piece, his back to her and his head in his hands. The dog whined again and stood up, and she pulled it by the collar to her and fondled its ears to quiet it, giving Paul time to regain control of himself, to calm his breathing and his pounding heart.

The silence settled again over the room, a listening, breathing silence. The two human occupants of it were more in sympathy with each other than either of them knew. At last Paul, without lifting his head from his hands, said,

'I must send you away. It is impossible for you to stay here—I would not leave you in the mouth of a lion's den.'

There was nothing she could say. Their souls would be in peril if they succumbed to these feelings.

'Would you like to go to Court, as Margaret did?' he said next. She did not immediately answer, and he turned to look at her. Their eyes met nakedly and they looked quickly away from each other. 'I could get you a place at Court, I think, if you would like it?'

'If it pleases you,' she said at last, 'I am content.'

'No, if it pleases you,' he said. 'The Court, I believe, is dull now. The King does not visit the Queen much since his conscience began to trouble him, and the Queen is not very gay since the Princess was sent to Ludlow. But the Court is still the Court. And you are very beautiful—it may be that one of the King's young gentlemen will fall so much in love with you that your lack of dowry will not matter.'

She stood up and curtseyed, still not meeting his eyes. 'I think I should be glad to go to Court, at least for the time being, if you can arrange it.'

'Then it shall be done. And, Nanette, be easy in your mind.'

'Yes, uncle. Thank you uncle,' she said. 'May I go now?'

'Of course,' he said. He wished he knew how upset she was by what had happened. He watched her walk to the door, her skirts just brushing the floor, her hair falling like a waterfall, a dark waterfall, from under the halo of her coif. 'God bless you,' he said softly. She faltered only minutely as she went out, closing the door behind her.

Outside Nanette turned without hesitation towards the chapel. Its breathless quiet calmed her at once, and she advanced almost to the altar rail, genuflected, and then turned aside to the prie-dieu before the statue of the Blessed Virgin. Kneeling, she wondered what was wrong with her. Since the death of her father it seemed that some part of her had been frozen, dead, until now; now she had looked immodestly upon two men, both of them forbidden to her. She had wished to impress Margaret's betrothed, wished to make him love her; and she had desired her uncle, her own father's brother. What had happened to her? What were these strange desires that fired her blood? Why did they seem mixed up in her mind with her father's memory? She was confused and ashamed—but another part of her mind sang with joy at the memory of Paul's touch, his response, the fact that he had wanted her as wildly as she had wanted him.

She was shocked with herself, and afraid. Holy Mother, she prayed, let me know myself, let me understand; then wash me clean and cool as a stone washed by the sea. Let me be pure and serene like you. Forgive me—give me grace.

After Christmas, in accordance with the arrangements that had been made, Nanette travelled, accompanied by Paul and Amyas and a large following of attendants, down to Kent to Hever Castle where she would stay for a few days before going to Court. The arrangement had been suggested by Sir Thomas Boleyn, for he was preparing to return his daughter Anne to Court—she now having been forgiven for her misconduct in the Percy affair—and he thought Nanette would make a suitable companion for her. They were both to enter the Queen's Household as soon as the Christmas season was finished.

The young women were introduced to each other by Anne's stepmother, eyed each other cautiously and then, apparently satisfied, smiled and kissed in greeting, and withdrew to the window-seat of the parlour to talk.

'I see at once that you are not like your cousin, and I'm glad,' Anne said nodding in satisfaction. 'I remembered her with kindness, for she was the one who introduced me to—a *certain person*—but I could never have been intimate with her. She was not my kind of person. She is married now, I believe? How does she fare?'

Nanette had still not quite recovered from the shock of meeting this extraordinary young woman, and did not at once answer. Margaret had described the large dark eyes, but no words could have prepared Nanette for the impact of them; shining, overwhelming, hypnotic, seeming more intelligent, more full of life than any human eyes could be, drawing you into their warm depths where you felt you could be sure of being understood. Nanette felt there was about her companion a withdrawness, some place in her mind she protected as one favours a wounded place to protect it from further harm. She had been hurt, and she bore a scar that was not yet quite healed; and Nanette felt a kinship with her that made her expand with sympathy.

'Margaret is well,' Nanette answered a little belatedly. 'She is very happy, having fallen in love with her husband the moment she saw him.'

'How fortunate for her,' Anne said. 'I hope he loves her too?'

'I doubt it,' Nanette said, smiling, 'but equally, she will never know it. He is too intelligent for that.'

Anne smiled too, understanding. 'A little deceit can be a good thing in a marriage,' she said. 'That is, supposing one does not marry for love, and who ever does? I do not know of anyone who loves their spouse—oh,' she added with a contemptuous smile, 'except my sister Mary, but she doesn't count.'

'Why not?' Nanette asked with interest.

'Because Mary would love anyone she was partnered with. She has no discrimination. Why are you not yet married? You are very pretty.'

Nanette liked the directness. 'Because my father died, and I was well cared for where I was, so nobody thought of it. I was brought up with Lady Parr's daughter, in Kentdale, until she was betrothed to be married.'

'I see. And now you are sent to Court to be seen. Who is the little Parr girl to marry?'

'Lord Borough,' Nanette told her. She nodded.

'Yes, a suitable match I suppose, though he is so old. Well, you must wonder why I am not married—I am twenty-three, you know.' It was said defiantly, and Nanette sensed the hurt underneath. She said gently, 'I supposed it was your own skill in avoiding matches you did not care for.'

Anne stared at her penetratingly for a moment and then laughed abruptly.

'No you did not, you sweet liar! You know perfectly well my sad, bad history. Well,' drawing her brows together in a frown, 'the end result is the same. Now I am too notorious to be married off against my will. Perhaps I shall remain a maid all my life. I sometimes think that is what I am best suited for.'

'I used to think that sometimes, too,' Nanette said. 'Katherine—Katherine Parr I mean, Lady Borough as she now is—and I used to talk about marriage, and I could never imagine myself married to anyone. We decided in the end that I should be a nun.'

'You are too pretty—and too worldly-looking—to be a nun,' Anne said. Her eyes grew distant and soft, and her voice dropped a pitch—Nanette was growing used to these abrupt changes of mood. 'He is married now, you know. He married last year. I hated him at first for giving in, but I don't suppose there was anything he could do. He was very ill for a time—I was too, of course, but he was sick even longer than I, and he is still weak and sickly. He hates her, and she hates him. A merry bedding they must have of it each night! Well, he has what he deserves. He could not stand up to the Cardinal. He was too weak. But I—I whom he despised as a puny girl—I shall stand up to him. I mean to pay him out one day.'

'The Cardinal? The most powerful man in England?' Nanette said doubtfully. Anne turned her glowing eyes on her.

'Yes, the Cardinal, the most powerful man in England, that great swollen spider! Powerful he may be, but I have one thing he has not—I have blood in my veins! His are choked and clogged with gold and rich food and possessions, riches and vanity and the desire for power. Mine throb with life, and with anger. I swore when they parted us that I should be revenged, and I shall!' And Nanette, looking into that vital, burning face, believed her. Then the great dark eyes filled with tears. 'I loved him, you know,' she whispered. 'I truly, truly loved him. I shall never love anyone ever again as I loved him.'

Nanette took her hand to press it sympathetically, and was startled when it was snatched back. The eyes now were wary, like an animal, just for a moment before she relaxed again.

'I'm sorry,' she said. 'I don't like anyone to touch my hand.' She regarded Nanette carefully for a moment, as if wondering whether she could trust her or not, and then with a little sigh she said, 'I like you. If we are to be friends you had better know the worst about me, I suppose. I don't like anyone to see it, even, if I can help it. You must never speak of it.'

'Of course not,' Nanette said. Quickly, her head slightly averted, Anne lifted back the hanging point of her under-sleeve and held out her left hand to Nanette. Nanette looked down, and the poor malformed finger filled her with pity. Anne turned her head back and looked at it cautiously, as if it might leap up and bite her.

'I hate it,' she said fiercely. 'I *hate* it.'

Nanette put her hand out very slowly and touched the tips of the fingers. The hand tried to wriggle away from her, as if it were a shy, wild animal. Nanette took hold of it gently and firmly and began to soothe it with her other hand. Her eyes met Anne's.

'You're afraid of it,' she said. Anne nodded unwillingly. 'Poor thing. Don't be. It's pointless to hate any part of oneself.'

'Aren't we supposed to hate sin, and try to root it out of ourselves?' Anne said through clenched teeth.

'It isn't sin. It's just a poor, hurt thing. You wouldn't hate a cripple, would you? You'd give him alms, and pity him. Don't hate your poor hand.' For a moment Anne looked at her, puzzled, as a child who has only ever known cruelty might look at someone offering kindness, and then she drew her hand away firmly, flicking down the sleeve and covering it with her right hand.

'I don't like anyone to touch it,' she said. But her voice was gentler than before, and Nanette knew that she was accepted.

In the Council Chamber Boleyn was telling Paul about the position at Court. 'We all thought last year, when the King made his bastard son Duke of Richmond, that he was going to legitimise the boy. It was his father's title, you remember, before he became king, and that seemed very significant.'

'I suppose it's certain, then, that the Queen can't have any more children?' Paul said.

'She hasn't conceived in seven years,' Boleyn replied. 'The King no longer cohabits with her, though he still visits her from time to time, and she still appears beside him on State occasions. But there would have been plenty of support for the idea of Richmond being legitimised—there are precedents, and it would clarify the situation.'

'So what was the objection?'

Boleyn shrugged. 'Who knows? The King loves to complicate matters. He loves secrecy and subtlety, and he hates anyone to know what he's about. First he said that he would accept James of Scotland as his heir, and then he made Princess Mary Princess of Wales as if he had decided to accept *her* as his heir. Then he made Henry Fitzroy Duke of Richmond for all the world as if *he* was going to be made heir. At the moment there's a suggestion being considered that Richmond and the Princess should be married and succeed jointly.'

'Marry? Brother and sister?' Paul said in horror. Boleyn shrugged again.

'There are precedents for *that*, too, but it's my belief that the King is only pretending to consider it. He is a very strict moralist. I don't think he'd consent to it for a moment. No, it's my belief that he's reconsidering a divorce. You know it's been mooted several times, and Wolsey would dearly like a liaison with France. A marriage with a French princess would please him mightily.'

'So being attached to the Queen's Household might be no more than a temporary appointment for my niece?' Paul said thoughtfully.

'I tell you these things because you ought to be aware of them,' Boleyn said, sitting back and smoothing the furred sleeves of his gown, 'but you needn't worry too much about it. If the Queen's Household was broken up on divorce, it would be reformed as soon as the King remarried, for the new Queen, and most of the same people would be reappointed. And a new household, built around a young French Queen, would be much livelier, you know—much more likely to lead to marriage for the young ladies.'

'I see,' said Paul. 'Thank you.' And Boleyn was left to wonder why the good news did not seem to reassure Morland exactly as it should.

Nine

$\mathscr{I}$T WAS A HOT SUMMER, AND THE COURT WAS GLAD TO MOVE out to the King's newly-acquired palace at Hampton. Hampton Court had belonged to Wolsey, was his finest residence, and a beautiful example of the new Italian style of architecture that was becoming fashionable. It was such a luxurious palace that the poet Skelton had mocked at it in one of his poems—'"Why come ye not to court?" "To which court—To the King's Court or to Hampton Court?"'—and the people, hating Wolsey more and more each day, had seized upon the words and made them into a vulgar song which was heard in every street and on every stretch of the river.

Wolsey was blamed for everything that went wrong in the country from the harvest onwards, and when the poor progress of the wars earned him the King's disapproval too, he bought favour back by presenting Hampton Court to the King as a gift—surely the most expensive gift ever given to him by anyone. So the Court idled away the hot days in the sweet water-gardens, the rose garden, the Italian garden, the orangery, the park, and the bowling alley. The King and his attendant circle of young men alternated idling with more energetic pastimes in the deer-park, the tennis court, and at the butts.

Nanette and the other maids were little occupied in duties, for the Queen kept to her own apartments for much of the time and was generally attended by her small circle of ladies who were also intimate friends. Nanette had the feeling that the presence of pretty young women disturbed her, and she felt rather sorry for her, but she was enjoying her freedom too much to think often about it. She and Anne and Madge Wyatt, a cousin of Anne's, made a trio of intimate friends, and to them, by bonds of relationship and also like-mindedness they drew a group of gentlemen who were some of the handsomest and wittiest in the Court.

Some of them Nanette knew already—Anne's brother George, of course, with whom Nanette was very happy to renew her acquaintance. He soon dropped into a way of teasing flirtation with Nanette that she found very pleasant. She sometimes thought to herself how good it would have been to marry George and thereby become Anne's sister as well as her friend, but sadly George was already married, to a crosspatch named Jane Parker whom George hated and treated with open contempt on the few occasions when she joined them.

Then there was Frank Weston, a little, hot-tempered man who was always full of loud oaths and boasts and whom the other men seemed to find very amusing; Richard Page, a quiet, scholarly man with an alarming cough; Francis Bryan, another cousin of the Boleyns whose sister Meg was expected to come to Court later that year; and Thomas Wyatt, yet another cousin of Anne's, and George's intimate friend. Nanette found him overwhelming, and in his company was disturbed and tongue-tied. He was small and stocky, with soft, thin chestnut hair, and a long curling chestnut beard flecked with gold which did not quite conceal a most marvellously sensitive mouth; and heavenly blue eyes that seemed as innocent as a child's until you read the wicked laughter in them.

'At last,' he said when they first met and he bent over her hand in a courtly manner, 'a rival for my cousin Anne. Anne has been tormenting me since her childhood with her beauty, but now at last I see the antidote. One sickness drives out another, you know, and your eyes infect me with the deadliest of all sicknesses.'

And he kissed Nanette's hand, and she felt the softness of his beard on her skin, and her heart fluttered. Anne was watching them, laughing.

'I'll have no rivals, Tom! I warn you here and now, you are expressly forbidden to love anyone more than me.'

Tom straightened up and, still holding Nanette's hand, he grinned wickedly at Anne, shewing his white teeth. 'Anne, dearest cousin, I always obeyed you in that, as you know. I even married a wife I could not love so as to be safe for you. But—' clasping Nanette's hand to his velvet doublet with a deep sigh, 'but what can a man do against the darts of the little blind god? Helpless! We mortals are helpless. And this divine young creature who stands before me now,' kissing her hand again, 'and regards me with eyes the colour of heaven itself—'

'Regards you with amazement,' Anne broke in, 'wondering if you can possibly be overcome with wine this early in the day. Nanette, I warn you, Tom is a poet and counts anything as fair game. Don't believe a word of his flattering lies or he'll break your heart.'

'Break her heart?' Tom said indignantly. 'Mine is the heart in danger—a softer organ could not be found in the breast of a maid even as tender as this little Nan whose hand I am privileged to kiss.' And he suited the action to the words.

'I think your heart is in as much danger from me as mine is from you, sir,' Nanette heard herself say, and was a little surprised that she had managed to draw enough breath to say it. Tom Wyatt had that effect, she learned later, on almost everyone. He looked at her now shrewdly, and nodded as if he had read her thoughts and agreed with them.

'I think you and I understand each other pretty well, Mistress Nanette. We shall be friends, of that I am certain.' And he took her hand and drew it through his arm, and taking Anne on the other arm in similar fashion, walked along one of the delightful alleys with them and amused them with his witty talk. He and Anne had played together as children, being, as well as distant cousins, very near neighbours in Kent; and listening to them chattering to each other Nanette learned very quickly that Wyatt was in love with Anne, and that Anne did not know it nor return it. When they joined the others, Nanette also perceived that George knew of Wyatt's hopeless passion, and that it made another bond between the two men who were married to women they disliked. It accounted, Nanette remembered, for Anne's remark about no-one she knew being married where they loved.

The whole group was sitting at its ease under the trees one hot day, while Tom and Anne worked on a song together, of which he had written the words and Anne the tune. She was picking it out on the lute which she held in her lap as she sat on a fallen tree-trunk. Tom stood behind her, one foot up on the log, leaning lightly against her shoulder and looking down at her bent head under its simple coif with an expression it was as well she couldn't see.

'Poor Tom,' George murmured to Nanette, beside whom he was lolling on the grass. 'Why is it we always fall in love with those we cannot have? Is there a natural perversity about fate?'

Nanette smiled. 'No, but there is a natural perversity about young men, especially about young men who are poets. What would you and Tom have to write about if your loves were returned? It's a dull man who loves his wife.'

George pretended to be shocked. 'Why, Mistress Morland, what a wicked thing to say! To suggest that Holy Matrimony makes a man dull!'

'Must I remind you that the Church teaches us it is the *lower* state, that celibacy is true bliss?' Nanette said with mock sternness.

'And must I remind you,' George countered, 'that the Church teaches us by example that celibacy is to be avoided at all costs? Why, even our great Cardinal has four daughters and a son on whom he heaps benefices.'

'Why are you two talking instead of listening to our delightful music?' Tom said, looking up. 'What is it you discuss so urgently, disturbing our shy muses?'

'The Church, my dear Tom, we discuss the Church,' George said.

'Then it will keep until another time. If it were something important, like love or poetry, I could forgive you, but please keep discussion of such unimportant subjects for another time.' Anne looked up at him, and he kissed her broad forehead and smiled. 'Play on, sweet cousin. If he disturbs you again, I'll make him suffer for it in the tiltyard.'

A roar of laughter greeted these words.

'You!' Frank crowed. 'In the tiltyard! I pray God I live long enough to see Thomas Wyatt in the tiltyard!'

'Then you will be as old as Methuselah,' Richard Page said, 'for it's certain a normal man's life-span would not be long enough to witness that event.'

'Poor Tom!' Madge broke in, defending her brother. 'For shame! You should not tease him so—he gives the world so much pleasure with his verses.'

'And himself so much pain,' Nanette added. Tom looked across at her and gave the ghost of a wink.

'You're right there, Mistress Nan—no-one but a woman in labour knows the pain a writer suffers in his writing.' There was a disturbance amongst the servants who were standing at a little distance, and Wyatt turned his head towards them. 'Who comes here? Why, it's Hal Norys. God's day to you, friend Hal! Now here is a man you may safely wager you will see in the tiltyard, Nanette. There's none so skilled with a lance as he.'

'Unless it be our sovereign lord the King,' George added quickly, and Nanette could not tell whether he meant it or was being politic, for she knew that Hal Norys was the King's closest friend, and greatly admired by His Grace.

'Stoutly spoken, George, and truly too,' Hal said. 'God's day to you all. You look so pleasant and happy here under the trees that I thought I'd join you, if you don't mind?'

'Of course we don't mind,' Madge said quickly. 'But are you sure His Grace can spare you? We never see you out of his company these days.'

'Has he let you off the leash, Hal?' George asked irrepressibly. Hal smiled and looked towards Nanette.

'I came to make myself known to my cousin Mistress Morland, and His Grace could hardly deny the rights of blood.'

'Your cousin?' Frank said, Nanette thought rather rudely. She didn't care much for Frank Weston. 'How is she cousin to you, Hal?'

'My cousin Amyas married Elizabeth Norys, Hal's cousin,' Nanette answered.

'That's right,' Hal said, 'and I hear that Amyas is to come to Court for the tourney at midsummer, though I fear my cousin Elizabeth will be too near her time to travel.'

'Amyas, coming here?' Nanette said, excited. 'I had not heard that news. It is very welcome. Are any more of my family to come?'

'I thought you would be glad to hear it,' Hal said courteously, 'so I came to tell you as soon as I could get away. I believe his brother is to come too.'

'His brother?' Nanette was puzzled for a second, and then realised he meant Margaret's husband. A pleasant excitement brushed her skin for a moment. 'Well it will be good to see my family again so soon. I hardly expected it.'

'There are more invitations going out for this tourney than any other before,' Francis said. 'For one, I am glad—one gets tired of seeing the same people tilting again and again.'

'One gets tired of seeing Hal beat the same people again and again,' George said languidly. 'Hal, you will have to retire from the lists and give the others a chance. It is hardly fair of you to enter at all, you know.'

Hal laughed and was about to reply when a giant shadow fell across the grass as a figure blocked out the sunshine that was striping the circle where they sat. A silence fell at once across the group as everyone jumped up in order to make their lowest bows and curtseys, and the familiar, terrifying voice was heard to say pleasantly, 'Well, Hal, so this is where you have got to. I can understand now why you hurried off, if it was to seek such pleasant company. Get up, get up, we are all friends here.'

Friends! Nanette thought as she arose slowly from her curtsey. The idea of being friends with the King of England! She risked a glance to take in the huge, glittering figure, standing with feet apart and hands on hips at the edge of the circle, the sunlight gleaming on the long red-gold hair. The handsomest prince in Christendom, she noted, was smiling genially, and his expression was obediently copied by a group of gentlemen standing behind him—his 'inner circle', consisting of spade-bearded, fat Suffolk, thin, hatchet-faced Norfolk, handsome Sir William Brereton, and lissom young Surrey, Norfolk's son.

'I almost forgive you for deserting me, Hal, when I see you in such good company—Tom, George—' He nodded to the two young men, gentlemen of his bedchamber, and his sharp eyes went on round the group, making mental notes. Hal gave an easy smile and spoke up.

'I came, Sir, on a mission I feel you must approve of—to welcome a kinswoman of mine to the Court. Mistress Anne Morland.'

The King's eyes came round to Nanette and stopped on her. Weak with confusion, she went down again into another curtsey and, feeling it safest, stayed there. A pair of broad, slashed velvet shoes came into her circle of vision, thus reduced to the grass, and she realised with faint horror that the King had come over to her and was extending his hand to her. She knew enough to touch the fingers and kiss the ring, but the King's fingers grasped her own and raised her to her feet. She was now standing before him and only inches from him. The rich fabric of his clothes, the hard gleam of the many jewels, the metallic sheen of the gold thread that embroidered his sleeves, were before her eyes, and her nose caught the sweet waft of perfume that came from him as he moved.

He was so close she could feel the warmth of his living body, and she could see his chest moving as he breathed. Cautiously she raised her eyes: he was so much taller than she that she had to tilt her head far back to see his face, and it was like looking up at a high building. Far above her was the long, smooth, hairless chin, and above that the small curly mouth, and above that the long flat nose, and at the far end of the nose the eyes looking down into hers with enquiry.

'Well, Mistress Morland,' the King said, 'you have stared long enough. What think you of your King?'

Nanette felt her face flush in a mixture of embarrassment and fear. Had she angered him by looking up? It was perhaps wrong to raise one's eyes to the King, even if he had spoken to one directly. She dropped her eyes hastily and, realising by the pause that some answer was expected of her, she stammered, 'I—I am—overwhelmed, Your Grace. If it please Your Grace—'

'It does please us, Mistress. We like to see prettiness combined with modesty in our maids. We knew your father, Mistress Anne, and your brother, I believe, was in the Household of our dear friend Cardinal Wolsey.'

'My cousin, Your Grace,' Nanette corrected him, and knew at once she should not have. The King's voice grew impatient.

'Well, well, your cousin. And it is that cousin who has married a Norys?'

'Yes, Your Grace.' She risked another glance upwards. The King was smiling again, she saw with relief.

'You are surprised that your King should know so much about your family, are you not?'

'Yes, indeed, Your Grace. That is—' she began to elaborate, realising her agreement could be misinterpreted, but the King went on, 'The King prides himself on knowing everything that goes on in the Court. I am like a father to my children, and I know everything about them. For instance,' and now at last he turned away from Nanette, and she felt herself relaxing with such enormous relief at ceasing to be the object of his attention that she thought she might fall down. He had turned now towards Anne, who was standing beside Tom Wyatt and holding her lute still in her left hand. 'For instance,' the King said, looking Anne up and down with great interest, 'I know that Mistress Anne Boleyn, lately returned to Court, has enticed away my friend Tom with her sweet singing. Fie upon you, Tom, for a false friend.'

Nanette watched her friend with admiration, for though Anne did not make so bold as to look up at the King's face (not such a stretch for her, for she was a good deal taller than Nanette) she did not look confused or ill at ease. She stood still with great composure, her eyes fixed somewhere around the King's chest.

'Not a false friend, Your Grace, I protest,' Tom said

pleasantly, 'but one who has a fatal weakness that sometimes makes him forgetful.' He darted a sideways glance at Anne, and Nanette saw her lips twitch as she tried not to smile. The King was still looking down at Anne, and the expression on his face changed as he looked at her; the smile faded from his mouth, and a kind of intensity filled his eyes. If he had not been the King, Nanette would have thought—

'Well, Tom, I forgive thee,' the King said. 'I think perhaps I suffer from the same malady.'

The tone of his voice made Anne look up for a moment in surprise, and her eyes met the King's for a moment before she dropped them, to look earnestly at the grass; and this time she did not conceal the smile that curved her lips. The King's face grew a little ruddier, and he took Anne's hand and kissed it with slow gallantry.

'You shall play your song for me, Mistress Boleyn, and I shall help you with it. Come, what say you to that?'

'Your Grace is too kind,' Anne murmured, keeping her eyes down. She did not sound at all overwhelmed.

'Not kind,' the King countered. 'You will see how kind the King can be when he has cause.'

'What should give the King cause?' Anne asked innocently.

'A glance from those eyes that are so determinedly cast down upon the earth.'

'Your Grace has expressed approval of modesty,' Anne reminded him. Nanette quaked inwardly at her boldness, but it seemed to please the King.

'That we have,' he said, reverting to formality, but smiling none the less. 'Well, keep your modest glances for the moment, Mistress Anne. When you know us a little better you may find you can look upon a King without being dazzled.'

And now Anne looked up—the merest flicker of a glance up and then immediately down—and Nanette knew it for a piece of coquetry. The King, seemingly satisfied, dropped her hand and turned away, gathering his attendants with a glance.

'I bid you adieu for the moment,' he said. 'Hal, come with us—we need you.' And then he was gone, and the shadow lifted from the gathering.

In the dormitory that night Anne and Nanette as usual helped each other to undress. They took off their coifs and their sleeves, and then Anne turned her back to Nanette to have her gown unlaced, and Nanette opened the subject that was on her mind.

'Anne, what did you think of the King's visiting us today?'

'What do you mean, what did I think?' Anne asked, as she stood, head bent forward, holding her long hair with both hands out of the way of Nanette's task.

'Why do you think he came?'

'Oh, I think for the reason he gave—he wondered where Hal had gone. Hal is never from the King's side—the King loves him dearly, you know, and will not part with him. He even has Hal to sleep with him now he no longer couches with the Queen. So he wondered what attraction could be so strong as to entice him away.' She turned her head to glance at Nanette. 'You should be proud that it was you.'

'Not I, but my cousin,' Nanette said. 'He has married—'

'Ciel! When you corrected the King, I thought I should die laughing,' Anne said, bursting in. 'Dear little Nanette, if only you could have seen your face!'

'I was terrified,' Nanette said, finishing with the lacings and helping to push the tight sleeves down Anne's arms. 'From beginning to end I was terrified. I was so amazed at your calmness. You didn't seem at all put out.'

'Well,' Anne said with a little Frenchified shrug, 'one learns Court manners. And my governess always used to say that Kings are like wild tigers—you must never let them see you are afraid of them.'

'When had your governess occasion to face a wild tiger?' Nanette said indignantly. Anne pulled her kirtle down to her waist and swung round to hug Nanette.

'Don't be so literal, child! Come Nanette, undo my corset, quickly, for it is cutting me in half.' She turned her back again for Nanette to untie the leather thongs that held the two halves of the solid iron corset that imprisoned Anne's tender torso. 'Oh, what we suffer for fashion,' she groaned, and then gave a great sigh of relief as the laces gave and she was left at last in her linen chemise. 'Come now, I'll unlace you. Turn round, and hold your hair away.'

'Did you notice, Anne,' Nanette said cautiously, 'the way that particular tiger looked at you?'

'Not at all as if he wanted to eat me,' Anne laughed. 'I should have thought eating me was the last thing on his mind.'

'You did notice, then?'

'Of course I did. But it doesn't mean anything. The King is a man too, you know, and will flirt like any other man. In France, the King was always chasing the ladies of the Court. That was why Queen Claude was so strict with us.'

'It didn't look to me as if it meant nothing,' Nanette said slowly. 'Are you sure you know what you are doing when you flirt with him?'

'*I* flirt with *him*?'

'I saw the way you looked at him and then looked away again,' Nanette said. She felt Anne shrug again.

'Oh well. One does it automatically, you know. It's all part of the game we play at Court.'

'Truly, Anne, I think you should be careful. I saw the way he

looked at you. I think he was serious. And then, remember—'
She hesitated.

'Remember my sister?' Anne supplied.

'I didn't want to say it, but—'

'I understand.' Anne's voice was hard. There was a short silence while her busy fingers alone moved. 'There, that's your gown, chuck. Can you manage the sleeves?'

Nanette turned round and took her hands, and the left one did not even struggle as she touched it.

'Anne—'

'It's all right, Nanette. Even if he does mean it, he cannot force me, and I should never consent. No, not even for a King would I lose the only thing women have to bargain with! If I have no husband, I shall go a maid to my grave, and face my God with a clear mind. There, does that satisfy you? Don't look so glum, dearest. I shan't be a slut like my sister, not even a King's slut.'

'I'm only afraid of what the King might do,' Nanette said. Anne raised her fine eyebrows in surprise.

'Why, what should he do? If he asks, I'll say no, and once he realises that I mean it, he'll lose interest and go and ask someone else. And then you will have to start worrying for yourself, for I'm sure you're the prettiest maid at Court. Now turn round and keep still and let me get your corset undone. And don't worry. Kings have higher things to worry about than their wives' maids of honour.'

The tourney was an occasion of joyful reunion for Nanette with her family. Margaret was there, looking radiantly happy and as proud of her husband as a peacock of its tail; and Amyas, and Paul, and they brought the glad news that Elizabeth had laid-in of another son, and both seemed well. The little girls had sent their envious love from the schoolroom to their elder sister, and her nephews and niece messages suitable to their ages and talents. There was also a delightful meeting between Nanette and Lady Borough, attending with her husband and her mother, and the only sadness was that there was not enough time to spend as long talking to her old friend as Nanette would have liked. She had the pleasure of seeing Amyas taking part in a joust, wearing the black-and-white Morland Arms on his surcoat, and the black lion crest surmounting his padded heaume. He fought two bouts, one against his old friend George Boleyn and one against his new relation, Hal Norys, and in both he wore Nanette's sleeve as her champion. Sitting at the front of the box with Anne beside her on one side and Margaret on the other, Tom and Paul and James Chapham behind them, their new friends all around, and even the King taking a keen interest; wagering on the result, listening to the excited chatter, drinking in the colourful sights; Nanette felt herself the happiest of mortals. What more could anyone want? Her champion won the bout against George at the third charge, but did not last even one charge against Hal Norys, who eventually won the entire competition, and was awarded his prize by the stout, ever-smiling Queen.

'It was no disgrace to be beaten by Hal,' Nanette told her sweating cousin when he rode up to salute her and return her sleeve. 'I'm proud of you, dear Amyas. You did so well.'

There was a feast that night and entertainments that went on almost until morning, and Nanette found herself delightfully much in demand for the dancing. She danced first with Amyas, and then with George Boleyn, then James Chapham, then Hal Norys, and finally Tom Wyatt came to claim her hand and lead her out. She had been enjoying herself so much that she had not had time to wonder where Anne was, and it was while dancing with Tom that she learnt the answer. As they walked down the set he nudged her and whispered, 'Look, there, little Nan. Thy friend has caught a bigger fish than she expected.'

Nanette looked, and saw the King dancing at the top of the set with Anne. The King danced well, and Anne was as graceful as a roe deer, but the space that was left around them seemed more than a respectful drawing-back by the other dancers. Whichever way he turned, the King never took his eyes from Anne's face, and she, laughing happily and tilting her lovely face back on her slender neck did not avoid his gaze. They danced as if they were the only two people in the room. Nanette could not help glancing towards the Queen to see how she reacted, but the Queen did not react at all. She sat on the dais, like a stone with a smile painted on it, and talked to the Spanish ambassador and the staider of the gentlemen of the Court, and of course the duller set of the maids who never joined in much of the fun—people like Jane Boleyn and Jane Seymour and Mary Howard and Lady Berkeley and Lady Oxford and Mary Saville.

'Tom,' she said abruptly, 'is it safe?'

'Safe? Why no, it is never safe to play games with the King, unless you are prepared to let him win or to face the consequences.'

'Anne does not intend to—to let him win,' Nanette said, looking into Tom's eyes. She said it more to reassure him than anything else, but she read in his eyes a fear that was not to do with his losing Anne to a rival.

'He has danced every dance with her,' he said. 'No-one knows better than I the power she has over men; but the King may not prove as easy to put off as she thinks. I wish—oh God I wish I had been free to marry her. Then I could keep her safe.'

'Safe from the King?' Nanette whispered.

'Safe from herself. If she gives in to the King, she will hate herself. And if she doesn't—'

He stared for a moment longer, broodingly, at Anne and her royal partner, and then seemed to become aware again of Nanette's anxious gaze and shook himself back to the present. 'Don't look so troubled, my dear little Nan,' he said. 'This is a festival time, and we should be laughing and happy. See how happy Anne is—why should you be less so, seeing that you were the queen of the tournament today, and that you are dancing with the most handsome man in the room? That's better—smile! I want every man to be jealous of me.'

After her dance with Tom, Paul came up to her, taking her hand and bowing. Nanette's blood was fired from the dancing and the touch filled her with too much excitement. She sought about for an excuse.

'Oh, uncle, would you mind? I am so tired, I don't think I could dance again.'

'I was going to ask you,' Paul said, 'if you would like to take a walk with me along the terrace and draw your breath there. It is a beautiful night, and very warm.'

'Why, I don't know—' Nanette said hesitantly. 'If it would be proper—' Paul raised an eyebrow. 'The Court is very strict. His Grace is very much against any sort of impropriety.'

'My dear child, they would not think it improper, surely, to walk with your uncle?' Paul said, and Nanette ashamed, could only agree. He drew her hand through his arm and they stepped outside into the summer air, warm as milk and scarcely dark, for it was the end of the longest day, when the sun hardly sleeps at all. They walked in silence along the terrace, and then Paul turned with her down into the yew walks where there were shadows and scented silence, where sometimes lovers would slip away to be alone together.

Nanette went with him without protest, but as they walked on in silence she became more and more aware of the warmth of his body and the touch of his hand. He did not look at her, and when she stole glances at him he seemed calm and untroubled; and when at last he spoke it was in a perfectly normal way.

'Well, my dear, I have been watching you today, centre of attraction that you were, and you seemed to me to be very happy. Are you happy here at Court? Is it what you expected?'

'I hardly know what I expected, sir,' Nanette answered, 'but I am happy here. There is so much to do, and the people are so pleasant. My friend, Anne, I love dearly, and the gentleman are so witty, and the ladies so charming—'

'And I dare say you have many admirers,' Paul added. 'Indeed, I saw you dancing with some of them. Has no man sought your hand yet?'

'Not yet, sir,' she said, thinking he was making a joke of it. 'I think most of the men in our circle are married already.'

'I see.' He was silent, and Nanette said to keep the conversation going, 'How are things at home? How are the children?'

'Your sisters grow prettier every day, and are as good as they are pretty,' Paul said. 'And Amyas and his wife continue to fill the nursery. Robert handles a sword with amazing skill now, and Edward is learning to ride. Their tutor speaks well of them both.'

'That must be pleasing to you.'

'It is. You can have no idea how much they please me. I spend a great deal of time with them—more, I may say, than their father does.' Nanette glanced up at him in surprise. 'Amyas, I'm afraid, is getting into some very bad habits,' he went on grimly. 'He spends a lot of time in the taverns of the city, even as my father did. I wonder sometimes if a taint like that can be inherited, passed on through the blood.'

Nanette was disturbed by this, not by the news that Amyas frequented low places—it never surprised her to hear that humanity was frail—but by the fact that in talking like this to

Paul was putting her on a level with him, destroying the safe uncle-niece relationship which protected her from herself.

'Do you think so?' he said when she did not reply.

'Surely not,' was all she could find to say.

'Well, perhaps not. But there was Ursula. You know about Ursula, do you not?' Nanette did not reply, and he went on as they walked, 'Ursula was my mistress. Yes, I had a mistress. I could not love my wife, you see, and Ursula seemed to me like a wife. I loved her. She was the purest thing that the earth ever bore. Does that seem strange to you, that a woman who laid with me in sin could be pure?'

'How can I judge?' Nanette said in distress. 'How can anyone judge?'

'I think as you on that—but everyone else judged, from the highest to the lowest. Well, the little bear is dead now, and past her pain. When she died, it was as if the light went out of the world. There was nothing left for me, nothing at all.'

They passed between the great hedges, and there at last it was dark. Nanette could hardly see his face, and there in the aromatic darkness he stopped and turned to her, and she felt herself beginning to tremble.

'I thought I would never find another human creature to love,' he said. 'But sometimes when you cut down a plant, it begins to grow again, in spite of you. It puts out buds, and the buds are stronger than the first growth was.' He took her hands in his and lifted them to his lips and kissed them, first one, then the other. 'Why do you tremble?' he asked. He slid his hands up to her elbows. 'Are you cold?' He passed them round her body and took the last step to her that brought her against him. She felt the hard muscles of his thighs against her legs, felt the warmth of his body, the sweetness of his breath stirring her hair, and she was overcome with the desire to yield to him. She pressed against him avidly, her face tipped back as instinctively as her arms went up around his neck. She could not see his face except as a white blur, but her mind's eye supplied the warm dark eyes, the lean features, the full, sensuous lips. For so long she had repressed the wild urges of her passionate nature, fighting them as her religion bid her, and now she had no more strength or will to resist. She was young and healthy, and she wanted to be made love to, here, amongst the scented shadows, and by this man whose sexuality made an almost tangible aura around him.

'Nanette,' he said, dazed by her response.

'Yes,' she said, not wanting him to talk, reaching up on tiptoe, her lips parted for him.

'You were the one who brought that second spring to my heart. I love you, Nanette.'

He kissed her, and the world went away, and they were spinning through a warm black void where there was nothing but themselves, the touch of their lips and hands, the taste of each other, the smell of each other, the sound of their breathing and the pulse of their blood. Thought fled before sensation. They sank to the ground, and Nanette was aware only of the fragrance of the grass crushed beneath her, the coolness of the air round her bare head as her head-dress was discarded, the scent of the yew hedges that framed them, the warm weight of her lover against her legs. Though armoured above, a maid's body was as defenceless below as a mouse's belly; the warm, strong hands on her legs, caressing her thighs, spanning her waist, were rousing her to a pitch of maddened excitement, filling her with a desire she did not know how to appease.

An awkward fumbling, and then the flesh touching hers was different, and the urgency lanced through her like lightning. Instinctively she knew what to do; and though she could not make any sound, no groan or cry could escape her frantic mouth that seemed to suckle on his tongue, in her mind she cried yes, yes, now!

A cool breeze scurried along the ground, rippling the grass and stirring Nanette's tumbled hair. A voice sounded very far away in her numbed mind, a voice that seemed only to say *now you understand*, but she hardly heeded it, only stored it for later, when her thoughts might not be so blurred. Her neck and shoulders were bare, for on formal occasions at Court the chemise that filled in the low square neckline of the gown was left off, and as the wind trickled past her she shivered.

'I'm cold,' she whimpered softly. The weight that was crushing her lower body shifted, moved sideways exposing her for a second to even more cold, and then her skirts were drawn down, gratefully, to cover her legs. The dark shape sat up beside her, and she prayed it would not speak and shed its anonymity; but it did, and became Paul.

'We must go in. You will catch an ague if you stay out here any longer. I should have brought a cloak for you. Come, stand up, my darling, give me your hand.'

Reluctantly she put her hand in his and he helped her to her feet. The shape had become undeniably, unshakeably her uncle Paul. She knew him intimately, there could be no mistake. She felt a little sick.

'That's better. Let me put my arm round you—you're shivering. Come, my darling—my darling—' He punctuated his words with kisses, kissing her unresisting face and then her lips, and as he reached her lips she felt him grow intense again, felt his hands harden on her shoulders. No, she thought despairingly, and swayed in his arms, thinking she would swoon. He desisted.

'I'm sorry—it is selfish of me. You are cold, and I must get you in. Hold, where is your coif? Stay still for a moment while I look…ah, here it is. Now let me put it on for you. I'm sorry I'm so clumsy—I have never been a lady's maid before. Is that right? Good, then come, my darling, my heart's heart, let us go in.'

They hurried across the grass towards the house, Nanette stumbling a little like a tired child, held up by his exuberant strength. Her mind was still blessedly numb, too numb to speak, but Paul's did not seem to be. He was buoyed with happiness, and she could feel it radiating from his body.

'Don't be afraid, my darling, everything will be all right. I swear it to you. I shall take care of you, everything will be yours. We shall marry and you shall be mistress of Morland Place. I shall do everything properly, never fear. I'll get a dispensation—I don't think it will take long, but if it does we'll marry without it, for I have a secret which will make everything easy for us. Your father was not my father's son. No-one else knows, but your father's mother laid with my father's cousin, and Jack was his son, not my father's. So if there is any delay we'll tell the priest that we are in truth no kin, and there will be an end to the problem.'

Scarcely hearing him, Nanette walked on towards the house. It seemed an endless journey through a strange semi-darkness, nothing seeming plain, nothing seeming like itself. The gargoyles under the roof edges seemed alive and leered hideously at her, and the wind moving in the trees seemed like voices just out of earshot talking about her, mocking her. What was Paul saying? She could not be hearing him right. She wanted only to escape. At the door of the house he took her again in his arms and kissed her on her forehead, her eyes, her cheeks, her lips.

'Goodnight, my heart, goodnight, my hinny, my little bird, goodnight. Sweet angels guard thy rest, sweeting. Go in now, go in, it's almost day. God bless thee, Nanette.' Twisting away from his embraces, she lifted her skirts and ran indoors.

Ten

ANNE WAS NOT IN THE DORMITORY WHEN NANETTE REACHED
it, stumbling-weary. She sat down on the edge of their
bed and tried to think, and her mind revolved dizzily from one
feeling to another. One part of her mind was elated, excited,
singing with joy at the pleasure she had taken and received and
at the knowledge that Paul loved her so deeply. She remembered the wild ecstasy of her blood and the small voice that had
said to her *now you understand*. She felt as if she had discovered
what she was meant for.

The other part of her mind was shocked and appalled. What
had she done? It was against every precept she had been taught.
To do what she had done was shocking enough, but to lie with
her own uncle, Margaret's father, who stood to her in the relationship now of father and guardian, was more shocking still.
And the knowledge of how paganly she had responded to that
profane love wounded her self-esteem. She had thought herself
to be in the main virtuous, certainly to be driven by virtuous
ideals. That the passionate part of her nature could so dominate
her was frightening.

Wearily she wondered what to do. Paul wanted to marry
her; indeed, in canon law they were married already, for
canon law did not distinguish between lawful and unlawful

consummation. And marriage with Paul would give her a secure home, a position in the world—mistress of Morland Place! An establishment was offered her better than any she could hope to achieve elsewhere, with her lack of dowry; a husband who would love and cherish her; wealth, status, power.

And if she did not marry him, what then? Marriage with any other man while Paul lived would be, in the strictest terms, impossible, would count as adultery in canon law.

Of course, it happened sometimes, and if the matter were to be hushed up, there might never be any difficulty. But on the other hand, if it should come to light it would invalidate any future marriage on the grounds of precontract—and even if it didn't, *she* would always know, in her heart, the truth of the matter. And if she should prove with child—what then?

So there was every reason for her to marry Paul, and very little to stop her; but even as she thought of it, she knew it to be impossible. To marry her uncle! A dispensation could be got, she knew, but how could she go through with it? How could she face Margaret, how could she bear Margaret addressing her as mother? How could she bear the servants' sideways looks, Amyas's censure, how live all her life wondering what Elizabeth was thinking behind that calm face? And Paul himself—once the fire of his passion cooled, would not even he turn against her? She could imagine a future in which they were to each other nothing but a constant, living reproach. Even now her feelings towards him were a mixture of desire and repulsion, as if he were the cause of her sensuality, and not merely its object.

She longed for someone to confide in. If only Anne were here! And as she thought that inner plea, the door opened softly and Anne's familiar slender figure glided in. Nanette jumped up to greet her, but before she could speak Anne had seized her hands and whispered in great elation, 'Dearest Nanette, what I have to tell you! Hurry and get into bed, and then we can draw the curtains and talk.'

'Something has happened? Anne, are you all right?' Nanette asked anxiously. Anne turned to look at her, and her face was answer enough. Her dark eyes were glittering, her cheeks were flushed, and she radiated excitement. This was no time for Nanette's anxiety. Silently the two girls undressed each other and climbed into bed, pulling the woollen curtains round to make a little, warm, dark privacy for their conversation.

'My dear Nanette, I wonder you didn't miss me before this,' Anne said, sitting up and clasping her knees to her chest. Nanette propped herself against the chaff-filled bolster, feeling the prickling of the straw-ends that poked through it, and looked towards the voice, for she could see only a white blur. 'Did you not wonder why I had not come up to bed?'

Nanette hesitated before answering. 'I have only just come in myself. I was walking in the gardens.'

'Were you, chuck? Let me guess—with Thomas? You must be careful of Tom, you know, for he breaks hearts as easily as a wrestler breaks heads.'

'No, it wasn't Tom—but never mind that—tell me what happened to you.'

'I have been with the King, Nanette, and, guess what he said?'

'I cannot,' Nanette said apprehensively.

'He said that he loved me!' Nanette did not reply, and Anne went on a little crossly, 'Why, have you nothing to say to that? Are you not astonished?'

'Yes, yes, of course I am—but—oh Anne, be careful! Tom was so worried about you. When we were dancing and you were dancing with the King, he said—'

'Oh, don't worry, I am safe enough. But Nan, it was so exciting! He was talking to me about music, and I was telling him about that poem that Tom wrote to me that he is trying to make into a song; and suddenly he took my hands—the King did, I mean—and declared the most passionate love for me. I had thought he was attracted to me—you know how one can always tell—but I didn't think it meant anything. After all, he *is* the King, and I only a knight's daughter, though my mother of course was a noblewoman. He said he loved me more than anyone in the world and that he would love me for ever—'

'But Anne, he is a married man!' Nanette cried, interrupting the bubbling talk.

'He is the King,' she said in lofty reply. 'It is different for a king. He asked me to become his mistress.'

'Anne!'

'Oh, it's all right. I refused him, of course, but I couldn't be angry. If it had been any other man, I should have been furious, but one can't be angry at such an offer from the King. He said that if I would be his mistress he would be as faithful to me as a husband and would take no other mistress while I lived. He was very stubborn in urging his case, you know, and very hard to resist. You can't imagine the things he offered me!'

'But you said no?' Nanette said, hearing the complacent smile in the voice. Anne gave a little sigh before answering.

'I refused, of course. It would be nice to have riches and power and jewels and to be acknowledged as first lady of the land—after the Queen—but it could not compensate for what I would lose. I told him that he could not love me, because I could not be his wife and would not be his mistress.'

'Was he not very angry?' Nanette asked.

'No,' Anne said musingly. 'I thought that he would be—I was afraid, really afraid, when I refused him, for he is the King, and one never knows what he might say or do next. But he seemed not angry, only disappointed. I think at first he thought I was playing a game and would say yes if asked often enough, but when he understood I meant it, he seemed suddenly sad. It disturbed me, you know, Nanette, because it made me think that perhaps he really does love me after all.'

'Would that make any difference?'

'No. I would not consent to be any man's mistress, not even the King's, but I should not like to think of him really suffering for love of me. But then,' she added briskly, 'that's nonsense. The King of England, suffering for Anne Boleyn! My confessor would chastise me for the sin of pride if he heard me say that.' She laughed, but the word 'confessor' had reminded Nanette again of her own problem. Anne had solved hers so simply by adherence to the paths of virtue. Nanette had strayed from those paths, and was being punished by the unease of her mind.

'Anne, something has happened to me this evening. I would I could tell you, so that you might advise me,' she said.

'Of course you can tell me. What is it, little Nan? You sound troubled. What has happened? How selfish of me to chatter away about my own affairs.'

'No, not at all. I should not burden you with my problems, but I do so need to talk to someone.'

'Tell me, then, dearest. I shall be glad to help if I can,' Anne said, and in the dark groped for and found Nanette's hand. 'Why, your hands are trembling! What has happened?'

Aided by that unseen contact, Nanette told her, slowly and unwillingly, of the events of the evening. When she had done, there was a long silence, so long that she was afraid Anne had been mortally offended by her behaviour, and she began to withdraw her hand in shame. But Anne's fingers tightened around hers, and she said, 'Poor, poor Nanette. Oh my dear, how you must be suffering in your mind.'

'You do not condemn me?' Nanette asked wonderingly.

'How could I condemn you? It might so easily have been me. I too have been tempted, you know.'

'But you have resisted temptation,' Nanette said bitterly. Anne stroked her hand.

'It was not the same for me. The temptation not so great—remember, I am older than you, and I have been in love. That protects me, for I shall never feel for any other man what I felt for Harry, so I shall never be tempted so strongly. But my dear, what will you do?'

'He wants to marry me.'

'Then you must marry him. It is the only solution.'

'Marry him? Marry my uncle?'

'It has been done before. A dispensation can be got—why, the King was considering marrying his son to his daughter, and if a dispensation can be got for that—'

'My own mind would not grant me a dispensation,' Nanette said. 'I don't think, I really don't think, I can do it.'

There was a long silence, and now when Nanette withdrew her hand it was not retained.

'Anne, don't blame me, please don't blame me,' Nanette pleaded.

'What will you do?' Anne asked at last. Her voice held disapproval and Nanette knew why.

'Anne, I shall never marry anyone else. I know that I cannot, after what I have done. That shall be my punishment.'

Anne's arms came round her suddenly, and gratefully Nanette yielded to the embrace.

'Little Nan, forgive me for judging you. I was wrong. Whatever you do, I am your true friend. I don't think I shall ever marry either, chuck—I am too old now, and who could marry me now that the King has set his eyes on me? It would be treason, I should think, at the least.' She gave a shaky laugh. 'We shall stay together, shan't we, Nan? We shall be friends, and grow old together in single blessedness. Say you'll stay with me, Nan?'

'I'll stay with you,' Nanette said. 'I'll never leave you, dear Anne.'

'Nor I you,' Anne said. 'My dear friend.'

They lay down to sleep, and Nanette was comforted by her promise. It was a means of escape, a way to avoid having to make the decision which was beyond her.

Never had the journey back to Morland Place seemed so long and so wearisome. Amyas had remained at Court for some time longer and Paul was travelling back alone, not wishing to remain any longer at the site of his hopes' demise. Amyas, it appeared, was pursuing a handsome young lady named Mary Holland, another of the Queen's ladies, and a close friend of George Boleyn's mistress, and there was enough hope of success to tempt him to remain. Paul could only be glad that Amyas's attentions were not fixed lower, for already at home he had a reputation for wenching amongst the lower orders.

Paul rode home in a gloomy silence that was almost tangible, not speaking to his attendants except to give them instructions, but his heart lifted a little at the first sight of Morland Place, its rosy bricks and tall chimneys set against a background of dark trees, the afternoon sunlight reflecting off its many windows. The comfortable sounds of habitation rose from it on the gentle air—a dog barking; the drowsy cluck of hens, and the cooing of doves from the pigeon-cote; the smack and thud of someone chopping wood, and voices calling cheerfully to each other in the inner yard. From the slight eminence where he had paused Paul could see some of the women coming home from the river with baskets of washing, and a boy driving the milch-kine up for the afternoon milking, ambling along lazily in the dusty heat. The air was thick with the creamy smell of meadow-flax and marsh-mallow, heavy with the sound of bees harvesting the rich clover, purple and white; and on the moat that encircled the house two swans dreamed motionless, breast-to-breast with their own reflections on the shining golden water.

It was home, it was the one thing that did not change, and though his heart ached no less at the sight of it, it was a sweeter ache, less restless. He was like a fractious child, calmed by the serene presence of the mother; Morland Place endured, the family endured, and that was what mattered. His own troubles were transitory, as was his life; and he was glad to be back. He called to Alexander, set his heels to his horse's flanks, and rode down towards the gateway.

The women saw him first, and set down their heavy baskets of washed and sun-dried bedlinen to curtsey to him and call out eagerly, 'It's the master, come home!' 'Welcome home, master!' 'God bless you, master!'

He waved to them as he rode past, and then he was clattering over the drawbridge and into the yard. Dogs barked madly in greeting and frisked about, sniffing at the horses' heels and snapping playfully at each other, and the steward and some of the servants came out to meet him while boys ran forward to take the horses. The only creatures undisturbed were the old woman who sat on a bench beside the door in the sunlight weaving baskets, and the tortoise-shell cat who was lying on her side at the old woman's feet, suckling a new litter. The old woman looked up briefly from her task, but her milky eyes passed over Paul without interest, for she was older than anyone knew, and had seen too many arrivals and departures to be concerned over one more; and the cat did not look up at all, but continued to lick the inside of one brindled wrist with her rose-pink tongue, oblivious to everything but the warmth of the sun and the tugging mouths at her seething flank.

Now the children came running out, shrilly excited, Robert and Edward jumping up and down and tugging at Grandpa's sleeves in a way their tutor would have deplored if he had been there, and behind them old Mother Kat carrying Young Paul and holding little Eleanor's hand as once she had held Nanette's bringing her to see her father. Eleanor was neither as pretty nor as merry as Nanette had been at the same age, but Paul's heart ached none the less at the reminder.

The steward gave his report in brief, assuring Paul that all was well. 'The shearing is finished but they're still packing the wool, sir, and Clem reckons there'll be twenty bales at least more than last year. The broadcloth is down at the wharf ready for shipping tomorrow, and Master Butts has got those bales of silk you ordered but he hasn't got a man to send with them until next week.'

'And the family—is everyone well?'

'Yes, sir, God be thanked. The young ladies are in the solar sewing, and the mistress is still in her chamber, of course, with the new babe, both quite well. And—'

And who was this coming out to greet Paul now? The grey bushy beard could not conceal the welcoming smile, the familiar long, brown gown, simple as a monk's, could not impede the haste of the wearer to embrace the returned traveller. Never had Paul been so glad to see anyone as he was now to see Great Uncle Richard.

'I have looked after everything for you in your absence,' he said as he kissed Paul heartily. 'Was the trip worth while? Did you enjoy it?'

'Oh, Uncle Richard, I am glad to be home,' was all that Paul could say. Richard stepped back and regarded him with his bright, pale eyes, took in the weariness and the dejected stance.

'You had better come in to the parlour where it is quiet and tell me. Steward, bring wine and bread! And see no-one disturbs us. Come, Paul, there is time before supper.'

It was cool and dim in the little panelled parlour and the rushes on the floor, changed on quarter-day not two weeks ago, were still green enough to scent the air like mown grass. Paul walked up and down as he spoke, and the smell of them bruised by his feet reminded him of that night in the yew-walk. Richard stood by the fireplace, staring unseeing at the Morland Arms painted on the panelling, his face grave. He was seeing in his mind's eye his own wife, Constance, dead these forty years, slender fairy creature that she had been. He had often thought, as she grew up, that Nanette looked a little like her; he could understand oh so well, how Paul could have fallen in love with her. The painful narrative came to an end, and Paul stopped in his walking as he stopped in his speaking, and waited for some word from Richard, something of reproof or comfort, he hardly knew what. Richard found the words with an effort.

'I'm sorry, Paul. God pity you, you have suffered, I know; but she was right. It would not have done.'

'Would not—? But why? Would she have not made a perfect mistress for Morland Place?'

'In some ways, yes. She is elegant in person and in mind, brought up in the best traditions in a fine and virtuous household. But—' He shook his head, not sure how to express the doubts he felt more through instinct than reason. His hand idly ran over the painted panel, tracing the lines of the white hare on the shield, his mother's device. 'My mother would not have agreed to it, you know.'

'Great-grandmother? What makes you think of her?' Paul said, puzzled and a little offended.

'Don't think that I do not take your troubles seriously, my son,' Richard said, 'but you know, she always knew what was best for the family. She brought you up not simply as a good Christian child, but as the heir to Morland Place. That was always the first consideration. And often, when I am in doubt about some course of action, I ask myself what Mother would have done. And she would not have let you marry your niece. Oh, I know you could get a dispensation, I know that it happens, but that is not always the rule one must follow. In your heart you know, too, that it would not do. In the end, you would hate each other.'

'You married against her wishes,' Paul reminded him.

'Yes, I know. But then, I was the youngest son. It was not important.' He turned to look at Paul at last, and Paul realized suddenly how old Richard was. The sunlight slanting through the window threw into cruel relief the lines and shadows of the old man's face. 'I never married again. I loved Constance in a way I can't describe. I can barely remember what she looked like, yet I can still remember how I felt about her when first she consented to come with me, penniless as I was, and walk the country with me. All my passion is spent now—I am old and hollow and loveless—but still I remember. And ever since she died, I have looked for her in other people. One can never really believe that a love like that can die; one always thinks it must have survived somewhere, in someone.'

Paul's eyes filled with tears, and he turned his head away, as the quiet voice went on, 'She is herself, Paul; she is not the person you are looking for; and sooner or later you would have come to recognise that, and then there would be no excuse for having violated God's laws. Morland Place has its heirs, the sons of your son, who was got upon your lawful wife, the wife my Mother chose for you. Be content. You do not need a wife to give you more sons, and you cannot have a wife to give you the love you have lost. She is gone for ever—let her rest, and be content.'

'And Nanette?' Paul said at last. 'What of her? I wanted to atone—'

'Atone?'

'For Jack—for hating Jack. I swore I would take care of his children.'

'He would not have wanted you to marry them,' Richard said, and his voice contained a smile. 'I believe you were mistaken about him, you know. Your father certainly believed Jack was his son.'

'It is a thing that can never be known, now,' Paul said.

Richard nodded. 'Of course. So put it from your mind. Jack never felt he had anything to forgive. See his daughters respectably married, and that is all he could want. Morland Place was never his, would never have been his. You do not need to give it to his daughter.'

Paul rubbed his eyes wearily. 'You may be right,' he said, unconvinced.

'I know I am. And now, if you have said all you want, shall we go and visit the young ladies before supper—you have not yet greeted them.'

'Later, Uncle Richard. I want to go to the chapel first. Do you go for me, and tell them I will see them at supper. I must be alone for a little first.'

'I understand,' Richard said. 'Go and make your peace.'

Make my peace? Paul thought. It is not I who can make it. Yet there was peace to be had all the same. The chapel's quiet seemed always to absorb a mere mortal's restlessness, and here, surrounded by the memorials of his family, he sought a definition of himself and his life. There were the tributes to Richard's brothers and sisters, dead before Paul's birth; and to Richard's father, whom even Richard did not remember, and Richard's mother, whom Paul could just remember. *In God is Death at End* ran the words beneath the double effigy. Then there were memorials to other members of the family—Jack and Edward and Mary, and Belle Butts, and little Jackie and

Dickon, all remembered here. One day there would be an effigy of Paul himself, and future generations of worshippers would stare at it and wonder what he had been like.

Life flowed through him, beginning long before his birth and continuing long after his death; Paul was a transmitter of the germ of life, one link in a long chain, one part of a pattern that no mortal man would ever see worked out. *That* was his worth, and in that there was peace to be found. Absently his fingers caressed the carved outline of the little bear. Her life too; perhaps there was justification for her life and death here too. He could hardly remember her face now; only the feeling he had when he looked at her. Perhaps Richard was right—that was what he had sought. Was it a betrayal? He thought not—he thought she would understand. Rest in peace, little bear. The peace dropped like slow balm into his wounds. He knew, because he was a sensible man, that he would not feel this peace for very long, nor very often, but it was there, and could always be sought again, and that had to be enough.

He knelt and folded his hands, and began the comfortable repetition of the Paternoster, soothing his soul with the familiar words as a bird-catcher charms a bird with the notes of his pipe until it will rest fearless in the palm of his hand.

The year that followed was, on the whole, a happy one for Nanette. It was long before she could forget what had happened, even longer before the image of Paul's unhappiness ceased to trouble her mind in quiet moments; but life at Court was gay, and the little circle of which Anne and Tom Wyatt formed the centre was the brightest and wittiest. It soon received an augmentation in the form of the King himself, along with Suffolk and Hal Norys, his inseparable satellites, and when the group had ceased to be nervous and tongue-tied at the King's presence, it preened itself instead, and enjoyed its own importance.

It was clear to everyone that the King was pursuing Anne with more than usual fervour, and many times Tom confided his fears to Nanette that Anne did not realise the danger of her situation. As far as he dared, Tom made himself a rival to the King, and the King, loving Tom almost as much as Hal, took it in good part; but even while Tom was trying to save Anne, she was busy defending Tom by telling the King, with her accustomed frankness, that she was not in love with Tom any more than with her sovereign lord.

Nanette spent much time with Tom while Anne was occupied with her royal admirer, and she tried to put his mind at rest by telling him that Anne had no intention of becoming the King's mistress. She chided him for supposing Anne to be worldly enough to give up her principles for the sake of the material gains that would come the way of a King's mistress, and he admitted, shamefacedly, that he ought to trust her more. All the same, the group was happiest on those occasions when the King was occupied with business, and Anne and George and Tom and Nanette and Hal and Madge could be free to laugh and talk, sing and play music, or play at cards or bowls, chess or merels together. Those were the times when Nanette was best able to forget the sadness of her uncle and lover, so far away in Yorkshire.

In the spring of 1527, just after Nanette's nineteenth birthday, the King arranged with the Cardinal to be called before an ecclesiastical court and tried on a charge of fornication with Queen Katherine on the grounds that she was his brother's wife and therefore not his. The court hearing was meant to be a secret, but in the event almost the only person who did not know about it was the Queen. The King was, as expected, found guilty, and as a result a demand was despatched to the Pope for an annulment of the marriage. The dispensation which had been granted by the previous Pope was stated to be invalid, since it was not within the Pope's competence to dispense with the law of Leviticus.

'Will the Pope grant it, do you think?' Nanette asked Tom one day as they walked behind the others in the grounds of Hampton.

'No doubt,' Tom said. 'The Pope has granted divorces on less sure grounds—to the King's sister, Queen Margaret of Scotland, for instance, and his brother-in-law Suffolk. The King should be free by the end of the year.'

'And then—a French princess, if my lord Cardinal has his way,' Nanette said. 'Well, at least a French princess will be more entertaining to serve than our poor Queen. I suppose she will go into a convent?'

'I suppose so. She will be happier in one, poor lady,' Tom said. 'I don't know why she doesn't save the King the trouble and retire of her own accord. It would be the best sort of life for her.'

'Anne says that a French Queen might turn out to be like Queen Claude, and that that wouldn't be any better.'

'Except,' Tom said drily, 'that if the King is married to a new wife and busy filling the royal nurseries, he won't have so much time or inclination to pursue Anne.'

'That would please you, wouldn't it, dear Tom?'

'You know it would. But I think it would please Anne, too, for it must be a strain to continue to think of witty ways of refusing a king. One never knows what might happen if she ceases to make him laugh.'

Nanette touched his hand. 'Try not to worry. I'll keep as close to her as I can. I promised never to leave her, you know. Between us we'll take care of her.'

'If only she would marry me,' he said gloomily. 'I have offered to divorce my wife and marry her, but she won't hear of it.'

'Perhaps when the King is married again and has lost interest, she'll change her mind. You know she thinks it dangerous for you to show interest in her,' Nanette said.

'Yes, I know—hullo! What's going on up ahead?' Tom said, seeing a servant run up to the group and give some message, waving his arms wildly. 'Come, Nan, let's catch up.'

The others had stopped and were questioning the servant eagerly, and when Nanette and Tom arrived, George swung round to give them the news.

'It seems a courier has just arrived from Italy,' he told them. 'The Spanish army has sacked Rome, and the Pope is a prisoner of the Emperor.'

Nanette and Tom exchanged glances. 'How does that affect things, do you think?' she asked. Tom shrugged.

'Not at all, I should think. Wolsey is a great favourite of the Pope's, and the King is a very prominent son of the church. He'll grant the petition just the same.'

'Oh, you are talking about the divorce,' Anne said. 'Do speak of something else—I seem to have heard nothing but that for months. I'm weary of it. I know—let's go and see if the strawberries are ripe!'

They set off towards the kitchen gardens, but Anne at least did not reach them, for another servant found them to say that the King wished to speak to mistress Anne at once, and she gave a small shrug to the others and followed the servant obediently. Nanette was troubled, and remained walking up and down the terrace for some time hoping that Anne would come back quickly. She did not, however, and it was not until she was on her way to the chapel for vespers that Anne rejoined her.

Nanette could see at once that something had happened, for Anne was deadly white, and her eyes were glittering strangely. She caught Nanette's arm, gripping it so tightly that it made Nanette gasp, and pulled her aside into an alcove.

'I must talk to you,' she said in a low voice.

'What is it, Anne? What has happened?' Nanette asked. 'You look so strange.'

'I have been with the King,' she said. She stared down at her hand, and Nanette, looking too, saw that Anne was wearing a new ring, a gold ring set with a large emerald, a very valuable piece of jewellery. 'He gave me this,' she went on, 'and he asked me again to be his mistress. I said that I would not, and tried to give him back the ring. I told him that I would never consent to be his mistress, and he looked so strange that I was afraid.'

'Oh Anne,' Nanette breathed, taking her friend's hand. Anne looked up then, and gave a peculiar, strained smile.

'He walked about the room for a while, muttering to himself. Then he came back to me and stared at me, and his face was grim and terrible. I trembled and wanted to run away, but of course I couldn't, so I just stood there and stared back at him. And then he said he would never ask me again.'

'Thank God,' Nanette said. 'Oh Anne, I have been so worried for you—'

'Wait, you haven't heard all yet,' Anne interrupted. She paused for a long time, so long that Nanette thought she was not going to speak again, and then she said, very low, 'He asked me whether, if he was free to marry, I would consent to be his wife.'

The blood drained from Nanette's face and she stared at her friend, unable to speak or move. Anne gave an uneasy laugh.

'Well may you be surprised! You may imagine how surprised I was.'

'Anne, what did you say? What did you answer him?'
Nanette found her voice at last. Anne held out her hand so that
the emerald in the ring caught the light.

'Need you ask, seeing this ring on my finger?' she said. Her
mouth twisted wryly, and with a sudden choking sound, almost
like a sob, she put her hands over her face. Her voice muffled,
she said, 'I told him I would.'

BOOK TWO

THE FALCON AND
THE CROW

Christ keep King Henry the Eight
From treachery and deceit,
And grant him grace to know
The falcon from the crow.

John Skelton
'Why Come Ye Not To Court'

Eleven

THREE WOMEN SAT IN THE SOLAR OF MORLAND PLACE SEWING, and though they were of an age, the difference between them was very obvious. Two of them were pregnant, and were dressed in the style of sober, well-to-do matrons—plain gowns of fine cloth, unadorned kennel head-dresses with the hood turned up to contain and conceal the hair, wealth displayed only by the depth of the rich lace frills at the wrist and the gold chains and ornaments at neck and bosom.

The other wore a gown of scarlet damask over a kirtle of green-brocaded silk. The scarlet sleeves were turned back to shew the undersleeves wired to huge fullness and slashed and puffed with the linen chemise-sleeves. She wore a scarlet French coif trimmed with peridots and a short hood to reveal the luxuriant hair falling to her waist. The neck of her gown was sewn with pearls and peridots, and the same stones clasped her sleeves and adorned her slender fingers. She looked every inch a lady of the Court.

'What was Katherine's wedding like?' Nanette asked Margaret.

'As dull as it well might be,' Margaret said, making a face. After five years of marriage she was at last pregnant, and it was making her cross and sickly. 'After one elderly widower, to choose another! Lord Latimer is as dry and grey and stick-like as Lord Borough, and it must be her choice, since her mother is dead. I can't imagine what she sees in him. She's rich enough by Lord Borough's Will to choose anyone she likes.'

'He's a Neville,' Nanette said, 'John Neville, and her cousin. He was often at the house when I lived with her. I dare say she loves him in a respectful sort of way. He is a very kind man, as I remember.'

'It is no bad thing to have a kind husband,' Elizabeth said. Nanette glanced at her, but she didn't look up, and Nanette wondered how pointed the remark was meant to be. Elizabeth was nearing the end of her seventh pregnancy, her two youngest sons having been taken off by the epidemic of the Sweat two years ago in 1528. She looked oddly helpless with her vast belly and swollen face and hands—she suffered from dropsy—but her expression was as mild and tranquil as ever. Could she really not know, however, that her husband was notorious in York for his sexual adventures?

'She wasn't widowed more than six months,' Margaret went on, ignoring Elizabeth's quiet comment. 'If it weren't for the age of her two husbands one would be tempted to think there was some other reason behind such a rapid remarriage. But there, I doubt whether pregnancy will ever trouble Katherine Parr. If she goes on marrying old men at four-yearly intervals she will be the richest old maid in the country.'

'That is unseemly talk, Margaret,' Nanette said.

'As well as being stepmother to a score of people older than herself,' Margaret continued unheeding. Nanette winced inwardly, remembering how nearly she had been in that position herself.

'Katherine Latimer is my friend, and I won't have you speak like that of her,' she said firmly. Margaret smiled sourly.

'Not so much of a friend that she would invite you to her wedding.'

'I must own that seemed strange to me, too,' Elizabeth said, 'to invite Amyas and me and James and Margaret, but not to invite you.'

Nanette shrugged, a habit she had caught from Anne. 'I'm afraid there's bound to be some notoriety attached to anyone from Lady Anne Rochford's Court.'

'People are bound to think that the King made Sir Thomas Boleyn Earl of Wiltshire in return for his daughter's services,' Elizabeth said.

'But it isn't true,' Nanette said, laying down her needle. 'I wish it could be got into people's heads that she is not his mistress. Up here, so far from London, the truth is harder to come by than rumour. And rumour starts with the Queen—she is convinced that Anne is just another such a one as Mary Boleyn or Elizabeth Blunt, however often the King tells her differently. She is a stubborn woman,' she finished bitterly.

'She has a right to be,' Elizabeth said.

'Has she?' Nanette said. 'I wonder. She talks often enough to the King about duty, but what about her own duty? She has failed to provide an heir to the kingdom, and by refusing to retire to a convent she is jeopardising the succession. She talks about virtue and duty, but all she has is pride and selfish stubbornness.'

'Perhaps she loves the King,' Elizabeth suggested.

'If she loved him, she would admit the truth and retire to a convent,' Nanette retorted.

'Perhaps she does not see it as the truth. I believe she has sworn in front of Cardinal Campeggio and to the Holy Father himself that her marriage with Prince Arthur was not consummated. She would hardly lie to such eminent people.'

'Oh, I don't think she is lying,' Nanette said impatiently, 'but she might be mistaken. In any case, how can we know precisely what God counts as consummation? It is evident that whatever she and Prince Arthur did together, God viewed it as a true marriage. Otherwise, He would not have taken all her sons from her. And her duty is clearly to make way for someone who can provide sons. She is wasting the best years of Lady Anne's life.'

'Who would have thought,' Margaret said, a little maliciously, 'that they would still be waiting for the divorce all this time later? When you wrote to us three years ago to say the King wanted to marry Lady Anne, you thought it would all be settled in a matter of months.'

'No-one, not even Cardinal Wolsey, thought the Pope would refuse. When he was taken prisoner by the Emperor, it occurred to no-one that he might take the Emperor's side in the dispute, and now he prevaricates and delays and wavers this way and that, not wanting to offend our King but even more afraid of offending the Emperor. And, of course, Cardinal Wolsey doesn't press him, seeing that's where his preferment comes from. As my lord of Suffolk said, it was never merry in England while we had Cardinals amongst us.'

'But surely the Cardinal is in disgrace now?' Elizabeth said.

'Yes, we heard he had been dismissed and was retiring to York,' Margaret added.

'True enough, but one never knows the next thing the King will do, and he is very fond of the Cardinal. My lady is worried sick that the King will take the Cardinal back into favour and that the Cardinal will somehow change the King's mind about marrying her. She says she has given her youth and her reputation to the King, and if they don't marry now she will be ruined. Poor thing, her temper is so frayed with worrying she gets quite hysterical sometimes.'

'Why should she worry?' Margaret said. 'Hasn't the King set her up in her own Court like a queen? We hear that Whitehall is grander than Greenwich even. And doesn't she appear at the King's side like a queen, and take precedence even over Mary of Suffolk?'

Nanette shrugged. 'It's true enough, but if the King changed his mind about marrying her it could all be changed in a moment. Oh,' she added hastily, 'he loves her as much as ever—more, I think, if that were possible. He is so good to her—when she gets into a rage, he soothes her and calms her, and when she weeps he cuddles her like a child. He is wonderful with her, and of course she clings to him more and more because she feels she has so many enemies. But the strain is terrible. I almost think she would rather now be his mistress than go on in this way. But the King would not do it. She will be his wife or nothing, by the King's will.'

The other two were silent for a while, thinking it over. Then Margaret sighed and said, 'Well, it's a strange situation, and stranger still for us, for we hear one thing by rumour and another by you. Rumour says that she is his mistress and holds him by power of the Black Art, that she has six fingers on each hand and six toes on each foot, and that she schemes to poison the Queen and Princess Mary. And another rumour says that she is the one who holds off the King, to make him so wild for her that he will marry her or die in the attempt. But from what you tell us, the truth is very different.'

'The truth would be hard for ordinary people to conjure for themselves,' Elizabeth said, 'since it is so very strange a situation. And a sad one—there are so many sufferers.'

'But Nanette has done well out of it,' Margaret said. 'She is lady-in-waiting to someone who, if not the Queen, lives like one, and will be the next one if she has her way. Look at her—decked and bejewelled! But it's a wonder to me, Nanette, that you aren't married by now. As Lady Anne's intimate friend you must be much sought after at the Court.'

Nanette smiled at this, knowing it to be a jibe. Margaret was jealous of Nanette's position at Court, and vented her spite by drawing attention to her maiden state. Nanette, at twenty-two, seemed an old maid to Margaret; but Lady Anne was nearing thirty, and Nanette felt, in comparison to her, very young and very lucky.

There was a commotion in the yard, and Elizabeth went to the window to look down.

'It is the hunting party returned. The girls will be up here directly, I am sure. You must go out with them tomorrow, Nanette. I'm sure you wished to go today. You do not need to sit with Margaret and me—we are quite accustomed to each other's company.'

'Well, I will go tomorrow, if you don't mind. I love to hunt—Lady Anne and I go out most mornings in the grease season. But what shall you do?'

'I have to visit some sick people in the village,' Elizabeth said. 'I should have gone today, but I did not want to leave you. So you see, you will be doing a good act by going and not keeping me from my duties.' She smiled as she spoke, so that Nanette might not feel rebuked.

'You are very good, Elizabeth, to take such care of the tenants.'

'They are mostly not the tenants,' Margaret said, 'but simply poor people in the surrounding villages. I cannot think why she spends so much time on them. They are not her responsibility.'

'I feel that they are,' Elizabeth said. 'I am mistress of Morland Place, as long as my father is not married. And while he takes the very best of care of his people, I cannot do less.'

'Oh, father has always loved playing lord of the manor,' Margaret said carelessly. 'But that need not trouble you. I wish sometimes he would marry again, and then you need not be dragging me round the hovels of the county so frequently. Nanette, you can't conceive of the smells!'

'But you need not come if it distresses you,' Elizabeth said. Margaret shook her head.

'I would sooner go with you than sit at home doing nothing. And I can't hunt in my condition. Besides, I like to have something to tell my confessor to offset all my faults. Ah, here are the girls! What a noise they make—like a pack of hounds themselves.' There was indeed a great deal of noise on the stairs, loud voices and much giggling. 'Now that Mother Kat's dead they run wild like animals, with no-one but a scatter-brained servant to keep an eye on them. They really are a disgrace. I've spoken to Father again and again about them. They ought to have been sent away years ago, or at least to have had a proper governess. Look at them,' she went on as the door opened and Catherine and Jane burst in, panting and dishevelled. 'Great girls of eighteen and nineteen, and not married! It's shocking.'

'Such a day we had!' Catherine exclaimed without troubling herself with formal greetings. 'Such a run!'

'We killed twice—two fat bucks,' Jane added, and turned to Nanette. 'Oh sister, you should have been with us! I'm sure you do not get such fine hunting as we have had in the south.'

'We have very good hunting in the south, I assure you,' Nanette said, mildly amused. The two girls had inherited the Butts fairness, and were very pretty in their hunting gowns of green velvet, with feathered green bonnets over their linen coifs. Their cheeks were pink and their eyes bright with the exercise, and there was about them an air of untroubled merriment which Nanette remembered, sadly, in Anne in the days before the King had chosen her to be his future wife. Margaret was not so pleased with their looks, however.

'Catherine, straighten your dress,' she snapped. 'And Jane, your hair is coming down at the back. Really, girls, you must try to look more like ladies and less like trollops. And must you run everywhere, and arrive out of breath?'

Catherine made a face at her. 'Oh don't fuss, Margaret. What does it matter? Nanette, we had the longest run ever today.

We hunted right out to Rufford and back round to the walls of Shawes.'

'So we stopped there and begged refreshments, and Ezekiel decided to come out with us for the rest of the run. Arabella was very cross. She looked just like Margaret—as if she'd been eating lemons!'

Jane laughed at that, and then exchanged a sly glance with her sister, and they fell into helpless giggles.

'Is Ezekiel here?' Elizabeth asked. 'Did he come back with you?'

'Yes, he's below with Uncle Paul. And Arabella and Great Uncle Richard are coming over to dinner too.'

'Then I must go and speak to the cook,' Elizabeth said. 'You should have said so at once, girls.'

'We came up to tell you,' Jane said indignantly.

'I'll come down with you,' Nanette said. 'I should pay my respects to Ezekiel. I haven't seen him since he married.'

At dinner there was a larger company at the table than was usual. Paul presided, with Elizabeth on his right and Nanette on his left. Amyas had not returned from York, and so Great Uncle Richard sat next to Elizabeth and engaged her kindly in conversation. Nanette was shocked at the change in him. Though still tall, he seemed to have shrunk together, like something collapsing inwards, and he had a strangely brittle look. His thick hair and bushy beard were silver now, and seemed somehow too virile for his frail body. His booming voice seemed lighter, and his eyes had a milky, far-away look in them, as if his attention was not entirely on things present and visible.

Beyond Uncle Richard sat Ezekiel and his wife Arabella. Nanette liked Arabella at once. Though not pretty, she had a pleasant, attractive face, and she had a brisk, sensible way of talking that seemed an admirable foil to Ezekiel's romance. Next to Nanette was James Chapham, whom she found as charming as ever. Margaret had not come down to dinner, since she felt suddenly sick, so Jane sat beyond James, and Catherine beyond Ezekiel. Nanette was disturbed to find how all through dinner her two sisters talked and laughed a great deal more than was normally expected of unmarried girls in their position. She also had opportunity to notice how blatantly Catherine flirted with Ezekiel—to his amusement and Arabella's faint scorn—and how Jane did her best to monopolise James's attention, failing only because he had sooner talk to Nanette about the Court and the London gossip than to Jane about the day's hunting.

After dinner when the nap was drawn the boy singers came down from the gallery and performed a ballet of the love of Semele and Jupiter, during which the other guests arrived, John Butts and his wife Lucy and their two surviving sons John and Bartholomew, now aged twenty and nineteen respectively. When the ballet was over they were also joined by Elizabeth's children Robert, Edward, Eleanor, and Paul in the company of the new nursery-maid and the chaplain, Father Fenelon, and when Margaret also came down to hear the singing the party was complete—except, conspicuously, for Amyas.

The afternoon was spent in pleasant pastime. Nanette played the lute and sang some of the new songs that were popular around Court, and little Eleanor, now seven years old, danced to them. The boys played a game of club kayles at one end of the hall, and Elizabeth and Margaret started a noisy game of Pope July which gradually drew in everyone but Paul and James, who preferred a quieter game of chess, and Nanette, who continued to pick idly at the lute and watch the group with contented eyes. This, she thought, was how life should be—a comfortable family scene, all the dear ones gathered together in one hearth, the servants and attendants beyond about their own business, innocent games and merriment, good company and good cheer.

And she looked across to where Paul was playing, his head bent over the board as he contemplated his next move, one hand caressing Alexander's head. Had she married him, she would have had the right to the central place in this happy scene. She would have been mistress of the house and all the inmates, her future assured and comfortable. And she would have had Paul, and his love, to lean on when she felt tired or discouraged or afraid, which was often. She looked for a moment longingly at the close dark curls of his head, the line of his pure profile, the droop of his eyelashes over those full dark eyes, his smooth lip caught in by his white teeth as he pondered the problem. She remembered with a little shudder how those long, strong hands, that now were reaching out to move a rook, had caressed her naked flesh, how—No, it was madness to think like that. He had been her lover; the memory gave her gooseflesh; she must forget it. All her life she had striven to deny that part of her nature and she had thought she had succeeded. But the blood pounded through her veins, and she longed to feel again the hard caress of a man's hands, the weight of a man's body pressing down on hers. Such wicked, carnal thoughts! Yet why did she feel only half alive? And then James looked up and glanced at her curiously, and she was instantly as scarlet as a boiled lobster, as if he could read her thoughts. She dropped her eyes hastily and fumbled a chord on the lute.

'Play something else for us, cousin Nan,' James said in a comforting voice. She risked a glance at him, and saw his eyes smiling sympathetically. He would not have looked so if he had been able to read her thoughts. 'Play us one of the King's songs.'

Glad to have something on which to concentrate, Nanette began to play and sing one of the King's favourites—'Pastance with good company, I love and shall until I die'. Very appropriate to the moment, she thought—and tried to ignore the fact that Paul's eyes were so often on her that he could not be giving much attention to the game.

It was good to go hunting the next day—the hard riding and the lust of the chase might drive the fever out of her blood, Nanette thought. She dressed that morning in hunting green, emerald-green velvet over apple-green silk, but she put on long leather boots under her dress, an innovation that Lady Anne had introduced into their little circle where, for love of the sport, the ladies rode cross-saddle. Catherine and Jane, mounting their side-saddled palfreys a little later, were perturbed to discover how far behind the Court fashion they were and each secretly determined to ride cross-saddle from then on. They were also a little mortified that Paul had seen fit to mount Nanette on one of his best hunters, a horse he would not normally have expected a woman to handle. It was a hard-necked bay gelding, and full two hands taller than their grey ponies.

It was a fine morning, cool but damp enough to put up plenty of scent. The hunt servants went ahead with the hounds, and the riders moved off after them, Paul and James, Nanette and Catherine and Jane, Robert and Edward, and the mounted attendants leading the spare horses. When they were half way to the first draw Amyas caught up with them, looking surprisingly fresh considering he had not arrived back at Morland Place until after the family had retired last night.

He greeted his sons with a cuff round the head apiece, stared at his cousins, and said to his father, 'I'm glad I caught up with you. Nothing like a morning's hunting for getting one out of the fog of virtuous reproach that fills the house these days. What shall we bring home today, do you think?'

Paul did not reply, giving him only a look of great disgust, and James filled the awkward silence with his usual social grace. 'There is a ten-point up on the moors, so I hear. It would be a fine thing if we could bring him home, to shew our cousin that we have as good hunting here as the King shews her at Richmond or Windsor.'

'Pooh! I know these fine folks' notion of hunting,' Amyas snorted. 'They keep their deer in a little park and chase them round and round at a gentle canter. The deer are so tame they come up afterwards to take titbits from the ladies' hands.'

'Amyas, you are as ignorant as you are unmannerly,' James laughed. 'What do you know about it?'

'More than you James, I warrant you. Remember I lived in the Boleyns' pockets for many years.'

'Then you must know that hunting can be as good sport there as here,' Nanette said. 'When did you canter round a park at Hever?'

'Do not compliment him with rational argument, Nan,' James said. 'He speaks only for the pleasure of hearing his own voice.'

'I grant ye we had some fair sport with George and old Boleyn—and the dark lady rode as well as a boy.'

'You mean Lady Anne,' Nanette corrected him, sensing some disrespect.

'Aye, the Night Crow as they call her now—'

'That's enough, Amyas. Curb your tongue,' Paul said sharply. Amyas stared.

'As you please. But even at Hever there was no real danger. Now here, you may lose a limb or even your life in the chase. You are right, James,' he clapped his brother on the back, 'the ten-point stag is the beast for us. We shall bring him back today or perish in the attempt.'

Paul consulted with the huntsman, and they rode up to the moors to the place where he thought it most likely they would find the stag. They harboured several deer, but they were all hinds, and Paul let them go. For some time they found nothing, and it looked almost as if they would not have any sport that day, and Catherine and Jane and the children were growing restless and whispering amongst themselves, when suddenly a silence fell across the group, and the ten-point stag appeared on the skyline five hundred yards before them.

The silence was broken in a crash of hound-music, and with the huntsmen calling their high, weird cries the hounds were off, their mouths like bells in the early-morning quiet. They were hunting by sight, but the stag soon lost them amongst the scrubby trees, and their noses went down for the scent and they set to work more methodically. The riders were close behind, weaving in and out of the branches, and then they were out into the open again and galloping. It was wonderfully exhilarating, and Nanette found she had been right—it put everything out of her head but the sting of the wind on her cheeks and the thunder of the hooves beneath her. She was at the front, only Paul before her, for her horse was the fastest, but Paul was not Paul any more, only another rider. She forgot everything but the hounds and the chase.

They checked in a small coppice, and the huntsman had to report that they had lost him.

'Gone through the water, master, that little peat-stream there,' the huntsman said shaking his head. 'I don't know if maybe he hasn't doubled back. He's a wise old one, is that stag. If we go back on our tracks maybe we'll pick him up again.'

'Well, we'll check now and take some breakfast, and then we'll try as you say,' Paul said. 'Let us have some wine and meat—we have been out two hours already.'

After a short rest and some food and drink they began again, and coming out of the coppice a little further over Nanette was surprised to see the walls of Shawes a little way in the distance.

'I did not know we were so close,' she said to James, who

was riding beside her. Instinctively she turned her head to look for Catherine, and she was not to be seen. Nanette dropped back and asked Jane quietly where she was. Jane looked sulky.

'I can't help it, it isn't my fault, so you need not look at me like that, Nan. I'm sure I told her she should not go, but she would.'

'Go where? To Shawes?'

'Of course,' Jane said, surprised there should be any question. 'She took our maid with her, of course, but Arabella is supposed to be going with Elizabeth to the village today, and I don't know what use Gatty will be.'

'Gatty?'

'Our maid. She just does what she's told, and if Catherine tells her to wait outside—well, she'll just fall asleep. She always does. I never knew any human being sleep as much as Gatty. But there wasn't anything I could do.'

Jane's voice was peevish, but there was an underlying smugness about it, and as she spoke she eyed James across Nanette's shoulder in a way that told Nanette she was only waiting for her own chance to behave as badly. With a cousin like Amyas, was it not to be expected that the girls would grow up wild? Nanette sighed and rode forward again, resolving to speak to Paul at the first opportunity.

They found the stag's trail again and after tracking him for a mile or more the trail became hot again and the hounds began to sing and pull at their leashes. They ran up a long gradual slope, and as they reached the top they saw him down below them at gaze. For one instant they regarded each other, and then with a bound the stag was away, and the hounds were running after him, and the hunt was up. They galloped down the hill, and as the hill grew steeper and steeper the gallop grew wilder and wilder. Some of them checked their horses, afraid they might stumble, but Paul and Nanette and Amyas and James went on full speed, hurtling madly down the hill oblivious to the danger. The terrain broke up into outcrops of rock and little gullies, and they hunted the stag until he turned at bay in a gully with no exit.

The huntsman held in the madly baying hounds, and let the mastiffs in for the kill. The stag went down kicking, and Amyas, excited beyond control, leapt down from his horse, his long knife ready.

'I'll dispatch him,' he cried. 'Stand back!'

'Have a care, Master Amyas—he's not finished yet,' the huntsman called. Amyas flung a glance back at Nanette and James.

'There is no joy in life without danger,' he shouted boastfully.

'Amyas, no!' Nanette called, for she could see, as could the others, that the ten-point was struggling back to its feet, shaking off the dogs. Amyas plunged on, the stag turned its head, eyes rolling madly at its tormentors, and tilted its deadly antlers towards the young man. Even as Nanette was crying out, Paul had flung himself from the saddle, and as the maddened beast struck he threw himself bodily at Amyas, knocking him out of the way and taking a glancing blow in the groin.

Nanette screamed, but the huntsman was on the stag's other side, and with a long tearing thrust of the knife he ripped its throat and its head fell back under the snatching mouths of the mastiffs. Nanette was in a state like delirium. She felt her feet hit the earth without any awareness of having thrown herself from the saddle and in a second she was kneeling in a billow of skirts at Paul's side. Amyas, just beyond, was getting to his feet, dazed but unhurt. Beside her the hart was still kicking feebly, and in her nostrils was the stink of its fear and the reek of blood, while her ears were dinned with the high-pitched worrying of the hounds, but these things were dim to her compared with the sight of Paul, his face white and pinched, drawing himself slowly up onto his elbow.

His eyes met hers, and pain and fright dissolved before some other emotion, something elemental and savage; his dark eyes shone with a feral brightness.

'Nan,' he breathed, so low no-one but she could have heard.

'Are you all right?' she asked. His hand was pressed to his groin, and as they both looked he lifted it slowly and they saw the bright stain spread across the cloth. Nanette's nostrils flared, and she heard herself whimper.

'It's all right—a flesh-wound only,' he said with an effort. The huntsman was whipping the dogs off now, and the worrying noise gave way before yips to silence. The stag sighed and stopped kicking. Its blood was darkening, and some of it was soaking into the skirt of Nanette's gown. 'I'll be all right,' Paul said, and he put his hand on hers. She looked down, her eyes wide, and saw the scarlet between his fingers, the smear on her own flesh. She looked up, and saw in Paul's eyes what her own expression must be, a savage lust. Horror overcame her. She sprang to her feet, and ran back to the horses. In a moment she had mounted, pushed her servant aside with the butt of her whip, swung her horse round on its haunches, snorting madly, and was galloping out of that bloody ravine. Dimly she heard shouts behind her, but they only spurred her on, fleeing before them as a hart flees the hounds.

When at last she rode home the rest of the party was there, and Paul was in the steward's room having his wound attended to. Nanette would speak to no-one, but waited outside the steward's room until Paul was dressed and able to see her. He dismissed the servant, and as soon as they were alone he made to step towards her, but she shook her head violently.

'Don't,' she said.

'Nanette, what happened?' he pleaded. 'There are servants out looking for you.'

'I had to be alone for a while. After what happened—'

'Then I didn't imagine it. You felt what I felt.'

'Don't. Please don't even think about it. Paul, you might have been killed. Why did you do it?'

'It isn't easy to stand back and watch one's son killed,' Paul said bitterly. 'Perhaps I should have let it kill him. Or perhaps I could have arranged that it should kill me.'

'Don't speak like that,' Nanette said.

'Why not? What is there to live for?'

'Everything,' she said. He looked at her in hope.

'Nanette, will you marry me? Back there when you looked at me, I thought—I knew—'

'I can't,' she said savagely. 'I can't give in to it. I don't know if I am sick, or mad, or cursed, or if God is testing me, but if I give in to these longings, what am I? I want you, and I know that I must not.'

The tears began to roll down her face. She was a pitiful sight, dishevelled, dirty and blood-smeared, the tears making clean tracks down her cheeks, and Paul stepped forward and took her in his arms, and she didn't struggle, but let him hold her.

'Don't say those things, chuck, you don't know what you are saying. Oh my dearest Nan, my hinny, marry me, and everything will be all right. What you feel is right, it's natural! You need me. We are intended for each other, and this is God's way of telling you. Don't go against it, my love.'

She did not answer, but after a while her trembling stopped, and gently, very gently, she released herself from his arms. He saw the expression on her face, and knew it was no use, and he let his arms drop to his sides. The movement had started him bleeding again, and there was a stain across the front of her dress as well as on the hem.

'I can't,' she said. 'I have to go back. Anne needs me, and I swore I would not leave her. So even if—I wanted to, I could not stay. But—' she swallowed and went on with difficulty, 'but I shall never marry anyone else. Paul—'

'Yes?'

'If only I could understand—'

There seemed to be nothing more to say, and in any case, speaking was difficult. She turned away, and then back, remembering what she had meant to say.

'Paul, my sisters need to be married. Catherine is behaving very badly over Ezekiel, and Jane copies her in everything. I don't want them to become like me. They are over-ready for marriage, and will be spoiled if they are not wed soon.'

He nodded, and then said, 'John Butts's two sons. They are not yet wed. I think John would not be too much averse to such a match, if I put it to him.'

'Do it,' Nanette said, 'and right soon. If he will have them, let it be done soon.'

'And what about you? You will go back to Court? Stay a little while longer.'

'I had better go. I don't like to be too long away from her.'

'I need you.'

'My lady needs me.' She looked around the small, bare room. 'I don't belong here. I will go at the end of the week, if you will arrange it.'

He could not speak, but he bowed his assent, and she curtseyed and went from the room.

Twelve

CARDINAL WOLSEY, THE GREAT PRINCE OF THE CATHOLIC Church, was dead. The common people rejoiced, for he that they had called the 'fat carl in a red hat' was a symbol of everything that was odious about the Church, its wealth and display and easy living, its preferential treatment, its evasion of the law. The eminent men at Court rejoiced, for he had blocked the way to advancement, and as long as he lived there was the risk that the King would recall him. The gentry rejoiced, blaming him for the taxes they hated to pay. And the King mourned.

He was at the butts at Hampton Court when Cavendish, Wolsey's gentleman-usher, brought the news. Wolsey had been arrested for treason, for allegedly having advised the Pope to excommunicate Henry and having planned a Spanish invasion on the Queen's behalf, and Harry Percy, recently become Earl of Northumberland on his father's death, had been sent with the warrant to bring Wolsey to the Tower.

'I hope Harry enjoys his revenge,' Anne had said to Nanette when she heard he had been given the task. 'He owes all his misery to that man.' But Harry Percy had been a gentleman-usher to Wolsey too, and there was that about the man, even aged and sick, which demanded reverence. Word came that he had not been equal to telling his former master he was arresting him, and in the end Wolsey, knowing full well what he was there for, had to prompt him. In a large train they had started for London, and had stopped the night at Leicester Abbey on November the twenty-ninth, and there, a few days later, the Cardinal had died of the flux.

Cavendish reported the story and repeated his master's last words to Henry with tears in his eyes, for Cavendish had been with Wolsey since his childhood. Henry's eyes, too were wet.

'I wish he had lived,' he said. 'He was my friend.'

Nanette glanced at Anne. Standing near the King, she had received the news pale-faced, and had managed to shew no gladness or relief, but now her eyes involuntarily closed, and Nanette saw her sigh. She knew that Anne always feared Wolsey, and even after his arrest there had been no surety that the King would not pardon him and take him back into favour. Indeed, his words now indicated that he had never intended his 'friend' to suffer the final penalty. Cavendish and Henry were talking now about the Cardinal's debts, and how they were to be paid.

'His servants' wages must be settled,' the King said and, clapping Cavendish's shoulder, added, 'Yours too, George, I'll be bound. How much does he owe you? A year? Ten pounds, is it not?'

Cavendish, still weeping, could only nod. The King shook his shoulder affectionately.

'You loved him too, didn't you, George? Well, his estate must be settled—will you take care of breaking up the Household and paying off the servants? Will you do this for him—and for me?'

'Of course, Your Grace,' Cavendish said shakily.

'And then, when that is done, will you join my Household? Will you serve me, George?'

'Oh Your Grace—'

'Now, now, George, straighten up, man. You loved your master and were faithful to him. Everyone has need of faithful servants, most especially a King. If you will serve me as faithfully as you served Tom, you will have repaid me a hundred-fold. Off with you now, I have much to do. Come, Anne.'

The King turned and walked away down the alley with Anne beside him, and Nanette and Hal Norys fell in behind them, the rest following at a distance.

'Well, my good servant is dead,' Henry said at length. Anne turned to look at him, and her face was angry.

'Your good servant? Now he is dead you choose to forget he was under arrest for treason! And that he worked as much against you as for you while he could. God preserve Your Grace from such servants as that!'

'Of course, you are right,' the King said thoughtfully.

'Now perhaps things will move a little faster, now that Wolsey no longer blocks the way.'

'There is no-one to replace him, you forget that. He was the ablest man in the Kingdom.'

'Perhaps several able men may be better than one alone. Master Cranmer has great abilities.'

'Your chaplain suggested one good idea, Anne, but that does not make him a man of great ability. I like him—he's a thinker—but he cannot replace Wolsey. Besides, his idea of asking the opinion of the Universities of Europe has yielded nothing. Despite being out all summer, and spending vast amounts on gifts, the commission has simply come back with the answer that half Europe is for us and half against, which we knew already.'

They said no more until they had mounted to the private suite, and were in the King's privy chamber, where no Household members were allowed except Henry's closest personal attendants. Hal Norys was the senior of these—he was the only member of the Household privileged to enter the King's bedchamber.

Anne faced the King now, misery in her face.

'What is to be done, Henry? It seems to me there is nothing left to try. The Pope will never grant the divorce, and I am wasting my life for nothing.'

'Now, Anne,' the King said kindly, placing his hands on her shoulders and looking down at her, 'don't you think I suffer as much as you from the delay?'

'No, not as much. Whatever happens, you are still King, but I, what am I? I have sacrificed my youth and my reputation. There is hardly a person of note in all Europe who does not think I am your mistress. I am shamed, and for what?'

'Shamed? Who thinks it shame to be a King's mistress?' Henry asked, frowning. Nanette feared for Anne, never having been able to accept that he was not as dangerous to her as to everyone else.

'*I* think so,' Anne replied. 'I would not be any man's mistress, not for the whole world, and yet I have that reputation. I think it would be better if I went home to Hever, and lived there in obscurity. Perhaps at last the world would forget the stories that attach to my name.'

She had threatened to leave him before, but never in this tone of great dejection. The King, to the surprise and distress of Nanette and Hal, burst into tears.

'Anne, don't leave me! Don't even talk of it!' he cried, taking her in his arms. 'You know that I love you, you know that everything I have done I have done for you. Dearest sweetheart, have I not given you this palace, do I not treat you like a Queen, do you not accompany me everywhere as if you were my Queen?'

'But I am not,' Anne said, crying too now.

'But you shall be! I swear it by God's Holy Rood. You shall be my wife and my Queen and the mother of my sons, and your son shall be King of England. I want no-one but you. Be patient, good sweetheart, and everything will be yours. Only do not, do not leave me.'

Anne leaned against him, and she looked exhausted, like a bird that has been flying against a storm.

'No, I won't. I can't. You are all I can cling to, Henry. I have so many enemies.'

'And many friends, too, darling,' Henry comforted her. 'Thank God princes may yet have trusty friends. Like my dear Hal, here, and your little Nan. You may trust them, you know.'

'And you, Henry? May I trust you?' She looked up at him suddenly, her eyes, brilliant with tears, devastatingly beautiful.

'You shall be Queen. I swear it,' he said. Anne gazed at him for a long moment, as if trying to read his countenance, and then she bowed her head.

'Then I am content,' she said. 'Have I Your Grace's leave to withdraw?'

She curtseyed and went out, and Nanette followed her. In the privacy of her own bedchamber, Anne sat down wearily, and Nanette poured a cup of wine and brought it to her.

'It is almost time to dress,' Nanette said. 'Shall I call for your gown?'

'Not yet—wait a while,' Anne said. 'Oh Nan, I am so weary of the situation.'

'I know. It is hard for you.'

'Harder than anyone can imagine,' Anne went on. 'Dear God, I am almost twenty-nine years old. If I do not marry the King, I can never now marry anyone. I shall have nothing, nothing at all. And the worst thing is—Nan, though I say I would never be anyone's mistress, I don't think I mean it any more. The King—we kiss and caress, but he will not go any further than that, and it rouses in me such feelings—Nan, you know about them, don't you?' Nanette, her feelings in turmoil, nodded. 'I don't want to die never having known love. If the King would take me as his mistress now, I would consent, but he will not. He wants me as his lawful wife, and he will do nothing to jeopardise that. He does not seem to feel the strain as I do.'

'He has many more things to do and think about,' Nanette said. 'He is busy all day long, whereas you—'

'I have too little. And you, Nanette, you have little also. If you had married as you might, you would have had a household of your own to keep. Don't you regret it?'

'I am happy with you, my lady,' Nanette said. 'I would not leave you for a hundred households.'

The winter was bitter, and even with braziers in every room in addition to the fires in the fireplaces, it was impossible to keep warm at Morland Place. If one had to leave the immediate vicinity of a fire to walk to some other part of the house, it was necessary to don a warm cloak as if one was going out of doors. And out of doors it was impossible to leave the environs of the house, for only where the servants had been able to clear the snow was movement possible. Morland Place was cut off even from the city, and remained so for weeks at a time.

Food ran low, and it was necessary to economise. Scurvy broke out, despite the fact that the salt-meat diet was augmented from time to time by fresh meat in the form of those stock animals it was impossible to keep alive. Scurvy was always a threat during the winter, but was normally kept at bay by the oranges and lemons that could be got in the city all through the year, brought in by ship from the hot countries of the world. It was no comfort to anyone to know that Ezekiel was probably in one of those countries at that very moment, having captained the *Mary Eleanor* for that winter's cruise in search of luxury merchandise.

Then, towards the end of January, during one of the temporary thaws, Great Uncle Richard insisted on making the journey from Shawes to Morland Place. As a concession to the weather he rode rather than walked, but the journey was difficult even on horseback, and he arrived chilled and exhausted and had to be put instantly to bed with hot stones at his feet and a draught of mulled wine to warm him inwardly.

'I cannot think what he would be at, to make such a journey at this time, and at his age,' Elizabeth grumbled softly. She was looking wan and pinched herself, for she had given birth just before Christmas to her seventh child, a son they named Henry, and because of the weather and the shortage of food she had not been able to regain her strength. Margaret, too, was suffering, for she was in her eighth month of pregnancy, and was not getting her nourishment she should. The baby was taking everything from her, and she was gaunt except for the greatness of her belly.

Elizabeth turned to the servant who had come with Richard, a young man in his twenties. 'What was your master thinking of, to come so far in this weather?' she asked him.

'I knaw not, Mistress,' he said respectfully. 'Awd Will, the maister's man, come to me last night and said "Jack," he said, "thy maister will to Morland Place int' morning, and I cannat tell him no. Therefore shallta go with him, for I am too old, and he s'd have a young man with him, against need." And so next day we set off.'

'Well, at least he had the sense not to drag poor old Will with him,' Amyas said. 'That would have finished the old fellow off for sure.'

'You forget, husband, that Great Uncle Richard is older than Will by ten years.'

'And you forget, wife, that there is a great difference between master and man. And the Morlands are a tough breed. You, Jack, did not your master say anything to you? Did he not say why he was coming?'

Jack scratched his head thoughtfully. There was scurvy at Shawes as well.

'Nay, Maister,' he said, 'he did not need to tell me owt.'

'Leaving need aside, carl, did he not say why he was coming?' Amyas said impatiently. Jack looked as if he did not like being called carl, but he thought for a moment and then said, 'I cannat think on owt he said, but that he would be at Morland Place. He said he must come.'

Elizabeth touched her husband's arm. 'We shall know when he wakens. He will tell us himself. Jack you had better go to the kitchen and get some soup and warm yourself. No, wait, I will come with you.' She glanced at her husband to explain, 'They might not give anyone a bowl of soup, without my orders— there is so little to eat anyway.'

Richard slept until supper-time, and as soon as he woke, the servant sent for Paul. He came in haste, to find his uncle weak and still a little confused.

'Paul,' he said in a weak voice. 'You are here, then? Or—no, I am at Morland Place, am I not?'

'You are, Uncle, and in my bed. Don't you recognise the carving on the bed posts?' Richard's eyes wandered to the great gilded supporters, and there, amongst the acanthus leaves and grapes were carved wine butts, canting device for the Butts family, and everywhere the hare-and-heather Morland device.

'Aye, the Butts Bed, made for your wedding to little Anne,' he said. 'As good a place to die as any, though I would have preferred my mother's bed, where I was born. Still, perhaps you can move me. Who has that bed now?'

'Amyas and Elizabeth sleep in it,' Paul said. 'But what is this talk about dying?'

'Come, Paul, come, don't sound so surprised,' Richard said, his voice growing stronger now as he came back more to awareness. 'Everyone comes to die at last. You must have been expecting it.'

'Uncle Richard, are you ill?'

'Not ill, only very old, and very tired. When this winter set in, I knew I could not survive it. But I did not want to die at Shawes. I never belonged there. So as soon as the weather broke enough, I set off for home. I want to die at Morland Place, where I belong.'

'But uncle, you may have brought on this weakness by that foolish journey.'

Richard smiled and shook his head. 'I may have hastened death by a few days, but I knew I should never last until spring. Don't be sad, child—I am content to die. This world has nothing more to offer me. I am seventy-two: I have beaten my mother by two years and more.' He chuckled, and Paul knelt beside the bed and took the old man's hand. He realised only then how important Richard was to him. He had been his friend and mentor all his life.

'Uncle, even if you are not interested in life, don't you know that we need you? You may live many years yet.'

'No, Paul, no, you must not be selfish. I have a little while before me to reflect on my life, and to repent of my sins, and to make my peace with God. Let me have tranquility now, if ever you loved me.'

Ashamed, Paul bowed his head.

'Paul, there is one thing that I would you could do for me. I wish with all my heart I could see Micah again before

I die. It is so many years since I saw him. He is my only living son.'

'It shall be done, uncle,' Paul promised.

Amyas, when he heard of the promise, was scornful. 'How could you promise such a thing, Father, when you know there is ten feet of snow outside?'

'If a messenger can get to the road, I think he will find it possible to get through to London. The road is used often enough to keep it fairly clear.'

'It would take weeks to get to London and back, and he may not live so long. And even if they get to London, there is no knowing that Micah will be there.'

'My lord of Norfolk is in London, and where should Micah be but with his master? Besides, would you have me refuse an old man's last request?'

Amyas shrugged. 'You can hardly order a servant to risk his life in this way. And who would offer to go?'

Paul smiled rather grimly. 'Uncle Richard did not bring a young servant with him for nothing. I shall ask him at once.'

Jack did not hesitate for a moment. If his master wanted his son fetched from London, Jack was the man to do it, and the risk was nothing to him. The weather was a difficulty, but no threat, for Jack was born and bred to it, and took it in his stride. It remained only to gather some more volunteers to accompany him, and that was not as difficult as Amyas had supposed, for the young men were thoroughly bored after weeks of being couped up in the house. Four sturdy boys were chosen to go with Jack, and another ten to accompany them as far as the road, for it might be necessary to dig a way through. The five messengers were given the best of the remaining horses, plenty of warm clothes, and a large portion of the entire stock of food, for Elizabeth agreed with Paul that a dying man's request took precedence over the demands of the living.

The men set off with the last of the better weather, and when they had gone the cold came down again like a grey pall, and Morland Place was once again wrapped in blizzards. There was so little to do that Paul was happy to spend much time with Uncle Richard, talking to him and listening to his tales of old times. As soon as he had recovered from his journey he was, by his request, moved into his mother's bed, and Amyas's complaints could not prevail. Amyas and Elizabeth moved into the Butts Bed, and Paul took a pallet on the floor in the same room. Uncle Richard's room soon became the centre of life at Morland Place, for it had to be kept warm, and the warmth attracted those who were not already attracted by the company. James came to hear stories of the Court of King Edward, Elizabeth for tales of the famous Queen, Elizabeth Woodville.

'Was she really beautiful?' she would ask.

'Beautiful, but cold—like the blizzard out there,' Richard would say. 'As white as snow, and as heartless. She used to dress all in white, like a virgin. And she loved only white or colour-less jewels, pearls and crystal and diamonds and moonstones. She was a breathtaking sight. Any other woman would have looked sickly, but in her white gown, glittering with crystal spars, diamonds at her neck and fingers, and with her white skin and silver hair she looked like some unearthly creature, a goddess of snow. Only we knew she was black inside.'

The children and Margaret, creeping into the chamber for the warmth, stayed for tales such as these. The boys wanted to hear about battles, the girls about balls. Only Amyas held aloof, and that was more out of opposition to his father than because he did not want to hear the stories himself.

The snow stopped, and a hard, breathtaking cold set in. The messengers had been gone three weeks. It was so cold that the surface of the snow froze hard enough for men to walk in snow-shoes, and some of Richard's audience deserted him.

Then one afternoon when all who could go out were enjoying the fresh, if bitter, air, Margaret went into labour. Weakened as she was with hunger, she could not bear the struggle to give birth. Elizabeth was with her, and held her hand through her brief agony, and before the servant who had been sent to tell James and Paul had brought them back to the house, Margaret was dead, the babe still inside her.

Her poor misshapen body was laid in its coffin on a draped pall in the chapel, and as many candles as could be found were stood around it, for there were no flowers for her, not even a bare twig. Her husband and father kept the vigil for her; there were no women to do it, for Elizabeth was too weak to kneel long in the cold, and Catherine and Jane were in the city, having been sent to the Lendal house before the bad weather set in to learn the ways of the household of their future husbands.

'It seems so hard that she should die now, in the middle of winter,' Paul said. 'If the young have to die, it should be in spring, when there is hope in the world.'

'There must be a special dispensation for women taken in childbirth,' James said. 'No time to make their peace—God must have a special law for them.'

They mourned her dry-eyed. Paul remembered her mother, whom she greatly resembled. He had never loved Margaret very dearly, because of that.

'Her life was short,' he said, 'but she had what she wanted. She wanted to go to Court, and she wanted to be married, and both of those things she had.'

James looked at him curiously. Paul went on, 'She is not to be pitied. You are the loser by her death. She gave you no son.' They resumed their silence, and the next day the coffin was consigned to the crypt, and only her maid wept for her.

Almost four weeks after they had set off, the messengers returned to Morland Place, bringing with them Micah in his priest's habit, attended by a tall young man in his twenties, a handsome young man with black curly hair and dark eyes, whose good plain clothes showed him to have a wealthy patron. No-one at first recognised him—no-one, that is, but Paul, whose winter-pale face blanched even more at the sight of him.

'Adrian,' he said. The boy fell to his knees and bent his head.

'Sir,' he said, and then, lifting his eyes shyly, 'Father. Will you give me your blessing?'

Paul placed his hand on the springy curls. 'God bless you, my son,' he said. Amyas, watching, seethed inwardly. The spontaneous gestures looked to him thoroughly rehearsed. He saw an air of slyness and calculation about the proud-faced boy, and his father, he felt, was too easily duped. But it was not the time to speak. Micah had to be welcomed and taken to his father. Micah was forty-eight, and his tonsured hair was going grey, but his face was younger, and tanned and healthy, and his blue eyes were very bright and alert.

'Cousin Paul,' he said, 'God's blessing on you and all of your house. I am glad you managed to send me word. Where is my father? How is he?'

'He is very weak, but neither ill nor in pain. He is in my son's bedchamber. You wish to go to him now?'

'Yes, at once, if it is convenient to you?'

'Of course. Come, I will take you.' Paul led the way up the stairs, prepared Richard with a few words, and stayed only long enough to see Micah cross the room and kneel by his father's bed. Paul closed the door and turned away, to find Adrian at his shoulder. Either he had grown, or Paul was beginning to shrink, for the boy was taller than him now—boy, indeed! Adrian was twenty-two, and a man.

'They will want to be alone together,' Paul said. Adrian made no answer, and Paul looked at him curiously. The dark, proud face seemed tight with some restrained emotion, and Paul was coming to realise that it was his habitual expression. Whatever passions raged inside Adrian, no-one ever knew of them. He rode his spirit always on a tight rein, and the strain of it made him seem as taut and quivering as a bow-string. 'How is it with you?' Paul asked at last. 'Are you getting on well? Are you happy?'

'I believe I am well thought of in my lord's house,' he replied. 'But happy—? I do not know.'

'No-one is unkind to you?'

'No sir.' A pause. 'I am happy to be home—to be here,' he corrected himself just too late. Paul was touched. This boy, so much like himself in looks, with that faint look of Ursula about him that made him dearer still, this boy seemed to feel those things for him and for Morland Place that were so sadly lacking in Amyas. Not for the first time, he wished Adrian had been his lawful son, and Amyas the bastard.

'I am happy to see you here. I wish that this could be your home.'

Adrian bent his head, and Paul went on his way, and Adrian's eyes followed him, filled with a longing for something that seemed always beyond his reach.

Richard grew weaker during the night, and the next morning Micah told him he should make his peace with God. The dead cold had not relented, but Richard, turning his failing eyes to the window, said, 'Spring is not far off. I am glad. Will you do what has to be done, my son? I would sooner it were you than any other priest.'

Micah heard his confession, gave him absolution, and administered the last rites, and then sat beside his bed, holding his hand. Richard's thoughts wandered from the contemplation of holy things once more to the world.

'I am glad to die,' he said. 'Already I am out of place. Men are changing. They do not work together for the common good, but strive and compete one with the other, to seize their own benefit. I think the world you leave, my son, will be a colder one than I leave now.' He was silent for a while, and then roused himself to say, 'I would like mass said for me in the chapel here.'

'As long as the chapel stands, it will be said for you, father,' Micah said. 'I promise you.'

The old man closed his eyes, contented. Micah signalled to the servant that the rest of the family should be fetched. Paul came first, for he had not been far away, expecting the call. He knelt and kissed Richard's cheek, and there was the slightest response of a smile. But the eyes did not open again, and even as Paul rose to his feet Richard's life went out gently.

Micah stood up too, and crossed himself, and looked at Paul. 'He made a good death, a good Christian death,' he said. 'I pray God I may go as easily when it is my time.'

'God speed his soul,' Paul said. 'He was a good man.' The tears rose to his eyes despite himself. There was nothing to mourn in a good death in the ripeness of years, yet it seemed somehow an ending, as if a light had gone out that could never be relit. 'With him ends an age,' Paul said. 'He was the last of his generation.'

Unconsciously he was echoing Richard's own words. As Paul wiped the tears from his face with the back of his hand, Micah searched for some words of comfort for his cousin.

'He was full of years,' he said at last. 'Don't grieve for him.'

'I think I am grieving for us who are left,' Paul said.

Richard was buried in the crypt under the chapel at Morland Place, near to the remains of his mother and of his childhood companion, Paul's father Ned. Micah was staying at Morland Place for a few more days in the hopes that the weather might improve and make the return journey easier, and Paul was doubly glad of this, for it gave him more time to get to know his bastard son. Adrian improved on him with each meeting. Paul spent long hours with him in the steward's room or the dining parlour or the solar, wherever they could be alone, and Adrian shewed him respect and affection, and revealed a good intelligence and sound principles.

It was not long before Paul was missing Uncle Richard more particularly, for he had always been used to seeking advice from him, and now he had no-one to consult over Adrian. Paul wanted to do something more for the young man than he had done already, and would gladly have consulted Richard as to what would be best. It was perhaps natural that he should turn, instead, to Micah.

'What do you make of him?' Paul asked Micah one day, finding him alone in the chapel.

'Adrian? It's hard to say. He is a young man of extraordinary abilities. He performs his duties to everyone's satisfaction, and leads a most abstemious life.'

'But?'

'I was not aware that I said "but",' Micah said with a smile.

'You did not, but the tone of your voice implied a doubt. What is it? You have some reservations about him. Is he not Godly?'

'He lives a very proper life, and observes his religion as punctiliously as he performs every secular duty. I don't know that I have reservations. I do not know of anything against the young man, and that is the truth. But there is something about him that makes me uneasy. What goes on inside him is a secret he keeps too well.'

'You have no evidence that he is not virtuous?' Paul said anxiously.

'None at all. But I worry about him a great deal. I wish I could love him.'

'I can love him,' Paul said. Micah raised an eyebrow. 'I am thinking of bringing him home, giving him some position here on the estate—what think you of that?'

'It would be good for him, in the worldly sense, and perhaps it would improve his heart to know himself loved and wanted. But what position can you give him? I think you esteem him too much to make a servant of him.'

'A servant? No, I would not have him a servant.'

Micah shook his head. 'I am sorry if I offend you, but anything else would be an affront to your other son.'

'It is not his business.'

'At all events I do advise you to speak to him first, before you say anything to Adrian.'

'Very well. I will do that,' Paul said unwillingly.

Amyas's reaction was violent.

'Have that bastard here? No! I won't hear of it.'

'*You* won't hear of it?' Paul, who had intended to be quiet and firm, caught heat from Amyas's anger.

'I won't have him in the house. Have you gone out of your mind, Father?'

'I think you must have gone out of yours. I am the master of Morland Place. What I do here is my business.'

'It is my business too, especially when it touches my honour.'

'It does not concern your honour. If I choose to bring a young man into the household, that is my affair. And this young man has great qualities, intelligence and virtue, which fit him for a position in the household.'

'This young man, you call him! Everyone knows he is your bastard, and everyone would talk about it. How you would favour him, even over your own son, your true son. I am heir to Morland Place, and my sons will have it after me. The inheritance is mine, and the family honour is part of my inheritance. I will not have my sons brought up side by side with your child of shame—if he is yours. Who can say whether you were really his father.'

Paul's eyes narrowed. 'Remember, if it comes to it, no-one can ever be certain who his father is.'

Amyas sneered. 'You may impute shame to my mother, as you ill-treated her when she was alive, but she was your lawfully wedded wife, and nothing can alter that. And I am your lawful son—your only lawful son—think what you like. If you have no care for me or for my mother's memory, or even for your own honour, remember your grandchildren, remember the Morland name. What will you give them? Will you have them despise you?' He knew he had hit home there. 'I say again, I will not have your bastard here.'

Paul was defeated, and he knew it. 'Though I was not wed to his mother, he is as much my son as you are. He is your own kin—does that mean nothing to you?'

Having won, Amyas could afford to be generous. 'I wish him no harm. All other things equal, I wish him well. Just so that my honour and my sons' honour be not touched.'

Paul turned away, sick at heart. 'I will send him away. It seems that I blight love wherever I find it, like a frost. From first to last, it seems that I cannot have what I love around me.'

Amyas looked at him coldly. 'Perhaps rather it is your fault that you cannot love what you have around you,' he said. Paul stared at him in surprise. But it was much too late now to wonder if Amyas missed his love; his name and his fortune Paul could give him, but not, anymore, his love.

'I will send him away,' he said again, and left the room.

The weather was still bitter, but it was better not to stay, Micah thought, and so the next day he set off again, with his attendants, for Court. Adrian went with him, and if he knew anything of the opportunity he had just lost, he concealed it along with every other emotion behind his proud, handsome, but inexpressive face.

Thirteen

HROVE-TIDE WAS LATE THAT YEAR, FALLING IN MARCH, AND the Lenten fast began and still the north was in the grip of the great cold. The Morlands went into the city for mass on the first Sunday in Lent, and they rode or walked along a road packed hard with frozen snow, between high white banks where it had drifted or been thrown by the men digging the path through. It had not snowed for over a week, but it was so cold that the last fall had not melted, nor any falls before that, right back to the beginning of the year.

After mass, despite the cold, the people stood around in the churchyard to talk, for more than ever in the isolation of winter this weekly meeting was welcome. The Butts and the Morlands gathered in the lee of the porch. Catherine and Jane were there, and greeted Elizabeth rapturously, demanding all the news she could give. They were to be married at Easter, and already there was a great improvement in their behaviour. Under the stern and watchful eye of Lucy their wild ways had been driven out of them like so many devils, and though they still chattered and giggled like a pair of starlings they were no longer likely to bring disgrace on the family. Their husbands-to-be, John and Bartholomew, were sensible, hard-working young men, both with the Butts fairness and light good looks, and the two girls were anxious for their approbation.

The talk was mostly about the weather and the difficulties it had brought. Ploughing was still impossible, so only quick-growing crops would be planted this year, which meant shortage next winter; more sheep and cattle than usual had died because of the extended winter, which meant shortage next year; hundreds of peasants had died, which meant there would be fewer people to do the work of the land, and that, too, would mean shortage. It was very bad. Master and man alike discussed the trouble, united by their common predicament; and master and man alike looked gaunt and pale in the bitter winter sunlight.

Paul had a separate problem to contemplate. A group of spinsters and weavers approached him in his corner of the churchyard to discuss it with him.

'We would have waited until the manor-court was called, Master,' said their ring-leader, a burly weaver called Will, 'only who knows when that will be, and things is very bad.'

'That they are,' Paul said. The factory closed for almost two months, no cloth made, and what there was was held up in the warehouses because of the weather.

'That's right, Master,' Will said, nodding his grizzled head, which seemed to balance on a neck grown too thin and weak for it. Will had always been a stout, even a fat man, but the famine had reduced him, and his skin seemed to hang on him in loose folds. Starvation haunted his eyes, but still he managed to be cheerful. 'It's hard for you, I grant, but it's worse for us, you see, because when we don't work we don't get paid, and then what are we to do when the price of grain goes up? We haven't starved because we've what we grow ourselves, our own cabbages, and what's left of t'pig we killed at Candlemas, God rest his soul for why should not a pig be a Christian too? And a few eggs—'

'How did you keep pig alive until Candlemas, Will?' asked one of his friends with great interest.

'Why, we brought him into t'house i' the warm,' Will said, grinning, 'and fed him off our table until he were ready to feed us. Aye, and we slept wi' him too, and right warm it were wi' him on one side and wife on t'other. But it doesn't change the fact that we have eaten all we can grow, and now we need money to buy bread until the new crops come in.'

'I do what I can for you,' Paul said, 'though God knows there is little enough for each of you, when what is given at the gates has to do for so many.'

'Aye, we know, Master, and we know you are a good, kind man, and your lady daughter too, God bless her,' Will said, 'for she's always about t'poor folks' houses doing what she can, and a blessed angel from heaven could not be more welcome than she is. But it's like this, Master—if we had worked at home instead of in your factory, we could have worked on many a day when it were too bad outside to go all the way to Brazen's Mill. And it's cruel hard to take a man out of his house on a bitter day to walk to his work, instead of him just going up the ladder to his loft and his loom.'

'Aye, and another thing,' said a woman, 'it's cruel hard to take a man away from his home, when there's work to be done there. I cannat chop t'wood and dig up t'clamps, as well as everything else I have to do, and when my man gets back from t'mill he is too cold and too tired to do it. When he worked upstairs he helped me with ploughing and sowing and tending t'beasts.'

'But what is it you want me to do?' Paul said helplessly.

'Close t'factory, Master,' Will said concisely, 'that's what.'

'Let us go back to the old way,' said someone else. 'It's not natural for a man to be working away from his home.'

'Nor for a woman,' said another. 'My bairns are growing wild for want of order.'

'But the factory is to your advantage as well as mine. If you all work at home, I have to employ men to bring you the wool and collect the cloth, and those men have to have horses or mules. It costs more, and so I pay you less. Don't you see that?'

'Aye, that's very well, but we had liefer be at home for all that. We have not been able to work for much of this winter. We could have worked if we had been at home.'

'Well I promise you that I will think about it,' Paul said. 'If I were to close the factory, it would take time to arrange matters, so for the time being you must continue with it the way it is. Does everyone who works in the factory agree with you?'

'Aye, Master, all are agreed, bar that wicked slut Maggie Finch that lives alone over to Highbury, and she does not signify. We are all agreed, and I was chosen to speak for us. We trust you, Master, we know you will not do us wrong. But we do not want to work at Brazen's Mill, and that's the truth on't.'

The family went for dinner at the Butts house afterwards, and John Butts listened with interest to Paul's account of the meeting, and then said, 'I cannot say I am very surprised. I know how the outlying people feel about being away from their homes. In the city things are a little different, of course, for most people no longer work on the old systems.'

'I am not surprised either,' Amyas said. 'Imagine having that long walk to Brazen's Mill every day to work when you know there are things to be done at home. And in bad weather it must be dreadful. I wonder the system was ever thought of.'

'It worked very well,' Paul protested mildly. 'It worked for Jack of Newbury—he died almost as rich as Cardinal Wolsey, and those who worked for him were very happy.'

'So it is said,' John Butts smiled.

'Our own people were happy enough with the arrangement,' Paul reminded him. 'It is only this very bad winter that has changed their minds. By summer they will have forgotten about it.'

'You mean you are not going to close the factory?' Amyas said disapprovingly.

'I promised them I would think about it, and I have done. In their own interests we must carry on as we are. To change back to the old way would be so costly that I doubt if there would be anything much for wages for them for some time. And, as I said, when the good weather comes they'll be happy enough.'

'Yes, and when next winter comes, they'll be unhappy again,' Amyas said. 'You don't care about the hardship to them, do you? You have no pity for them, dragged away from their houses, forced to walk for miles through any weather, neglecting their land and their animals, hardly ever seeing their children, just so long as your precious cloth gets made—'

'Amyas, stop,' Paul said sharply. 'You are talking nonsense, and you are being impertinent. Apologise.'

Amyas muttered something sullenly, and John Butts said reasonably, 'After all, it is only the spinsters and weavers who are complaining. The carders and washers and tenters, the dyers and shearers and millers and fullers all have to work away from their homes anyway, and always have, and they don't find it wrong or unnatural or very much of a hardship. I shouldn't worry about the weavers, Amyas. They'll settle down again, as Paul says, when the good weather comes.'

'Whenever that will be,' Paul said with something of a sigh. 'It seems as though this winter has been with us for ever and will last until the Second Coming.'

Strangely, after those words, the thaw started the very next day. As soon as Paul poked his nose outside the bed-curtains he could smell the change in the weather. The sun, when the shutters were opened, was less brilliant than it had been yesterday, but was much warmer. After a hurried breakfast he set off with an attendant for the factory, anxious to see what the mood of the weavers was in view of the change in the weather.

The factory was set up at the side of the tenter-field, a little downstream from Brazen's Mill on the bank of a tributary of the River Ouse which the local people called Akburn. The journey on horseback was a little complicated by the beginnings of the thaw, for the melting snow was slippery and once or twice the horses sank into pockets of soft snow and had to flounder their way out, and Paul guessed that by the time he went home again it would be even more difficult. He sighed inwardly, wondering if it meant yet more days when the factory would have to be closed.

Work was going on when he arrived. The factory was a simple rectangular building of stone with a deep thatched roof and a great chimney at each end, and was chiefly famous for having glass windows, unlike any building in the area except Morland Place. These had been put in by great-grandmother Eleanor Courteney in order that there should be light enough inside to work even during the worst weather. Inside was a single, long room, kept warm by a huge log fire in the fireplaces at either end. There were rushes on the floor, and placed in two even rows down the room were the great looms, and the spinning wheels. As Paul had said, on the whole the people who worked in the factory had been happy enough. It gave them a sort of status amongst their neighbours, other than those who thought everything modern came straight from the Devil, and it gave them an opportunity for friendly intercourse every day instead of just once a week at the Sabbath Mass.

Paul spent some time there, inspecting and encouraging, and evading questions, and then went on to visit the dyeing-house and finally the mill itself. The mill-keeper was a small, lively man who had grown old in possession of his present job, and he loved the mill like a child, and he loved the Akburn like a mistress. Paul found him in gloomy humour.

'It's a bad business altogether, Master, that it is,' he said shaking his head. 'This weather has been sent by the Almighty to test our faith, in my opinion. And tested we shall be. First the snow, then the long freeze, and now this thaw—we shall have trouble before the week's out, mark my words.'

'What sort of trouble?' Paul asked, wondering if he had heard of the weavers' discontent. The mill-keeper raised his eyebrows in surprise that Paul had not already considered it.

'Why, Master, with the water, of course. Look, come look.' He hobbled nimbly up the stairs and Paul followed him to the upper storey where a platform ran round the outside of the mill for the purpose of servicing the windsails. Though the mill was a water-mill, it had subsidiary windsails which worked a small mill for grain, mostly used by the local villagers. The mill-keeper led Paul to the parapet and they both leaned over and looked down at the churning water. The great mill-wheel, its wood dark with water and glistening with green slime, turned endlessly, the white of the broken water almost too bright, by contrast, to bear.

'See, now, Master, see how angry she's getting.'

'Is she?' Paul asked, puzzled.

'Th'Akburn,' he elucidated. 'She's a lot faster already, and the thaw has only been with us a few hours. Don't you see, Master, all that snow that's been lying about for week after week, it'll all melt now and drain into the rivers, and down they will come, faster and faster.'

Paul considered it. 'But that will be good, won't it? It will give you more power in the mills.'

The mill-keeper nodded, but went on, 'Aye, that's so, and as far as it goes it's very well. But up yonder,' he nodded upstream, 'there are two or three little streams that run into her, and there's also the Wake Dyke, that keeps the water back for the Wake Mill. Unnatural that is,' he said in disgust, contemplating his turning wheel, 'interfering with the run of a river, and such a river as this, who is as sweet and obliging as ever a Christian soul could be. Why, I've known this river since I was a child, played by it—and in it, God knows! Many's a time I've tumbled in, and many's a time she's carried me safe on her bosom to the banks. Why—'

'Yes, of course,' Paul interrupted, trying to bring him back to the point, 'but what is it you fear from the thaw?'

'Why, Master, I s'd have thought it were obvious. When the great weight of thaw-water presses against that dyke, it will very likely break, and then all the water will rush down here, and my mill-wheel will not be able to turn fast enough, and it will be smashed.'

'And is there nothing you can do?'

'I shall do what I can, to be sure. I'll watch her like a hawk, and I'll open the paddles up to their widest as the water comes faster, but if that dyke breaks—' he shook his head. 'It'll be a bad thing, Master, and I won't deceive you.'

It was another thing to worry about. Paul dreamt that night of rushing water, and the next morning he rode through mud and slush back to the mill to check on the condition of the water. The difference was already apparent. Where yesterday the Akburn had been a busy, swift-flowing river, seemingly bent on its task of turning the wheel, today it looked angry and swollen. Its surface was touched with foam and bits of debris floated past, twigs and other frag-ments rushing downstream and spinning a little as they went. The wheel was turning faster too, and Paul could hear it groaning as he climbed the stairs to the platform. The mill-keeper was anxious.

'If it gets no worse than this, it will be all right,' he said, 'but the paddles are open almost to their limit, and I cannot answer for it if the dyke goes. There are things coming down the river I have not seen before. A dog went through this morning, and only by a miracle it did not get caught in the paddles. Look at all these twigs and branches! I am up and down with the pole all day, clearing stuff away.'

Looking down, Paul shivered. The sight of the great, black, dripping wheel was today somehow ominous, and the water that churned and raged through it was streaked with yellow, turgid and oily and wicked, its foam like bared teeth. Paul decided not to go home. 'If the mill-wheel was smashed, it would be a very bad thing—there would be great expense and much time involved in replacing it. But perhaps the dyke would not break. Why should it?'

'Because it is badly made, Master, that's why,' the mill-keeper said. 'Built by a Dutchman, so they say, and how is he to know what our rivers are like here? I've seen it, and I wouldn't give a plucked hen for it, no, nor for its chances of staying together against a thaw-flood.'

At dinner time Elizabeth, who had been visiting some sick villagers nearby, rode to the mill with her maid, for Paul's talking about the river and the mill last night had made her anxious.

'It looks bad,' Paul told her. 'The keeper thinks the Wake Dyke will go, and then the mill-wheel will surely go too.'

Elizabeth looked anxious. 'There seems no end to the troubles the thaw is bringing. With the warm weather and the damp, there were fogs down below yesterday and today, and you know how fogs breed pestilence. I was visiting today, and I'm much afraid there will be fevers of all sorts before the week is out.'

Paul was concerned. 'You must take care of yourself, Elizabeth. You do too much, and you are not strong. If there is fever in the village, you must avoid it. You could not resist it in your condition.'

Pale, thin Elizabeth smiled wanly. 'If it is my time to go, God will take me, and if it is not, I fear no ill. There is much consumption there already, and I cannot turn my back on the suffering.'

Paul put a hand on her shoulder. 'You are a good woman. You make me ashamed. Will you go home now?'

'No, I think I will stay here,' she said. 'I cannot be easy in my mind while the fate of the mill is in the balance. Will you come with me now and eat something, Father? I have some bread and some cheese and some pasties in my saddle bag.'

They ate in the mill-keeper's quarters in reasonable comfort, and asked him to join them, but he would not, for he could not bear to leave his observation post for a moment. The paddles were now wide open, and inside the millhouse the groaning of the wheel and the machinery had become a cacophony. It was like being inside a drum that was being beaten. With great labour the mill machinery was uncoupled from the wheel, otherwise the mill might have flogged itself to bits.

Through the afternoon they waited, staring at the river from the platform and willing it to recede. But it grew more and more swollen, and began to lap over its banks. It was only then the possibility of flood suggested itself to Paul, and he hastened to send the factory workers home. He was still supervising their departure when there was a faint but anxious shout from the direction of the mill. Looking over his shoulder, he saw the small figure of the mill-keeper dancing on the outside platform in his effort to attract attention.

'It must be the dyke!' Paul cried. 'Go on, all of you, get away as fast as you can.' He flung the words over his shoulder as he ran, faster than he had ever run before, towards the mill. His breath sobbed as he ran up the stairs, to encounter the mill-keeper and the two women on the platform.

'Look, Master, look! It's coming. I told ye! It's coming! Oh my poor river, oh my poor wheel! What's to do? A curse on the fool that made that dyke!'

Even while he was jabbering out his distress, his Master had rushed to the parapet and leaned over. It was a terrifying sight. Upriver, and rushing down towards them like a galloping horse, was the crest of the running wave of the banked-up floodwater, a dark wave edged with yellow foam.

'Jesu preserve us,' Paul cried, crossing himself. It was terrible, and frightening. What could withstand it?

'The factory,' Elizabeth said. 'The weavers—they'll be drowned! The villagers—everybody will be drowned. I must help them.' And she darted for the stairs.

'No, Elizabeth, no, stay here! I have sent the weavers home, and you cannot help anybody now.'

'Stay here Mistress—you'd have no chance outside,' the keeper said. 'The millhouse is sturdy built, we'll be safer here.'

'We'd better go inside,' Paul said, grabbing for Elizabeth's arm.

'Hold on, here it is,' the mill-keeper yelled, and flung himself towards them, gathering the maid Betty in a surprisingly strong arm as he did, and then the wave hit them. There was a tremendous crash, and a shrieking, tearing groan like the earth being torn open as the force of the wall of water smashed through the mill wheel. The four people grabbed for posts or rails, as with a shudder that shook the whole building the wheel was wrenched from the mill and smashed against the bank. The flood-wave leapt up the walls like a ravening wolf, and with a rending noise the outside platform collapsed. Soaked, shaken, with bleeding hands they scrambled and fought for the door as the platform slid out from under their feet, and as the upsurge of water hit him, blinding him, Paul felt the edge of the door jamb under his fingers and clung for his life. He was almost jerked loose as the last of his foothold fell abruptly away, and dimly he heard the cries of the others, dimly he realised they had gone, fallen with the wooden platform into the murderous flood. But he was too exhausted and stunned to understand. For minutes he clung to the door frame, his body dangling over the river, his feet in their soft leather boots scrabbling for a hold, and then as his raw hands grew numb, he let go, fell briefly through the air, and into the water.

He had had a long dream, a confused and horrible dream, and the black, bitter taste of it was in his mouth as he drifted back into consciousness. He did not know at first where he was or even when it was. His head ached so savagely that thought of any kind was difficult, and every breath seemed to be made of pure fire, and dragged into lungs that were pinned with sword-blades to his back. It was dark, only a small glow from a candle lighting his immediate surroundings, which were dark red. Was he in Hell? Was this the beginning of the eternal torment? Yes, that must be it—he was hot, consumed with heat, and breathing pure fire. Despairing, he drifted back into unconsciousness.

When he woke again, it was with the sense that a long time had passed. It was daylight, and he was rational. He was in his own bed, with the crimson cover and curtains, in his own room at Morland Place. His head ached, and his chest ached and he felt very weak and spent, and he could not move any part of his body, but he knew where he was. Somehow, by some miracle, he had survived the flood. Painfully he turned his head and discovered a servant dozing by his bedside with Alexander at his feet. He tried to speak but made only a croaking noise. It was enough to make the dog whimper, waking the servant, who ran to fetch Amyas.

Soon, Amyas was there, bearing a cup from which wonderful smells arose.

'Hot spiced wine,' Amyas said. 'Drink first, Father, it will revive you.' As gently as a woman, he lifted his father's shoulders and held the cup for him to drink. The hot, invigorating liquid made Paul cough at first, but soon sent a wonderful tingling through his limbs and brought life to them. His left arm, he discovered, was tied rigid and immobile to a splint, but otherwise he seemed undamaged.

Amyas put the cup aside, and then beckoned forward a page with a bowl and spoon, and when Paul was propped comfortably in a sitting position with the softest, feather-filled pillows the house could provide, Amyas sat beside him on the bed and fed him, spoon by spoon, with broth, and in between mouthfuls, told him what had happened.

'How long have I been in bed?' Paul asked first.

'Ten days,' Amyas said. 'You were close to death. The doctor said you had a fever in the lungs, and that it almost always proved fatal, but God spared you, for which we have given thanks in the chapel at every spare moment of the day and night. Your left arm is broken, but healing, and you had a terrible wound on the head. We feared you might have lost your reason by it, but that, too has healed.'

'What happened?' Paul asked.

'The flood waters came down, it seems, in a great wave.'

'Yes, I saw it. It hit the mill,' Paul said. Amyas hurried on.

'The wooden structures outside the mill collapsed. The water flooded the tenter-field. The factory is damaged, all the looms smashed to splinters. Three villages have been flooded, and God only knows how many villagers are missing. We have given alms to many who have lost everything they had, and I hear there are hundreds homeless. The abbeys have taken many of them in, but what they will do afterwards I cannot tell.'

There was something Paul was trying to remember, but it would not come to him. 'I fell into the river,' he said, frowning. His mouth closed automatically over another spoonful of broth.

'You were washed downstream a long way, and finally brought up against a tree-trunk growing out of the bank. That's what broke your arm, we think, for you seemed to be trapped by it, wedged in the roots. Our men were already out looking for you, and a party of them found you and brought you in.' He shuddered. 'They brought you in on a hurdle. I shall never forget it.'

But Paul was not listening. A voice had floated up from his memory, a voice saying, 'Many's a time she's carried me safe on her bosom to the bank.' That was what he was trying to remember—what—who—? Suddenly it came to him in a terrible illumination of anguish. 'The mill-keeper. Elizabeth. What happened to them? There were four of us—what happened to Elizabeth?'

'They were killed,' Amyas said, and passed a hand over his face. 'Their bodies were found when the flood started to go down. The mill-keeper and Betty were not far away, tangled up in the wreckage of the wheel and the balcony. Elizabeth—' He paused and swallowed—'Elizabeth was carried downstream. They found her on the shingle beach at the curve where the Akburn meets the Ouse. They were all—horribly broken. We don't know how you escaped.'

Paul's mind was working fast now. 'They fell before me. They went in at the same time as the platform collapsed. It must have been being tumbled about in the water with the wreckage—' He couldn't finish. 'When I fell, the water was clear. I suppose that's what saved me.'

Amyas wiped the tears from his face with his sleeve. 'Father, I can't tell you what I have been feeling. I know that I have been punished. Elizabeth—I loved her. She was a good woman, mother of my children, and I loved her truly, but I treated her so badly, and God has punished me by taking her in this way. I have spent so long on my knees I hardly know how to straighten up, begging for forgiveness. Oh Father—' He broke off, and it was a while before he could resume. 'And I have behaved badly towards you, too, Father. I have been undutiful, and God has opened my eyes to that, too. I have brought suffering on so many. I do not know what I can ever do to atone.'

'My son, my son, do not give way. Calm yourself, my dear child,' Paul, said, reaching a hand to stroke Amyas's arm.

Amyas seized it and pressed his face to it, still sobbing, and as Paul watched him a feeling of revulsion came over him. Why did Amyas's words ring so hollow? It was as if Amyas were playing the part of the grief-stricken husband to the enthralled audience of himself, saying and doing what he imagined fitted the occasion, flinging himself into the role with as much abandon as he had brought to the role of rake and debauchee about the taverns of York.

Even as a child, Amyas had always wanted to be the centre of attention, and as his father's darling and his tutor's pride he had found it easy. Now in adulthood it seemed he would adopt any part that fitted his purposes or his image of himself. That was why the grief did not ring true. Amyas loved only Amyas. Paul tried to withdraw his hand, but Amyas had it in a tight grip, and he could only wait until the show of anguish was over.

By Lady Day the flood waters had receded, and it was possible to begin to assess the damage. The factory was not damaged beyond repair, but the weavers more than ever did not want to work in it, and there was no alternative but to restore the old, time-consuming method of home-working. The mill-wheel would have to be replaced, and the banks of the river from the mill all along the tenter-field needed to be rebuilt and strengthened. All that would cost money.

There was great loss of life in the three villages that had been drowned, and several of the workers who had not fled quickly enough were also lost. The fever—some called it marsh-fever, some smoke-fever—which sprang up in the wake of the flood-water took off many more, amongst whom was Amyas's youngest son Henry, who sucked the fever from his wet-nurse.

Another loss to Paul was that of thirty breeding ewes who had been drowned in the floods. They would have to be replaced, and that would cost money. And then there was the prospect of his nieces' wedding in April, when their dowries would fall to be paid—where was the money to be found? But here, at least, relief was at hand—John Butts, good Christian soul that he was, married his sons to the girls without dowries, and still made settlements on them.

'You can pay the dowries when you have money enough,' he said. 'We are all one family—how could you imagine I would press for the payment?'

So Catherine and Jane were married one sunny April day at All Saints by the Roman Bridge to the handsome Butts boys. Almost immediately Jane and her Bartholomew set off for Calais where Bartholomew was to study and eventually take over the Staple office; John was to remain in York to help his father in the business. Paul, after much thought, sold one of the outlying estates over towards Osberwick, and with the money paid the dowries and bought new stock, and with what was left began the rebuilding of the mill-wheel.

His arm healed, but it healed crooked and almost useless;

his head healed, but there was a jagged scar across his forehead which he would carry for life; and when he finally rose from his bed and took a first look in the mirror, he was shocked to see that his hair had turned quite grey. The most noticeable change, however, was in his relationship with Amyas. Amyas ceased from that time to haunt the city, and Paul in return gave up much more of the running of the estates and the business to Amyas. They still argued about most things, but it was not so rancorous as it had used to be, and Amyas no longer disagreed simply for the pleasure of taunting Paul. Amyas the reformed rake and dutiful son might not be any easier to love than Amyas the sinner, but he was certainly easier to live with.

Fourteen

*N*OW AT LAST THINGS WERE MOVING ALONG; NOW AT LAST it seemed as though the thing they had waited for these six years might truly be within their grasp. Queen Catharine had been sent away and was living in a small house near Dunstable with what she considered a paltry household of only four hundred servants. The Princess Mary was at Richmond, and not allowed to see her mother. Neither of them would yet accept that they had lost the battle, supported and encouraged as they were by the two Spanish ambassadors and a number of bishops, and ultimately by the Pope himself who continued to plead, if quietly, with Henry to take back Catharine to his bed.

Christmas was spent quietly, and the new year of 1532 came in, accompanied by the usual gifts. Queen Catharine sent the King a gold cup, which he put aside without acknowledging. His gift to Anne was the redecoration of her apartments in Whitehall with hangings of crimson satin and cloth-of-gold, hers to him a set of ivory chess-men, and each was delighted with the other. Nanette gave Anne a cushion covered with black velvet on which she had embroidered a design of pansies in the dark, rich colours that Anne loved, purple and crimson and tawney; and Anne gave Nanette a chestnut-and-white spaniel puppy. Nanette named him Ajax, which made Anne laugh.

'You could hardly have chosen a more inappropriate name,' she said. 'If he is anything like his mother, he is no mighty warrior—more like a coney's kitten.'

'Hush, you'll hurt his feelings,' Nanette protested. 'It is to comfort him for his small stature that I have given him such a large name.'

The two of them were sitting in Anne's apartments at their embroidery. Close by were Madge and Mary Wyatt, and at a little distance a number of other lady attendants, for now Anne kept state like a queen and one of the trials of that state was always being surrounded by attendants. Anne now, however, did not seem to mind it. She had grown gentler, more digni-fied, and her wild hysterical rages, that had stemmed mainly from frustration and helplessness, had disappeared. To Nanette she seemed already a queen.

The difference had been made by one Master Thomas Cromwell, who had been secretary to Cardinal Wolsey who had changed to the King's service just before the Cardinal's death—by, it was said, the Cardinal's own command. Cromwell was a very different kind of person from his old master. He was a dark, sleeky handsome man in his mid-forties. His origins were obscure—his father had been a blacksmith—but under the Tudors these things did not matter too much. Cromwell had studied banking and commerce in Italy and Holland, and law in London, and had a brilliant and shrewd brain and an innovative method of thinking which made him as much a creator as the artists he so deeply admired.

He was, besides, a cultivated man, with polished manners, able to put people at their ease; a witty man with whom it was a pleasure to converse; a great patron of the arts, whose house in Throgmorton Street was stuffed with paintings and books and objets d'art, each of which he knew and loved with the inti-macy of a true connoisseur. He kept the best table in London, and even those stiffest-necked of the nobles who resented the progress of a self-made man did not refuse an invitation to dine there, and Cromwell was notable as the only man in London able to dine protagonists of each side of the Secret Matter simultaneously. He was also just and humane, a great giver of charity, and a promoter of many an honest man; his servants spoke well of him, which said much.

Cromwell's arrival as the King's adviser had led to the subject of the divorce being dropped, for he had another matter for his master to consider. One of the books in Cromwell's library was an Italian work called *Defensor Pacis*, written two hundred years earlier and containing such revolutionary material that even Cromwell did not dare have it translated into English. One of the points the author made was that since St Peter did not precede the other apostles, he had no claim to supremacy, and since there was no evidence that St Peter had even been in Rome nor had ever been a Bishop, no pope could claim supremacy on the grounds of being his successor.

The logical conclusion of that was that no allegiance was owed to the Pope, and that therefore all the people of England, lay and clergy alike, owed their obedience to the King alone under God. The clergy as a group were so well hated by the contentious English that the King had no worries about there being a general revolt against the idea. Large sums of money in the form of fees and tithes were being paid to the see of Rome which the payers thereof would be glad to retain for their own uses. The lower clergy would be easily brought to accept the edict; the only resistance might therefore be expected from the bishops and from one or two of the nobility and the educated gentry for whom religion was more than a matter of custom.

Cromwell was a lawyer, and the law was his natural element and his weapon. If the clergy were to be subdued, it would be by law, and if the country were to be severed from Rome it would be through the pronouncements of Parliament. The King should be the supreme head of the Church, and anyone who thereafter acknowledged allegiance to the Pope would therefore be guilty of treason, and could be dealt with by the law.

It was a simple, masterly, and utterly revolutionary plan, and while, through the spring of 1532, Cromwell and the King took it through Parliament and slowly brought irresistible pressure to bear on the recalcitrant bishops, Anne sat quietly in her apartments, serene and dignified, and ceased her railing and crying.

'For you see, Nan,' she said to Nanette, 'if the Pope no longer has authority in this land, then he cannot either permit or deny the divorce. It will be for the King and the Primate to do. The end is in sight, my dear friend.'

'But I thought Warham was on Queen Catharine's side,' Nanette said. 'Surely he won't agree to a divorce?'

'No, I believe that silly old man would hold out in the mouth of Hell itself,' Anne said, but without her usual rancour. 'But he is very, very old, and sick into the bargain, and he will not live much longer. And then Henry will appoint my dear Thomas Archbishop of Canterbury, and he will pronounce the divorce. Oh Nan,' she put down her work and looked across at her friend with a sudden smile, 'I am so happy.'

'I have noticed it,' Nanette said, 'And gladly. But—' she hesitated.

'What is it?' Anne asked.

'I should not ask you,' Nanette said. 'It is the idlest of curiosity, and I have no right to ask such a question of you.'

Anne glanced at Mary and Madge who were talking quietly together on the other side of the circle they made around the little Italian table on which the embroidery silks were laid out.

'Ask me,' Anne said. 'Are you not my dear friend? I have no secrets from you.'

'Nor I from you,' Nanette said. 'Then, dearest mistress, I was wondering if you were happy only because the end of the struggle is in sight or if—if you were happy to be going to marry His Grace.'

'Are they not the same thing?' Anne said, raising her eyebrows, and then shook her head slightly, making the light glint from the emeralds that decorated her coif. 'No, no, I understand you. You are right, of course—I do love him. How could I not? No-one who has ever spent any time with him has been able to withstand his charm. God knows, I had little enough cause to love him in the beginning, but—Nan, only consider how good he is to me! How gentle when I am unhappy, how patient when I am angry. I scream at him and abuse him, and he only gentles me and soothes me, as if I were his kestrel bating on his fist.'

'And consider, too, how he loves you,' Nanette said. Anne's face grew tender at the recollection.

'Yes, he does love me, Nanette. I believe never was anyone loved as much as I am by him. All these years he has held by me, protected me, fought for me, and never demanded anything of me. *You* know how often I would have given in to my feelings, to my—my animal nature if he had not loved me well enough to guard my purity like my life.'

'Yes, I know,' Nanette said. So much of Anne's hysteria had stemmed from the repression of her feelings, from the dreadful torment of those times alone in her chamber with Henry, when he would kiss and caress her until she was as wild as a she-cat in season, and then draw back before they could be tempted into the final act. He seemed able to live with this half-and-half state of affairs, but Anne was kept perpetually on the borders of frenzy. No-one but Nanette knew about this, but to Nanette Anne could confess all and be sure of understanding. For had not Nanette felt those same feelings?

'It is the Devil in us,' Anne had said once when they talked of it. 'Men say that women belong more to the Devil than men do, and sometimes I think they may be right. The Devil in us prompts us to these wild longings.'

'You are right,' Nanette said. 'I had not the power to withstand them. You know, dear mistress, how I have sinned. I have prayed and done penance again and again—'

'And I have too,' Anne said. 'I have told all to Master Cranmer, to my dear Thomas. He forgives me and makes me comfortable again, makes my sins seem bad without being overpowering, makes me hate them but without hating myself. And I would have sinned like you, Nan, if it had not been for my dear lord, the King. So you must not think you are more wicked than me. Why do you not change your confessor, go to Cranmer instead? He would make you easy, I know it.'

Nanette agreed, and made the change, and found that Master Cranmer could give her peace too, and for the first time she began to be able to forget the past. The news from Morland Place was all sadness, and when she allowed herself to think of home, she was seized with pity for her uncle's loneliness, and only her oath and her loyalty to her mistress prevented her from going to comfort him—for he loved her, she felt, almost as much as the King loved Anne.

The ladies were sitting thus one morning in the middle of May when the King was announced, and they had barely time to get to their feet before he came in at the door, as always seeming almost to fill the room. Nanette always found his sheer size overpowering. He was heavier now, middle-aged, but it seemed almost sacrilege to think in those terms of a King; and he was still the handsomest prince in Christendom.

'Henry!' Anne exclaimed in pleasure. She did not curtsey—in private she maintained intimacy with him, and he liked it. Only two people in the whole world called him by his Christened name—Queen Catharine, and Lady Anne Rochford. It was a lonely thing to be a King, and it was well to have one person with you on that high eminence you inhabited. 'How good it is to see you. You bring news for us?'

'The best,' the King said, taking her hand and looking down at her with a jubilant smile. 'Today the Bishops returned their answer—they have agreed to enforce the Accusation against the Clergy.'

Anne had no word to say, but her face expressed all.

'So now it is all but done, my lady. Their privileges are removed, their allegiance to Rome removed—Chapuys says that now the clergy have no more status than shoe-makers!'

'Less,' Anne laughed, 'for a shoe-maker who does not perform his craft well will not remain long a shoe-maker, while a priest may be as bad a priest as he will. I would sooner trust a shoe-maker.'

'And sooner promote him?' the King added. 'Ah, but our good friend Thomas is skilled at his trade. His patches souls very neatly, does he not? And he shall sew us together a fine marriage, once we have given him his office.'

'Shall we?' Anne said. 'Shall we truly?' The King lifted her hand to his lips and held it there a long while, and said tenderly, 'We shall, my darling. I promise thee there is not much longer to wait. And then thou shalt be entirely mine, as I am already entirely thine.'

And then he took her other hand, too, and with his eyes on hers kissed her malformed little finger. It was his greatest gesture of love, saying that he loved even her imperfections, as it was Anne's greatest gesture to allow him to do it, she who could hardly bear to touch her hand herself.

'It shall not be long,' the King said again. 'I have spoken this morning to Du Bellay. This autumn we shall go to Calais and meet King Francis, and he shall receive you as my Queen. And you shall have a title, too, my darling.'

'Another title?' she laughed. The King waved that away.

'A title of your own,' he said, 'not merely a small piece of your father's. You shall have a title in your own right, so that all the world may see how much I value you. Especially so that Francis may see how I value you.'

'If I am to go to France I shall need—'

'A hundred new dresses,' the King finished for her, laughing. 'Well, well, and you shall have them. But think of that later. Look, how the sun shines, chiding us for being indoors. I have been closeted all morning. Come with me, and let us go down to the bowling alley for some exercise. George and Hal are growing too cocky since I have not had time to beat them for a week or two.'

'That will never do. They must acknowledge at all times that as well as being their King you are the best bowls-player in the world.'

'Except, perhaps, for your cousin Tom?' the King asked shrewdly. Anne would not be baited. She shrugged it off gaily.

'Who knows how good or bad Tom will be when he comes back from France? They do not play bowls there.'

'You shall find out,' the King said. 'I have more news for you—Master Wyatt will be back at court by Lammas-tide. How like you that, sweetheart?'

Anne's smile was his reward. 'You know well. My dear cousin! How I have missed him!'

'And I too,' the King said sincerely. 'He is the only man I would ever allow to beat me at bowls, and that is only from my great love of him.'

The party went out into the sunshine, and Nanette reflected again on how lonely it must be to be a King.

For Paul, Morland Place had become very melancholy, full of shadows, silences where once there had been speech and laughter and the sound of everyday life. There was no woman of the house now. He promoted one of the older women servants to housekeeper, and she took orders from him and from the steward, and somehow things were done, but it was not the same. His crooked, useless arm confined his activities. He, who had been the best archer, the best tennis-player, the best lutanist for miles around, could no longer do those things. He had also been the best dancer, but there was no dancing now at Morland Place, for there was no-one to dance with. Often and often he thought of Nanette, dancing at court and acting in the masques, conversing and laughing and singing; she represented for him all the things in life he had lost, and at night as he drifted off to sleep he would imagine her coming home to Morland Place, bringing with her all those things that were missing.

He spent much time hunting and riding, for on horseback he could best forget his disability. He could still handle his hawks, but there was something in the death of small birds that now distressed him, and he rarely visited the mews, giving his own birds over to the care of Amyas and to his grandsons, who were learning the gentlemanly pursuits. Paul's closest companion these days was often James Chapham, and the two widowers would ride out together to hunt the deer or the boar or the badger. No Morland for a hundred years had ever hunted the hare.

It was not many months before Paul and his son were quar-relling again, and that summer of 1532 it was religion which caused the falling-out between them. After Elizabeth's death Amyas had given up whoring and gambling and almost given up drinking and had adopted the role of the fanatical upholder of religion. He heard Mass four times a day and more on feast days, spent long periods in silent prayer and contemplation, and generally made everyone's life a misery by his censorious interference with their innocent pleasures.

Parliament's attack on the Church that summer, which Paul in common with most of the people saw as a welcome reform long overdue, Amyas chose to see as the most terrible blasphemy, likely to herald unprecedented horrors by way of divine retribution, and certain to involve anyone consenting to the attack in eternal damnation. He ranted and raved indiscriminately and most indiscreetly against Cromwell, Parliament, the Council, and the King, and condemned the Divorce in the roundest of terms. Paul did his best to curb his excesses, but opposition only made him shout louder, and Paul lived in terror of being implicated in Amyas's treasonable utterances. It was all very well to denounce the attack on the clergy, but when it came to questioning the King's supremacy and putting oneself on the wrong side in the matter of the Divorce, the next thing that might happen was an arrest for treason.

Furthermore, Paul, though he had learnt to despise the Tudor dynasty at his grandmother's knee, could not wish for a female heir or a minority, and thought that Queen Catharine should long ago have resigned herself quietly to the life of a convent. He was a friend of the Boleyns, and of the Norfolks, and his own niece was in a position to be much damaged by the knowledge that her family had arranged itself on the wrong side of the dispute. So he and Amyas quarrelled, and it added another unpleasantness to be borne in that hearth-cold house.

The children were Paul's comfort. They had not learnt to like their father, though they accorded him the respect that was expected of them. It was their grandfather who had always shewn them attention and love, and to him they shewed a deference that was mingled with, and that sprang from, their genuine regard for him. He heard them say over their lessons, listened to their chatter, watched them training their hawks, played with them during their recreation hours, and told them stories when, tumbled sleepily on the hearth with the puppies at the end of the day, they begged for Jack the Giant Killer or Robin Hood and Little John.

Paul taught Robert to ride and to joust, in preparation for the time when he might wear the black lion crest on his helmet at some feast-day tourney. He corrected Edward's grip in archery and his style when he wrestled with Barnaby, the elder boys' page. He taught Young Paul to play the lute, the harp and the gittern, and helped him to polish up the little songs he invented out of his own head. Eleanor he could do little for, except to hold her on his knee at story-time, and hear her say her French. She was not very bright nor very talented, but she had a sweet nature, and she was the only female of the family at Morland Place, and she queened over them in the gentlest way.

He loved the children and James was a good companion, and he had plenty to do in trying to restore the health of the estate, but at night as he lay trying to sleep, often kept from it by the pain in his damaged arm, even more often by the emptiness inside him, it was to Nanette his thoughts turned. If she would but come home, the darkness would lift, the bitterness leave him. She was light, and warmth, and comfort. He prayed to the Holy Virgin for her, never thinking that that might be an unacceptable irony. The deeper recesses of his mind prayed wordlessly to a nameless earth-mother, she who gave birth each spring to the tender, the thrusting green shoots. She had said she might come back, when her mistress no longer needed her: then everything would grow sweet again, and green, and new. He clung to that for his main comfort, not even second to that of the Mass. She had said she would come back.

The light shone against the silk of the tent, throwing strange shadows across it as people inside moved around, passing the torches and candles, and the sound of voices and music was barely muted by the thin fabric. Two liveried boys waited for their musical cue to draw back the two curtains. Their surcoats were blue, and decorated with the lilies of France, and they rolled their eyes nervously towards the group of eight masked ladies who waited to make their entrance.

The ladies, too, were nervous, but if they shivered it was more likely because Calais in October was cold, and their clothing had been designed for show and not for comfort. They were all dressed alike in crimson satin gowns over cloth-of-gold kirtles, and their masks and headdresses were of gold sewn with pearls, and they wore no veils, their hair streaming loose down their backs in a way calculated to rouse men's passions. Inside the tent was a great company presided over by two kings—the King of France and the King of England—before whom they would have to dance.

Nanette stood second in the line. In front of her was Anne, Marquess of Pembroke, who would one day soon be Queen of England, and beside her was Mary Howard, daughter of the Duke of Norfolk and betrothed of the King's bastard son, the Duke of Richmond. Nanette's proximity to this great lady was a tribute to her beauty. Lady Anne had chosen the seven most beautiful of her ladies for this occasion, regardless of rank, for, she said, the King of France would neither know nor care who had precedence over whom, but beauty he would appreciate and acknowledge. He had not actually agreed to receive the Marquess, and so this masked entertainment had been arranged.

Nanette shivered a little as the damp sea-breeze trickled over her bare chest and shoulders and stared at the two little pages.

Irrelevantly she thought of her brothers, long dead now, little Jackie and Dickon—these pages could not be much older than her brothers had been when the Sweat took them. And her father—how proud and pleased her father would have been to see her now! She doubted not, had he been alive, that he would have contrived to be here in some capacity. But then had he been alive, she would probably not have been here at all—she would have been married long since, and at home with her children.

Inside the tent there was a sudden cessation of noise, and then, startling them all with its loudness, a braying fanfare of trumpets, and jumping like guilty mice the two children drew back the silken curtains and the light flooded out like golden water. Head up, without a tremor, the Marquess walked forward, and two by two the ladies followed her. The tent was hot and redolent of food and burning fat from the torches, and the air was thick with the reek of sweat and perfumes. Directly ahead of them was the dais on which, under a silken, tasselled canopy, were the two great chairs occupied by the anointed kings. The space in front of the dais was empty; all around the sides of the square was the press of attendants, all male, the nobles and notables of two countries.

It was all rehearsed, and they knew exactly what to do. The ladies walked up to the dais, curtseyed low, and spread out into their dancing formation. Nanette had time as she waited for the music to begin to look, from behind the safety of her mask, at the two kings. There was their own King Henry, glitteringly magnificent but comfortingly familiar, leaning on his elbow and smiling with satisfied pleasure. The French king, as tall as Henry, was thin, dark-faced and ugly; a thin black moustache underlined his long, bulbous nose; his skin was pitted with pox-scars and sallow; his mouth a long inflexible scar above his scanty-bearded strong chin. He was smiling with cynical amusement. He looked, to Nanette, dangerous, and she thought that, though their own King was more magnificent and more handsome, he yet looked like a child beside an adult, the merest apprentice beside a far-too-experienced master.

Then the music started, and Nanette had no more time to think, for the dance they had rehearsed was complicated and energetic, involving much controlled grace as well as virtuoso leaps such as French ladies neither could nor would perform in a dance. At last, breathless, they came to the end and sank to the ground before the dais to a roar of appreciative applause, and the King, jumping up from his chair with a shout of delight, bent over the Marquess and twitched off her golden mask. He took her hand and raised her and led her to King Francis.

'Brother, may I introduce to you Lady Anne Rochford, Marquess of Pembroke, the originator of this ballet which has so delighted us?'

There was no more than the briefest moment of hesitation. Of course, King Francis had known all along who was entertaining him, had known this occasion was designed for the express purpose of having him receive her, but he had never officially said he would receive her. From the position of her deep curtsey Nanette could see the faces of all three protagonists, and she wondered, admiringly, at Anne's calm dignity. In her face there was neither fear nor ingratiation. She might have been a Queen looking at the ambassador of an unimportant country. What if he rejected her? But no, he could not. His long moment of gazing was because he had forgotten, if he had ever known, the potency of Anne's spell. He was overcome by the dark magic of her beauty.

Now he was smiling graciously, his eyes glittering with some hidden emotion, and bending over her hand like a courtier.

'We have met before, I believe,' King Francis said. 'I could not forget such a face. But the beauty of Mademoiselle de

Boulans was as a candle flame against the sun of the beauty of Madame la Marquise.'

'You are right, you are right,' King Henry exclaimed in pleasure, and turning to the rest of the ladies he cried out, 'Unmask, every one! I would shew my brother of France how we breed beautiful women in England.'

This too was rehearsed. Nanette stood up with the others and peeled off her mask and there was a gasp of appreciation from the onlookers—no doubt that was rehearsed too. Francis looked them all over slowly. Nanette felt her skin burn as his eyes passed over her. He bestowed on each of them a glance which though brief was minute and knowing. He might have been a horse-merchant looking through a paddock.

'Any one of these ladies, brother of England, could hold her own in any company, and yet, I believe, this star outshines them all. France is honoured by your presence, Madame. Welcome, ladies, welcome.'

Henry sat down again, and the three of them spoke in low voices for a few moments. Nanette could not hear what was said, though she could see, even from that distance, that they spoke French, and that most of the talking was done by King Francis and Lady Anne. Their speech was rapid and fluent, and for a moment she wondered whether King Henry had difficulty in keeping up with them. His French, she knew, was excellent, but he had never lived in France, nor spoken it as his native language.

Soon, however, the moment was over, and the ladies must withdraw again. There were no women present at the feast, and therefore it would not be etiquette for them to stay. Taking their cue from the Marquess, they all curtseyed very low, and backed out, and the silken curtains dropped again into place, shutting them out in the salty darkness. At once their serving women came forward with cloaks to fling over their bare shoulders, and they hurried back towards the grim grey walls of Calais Castle where they had their quarters. It was a walk of no more than a hundred yards, and it was done in silence. No-one felt inclined to talk.

In her anteroom, the Marquess dismissed all but Nanette and Mary Wyatt, and when they were alone together she flung off her cloak and almost ran to the slit window in the thick stone wall and pulled aside the hide curtain to look out.

'You can see the camp from here,' she cried. 'Little muted lights, like glow-worms. And smell the sea—mild and sweet it smells, more like spring than autumn.'

Nanette went towards her, and she turned, and Nanette saw how her eyes were huge and glittering with some unnatural excitement. Her face was white, with two red spots above her cheekbones, and her body was quivering like some creature driven beyond endurance either by pleasure or pain.

'My lady,' Nanette said anxiously, and then glanced back at Mary. Mary came forward too. Nanette could feel the heat radiating from her mistress's body like the heat from a brazier. 'You are feverish, my lady, you have caught a chill. Come, let us put you to bed.'

'No, no, I am not feverish. I am—' She stopped abruptly and turned again with a sharp, restless movement, to breathe in the night air. Mary Wyatt said, 'You are overheated, my lady, and the night air is not good for you—'

'Peace, Mary. Smell it, only smell it—it could not harm anyone. I am strangely elated tonight, as if I had drunk too much wine. But it was not wine I was drinking—it was nectar. I have sipped in something from the air surrounding a king. Do you not think perhaps, that they carry their own air with them, a small sphere surrounding them of rarefied air? Oh, my dear friends, tonight I do not step upon the earth. Tonight I am air-borne.'

She spun around on the spot and danced across the room, and her feet made no sound, scarcely disturbed the rushes. At the other side of the room she spun again, stretched wide her arms, and laughed wildly, drawing in great breaths of air as if her lungs were starved.

'My lady, will you take a little wine?' Nanette asked, wonderingly.

'A little supper,' Mary added eagerly. 'Take a little supper and let us undress you for bed. There is a brazier in your room, and it is warm and snug. Let us call for some supper for you.'

She looked at them quizzically, her mouth still laughing as a dog will laugh at some secret pleasure of its own. 'Well, well, you do not understand, and how can you?' she said. 'You shall have your way, my dear, dear friends. Mary, let you go and get me my supper. Do not call the servants—I don't want servants by me. Bring wine and a little cold fowl, and you shall eat with me. And Nan, do you come with me into the bedchamber and make me ready. For tonight, I think, Jove himself may take on the form of a mortal and visit me.' Nanette and Mary exchanged the swiftest of glances before Mary ran out of the room on her errand. 'Aye, you understand now, don't you,' Anne said, almost under her breath. She went through into the bedchamber, where the servants had already placed the glowing brazier and lit the candles and left hot water.

Anne stood like a graceful statue while Nanette undressed her, remembering as she unlaced the gold sleeves how they had undressed each other all those years ago in the maids' dormitory. Anne's face was turned towards the window, as if she could see through the covering and out to the sea. Nanette looked at her in wonder. She was thirty years old, and yet she looked, slender and white and cloaked in her magnificent hair, like a young girl still. Her great eyes shone like dark lamps, her subtle mouth was touched with shadows of unsubstantial laughter.

The column of her neck bore her head as a stem bears a flower, and below it her body sloped away virginal, untouched, as little and unformed as a child's, small round breasts, flat belly, long straight thighs like a foal's. She turned her head towards the window, and her body quivered minutely, stirred by some awareness only she could feel as she waited for the god to put on human flesh to come to her.

Nanette bathed her and dried her carefully, anointed her with delicate perfumes, and dressed her in her simple white bed-gown of a silk so fine and soft it could have been drawn through the ring on her little finger. Then Mary came back with the supper, and on Anne's instructions they took off their coifs and sat with her and shared the food and wine with her, and they laughed and chattered together like carefree girls, and for a while Anne's strangeness seemed to desert her, and she charmed and entertained them as she had used to do in the old days before the King noticed her.

They did not notice the time pass, but it was nevertheless a long time later that Anne suddenly stopped in mid-sentence, looked away towards the window, and said, 'Hush! Listen!'

They listened.

'I hear nothing,' Mary said. 'What is it?'

'He is coming,' Anne said. She got up and moved as if drawn by some invisible cord to the window, drawing aside the covering. Outside it was grey with the first light of dawn. 'Look,' she said. Mary and Nanette went to stand behind her and looked too. The grey sky, soft with mizzle, reached down to the grey sea, so calm it barely moved, shewing no speck of white, no turning wave, and below them the dark roofs of Calais town shone wet in the pearl of first light. There was no sound or movement anywhere, and the lights were out in the camp of tents at last, though near the harbour a flag or two of grey smoke hung above the houses, unmoving in the still air.

'How beautiful it is,' Anne whispered. 'I shall never forget Calais. Never forget this—' She lifted a hand to indicate all she saw, and it never completed its gesture, for there was a knock at the outer door. Her eyes widened as she turned her head. The feverish excitement was gone, and yet she was still taut with some emotion. Nanette saw the corner of her nostril flare, and thought perhaps it was fear.

'Go let him in,' she said, not looking at them. Nanette caught up her hand and kissed it fiercely before she left to do her bidding. She wanted to bless her mistress, but she had no words. They closed the inner door and crossed the cold ante-room to open the outer door. The King stepped in, ducking under the low door, bringing with him the damp, fresh smell of morning. The fur of his mantle was white with beads of mist. His eyes went to the closed inner door and he opened his mouth and shut it again. He looked curiously afraid; very young, very handsome, but somehow nervous and apprehensive, as if he were a young boy afraid of being rejected by his first ever lover. Nanette's heart went out to him in a warm flood of tenderness, forgetting for that moment that he was her lord and King. She put out her hand and almost committed the enormity of touching him, but he looked at her in time to prevent her. His lips twitched as if he would have liked to smile but could not just then remember how it was done.

'Ladies, you have leave,' he said. 'You will not be needed again tonight.'

They curtseyed, and were about to go when the inner door opened, and their mistress stood there, white gown, black hair, white face, black eyes.

'Henry,' she said. The King's face blanched, and for a moment he could only stare at her, in the grip of more emotion than he could express. Here was the end of a long, weary road. 'Henry,' she said again, and this time it was a plea. She began to quiver, and as the shaking grew worse, threatening to overcome her completely, he was across the room in two strides and had taken her in his arms, pressing her little narrow body against him, laying his cheek on the crown of her shiny head. He closed his eyes and tears broke past the barrier of his eyelashes and shone for a moment on his cheeks.

'Oh my lady,' he said.

Nanette and Mary slipped out quietly, and closed the door behind them.

Fifteen

ANNE'S FLUX WAS DUE IN NOVEMBER JUST AFTER THEY ARRIVED home in England. She and her intimate ladies awaited it anxiously. It was late, but then the strain of the journey might have affected it. November passed away, and December, and there was nothing. Anne began to be nervous, the King elated. He, at least, had no doubt of the issue, but Anne, who spent much time in prayer, felt it unchancy to talk about it until it should be certain. Nevertheless, the King had the Queen's apartments at the Tower redecorated in her honour for, he said, she should occupy them before midsummer.

January came, and the third expected flux did not appear, and it was certain that she was pregnant. She was sick in the mornings, sometimes at night as well, and her little breasts had begun to grow and feel tender. So on the twenty-fifth, early in the morning, the King married the Marquess in a secret ceremony in an attic in the west turret of Whitehall. The King was attended by Hal and George, the Marquess by Lady Berkeley and Mary Wyatt, and the ceremony was conducted by the Bishop of Lichfield. The Bishop had not been told the purpose of his summons to that particular attic, other than that he was required to conduct mass. When he knew he must marry the King to the Marquess, he was so overcome by terror that he could hardly speak, and to hasten matters the King intimated, without precisely saying so, that the Pope had agreed to a dispensation. It was enough for the Bishop's conscience; the Mass was said, and Henry and Anne were man and wife.

It had to be kept secret for the time being, since all the required legislation had not gone through Parliament yet, and the Pope's approval of Cranmer's appointment as Archbishop of Canterbury was still awaited, but the inner circle knew of it, and spoke of the *forthcoming* marriage between the King and the Marquess of Pembroke with much solemn glee. It became another of their esoteric jokes, of which they had so many it amounted almost to a secret language.

Elsewhere, it was thought that the King's new marriage would take place at Easter, but in mid-April the rumours that were flying up the country were confirmed at Morland Place in a letter from Nanette.

'You must by now have heard the news,' she said. 'On Monday last it was announced in Parliament that the King's marriage to the Lady Catharine was not valid, and that he had married our beloved Marquess in January. Then on Tuesday my lord of Norfolk and my lord of Suffolk went to Lady Catharine to tell her of this, and that her title and status would henceforth be Princess-Dowager of Wales. If she would accept the title, they were instructed to tell her, she would have a large palace, and an income in accordance with her dignity, and that the Lady Mary her daughter should live with her.

'This last, it was supposed, would sway her if the other matters did not. The King could not have been more generous in his offer, but the ungrateful lady refused all, and said that she would rather beg her bread from door to door than accept the title, knowing full well as she must that the King would always provide for her. We were all outraged when we heard of this. The Lady Catharine may have been in her time a good and pious woman, but she is also ungrateful and stubborn to a degree, and has caused my dear mistress much suffering.

'However, the Princess-Dowager could not prevent the King from doing what he would, and on Sunday my lady attended chapel in Royal state, attended by sixty ladies and dressed all in cloth-of-gold, and wearing the royal jewels. My lady of Richmond carried her train, and I was in attendance walking beside Mary Wyatt. My mistress was prayed for as Queen, and afterwards held court and everyone knelt and paid her homage.

'The Coronation is to be in May, which is very short notice for all to be made ready, but the heir to the Kingdom is expected in September, and the King would not have his beloved Queen bear the strain of the ceremony in high summer when the child is so near. She looks more beautiful than ever, and the King loves her to distraction. I believe now that all her troubles are over, and my duty to her almost done. I must stay with her until her son is born, the Prince we all so eagerly await, and then I believe I might come home. I love court life, but sometimes I miss the quiet life of the country more. Tom Wyatt and I talk about it often, for he believes there is nothing on earth so valuable as what he calls "the green life" as opposed to the gold.'

Paul read this letter with an eagerness he could barely conceal. She would be coming home! Life seemed to spring up anew in him at the thought, and the April weather seemed to brighten perceptibly beyond the windows. Bellowing for his steward, he began to plan an enormous spring-cleaning, and not before time, for the house had been neglected since Elizabeth died. The household would move at once to Twelvetrees, and Morland Place would be stripped to the bare boards and scrubbed and sweetened; painted walls and panels would be touched up, hangings beaten, bed-covers and curtains washed, sweet herbs sprinkled with the new rushes; every piece of gold, silver and pewter in the place would be polished until it shone like a star, and he would order a hanging cupboard to be made for the wall of the winter-parlour so that the best pieces could be displayed in the manner that was newly fashionable at Court.

And for when Nanette came home there should be a new tapestry for the wall of his bedchamber, he decided. The Garden of Eden tapestry of his great-grandmother hung in the great hall, and the hanging in Paul's chamber was merely a coloured design of red and blue wool, not fine enough for a lady who had lived at Court and was now personal attendant to the Queen of England. It should be something very rich, but delicate and allusive as suited Nanette—something to do with unicorns and white harts and maidens. He would go that very day into York and see the best of the tapestry-makers.

A new horse for her, too—a white palfrey he thought—and a hound of her own to make hunting more interesting. He had heard, from one of her letters, of her little spaniel, but she should have a great deerhound too, one of Alexander's offspring. He told Amyas of his plans, and Amyas was merely sour. He was against the new marriage, would not hold it to be legal, refused, until Paul threatened him with personal violence, to stop calling the Lady Catharine 'Queen', swore he would not recognize any issue of Queen Anne's body and, by his own illogical method, regarded Nanette's homecoming as part of the new order of things and would not be glad about that either.

The regeneration seemed to spread outwards from Morland Place. There were more twin lambs born that year than anyone could ever remember, and the blossom was so thick on the fruit trees that it portended the heaviest fruit-crop for years. The spring weather grew bright and brilliant, trees burst into tender leaf, birds sang madly in every tree and bush, the swans on the moat at Morland Place hatched five signets, and hares played almost under its walls at sundown. Paul's niece Catherine, who had married young John Butts, had a son, whom they named Samson, and news came from Calais that her sister Jane was expecting a baby in the summer. Ezekiel's wife, Arabella Neville, was also pregnant, which was a matter of great joy to them, for they had been married five years without her having ever conceived. Arabella attributed her happy condition directly to the pilgrimage she had made last autumn to the shrine of Our Lady at Walsingham, for it was the month after that she had conceived. Amyas, in his new role as guardian of family piety, encouraged that view, and Paul in his happiness refrained from teasing his son by pointing out that the ex-queen Catharine had made more pilgrimages to that same shrine than there were years in Amyas's life.

The new burst of energy also encouraged Paul to consider his grandchildren's future. Robert was now thirteen, and in need of rubbing shoulders with more gentlemens' sons than he was meeting under his tutor. The cloth trade was doing well, despite having had to revert to the old system of working, and, with the large crop of lambs, wool was likely to do well this year too, so Paul felt they could afford to send Robert away to school. After some consideration Winchester was chosen for him. The school there was a good one, and it was a reasonable distance from Dorset where the Courteney cousins lived. John Butts's wife had been a Courteney, and Paul's great-uncle John, who had been ejected from the family in disgrace on marrying a very low woman, had re-established himself by his second marriage to a wealthy and respectable widow whose estate in Dorset adjoined that of the Courteneys.

Edward, who was eleven, was more easily settled. His schooling was to continue under his tutor, but he was to spend part of every week with James Chapham, learning his business and anything else that gentleman might teach him. It was quite likely that James would marry again, in which case the settlement would cancel the previous settlement made on Margaret, but the experience could not be anything but useful to Edward and therefore to the family. Finally, there was young Paul. Amyas wanted him to become a priest, and despite the current climate of anti-clericalism, Paul considered it a good career for a third son. A lawyer might be more useful to the family, but Amyas did not wish the boy to be ordained against his will, and so Paul saw no harm in sending him for a year to St William's College, where great-uncle Richard had once served. Young Paul, now seven, had a very beautiful voice, and it seemed likely that he would be chosen to sing at the Minster, which would be a great honour.

There was no need to make any change in Eleanor's situation. She spent some of her time with Arabella and some with her governess, but though she was lacking female company, there was no way of securing her companions of her own age unless she was sent away from home, and Paul did not want that. Girls of good family could not be sent to be brought up at Morland Place when there was no Mistress there, so Eleanor's lonely status as sole representative of the distaff side of the family must continue until Nanette came home, or Amyas remarried, or Eleanor's brothers grew old enough to have wives themselves.

In August, when the Court moved from Greenwich to Windsor so that Queen Anne and King Henry might have a little hunting and so that Greenwich might be prepared for the lying-in of the Queen in September (the first such event for seventeen years, for after the birth of the Lady Mary, Lady

Catharine had never carried to term), the Morlands were also on the move. Robert was going to Winchester, and Paul decided to accompany him in order to pay a visit to the Dorset Morlands, a visit which he felt was long overdue. James Chapham had business in Southampton, and would ride with them, and then John and Lucy Butts announced their intention of travelling with them also, so that they could visit Lucy's family, the Courteney cousins.

The journey to Dorset was easy, for it had been an exceptionally dry summer. The only trouble to be encountered was the dust, which in some parts rose so thickly under the horses' hooves that it was like a sea-fog, and made it difficult to breathe, and the fact that the road was so hard that by the time they reached Leicester the legs of one of the horses had swelled up and they had to rest there for a day until it recovered.

They made a leisurely journey through Nottingham, Leicester, Oxford and Salisbury, and on the tenth day set out from the beautiful old city of Salisbury into the hills of Dorset which, despite the dry summer, were still green. Here they parted with James, for he took one road, heading for Southampton, and they took another, heading for Netheravon, the estate of the Courteneys. They arrived at supper time, and while Lucy was thrilled at the thought of seeing her family again, and Robert, despite his tiredness, was very excited, Paul could only be relieved, for his arm was aching savagely.

The family was all there assembled to greet them, having been warned of their coming by the servant sent on ahead. Netheravon was a large, old, rambling house, much added to and altered, and as Paul dismounted stiffly in the courtyard, the first thing he noticed was the carving over the door, very crude and much weathered, of a hare. It made it seem something like a coming-home to him, for Netheravon was where his great-grandmother had been born, and the hare had been her device which, modified, had formed the basis of the hare-and-heather device of the Morlands.

Servants came forward to take the horses, a very stately steward in a smart green livery brought the welcoming-cup, and at the great door were the members of the family come out to greet them. Everything was done properly and formally, putting Paul in mind of Morland Place when he was a boy and his great-grandmother would have been horrified if any point of etiquette had been overlooked. The first greetings had to be between him, as head of the Morland family, and George Courteney, master of Netheravon.

'God's greeting to you, cousin. You are very, very welcome here. We are honoured by your visit,' George Courteney cried, embracing Paul. It was not particularly easy to do, for George Courteney was startlingly small, and Paul, stooping from the habit of a man used to being taller than everyone else, had abruptly to double himself.

'God's blessing on the house,' Paul said, straightening, and added, seeing George's wife a step behind him, 'and the woman of the house.'

'My wife, Rebecca,' George said. The woman came forward to kiss him.

'We have looked forward so much to this visit, cousin Paul,' she said, and Paul felt, warmingly, that it was not just a form of words. They all trooped into the great hall, and there was a confusion of greeting and kissing as everyone was introduced to everyone. Lucy Butts was the centre of attention, for she was coming home to the place of her birth.

'I never thought,' she said with tears running down her cheeks to her laughing mouth, 'when I went away from here to be wed that I would ever see the house again. I am so happy. George, kiss me again. You have not changed the least bit.'

Paul discovered on closer scrutiny that George and Lucy were very alike in feature, and that George's smallness was not from deformity or disproportion but simply that he was built smaller all over, like a different kind of human being. This latter discovery came when Paul was introduced to George's twin sons, Phillip and James, who were fourteen years old and identical to their father in stature. It was as if his body had ceased to grow after that age. The twins were the image of their mother.

'Born on May-day,' she said, 'so we named them after the Saints whose feast day it is.'

'And sorely sorry she was to be missing the May-day celebrations,' George added, smiling at his wife. 'We always have a glorious day here, and 'Becca is out from dawn to dusk—but not that day.'

'I was a-labouring from dawn to dusk that day,' Rebecca said without rancour, and Paul glanced in surprise at Lucy, for such things were not usually spoken of in public. But Lucy did not seem to be embarrassed, or at least, if she was, she did not shew it.

'And have you any other children?' Paul asked, to change the subject. He failed miserably, for 'Becca said with broad cheerfulness, 'No, just the two great lads there. It was so hard a labour bringing them into the world that I had to stop at two. They broke me inside and put an end to my childbearing.'

The two boys looked at each other and then at their mother and grinned shyly. They had not spoken a word since they had come in, and Paul was to find that they very rarely did speak. It seemed that they had enough silent communication with each other to satisfy them.

'We are only waiting for our neighbours to arrive, and then we shall have supper. We sent a servant to Hare Warren as soon as yours arrived, so they should be here at any moment. You will find Alice little changed, Lucy—'

'Except that she is with child,' Rebecca broke in, 'and the size of our barn with it. I dearly believe she will have twins again.'

'Is she like Lucy and George—in looks?' Paul asked.

'You find us alike?' George asked, interested. Paul did not have the chance to answer, for Rebecca said, 'You know that you are, husband. All three of you are as like as if you were twins yourselves. Peas from the same pod could not be liker, cousin Paul, and I say truth. If I did not know for certain sure there was two years between Lucy and George, and another two between George and Alice—but here they come now, if I am not much mistaken!'

'You could hardly mistake the noise the children make, 'Becca,' George said pleasantly, and at that moment the door to the hall opened, and in ran four little girls, identically dressed and so alike each to each that at first Paul thought the weariness of the journey must be affecting his sight. They were all about six or seven years old, diminutive, very pretty, dressed in gowns of green velvet with white linen chemises and white starched caps under which their hair hung in dark chestnut curls. They ran in chattering like starlings and rushed to greet their uncle and aunt before, just as suddenly, spying the strangers and falling silent, dropping startled curtseys and lowering their eyes bashfully. They were followed, more sedately, by a small woman, enormously pregnant, who could only, by her features, be Alice, and a tall man with the same dark chestnut hair who, by his vivid blue eyes above high cheekbones, could only be a Morland—Luke Morland, Paul's cousin.

Greetings were exchanged and introductions made. Luke and Paul embraced cautiously. 'It is too long since our families met,' Paul said, 'Your father, I know, was something of an outcast, but that need not make us strangers to each other.'

'I feel as you do, cousin,' Luke said. He did not smile easily, and there was a way he had of closing his lips after each sentence that made Paul think he did not love easily, or forgive easily, either. 'My grandmother cut my father off because of his first marriage, and when she reinstated him for marrying my mother, he did not particularly want forgiveness of that kind. But blood is thicker than water, they say, and I have no quarrel with you—or with my wife's kin,' he added, turning to embrace John Butts.

'Now, Luke, don't bring up the past in that way,' George said and clapped him on the back with an easy familiarity which Paul did not suppose Luke much liked. 'From what I hear your father and your grandmother were cut from the same cloth, both of them proud as the Dark Gentleman and as unforgiving. And you are like to have gone the same way, if it was not for the gentling influence of the Courteneys.' Paul saw that Luke, far from resenting this kind of talk, seemed almost to like it. He did not actually smile, but the grim line of his lips relaxed a little, which was as near as he ever came to smiling.

'You are very like my great-grandmother, as I remember her,' Paul said to him now.

'You remember Eleanor Courteney?' Rebecca exclaimed irrepressibly. 'Lord, that seems hardly possible! She's like a character from an old tale to us here. Was she very beautiful, as they say?'

'I danced with her at her birthday feast, the day before she died,' Paul said, 'and she seemed very beautiful to me then. But I was only a child. I remember best of all her eyes—and they were very like my cousin's here.'

'I do not know what she looked like, but my fancy is always that Elizabeth here resembles her. What say you to that? 'Lisbeth, come forward child, where are you?' Rebecca turned towards the four identical little girls and pulled one forward towards Paul. The child dropped a curtsey, and then raised her eyes for a moment, boldly, to his face. The vivid flash of blue reminded Paul painfully of Nanette, and he bent down and kissed the child gently and said, 'God's greeting to you, little cousin.' Then to Alice, 'They all look so alike to me, I cannot imagine how you tell them apart.'

Alice laughed. 'At first glance all sheep look alike—but the shepherd knows them all. Elizabeth, here, is the oldest—she is seven—and she is also the biggest—'

'Big and bold and wicked,' Rebecca added with a laugh, 'and as wild as a fox. There's no holding that little mistress when she has a mind to ride off into the woods. The times she's been beaten—but to no avail!'

'And Ruth,' Alice continued, unperturbed, 'is Elizabeth's twin, and she's much thinner and smaller, and her hair doesn't curl. Mary and Jane are only five, rising six, and they are smaller and stouter and to my mind look more like me than like Luke.'

Paul looked at them doubtfully. 'Of course, now you mention it, they are all very different, but I fear it will take me time to know them one from the other.' Except Elizabeth, he thought silently.

Shortly afterwards supper was served, and they took it in the great hall in a very simple, homely way. The Courteneys obviously lived in a much less grand way than the Morlands of Morland Place. There were no singers or musicians to perform while they ate, and when the cloth was drawn the family soon left the table and gathered around the hearth in the centre of the hall for a domestic evening of conversation, each of them taking up some piece of work to keep their fingers busy, while the little girls, on command and obviously reluctantly, each performed in turn one song which they would have sung unaccompanied had John Butts not offered to accompany them on the lute. Paul nursed his crooked arm in silent regret. He would have liked to accompany little Elizabeth, for her voice, though untrained, was sweet.

The next day, since it was the grease season, they hunted the deer. On the way to the first draw Luke rode alongside Paul and questioned him in an abrupt but not unfriendly way about the family and in particular Morland Place, which he had never seen.

'You must come and visit us,' Paul said at length. 'You would be welcome. Our house is too quiet now, though I hope my niece may be coming back soon, once the Queen has laid-in. She is in service to Queen Anne.'

Luke looked at him curiously. 'Queen Anne?' he said. 'That sounds strange from your lips, cousin. What think you of this business of the King's?'

Paul looked at him sideways. 'What business?' he asked cautiously.

'Why this divorce and nonsense. The men in the city say it will not affect trade with Spain, and the Hanse care not one way or the other, though it is said they insulted her at the coronation by putting the arms of Spain above her white falcon on their display. But how can a man take another wife, and his first yet living? Whatever the offspring may be, it will be another bastard to cloud the issue. Though I suppose if you call the Bullen woman Queen Anne you must be for it.'

'I would be sorry to fall out with you so soon after making friends,' Paul said, 'but if Parliament says she is Queen and Lady Catharine is not, then I accept it, for it is the law of the land.'

'Aye, that's what More says, Sir Thomas More. But Parliament cannot say the Pope is not head of the Church, can it? And if that is not so, then the rest cannot follow.'

Paul shifted back from the quicksand. 'I do not thoroughly know what Parliament may be competent to judge and what it may not. I only know that I am the King's subject, and obey the law of the land.'

'And I am God's subject, and obey the law of Christ,' Luke said.

'Perhaps that is the same thing,' Paul said. Luke looked at him sharply, and then away.

'Let us not quarrel over it,' he said. 'We will see soon enough who is right. In the event, we may have nothing to quarrel over. But if your niece is at Court you will need to be careful of your opinions, I doubt not.'

Paul said nothing. Let Luke think what he liked for the time being. He wanted to repair the breach in the family if he could, and above all he wanted friendship with Luke Morland, for he had already decided that his grandson Robert should marry Elizabeth Morland, and he wanted nothing to come in the way of that design.

Queen Anne retired to the prepared birth-chamber in Greenwich Palace on the first of September, and thereafter no man was allowed across the threshold except her chaplain and the doctors. It was swelteringly hot, and Anne was uncomfortable, peevish, and bored. Even the glorious decorations in the suite of rooms and the magnificent French bed that the King had given her for lying-in did not satisfy her.

'Did you hear what that wicked woman said when I sent for the State christening robes?' she said to Nanette one morning as they and some of the other ladies sat sewing. At least, the ladies were sewing. The Queen had long ago given up any pretence of working, and was walking around the room fidgeting. She held a cup in her hands from which she had long ago drunk a draught of lemon-juice and she flicked the rim irritably with her finger-nail as she walked. The dogs, lying panting in the scant shade below the window looked at her resentfully as she passed. It was an irritating sound.

'Yes, Your Grace,' Nanette said. 'She refused them.'

'She had no right. They were not hers to refuse,' Anne said, working up her rage. 'They are Crown property. And to say she would not give them up for so abominable a case—! To call me and my son abominable!'

'Your Grace, it isn't good for you to talk like that,' Mary Wyatt said. 'You will spoil the baby's temper.'

'Has His Grace decided on the name yet?' Nanette asked, to change the subject.

'No, he still cannot decide between Edward and Henry,' Anne said a little more calmly. 'But he has had the birth notices written out all the same. They just say "the prince" and nothing about a name. I wish I could be as sure as he is that it is a boy.'

'All the soothsayers—' Mary began, but Anne shrugged it off.

'Soothsayers have been wrong,' she said. 'I just have a feeling— but it is nothing. Just this abominable waiting, I suppose.'

'Even if it were to be a girl,' Madge Wyatt said, 'it would not matter so much, dear Your Grace, would it? So long as it is healthy.'

Nanette threw her a frowning glance. It was not well to talk of such things so near the time.

'Sometimes I simply no longer care if it be a girl or a boy,' Anne said, resuming her walking. 'Just so that it is over and done with. But if it be a girl, I will have to go through it all again, and that would be so wearisome!'

The penalty of being a wife, Nanette thought. And girl or boy, Anne would have to go through it again, and again. Her hand went up to cross herself, and Anne turned in her walk just in time to catch the tail end of the gesture. Her eyes narrowed, but she did not ask the reason. There were things at this stage of her pregnancy she did not want to know.

'Oh I am so bored!' she cried instead. 'I feel as if I have been here for ever. What date is it? How long have I been here?'

'The seventh of September, Your Grace. Tomorrow is the

feast of the Blessed Virgin Mary,' Mary Wyatt said. Anne gave a strange grimace.

'An omen, think you? I wonder. I remember one of the displays in my coronation procession was of the blessed St Anne, mother of the Holy Virgin. St Anne had only one child, and that a girl. Do you think it was deliberate, a reminder of the Lady Catharine?' She did not wait for an answer but turned again restlessly towards the window. She stepped accidentally on Ajax's tail, and he yelped. Anne kicked at him crossly.

'Be silent, beast. Oh dear God, I am so tired of being pregnant. I wish this child were born. I have not seen a soul but you for a week. I wonder what my dear Tom is doing now? And George, and Hal—hunting still, I warrant. Oh I wish I could be out there with them, riding. I long to feel the wind in my hair and a horse beneath me!'

'You will, soon, Your Grace. Have patience,' Nanette said, and in a quiet voice, 'Remember that you are the anointed Queen of this land. Your life is no longer your own. You have your duty to the people of the realm, just as the lord King has. His life is given to rule and defend them, yours to give them an heir. That is your sacred duty, and God brought you to this point to perform it.'

'Yes,' Anne said, looking at Nanette with wide eyes, seeing the truth of it. 'You are right, dearest Nan. It is the penalty of being a woman. I should have been born a man,' she smiled, but gently. 'But I must not question the will of God. His will be done.'

It was shortly after that that her pains began, and Nanette, along with all her ladies who loved her, stepped from the real world into a nightmare. A Queen could not give birth in private, like a gentlewoman, nor in quiet, like a beast. The birth chamber was thronged with women, not only her serving women and the midwives but all the women of the Court who cared to watch and all the noblewomen whose duty it was to be there. Nanette's only comfort was that she was sure Anne soon became unaware of them. Her suffering was terrible. At first she shrieked with abandon when the pains seized her, but after a while she only groaned, rolling her eyes from one face to another like a goaded animal, seeking pity where there was none.

There was nothing Nanette could do but hold her hand when the spasms came and wipe her forehead when they were over. 'She's very small, more like a child than a woman,' one of the midwives whispered to Nanette during one pain. 'She will have trouble.'

The penalty of being a woman, Nanette thought. The birth-pain, given to woman because of Eve's wickedness in the Garden of Eden. The Garden of Eden tapestry at Morland Place. Her wickedness, but not at Morland Place. The Church said that marriage was the inferior state, that celibacy was the higher. Why then did one have these longings? It was the Devil in you. Women had more of the Devil in them. Eve in the Garden of Eden. The penalty. Birth-pain, the suffering, the blood, the smell, the death. But why? Why? Anne groaned again, an inhuman sound, and her great dark eyes, protruding with agony and fear, stared up at Nanette, pleading silently for her to take away the pain.

Nanette was weeping, though she did not know it. 'Hold on, Anne, hold on,' she whispered. Thy will be done, Lord, but why? Anne was not wicked. She, Nanette, was wicked. Paul. Hampton Court, the yew-walk. Wickedness in such a pleasurable guise. No, that was a sinful thought. But Paul loved her, would do her no harm of his will. He had come to see her last week in Windsor to ask if she would come home. 'When my mistress is delivered of her child,' she had said, and she had thought longingly of Morland Place, the orchard, the Italian garden, the herb garden, the cool, panelled winter-parlour, the Garden of Eden tapestry with the knowing, smiling hare jumping out of the middle. No serpent there. No serpent at Morland Place.

'That's right, Your Grace, you're doing well.' The midwife, cheerful and professional. 'His Grace is outside the door, waiting for news. As eager a father as ever I saw. So bear up, my lady, bear up.'

'Henry?' Anne said hoarsely. Nanette leaned closer.

'He is outside, Madam, walking up and down. He suffers with you. He loves you, Anne, so much.'

'Yes,' she said, and closed her eyes, seeking to escape the pain. But it was there, too, bigger in the darkness. She opened her eyes, and sought Nanette's face, 'My duty—to the State—' she said with difficulty. Nanette nodded, unable to speak. 'His will be done,' she said, and Nanette wondered, afterwards, whether Anne had meant God's, or Henry's.

The pains were terrible, but in proportion they were short. Between three and four of the clock in the afternoon the baby was born, a large, healthy girl.

Nanette took the word to the King, who waited in an anteroom, just far enough away not to hear the groans of the Queen in labour. He started up as she entered and the suffering in his face was terrible.

'Is it over? Is she all right?' were his first words, and Nanette felt for him as a human being, that his first concern was for his wife. He really loved her, she thought.

'Her suffering was very great, Your Grace, but she is resting now. She will be all right.'

'And the babe? He is healthy?'

Even now, she thought, he is so secure. She looked into his eyes.

'It is a girl, Your Grace. She is large and healthy.'

For a moment, he was stunned. He stared at her, uncomprehendingly, and only when she stepped aside to allow him to pass did he recollect that he must go into the birth chamber to see his wife and child. He moved forward automatically, but stopped again as he reached Nanette and looked at her questioningly, as if he was not sure whether or not he had asked the question he had asked or received the answer he had received. Nanette met his gaze steadily, and he turned his head away and walked past her.

The walk to the chamber was very short, but it was enough for him to compose himself and his thoughts. He went straight to the bed, and looked down at Anne with tenderness and a sudden, painful pity. She looked so exhausted.

'I did not know it would be like this for you,' he said. He took her hand, and chafed her crooked finger with his thumb, absently in the old gesture. Her eyes seemed more than ever to fill her face, suffering having drawn back her skin to her skull. 'Thank God you are all right. Oh my darling—'

'The babe, Henry,' Anne said. He kissed her hand to silence her.

'A healthy girl,' he said. 'We must add an "s" to the birth notices.' He smiled to shew it was a joke, and she closed her eyes and tears ran out from under the lids. 'Anne, don't, please don't,' he said gently.

'She's only tired, sir,' the midwife said from the other side of the great bed.

'You are all right, and the babe is healthy, and we have all our lives to get sons,' the King said, ignoring the interruption. Anne opened her eyes again, and tried to smile, and he kissed her hand and laid it down on the counterpane. 'Rest now, sweetheart. I will come again soon.' He turned away from the bed, and Nanette gave the baby, lying on a velvet cushion, to Anne's cousin, Mary of Richmond, to bring to the King. He loved babies, all babies, as sometimes big men will love small helpless creatures. He put his finger to its fist, and the starfish hand opened and closed around it. A smile of foolish delight spread over his face.

'My daughter,' he said. The baby, eyes firmly shut, opened and closed her small pointed mouth, swallowing and gaping in preparation for the knowledge of food. The King watched her, enchanted. No child had been born of his body for seventeen years. There had been no need to fear, Nanette thought, that he would not love her. He picked up the baby, his big hands sure as they would have been handling a puppy, and held her up, one hand under her buttocks, one hand supporting her head, and she drew up her knees and flexed her hands, looking for the thing she had been holding.

'My daughter,' the King said again, and this time it was in benediction, and he kissed the bony forehead where the gingery thatch of hair ended. 'We shall call her Elizabeth, after my lady mother.'

The onlookers murmured approval, and the King gave back the baby to his cousin almost with reluctance. The penalty is all the woman's, Nanette thought; and yet there must be satisfaction of some sort in giving so very innocent a joy to a man as I have just seen in the King's face. That love was purity itself.

Sixteen

$\mathcal{T}$HE BABY WAS CHRISTENED WITH GREAT POMP AND CEREMONY
in Greyfriars church within the Palace of Whitehall,
and the King gave orders for the celebrations that Londoners
loved—bonfires, torchlit streets, wine running in the fountains
and conduits, dancing, fireworks, street banquets, illuminated
and decorated craft filling the river. The Spanish party rejoiced
that the child had turned out to be a girl, but the parents of
the new princess were not perturbed, and showed it. The
next would be a boy—there was plenty of time; but the King
dismissed those soothsayers who had so misled him by promising him a son, and swore never again to consult them.

Nanette was astonished by how quickly the Queen recovered, for the birth had been difficult, and thirty was perilously
late for a woman to bear her first child; but by the middle of
October she had resumed her normal occupations. By the end
of that month Parliament had settled the succession on Anne's
children, and the Lady Mary was proclaimed illegitimate.
Princess Elizabeth continued to thrive, and was brought to
Anne in her private apartments every morning, for Anne hated
to have her out of her sight.

'Ah, here she is!' she cried as soon as the wetnurse brought
her in. 'How is she, nurse? Has she been feeding well?'

'Lord bless you, Madam, she is as lusty as can be,' the midwife said. Nanette always looked with a kind of horror at her uncorseted shape, the great round breasts bulging under the bodice of her dress and making wet patches where her milk leaked through. She glanced, by comparison, at the flat, smooth cloth of the Queen's bodice, drawn over her iron corset, and her tightly nipped-in waist. Another of the penalties of being a woman—but thank God a gentlewoman did not need to suffer it while she could hire a wetnurse to suckle her babes.

'Give her to me,' Anne commanded, and took the baby, lying on a cushion, into her arms. 'Isn't she beautiful?' she said with vast satisfaction, looking down at her daughter.

'She is that, Madam, and she has such a powerful suck that I doubt not she will grow to be a buxom maid. I never nursed such a lively baby.'

'Nanette, come look—isn't she beautiful?'

Nanette went across to look down over the Queen's shoulder and said automatically, 'Yes, Your Grace,' but privately she was puzzled. The baby was dressed in a long white gown tucked and ruffled with the finest Flemish lace, so that all of her that could be seen was her small red face and her clenched fists. She had a little thin gingery hair on her skull above her alarmingly blue-veined forehead. Her eyes were almost always screwed tightly closed, but her eyebrows were perpetually on the move above them as if she were thinking out complicated problems. She had an indeterminate splodge of a nose, as had all babies, and a pink, pointed mouth like a mouse, which chewed toothlessly on nothing, like an old woman's. Beautiful? Well, she could only suppose one felt differently when it was one's own.

The baby opened her eyes for a moment, and they wandered in an unfocused way across her mother's face. Anne was delighted.

'She looks at me!' she exclaimed. 'She heard my voice. Nurse, will she have blue eyes, think you, like His Grace?'

'They will be dark, Madam, without a doubt. They are so dark a blue, they will turn in a few weeks and be as dark as your own.'

Anne seemed not to know whether to be pleased about that or not. 'But her hair—that will be red, I suppose, like the King's?'

'It is red now,' Nanette said, to please her.

'But if the eyes will change colour—and I have heard that a babe's hair often changes quite from one extreme to another,' Anne said anxiously.

'Sometimes a babe will have a lot of hair when it is born, Madam,' the nurse explained, 'which comes away when it is a few weeks old. We call it birth hair, and it is generally very dark. But the hair my lady Princess has now is not birth hair— that is her true hair. It will be as red-gold as—' She stopped in some confusion, and then went on, 'as His Grace's.' Anne did not seem to notice the hesitation or the nurse's confused blush, but Nanette threw her a sharp glance and guessed after a moment she had been going to mention the Lady Mary. It was so sad that that poor young woman, who as a baby had been as beloved and as feted as Princess Elizabeth, should now be suffering so much misery and rejection through no fault of her own. It was said that when she had been told she was now a bastard, she had burst into tears; but she had refused to acknowledge the Princess Elizabeth as heir to the throne.

'Well, I'm glad of that, for I would not want her to have her mother's unfashionable looks,' Anne had been saying. 'I should like her to be a true beauty. Dark eyes and red-gold hair—it will look well. Very well, nurse, you may go for the time being. I wish to keep the Princess with me for a while. I will send for you if you are needed.'

The nurse left with an obedient curtsey and no more than one anxious look back, and Anne placed the cushion and the baby on the floor at her feet and simply gazed, enraptured, at the tiny creature. Ajax and Anne's spaniel, Purkoy, came forward to sniff at the baby, and Anne pushed them away, but gently.

'Away, it is not for you to look at a Princess. Nanette, truly, do you not think she is beautiful? No, don't answer, I know you cannot understand me, I see it in your face. You would never be a successful liar—you shew too much of what you feel. Oh Nan, it pulls and tugs at my very soul to see her. I would not change her for a son, and I believe the King would not either. And I shall soon be pregnant again—next time it will be a boy.'

'You can talk so eagerly about being pregnant again, after all you suffered?' Nanette asked. 'I know that you must want to be pregnant again, for duty's sake, but you sound so—glad about it.'

'I am,' Anne said. 'It is a hard thing to explain, but I have quite forgot the pain of bearing her. Oh,' seeing Nanette's look of disbelief, 'I remember that it was, but not how it was. I used to wonder, when I was a child, how a woman who had once had a child could ever want another, but I understand now. I would not be afraid of the pain, because I do not remember it, and the reward is so great—so very great.' She leaned down to touch the baby's hand. Her long hair swung forward over her shoulder as she did, and the baby's hand locked round a strand of it. Anne disengaged herself gently.

'It is dreadful that so soon I shall have to send her away. Henry says she must go out of London before Christmas, for health's sake.'

'Where to, Madam—is it decided?' Nanette asked.

'She shall have a household at Hatfield, and Mary will share it with her. Strange to think of that girl being my stepdaughter. When I think of my own stepmother and how much I love her and she me, I wish there was some way in which I could reach Mary—but it is impossible. She hates me, and while she disobeys her father too—'

'I am glad at least that you no longer hate her,' Nanette said.

'Hate her? Oh no, I could not hate anyone now—except That Woman, and then only because she threatens my baby. I feel so full of love, I wish I could do everyone good. I have increased all my charities, and I am going to set up a sewing school to make clothes for the poor. I shall think of other things too, but I wish I could do some great, permanent good, to show how grateful I am for my little princess.'

'The greatest good you can do this realm—' Nanette began. Anne laughed.

'Oh yes, I know—is to give it a male heir. Well, I shall do my best, Nan, you may be sure of that. At the end of this month Henry and I—' she did not finish the sentence, but nodded significantly, and Nanette knew what she meant—they would resume married relations. Nanette thought it time to introduce the subject of her own future.

'It seems to me, Your Grace, that the time has come when you no longer need me. You are crowned and anointed Queen, you have born a healthy child, and your feet are settled upon the path your life was meant to take. You know that I promised to stay until you no longer need me, and then go home to Morland Place—'

She faltered and stopped as the Queen's eyes came round to look at her with distress. 'Oh Nan—you don't really want to leave me?'

'No, of course not,' Nanette said uncertainly, 'but seeing you so happy with your husband and your babe has made me think—Your Grace, I am twenty-five years old.'

'I was not wed until I was nearly thirty,' Anne pointed out.

'It is different for you,' Nanette said a little stiffly. Anne considered.

'Yes, it is. You are right. But Nan, don't go yet. There is still trouble to come. The Spanish woman still has friends. Go home for a visit at Christmas, if you will—I can do without you for a month or six weeks then if you like—but then come back, at least until my son is born.'

Nanette was very still, for she did not want to shew the sigh or the sadness that were inside her. At length she said, 'My dear mistress, you know that I said I would not leave you until you had no more need of me. You do not have to beg me to stay—I will stay, and willingly, until you give me leave to go.'

Anne jumped up and embraced her, her bubbling good humour restored, and so it was settled. Another year, Nanette thought. But I will go home at Christmas. I will have that, at least.

'—and now the Queen is pregnant again,' Nanette said. She was sitting near the window in the solar, illuminated by that particular, strange light that is reflected from snow. Paul thought it made her look more beautiful than ever.

'Already?' he said. 'That is good news indeed. It proves that she is fertile.' He cast a glance at Amyas, who was lolling against the fireplace, toasting his legs at the roaring fire of logs. With a brazier on the other side of the room, and a thick curtain over the door, the solar was as cosy as anyone could wish.

'Aye, fertile,' Amyas said with bad grace, 'but if she do not get a son, what good is it? The child she has only complicates matters.'

'The King does not look upon it that way, and nor would you,' Nanette said firmly. 'Does your daughter Eleanor compli-cate matters for you?'

'No, but then there was no uncertainty about my marriage.'

'Nor is there about the King's. He never was married to the

Lady Catharine. Queen Anne is his only and true wife. What is complicated about that?'

'Because a girl-child cannot inherit the kingdom,' Amyas said. With the tip of his toe he absently rubbed the belly of the basking Alexander, and the old hound groaned in his half-sleep with pleasure.

'There will be no need for a girl-child to inherit the kingdom,' Nanette began, but Paul cut across the argument which in one form or another had been going on with Amyas since the Princess was born.

'It is so good to see you looking so well, Nanette. You have such an air of fashion about you—' he waved his hand in a circular movement—'with your little dog and your elegant poses. That shade of blue suits you well—what is it called? Is it the latest thing?'

'We call it French blue,' Nanette said. 'The Queen favours it, but she says in her kindness that it suits me better because I have blue eyes.'

'And what else is new in fashion?'

'They say that five-cornered head-dresses are coming back into style again, but I still think the French hood is prettier, and I shan't adopt it.'

'I like the way you ladies of Court shew your hair,' Paul said, smiling. 'It makes you all look like little girls.'

Nanette heard this with some pain. She had told Paul that she was only here for a visit, but she had not yet told him she was still not free to leave her lady. She was shocked by the change in him, which she had barely taken in on his brief visit last autumn. His hair was quite grey now, and he seemed much thinner, and his face was lined with sadness and pain, which made him seem gentler in a way that grieved Nanette. He was still a very handsome man, but he had lost that air of certainty, of mastery, he had always carried with him.

'Tell me about Morland Place,' she said now. 'How have things been here—I have hardly heard anything from you. Are things going well?'

'The harvest was bad,' Amyas said at once, 'but I dare say you know that. We hear it was bad all over the country.'

'Yes, so it is said. There was not enough rain anywhere,' Nanette said.

'The rye harvest was good enough,' Paul said, 'but the barley did badly. Luckily we planted no wheat this year, though it generally grows well on the sheltered side of Shawes. But further south, where they grow more wheat, we hear there is a regular famine now.'

'But the sheep—they did well, did they not?' Nanette asked anxiously. There must be something cheerful to be said.

'There was a good crop of lambs,' Paul began, but Amyas, determined to be gloomy, said, 'There was less wool than usual, because of the weather. And the wool prices being fixed, there is little profit in selling it.'

'But cloth prices are rising all the time,' Paul pointed out. 'We can hardly make enough for all the demands there are. Why, we made twice as much Morland as last year, and more than twice as much fine broadcloth, and sold it all. I wonder sometimes if it is worth our while selling wool at all. We might as well make it all into cloth.'

'Morlands have always been wool merchants,' Amyas said. 'It is the tradition. And I want to die a Master Stapler as my grandfather and great-grandfather did. Wool is an old and honourable trade.'

'And cloth, being a new trade, is dishonourable, you would say?' Paul asked, but he smiled to rob the jibe of its sting. 'One day, Amyas, you will learn that not all new things are bad, nor all old things good. But for the moment we will carry on as we are. It would be hard to make more cloth now, seeing that we can no longer work with the factory. You cannot imagine, niece, how much time is spent by my factors taking the wool to the spinsters and the spinnings to the weavers and the cloth to the finishers. The roads are full of horses and mules loaded with Morland wool being taken from one place to another.'

'Has the new mill-wheel been finished yet?' Nanette asked. Paul shook his head.

'Not yet, though we hope that it will be ready by March next. For the moment we have set up a small wheel alongside the mill for the fulling, but much of it still has to be done by hand. It has been a costly business altogether, the loss of the wheel.'

'More costly than you know,' Amyas muttered, and Nanette looked across at him with an exasperated pity. His loss had been terrible, but he always managed, somehow to turn pity into something else by his attitudes and words.

'Tomorrow, if you care to ride out, we will go by the mill and you shall see how the work is coming along,' Paul said. 'Amyas, what have we for Nanette to ride?'

'She can ride my Falcon, if you like. I shall not go out. Tomorrow is a Saint's day, and I shall spend it by the fire keeping warm. I am glad you have come, cousin, for my father never kept such good fires for me. He said a lady of the Court would need to be kept warmer than us, being more delicate.'

Nanette laughed, glad that his humour seemed to have improved, and then Paul said, 'Will you come and see the new tapestry I have had made? It is not hung yet—I would welcome your opinion on the best place for it. It is in a storeroom along the passage—will you come?'

Although she guessed it was an excuse to have a private talk with her, Nanette agreed, and rose at once. Paul called two servants to bring the brazier, and Nanette picked up Ajax and followed him with Alexander padding behind, leaving Amyas still lolling by the fire.

When the servants had placed the brazier in the storeroom Paul signed them to wait outside, and led Nanette over to look at the tapestry, which was hanging over a frame. The snowy light from the window was good enough to examine it by.

'Why, uncle, it is beautiful,' Nanette said. 'It must have cost a great deal of gold. It is as fine as anything in the Palace, though it is small.'

'It is made for a small wall,' Paul said absently. Nanette looked at him sharply.

'Then you have already decided where it is to hang?' she said. Paul did not immediately answer and, beginning to understand, she looked away from him in embarrassment and stared again at the tapestry. It was a fine piece of work, delicately done, of a green hummock sewn all over with a profusion of flowers, on which sat a maid in a blue and silver gown. She had long dark hair, uncovered, to shew she was virgin, and long slender hands, one of which held a silver mirror. Beside her, with his forefeet on her lap, lay a unicorn wearing a golden chain, and he was looking at his reflection in the mirror the maid held. Her other hand rested on one of his forelegs, and she looked at him lovingly. The background was dark red, and sewn all over with flowers and bright birds and small beasts, foxes and conies and squirrels and mice and the like, all very lively and gay.

'It is for you, Nanette,' Paul said. 'It was for you I had it made. Have you not guessed? It is for the bedchamber, to hang on the wall opposite the bed, to be the first thing you see in the morning when you rise. The maid is you, and the unicorn is love. Do you like it?'

'It is beautiful. More beautiful than I deserve,' Nanette said slowly.

'Nothing is too beautiful for you. Nanette, when are you

coming home? Your mistress must release you from your oath, now she has her husband and child and is crowned Queen. You said that you would—'

'I know what I said,' Nanette said, and she sounded angry. She did not want to have to refuse him. 'She has asked me to stay until her son is born.'

'When will that be?' Paul asked. His voice was flat and carefully without expression.

'The babe should be born in August,' Nanette said. She turned to look at him, and he took one of her hands and chafed it absently.

'Nanette—' he began with difficulty, 'Nanette, do you want to come home? No, wait, don't answer yet. I am an old man now, and have a useless arm into the bargain. It would be no more than natural if you did not want to marry me. I want you to know that this is your home, whatever your feelings for me.'

'Oh Paul,' Nanette said helplessly.

'You will tell me, won't you, if you have changed your mind? I want to know.'

'You are not old,' she said, despairing of being able to sound as if she meant what she said. 'And your arm—that is nothing. Hard for you to bear, but not for anyone else.'

'I can't play any more,' he said. 'You remember how I used to play the lute?'

'There are other things,' Nanette said. 'You could learn the harp. There is a harpist at Court who has only one arm. You must not despair—life is not over. You are strong and healthy and able. This sadness is a poison and you must not let it overcome you.'

'But you, Nanette—what do you want?'

'I want to come home,' she said. She met his eyes steadily. 'I want to be married and have bairns of my own. You know you are the only man I could marry.'

'And is that the only reason you want to marry me?' he

asked quietly. She looked at him for a long time, at the lined, handsome face, the broad shoulders not yet stooped, and she thought suddenly of Anne and the King. 'How could I not love him?' Anne had asked. 'He is so good to me.' Consider, Nanette had said, how he loves you. Paul was the only man she could marry, but that was not all there was to it.

She saw the agony of waiting in his face, and wanted to end it for him. She put out her free hand and touched his hair, that she had remembered all along as so dark and curling.

'It looks as though frost has covered it, as though it might still be dark underneath, if one could brush the frost away. No, Paul, that is not the only reason.'

His lips smiled, but his eyes were still anxious. 'The frost has touched more than my hair,' he said. 'What is the other reason?'

'I love you,' she said. She saw the gladness pass across his face like sunlight crossing the hillside in the wake of a cloud-shadow. He released her hand and put his arms round her.

'This arm is still good enough to hold you with,' he said, and now he was really smiling. She looked at his mouth, and shivered. More true than I know, she thought. I really do love him. They kissed in all gentleness, but they were both aware of other feelings stirring in the darkness behind their closed eyes.

'I will wait for you,' Paul said at length, and Nanette rested her face against his chest, satisfied for the time being merely to stay there in his arms, protected, at peace.

Once she was back at Court, Morland Place seemed to Nanette to be very far away, and almost part of a fairy land with no substance in the real world. She came to look back upon that quiet Christmas with longing, for trouble was never far away from the Queen and her household, and it seemed sometimes that as long as Lady Catharine and Lady Mary lived, it would never retreat very far. Lady Mary was Anne's greatest fear, for Catharine was sick, and though many people felt sorry for her, few any longer resisted the validity of the new marriage; but Lady Mary had been England's Princess for a long time, and she was much beloved by the people, and many of them felt that, bastard or no, if there had to be a female heir to the throne it might as well be the King's firstborn.

Lady Mary herself continued stubbornly to cling to the belief that her mother's marriage was good and that she was Princess of Wales, to the extent that when Anne sent her two trunks full of new clothes just after the New Year, clothes which she badly needed and which would normally have delighted the fashion-conscious young lady, Mary refused to accept them because the trunks were not labelled for the Princess of Wales.

Fear, and the sickness that accompanied the early stages of her pregnancy, made Anne's temper shorter, but she did her best to control it, and in March went with the King to Hatfield to try to make peace with her stepdaughter. She returned to Greenwich in a rage.

'She is impossible!' she exclaimed furiously to her brother as she walked around her presence chamber, unable to keep still for irritation. 'She behaves out of all reason! I am past patience with her!'

'Be calm, dearest,' George said gently. He was lolling on the windowseat, playing with the trinkets in a lacquer box which had been left there, running the strings of beads again and again through his fingers. Tom Wyatt was there too, sitting on the floor with his back against the wall, picking very softly at a lute. He had come to visit Mary and Madge, who were sitting with Nanette sewing shirts for the poor—at least, that was his excuse. They all knew it was Anne he really came to see. 'You could hardly expect anything else from her, could you, knowing whose daughter she is? What would you do in her case?'

'We were taught to be obedient to our father, George—but she doesn't seem to have thought of that,' Anne said. 'It is the Spaniard in her. The Spanish blood. But I'll bring down that abominable Spanish pride!'

'Anne, you must guard your tongue,' George said, holding a string of jet up to catch the light. 'Don't you know old Chapuys has written to his master that you intend to poison Mary.'

'The old fool!' Anne hissed.

'Aye, but what he tells his master is heard by many before it crosses the water. Your best path is to be pleasant and patient with the girl.'

'But George, you don't know what she is like,' Anne said, turning on him. 'I went to Hatfield with the intention of being kind to her. I invited her in the politest possible way to visit me at Court as Queen—'

'Tactless of you, sweetheart,' Tom murmured. Anne's eyes seemed to get larger when she was angry.

'Everything is tactless to that girl. She said she knew no Queen but her mother, and then the insolent slut went on to say that if I as her father's *mistress* would like to intercede for her with him she would be grateful!'

Both Tom and George laughed at that, and Nanette looked apprehensively at her mistress. It really was not good for her to get so angry.

'It isn't funny!' she shouted.

'No, but it's bold,' George said. 'Did you slap her face, darling?'

'I wanted to,' Anne said, 'but I restrained myself. I told her that was impossible and said I would be her friend in any way I could, and she just looked at me—sweet Mother of God the look on her face! As if I were a servant who had just spilled slops on her best velvet shoe! And she said not a word. How dare she treat me like that? And when I complained to Henry, he just shrugged it away.' She imitated the gesture, and Nanette thought how little it must become the huge form of the King, who had only caught it from Anne. 'He said he was too busy to worry about her, what with trying to get all the attainders through Parliament. Cromwell was there, looking patient—you know the way he does when he thinks something is unimportant and troublesome—and—'

'Anne, listen,' George said, getting up and dropping the beads abruptly back into the box, 'you must try to be calm and not let it show how much you hate Mary. The people are not all behind you. Some of them blame you for the Nun of Kent's being arrested—'

'They blame me for last year's bad harvest too,' Anne said, but she was listening.

'—and when More and Bishop Fisher are imprisoned they are going to blame you for that, too. You know how More is a popular hero.'

'Well, well,' Anne said. 'You are right, I suppose.'

'You know I am,' George said, putting his arms round her, and nibbling the side of her neck. She jerked her head away irritably.

'Don't do that! What would have have me do, then, brother?'

'What you do so very well—be gracious, dignified, queenly. You are the Queen. You carry the heir to the throne in your belly. Nothing can touch that, not all the proud little Spanish bastards in the world.'

Anne rested a moment against him and closed her eyes. Tom's hands had stopped, and the lute was silent. Nanette looked at him, and saw his sadness. He should have married her, Nanette thought, and kept her gentle.

'All the same,' Anne said after a moment, 'I wish they were

both dead.' And her voice was quiet and flat, and Nanette could not prevent her hand from crossing herself.

The next day, as if in judgement, Anne was seized with gripping pains, and by the afternoon she had miscarried of her child.

It was a blow, but not overpowering, and by the end of April the Queen suspected herself pregnant again. In May the suspicion was confirmed, and all was well once more. She evidently conceived easily; nonetheless, when the King went on progress that month he left Anne behind at Greenwich with instructions to rest and be careful. Nanette was glad that the King had, temporarily at least, left her alone, for she had a suspicion that it was Anne's temper that caused her to miscarry, and it was sure that she was more irritable when the King was there than when he wasn't.

The summer passed pleasantly for them, though there was trouble elsewhere—there was a rebellion in Ireland and, more seriously, on the Scottish border where some Scots nobles with the support of Chapuys and under the leadership of Sir Thomas Dacre—another Neville connection—succeeded in capturing Carlisle. The so-called Nun of Kent was executed, along with the five friars she had duped into supporting her, and Sir Thomas More and Bishop Fisher were imprisoned in the Tower for misprision of treason in not reporting her activities.

In September Anne was five months pregnant, the baby had started to move, Lady Catharine and Lady Mary were both suffering from ill-health, and the King was as attached as any man could be to Princess Elizabeth, playing with her for hours and carrying her about with him as a fashionable lady carries a dog. Nanette began to think that it might not be too much longer before she was home again. But then the Queen discovered a mild flirtation between the King and one of her ladies and, ignoring the fact that such flirtations were commonplace and that she herself flirted in much the same way with the gallants in her own circle, Anne flew into a rage and quarrelled violently with the King; and a few hours later she miscarried swiftly and painfully of her third child.

Their quarrel was soon patched up. There was too much love and dependence between them for such a thing to cause more than a few days coldness, and as soon as the doctors decided it was permissible, the King was again making his nightly trips along the anterooms and corridors that separated his chamber from the Queen's, accompanied by his pages and gentlemen of the bedchamber. The journeyings were so public that even the Spanish ambassador soon had no doubt that the rift was mended, and was reporting gloomily that the King and the Lady were together again.

She would be pregnant again before long, of that there was no doubt. But Nanette, torn between her love for her mistress and her love for Paul, longing to be home, began to wonder if there would ever come a time when the Queen would no longer need her, and would release her from her service.

Seventeen

HE NEW WHEEL FOR BRAZEN'S MILL WAS FINISHED IN MARCH, and it was one of the major items of discussion at the manorial court which Paul held at that time. Amyas did not attend it, and Paul had a feeling that as soon as he was dead and Amyas was master, he would discontinue the practice of consulting his tenants and merely send out edicts like an Emperor. Amyas was once again causing Paul great anxiety: the Treason Act, passed last November, had made it a crime to impugn the new marriage or the legitimacy of the Princess Elizabeth, and it was well known that Cromwell had a very efficient system of information-gathering.

The month before, a man had been brought before the magistrates in York and fined for referring to the Queen as 'The Great Whore' during an argument in a tavern. Amyas had recently taken to frequenting taverns again, though to his credit his consumption seemed still moderate, and if his conversation at the tavern was anything like his conversation at home, it was highly treasonable matter. It would only take one person to report Amyas's words (and not to report them was a crime too—misprision of treason was the charge on which Sir Thomas More was still languishing in the Tower) and he too would be up before the magistrates; and the fine imposed on a

Morland would be much heavier than that imposed on a mere butcher's assistant.

To add to Paul's worries, the latest news from Court through Nanette's letters was that the Queen, who had conceived during Christmas-tide, had miscarried again, and that Chapuys was spreading rumours that the King was being unfaithful to the Queen, pursuing other ladies, and thinking of discarding her.

'It is not true, and I hope that you will deny the matter whenever you hear it,' Nanette had written. 'Chapuys does not understand the way things are with us. At least, Master Paget—the King's secretary—says that he does understand and falsifies things for his own ends, but I think he is merely misguided. It is all a form of words, the flirting, and means nothing. Everyone does it. The King is as much in love with Her Grace as ever; but she has many enemies, and worry makes her temper short. I am sure she will conceive again soon.'

These matters ran through Paul's mind as he conducted the manorial court, and more than once he had to force his attention back to the present in order not to slight his tenants. He was aware, as his grandfather and great-grandfather had been, that it was upon them as much as upon the sheep that the Morland fortune rested. There were fewer faces before him since the flood and the following drought, and in consequence there seemed to be more requests to buy up vacant strips than ever before.

'I have a different sort of request to make, Master,' said the next petitioner to remove his cap and stand before Paul. It was a grizzled sexagenarian called Granby who had three grown sons and a large holding, much of it on the borders of the demesne lands near Akcham. The tone of his voice called Paul's attention fully to him, and he noticed something alert in the attitude of those men and women standing near Granby. This was evidently to be something unusual.

'I am listening,' Paul said. 'What is it?'

'Well, Master,' Granby said, 'you know that Foley's strips lie vacant, and they are all that lay between two of my holdings on the south side of Popple Height.'

'Yes—say on,' Paul prompted.

'Then there's four strips of Will Weaver's lying above them, on the cross. I've spoke to Will, and he's willing to sell them to me, if you're agreeable, Master, but the thing is this—the top of Popple Height is waste land, and the Akcham folk run their goats and pigs there. And then there's the deer that come down from the woods across the river. Hurdles don't keep 'em out—I never knew a deer that couldn't get over a hurdle like it were stepping over a fallen twig.'

There were murmurs of agreement from the listening crowd.

'So, what is it you want to ask me?' Paul asked, though he had something of an idea by now.

'Well, you see, Master, it's like this. If I were to sell some of my strips in other places, and buy up Foley's and Will Weaver's, and then if I were to enclose them with a hedge—why then I'd have one big field that the deer and the beasts couldn't get through, and I could plough it all up, Master, leaving no trenches to mark the strips, 'cause I wouldn't need 'em. I'd get that much more land out of it, Master, and I could plant all the one crop, and tend it that much easier, wi'out all that traipsing back and forth across the hill. My sons could work together with me. The crop would be bigger, and then—'

'Master's rent'd be bigger too,' someone called out, and a ripple of laughter ran round the great hall. But the matter was very serious. Paul's expression was far away as he thought out the implications.

'What sort of a hedge?' he asked. Granby had obviously thought about it, for his answer was pat.

'Hazel, mostly, and whin and whortle, and here and there some small crab-trees to strengthen the line, and wild-rose to keep the beasts out. That way, you see, Master, the hedge would be a crop in itself, hazel-nuts and apples and whortleberries and rose-hips, so it wouldn't be a waste of the land it grew on.'

Paul nodded slowly. 'And inside the hedge, a ditch to channel the water?'

Granby hadn't thought of that. He looked from face to face and nodded. Paul could see by the interest on the faces around him that the idea appealed to more than just Granby. Over the years many of them had amassed holdings contiguous to each other, which made it seem wasteful to farm them in strips.

'And you really think this will give you a bigger crop?' he asked at last.

'No doubt about it, Master. Why, the things we hear about the enclosures further south—you'd only have to believe half of it to think it were worth doing.'

'I've heard the peasants aren't too pleased about the enclosures in some parts of the country,' Paul said with a small smile. Granby was not put out.

'Aye, Master, you say true, but that's in places where the land-lord—saving your honour, Master—has enclosed the peasants' own land and took it from them for the reason of grazing his own sheep. Now we know you would not do that, Master. It is a different thing quite, this.'

'Well, I will think about it and let you know very soon what I decide,' Paul said. 'I cannot see any reason why you should not do this, if the others are all agreeable, but I must think about it first, to see that there are no points against it that we have overlooked.'

They were satisfied with that answer, and matters moved on to other areas, but it gave Paul much to think about, and on the closing of the court he went into the city to visit John Butts and ask his opinion. The house on the Lendal was in as much of a bustle as ever, and having greeted his niece affectionately and admired her babies—she had just had another child, a son they had named Joseph—and accepted an invitation from Lucy to stay to supper when he had finished his business, he was shown into a small chamber to the rear of the hall where John conducted his business.

'What do you think of it?' Paul asked John when he had related the request that had been made to him at the court. 'I know that in some parts of the country the very word "enclosure" is like to cause an uproar, but I cannot see anything against it here, for my people. And as someone remarked, it will put up my rents.'

'I cannot see why they should not do it, although it is impossible with any new idea to know what the drawbacks may be until you crack your shin against them,' John said, thoughtfully scratching his beard. 'What is your own opinion?'

'It has given me the idea of enclosing some of my own outlying fields. The higher land is thin and poor, and it seems to me that a good stout hedge would protect the field from the wind, and perhaps enrich the soil, by stopping the wind from blowing it away in the summer. And then—a hedge might hold the water in, do you think?'

'Anything that held the water in would be a Godsend,' John said shaking his head. 'I sometimes wonder if we're being punished by this drought, though what we might be punished for, I cannot tell.'

Paul sat down on the window-seat and rested his aching left arm, cupping the elbow with his right hand, and Alexander sat by him and rested his grey muzzle on Paul's knee. 'Amyas would be able to tell you,' he said bitterly. 'He would say we are being punished for the break with Rome.'

'Ah, yes, Amyas,' John said thoughtfully, regarding Paul as if wondering whether or not to go on.

'What is it now?' Paul asked. 'What has he done that I have not yet been told about?'

'Oh, it was just that I was wondering whether enclosing your fields might not be a dangerous precedent to set for Amyas. The troubles down south have been caused by the land-lords enclosing the fields against the tenants' wills or interests. Forgive me—but when you are gone might not Amyas take your action as excuse enough to do the same?'

'When I am gone—aye,' Paul said, staring at the floor gloomily. 'I think I have stopped wondering what he will do when I am gone, for my imaginings must fall short of anything that boy can think up.'

'He is not a boy any more, Paul, he is more than thirty years old. Perhaps that is the problem,' John suggested gently. Paul did not notice the hint.

'All I can hope is that I will outlive him, and pass on the estate to Robert. Robert will follow in my footsteps, in the Morland tradition. That is a good boy, you know, John. He will make a good master of men, if only he gets the chance. Amyas seems set to ruin us all. But he also seems set for martyrdom—perhaps that will happen first.'

'Paul, I don't like to see you in this humour,' John said. 'It is perilously close to wishing your own son dead. Come, be more cheerful. Amyas has escaped being overheard, and he is not so important that Cromwell's spies will follow him and record his words for their master.'

'I wish I knew where he was now,' Paul said. 'He went out this morning because he would not attend the manor court, and in such a mood that I am afraid he may be working our ruin at this very moment.'

'You exaggerate—' John was beginning, when there was the sound of a distant commotion, and in a moment the door was flung open and Amyas himself burst in. He pulled up short when he saw his father, and then rounded on him angrily, and Alexander bristled and growled softly in warning.

'Now perhaps you may be satisfied!' he shouted. 'This is the doing of The Concubine, you may be sure—she and her Lutheran friends, and the blacksmith's brat they call Vicar General—Vicar of Hell would be more appropriate. Despoilers! Their work has begun at last, as we knew it should.'

'Enough! You have said enough—these words alone could bring us all to ruin, don't you realise that?' Paul interrupted him, standing up and drawing himself to his full height so that he towered over Amyas. His patience with the boy (boy? John was right, he was old enough to know much, much better by now) was finished. 'Do you want your sons to be orphaned and destitute? Do you want your family to be implicated in your crimes? What about your cousin John, here, and his family? What have they done that you should endanger them with your treasonable words? If you have a longing to die, go fall on your sword. Take me with you, if that's your plan, but I will not stand by in silence and let you attack the innocent with your headstrong, wild stupidity!'

He had never spoken so forcibly to Amyas, and when he replied it was more in astonishment at his father's ignorance than in anger at his wickedness.

'But you cannot have heard—Cromwell's commissioners— the investigation—inquiring into the religious houses—'

'It has been going on for three months,' Paul said. 'What can rouse you now to this passion? It is an investigation long overdue. We have all been talking for years about the reforms that are necessary—'

'They are not sent to gather information for reforming the houses but for destroying them,' Amyas said bitterly. 'You are blinded by your own interests if you think that.'

'The houses that do not need reforming will not be interfered with,' Paul said firmly. 'The King himself has stated that.'

'And with Cromwell choosing his own agents, can you

believe any house will be found not in need of reform?' Amyas
said. 'Where there is no fault, they will invent one.'

'I doubt it,' John said calmly, trying to bring a little ratio-
nality to the exchange. 'But I doubt whether there are many
religious houses in the country that do not need reform.'

'There is one that will never need anything again,' Amyas
said now. 'And it is on your doorstep. I have just come from
there. An order has been sent to St Clements Nunnery that it is
to be closed and disestablished, and its goods confiscated to the
State. Now what have you to say?'

There was a moment's silence, for the news was a shock to
both listeners. St Clements Nunnery seemed a part of their lives,
for it was close by their own Holy Trinity Church in Trinity
Lane, and most of the houses in Trinity Lane were owned by
it. For Paul it brought back a sudden, painful memory, for the
house he had rented for Ursula after she had left the Shambles,
and in which she had drawn her last breath, had been owned
by the Nunnery. He recovered himself, and said,

'It must be obvious even to you why St Clements is to be
closed. It no longer serves any useful purpose. Besides the old
Prioress, there are only two novices there, and I believe they
are both children.'

'There are many such places in the country,' John Butts said.
'With a few exceptions, the religious houses no longer draw
new members as they used to. Their day is done. It is right that
they should be investigated.'

'What would have happened to all the folk made homeless
by the flood if the monasteries had not taken them in?' Amyas
asked. 'How can you say their day is done?'

'There are some, I grant you, in the wild lands to the north
that are still useful—but as to the villagers who suffered from
the flood, I am sure more was done for them by the great families hereabouts than by the monasteries. And I am sure there are

none of them still supported by the monks. Their refuge was very transitory. St Mary's Abbey took none of them in, and the monks there never entertain any but the rich and the noble.'

'You are blinded to the truth,' Amyas said. 'The religious houses will all be destroyed before your eyes, and you will convince yourselves that it is for the best of reasons. But the truth is, it is their wealth that is wanted—their lands and gold and plate and riches—all will be confiscated to swell the Exchequer, and that will be the true reason for their destruction, whatever you want to tell yourselves.'

And with that he turned and went out, leaving the older men not entirely comfortable. At last John Butts said, 'He may be right. But we are right too. If it was their wealth alone, they might have been seized at any time in the past hundred years or more. The world is changing, and men are changing too. Their day is done, as I said. You and I, Paul, will leave behind a very different world from the one we were born into.'

The harvest was bad again that summer, worse, in fact, than the year before with the cumulative effect of the two-year drought, for the seed that was put into the earth that spring had been the poor, shrivelled product of last year's failed crop. All over the country people looked forward despairingly to another famine-stricken winter, and predictably they muttered and murmured, seeing it as a punishment from God. Surprisingly, they no longer blamed the Queen for it, but the King. It was his actions, his policies, which had brought this disaster upon them.

The Pope continued to protest against the King's actions, and to spite him sent a Cardinal's hat for Bishop Fisher, still in the Tower along with Sir Thomas More. It was too open an affront to the King. Now was the time, he discovered, to make them both take the oath of allegiance to the Princess Elizabeth. Both refused, and the King had them executed, along with nine monks who also refused to take the oath. The Pope then announced that he was going to excommunicate the King, which would not have worried the King one jot but would have absolved his subjects, those of them who still felt the Pope to have any authority over them, from obeying him. Cromwell's tentative suggestion for a compromise was to make the Lady Mary the King's heir; the Duke of Norfolk meanwhile had a plan to marry his son Surrey to Mary and make them joint heirs since, in the eyes of many, Norfolk was more royal than the King himself.

To add to all these troubles, foreign ambassadors were openly rude to the Queen and referred to the Princess Elizabeth as 'The Bastard', while attempting to pay court to Lady Mary. The Queen seemed on the brink of disaster, and the King had been cold and distant to her for some weeks, but she had not been endowed with determination and courage for nothing. In the middle of June she gave a great banquet followed by a play and various other ingenious entertainments of the sort the King loved best. He remembered again how he loved her, how there was no-one like her. By the end of the month, the Queen was pregnant again.

Those who loved her held their breath and waited. By the end of September she had safely passed the dangerous three-month mark, and the King took time to go hunting in Wiltshire with Jack Morland's old friend, Sir John St Maur, or Seymour, as it was now more commonly written. Anne did not accompany him, but when he returned in October they went on progress for a month and were seen everywhere together, reported to be merry and in good health as they hawked and hunted and feasted and danced. In November they returned to London, for it was necessary for Anne to be quiet until the other danger-point, the fifth month, was past, but in December she entered the sixth month of her pregnancy in good health and good spirits, and the Court could look forward to the Christmas revels with light hearts.

The King was anxious to please her in every way, and even dismissed his jester, Will Somers, whom he loved dearly, because he had continued to make coarse jokes about the Queen's virtue and the Princess's legitimacy; and he brought to Court again the eldest daughter of Sir John Seymour, because Anne had served with her in the old days when Catharine was Queen and their fathers were friends. In fact, though Anne accepted her as lady-in-waiting with a show of pleasure, she really did not care much about her.

'She is not one of us,' she confided to Nanette. 'She is a terrible prude, she can't sing or play any instrument, she barely talks, and she can't read or write.'

'Then why did you want her for lady-in-waiting?' Nanette asked, pausing in her stitching. They were engaged in getting together a new wardrobe for the Princess, who at just over two years old was ready to be dressed in adult clothes instead of baby petticoats. Kirtles and gowns, fur-trimmed sleeves, coifs, cloaks, velvet shoes were ordered, the colours and materials chosen with great care by Anne for her beloved daughter. Dressmakers were to provide them, but Anne wanted something to come from her own hands, and she and Nanette were therefore engaged in sewing lace trimmings on to the child's new chemises.

'Catharine used to sew Henry's shirts for him, and while I do not intend to copy her in that, I should like Elizabeth to wear something I made myself,' she had explained.

'Oh, to please the King, and my father,' Anne said, referring to the new addition to Court. 'And she might keep George's wife happy—they are two of a kind, those two Janes. Anything that will stop Jane Rochford spying on me will be a boon.'

'They don't seem alike to me,' Nanette said doubtfully. 'Jane Rochford is genuinely spiteful and unpleasant. Jane Seymour seems merely good and dull.'

'She may seem so to you, but believe me that one is as sly and scheming as my dear sister-in-law. It is a fashion to suppose that ugly people must be good, but I think what you are inside shews on the outside. And that one is, underneath it all, a spiteful little prig.'

'But dear Madam,' Nanette said, dismayed, 'if you believe that, why did you not refuse to accept her? You don't need any more enemies around you.'

Anne laughed and patted her belly. 'I won't need to worry when this babe is born. The mother of the King's son will be too secure for any enemy to harm. And I really believe this time, Nan, it will happen. I feel so well!'

'You look well,' Nanette admitted warmly. Anne was dressed in a velvet gown of a warm carnation shade, with great sleeves furred with black fox, and the folds fell gracefully over the swell of her belly. She had taken to wearing the new five-cornered head-dresses, which were much like the old kennels that were worn when they were girls, except that the side-pieces were much shorter. The gauze bands at the front and the folded-up veil at the back covered the head entirely so that no hair could be seen, but the style suited Anne's strong features and set off her great shining eyes.

The Court was gay that Christmas, and the Queen's intimate circle excelled itself in producing entertainments for the King, who had been suffering for some time from a pain in his leg which tended to make him short-tempered. Anne and George were at the centre of all the revelries, and around them circled the brilliant and beautiful satellites they attracted—Tom Wyatt, Hal Norys, Frank Weston, Will Brereton and young Surrey, and the ladies, Mary and Madge Wyatt, Meg Bryan, Nanette,

Madge Shelton, and Mary Howard. The new maid, standing on the edge of things and staring with her bulging pale eyes, might well have thought they were all mad. No-one much cared for her—she was stout, plain and very dull, and at thirty well past marrying age.

After Christmas Nanette received a visit from Paul, this time in the company of Amyas and young Paul, for the latter was now ten and it was time for him to enter a household, since he did not seem to have any desire to become a priest. The family was under the patronage of the Duke of Norfolk, and so it was into his household that young Paul was to be received, and he was brought by his father and grandfather to Hampton where the Duke would meet them.

The Duke was very affable to Paul, for they were of an age—in fact Thomas Howard was just three years older than Paul—and they had many experiences in common. Norfolk had spent a great deal of time in the north, for he was the King's premier general, and fighting the Scots and the Borderers had meant that he had spent a good deal of time in and around York. He greeted the child, too, pleasantly, and young Paul tried to remember what he had been taught to do and say on this occasion but he was too overawed by his surroundings and the forbidding aspect of his new master to do more than bow in terrified silence, but it did well enough.

'Tongue-tied, eh?' Norfolk said with what served him for a smile. 'Better say nothing than the wrong thing, that's always been my motto. You will do well enough, lad. And now, Master Morland, we had better in courtesy let the child pay his respects to his cousin, Henry Norys, since he is here. Norys is held in high regard by the King—I believe the King hardly lets him out of his sight—and if the lad is to get on, it will do him no harm to be polite to the right people.'

'Indeed, Your Grace, I should be glad myself to pay

respects to Master Norys—as would my son,' Paul said, with a prompting glance at Amyas. Amyas bowed his consent and muttered something about his 'dear wife's cousin'. He was finding it hard to know how to conduct himself, for the Duke was the uncle to the woman he still thought of as The Concubine; but on the other hand it was said that he disliked his niece and was working for her downfall. Amyas did not know whether to regard him as friend or enemy.

'Very well—the long gallery I believe should be empty at this time. We will go there, and I shall send for Norys to join us,' the Duke said, and beckoning an attendant, sent him on the errand. The Morlands went with the Duke as he led them briskly through the corridors and anterooms to the long gallery, and behind them came the crowd of attendants and servants without which no person of any note ever moved in the Palace. The long gallery was not, however, empty when they arrived. At the far end someone was sitting on the window-seat in the last window, plucking a tune upon a lute and someone else was singing a thread of melody in a dark, sweet voice. The Duke approached them with a frown between his eyes, ready to send them packing, the seated man and the two women standing.

He neared the group; the woman with her back to them turned; the Duke stopped and swept a low bow and the dark voice said with sweet irony, 'Well Uncle? Well met.'

'Your Grace,' Norfolk said, straightening. The seated man was Sir Thomas Wyatt, the smaller of the two ladies his sister Mary; the tall woman in black velvet was unmistakably, even at this distance, the Queen. The Morlands in their turn swept a bow, Paul doubling his petrified grandson with a firm hand on the top of the head. 'I didn't know you were here, Your Grace,' Norfolk went on, managing to make it sound like an accusation instead of an apology. 'I had thought to meet your cousin Norys here on a private matter.'

'It is no matter, Uncle—we were just going,' the Queen said, and flicked a glance across at the waiting trio. 'But let you present your guests to me. If they be friends to my cousin they must be friends to me.'

'As it pleases Your Grace,' Norfolk said curtly, and, turning, beckoned them forward. Paul went forward willingly, propelling the child with a hand on his shoulder, and Amyas followed just behind. They reached the group and bowed again, and on straightening up Paul found his eyes held by the glowing dark eyes of Nanette's mistress. Her astounding beauty had not been exaggerated, he discovered. She was dressed all in black velvet, which made her skin seem almost supernaturally white by contrast. Her head-dress was a halo-shaped French hood, trimmed simply with pearls, and from under it her black hair hung loose and lustrous to her waist which made her seem somehow girlishly young. She was noticeably pregnant, and she seemed to glow with good health.

'Master Paul Morland, Your Grace, and his son, and grandson whom I have just taken into my household,' Norfolk made the presentation.

'Master Morland! Of course—my dear Nanette's uncle! I am very glad to meet you, Master Morland. When last I saw you it was at Hever, I think, when Nanette was first going to Court.'

Paul was flattered by the kindness of his reception, and bowed again, saying, 'Your Grace does me honour by remembering. May I enquire how my niece does?'

The dark eyes held his with a searching look before she replied, 'She is very well. We are having our portraits painted by our dear Holbein—I have just finished my sitting and perhaps rather cruelly have left Nanette to sit alone. I was on my way to my chamber to change when I met my cousin Tom, and stopped to talk, so now, if you will forgive me, I will leave you to the good offices of my uncle. Master Amyas,

God's greeting. I know you for my brother's friend.' Her words were cool, as if she knew him for something other than that. Her eyes turned to young Paul, who had been staring at her in astonished wonder, and for a moment her expression softened and became both tender and sad as she smiled at him.

Then she swung on her heel and walked away, her heavy velvet skirt hushing against the bare, polished boards. 'Come, Mary,' she said. 'Tom, will you wait on me? Oh—' she turned again, and looked at Paul. 'I will tell Nanette you are here. When you have finished your business, you must visit her. I will send a servant to bring you where she is.' And then she was gone. Paul looked at his son and grandson, and saw on their faces almost identical expressions of stunned admiration; might it be hoped, he wondered, that Amyas would cease his hostility now that he had actually seen the Queen and had been reminded that the Queen's brother had once been his intimate friend?

A servant in the Queen's livery came into the gallery while they were talking to Hal Norys, and when Paul had excused himself, leaving Amyas to take care of the boy, the servant bowed to him and said, 'Her Grace the Queen sent me to bring you to Mistress Morland. Will you follow me, Master?'

Paul was led to one of the anterooms to the Queen's apartments, and there was Nanette, all in dark-blue velvet, her hair loose under a halo cap as the Queen's had been. She stood up as Paul came in, and curtseyed, and said 'Uncle,' much as the Queen had done a little while earlier. Then she dismissed her waiting-woman to the next room with a wave of her hand, and as soon as they were alone she ran to him to be embraced.

'Oh, Nanette, it has seemed so long since I last saw you.'

'It has been a long time. So you met with the Queen—do you not think she looks well?'

'I never saw such a fine glow of health in a woman.'

'I am sure this time all will be well. It will be a boy: the Queen says she feels it as sure as fate. She is past the dangerous time. And the Lady Catharine is dying—God forgive me for being glad for it, but it will be a release for her as well as for my mistress.'

'So you think—this might be the end?' Paul asked hesitantly.

'I do, I am sure of it,' Nanette said happily. 'The bairn will be born in spring, and I shall be home in the summer. And then—'

'And then?'

'There will be nothing more to wait for, will there?'

'No, indeed. Nanette—I can hardly believe it. Do you really want to marry me?'

'Yes, really. I am sorry she told you about the portrait. It was to be a surprise for you. I meant you to have it as a wedding gift.'

Paul smiled and stroked a stray hair from her smooth brow. 'I promise to forget about it. I understand Master Holbein is painting it?'

'Yes—I am very honoured. The Queen was having her portrait taken, and she asked me if I had ever had mine done. When I said no, she bid Master Holbein paint me at the same time, and said she would pay him for it. And, look, he has given me one of his sketches for the Queen's portrait, for a gift.'

She picked up the paper that was lying on a chair and showed him. It was a head-and-shoulders sketch of the Queen in the dress he had just seen her wearing, but—

'But that is not the same head-dress.' It was, a five-cornered, matron's cap.

'She was trying them on, to see which she thought would be the best. I thought the French hood was better, but she thinks the King would prefer her like this. He is to have a new portrait done too, now that he had grown his beard.'

'Grown his beard?'

'Oh yes, and cropped his hair. It was in honour of the King of France. He has made an order that all the men in the Court shall crop their hair and grow their beards. I think, though, that he has done it because he thinks it makes him look younger.' She glanced around her as she said it, and then smiled at him. 'You see how cautious we must be at Court. Oh Paul, I am weary of this public life! Sometimes I feel ashamed that I have wasted so much of our lives in this way. I should not have refused you all those years ago.'

Paul took her hand. 'All things that happen were meant, and perhaps we both had to suffer before this could happen. It will not be long now. In the summer, you will come home. In June, do you think?'

'The Queen's child will be born in March. Perhaps I shall be home even earlier—perhaps in May.'

'Oh yes, come in May if you can. May is the loveliest month.' He kissed her, and at once Ajax ran forward and began to bark at his feet. Nanette drew back, laughing, and picked up the little dog.

'He is jealous of you!' she said. 'He hardly likes anyone to come near me, especially since Anne's little Purkoy died, and he has no other dogs to play with.'

Paul stroked the spaniel's silky head and spoke to it firmly. 'You will have to get used to me, Ajax, for I am going to be doing this very often once your mistress is home. We'll have to buy him a playmate. Perhaps if we get him a bitch—?'

'Happiness makes you generous to all creatures,' Nanette laughed. 'Come, we must go. My mistress awaits me: it is almost time for mass. And I believe you are expected by my lord of Norfolk. Do you stay with him?'

'This night only,' Paul said. 'Then I am going to Dorset to see my cousin Luke. Once Morland Place has a mistress again, I can acquire a companion for Eleanor at long last. I intend to ask him to send his two eldest daughters, Elizabeth and Ruth, to Morland Place to be brought up.'

'Do you, indeed? That is a good plan. They can attend me. Nothing teaches a girl so fast as waiting on a lady, as I know from my own experience.'

'And nothing prepares a wife better than being brought up with her husband,' Paul added. 'Robert will be home from school this summer.'

'Robert?'

'Luke Morland doesn't know it yet,' Paul said with a smile, 'but Elizabeth is going to marry my grandson Robert.'

Eighteen

*A*FEW DAYS AFTER PAUL HAD LEFT FOR DORSET, NANETTE was running along the corridors in answer to an urgent summons from the Queen. The message had been to come with all haste, and at first she had been afraid that it was the start of another miscarriage, but the messenger had said that the Queen appeared in good health, only rather agitated. Probably, then, there was no need to run; but anxiety sped her feet, and lifting her skirts clear of them, and with Ajax bouncing behind her with his tail up like a banner, she flew round a corner and bumped fair and square into a tall young man coming in the other direction.

He staggered but kept his footing, and strong hands grasped her arms to hold her up.

'Oh! I beg your pardon, sir—I did not—' Nanette's breathless apology died on her lips as she looked up into the face of the man who held her. It was a lean, handsome face, with large, dark eyes, a beautifully sculptured mouth, thickly-curling dark hair—only the chin and the nose were wrong. He got those from his mother, probably.

'But surely—you must be my—' She paused again, hardly knowing what relationship to claim, and went on hastily, 'my uncle's son? Are you not Adrian?'

A smile curved the sensuous mouth, but it was a sad smile, and the eyes, though they brightened, remained distant; not precisely hostile, but watchful.

'You remember,' he said. 'You acknowledge me. Well, cousin, I must thank you for that. It is a courtesy, even if you did precede it by trying to knock me down.'

The words and the tone of voice should have made it a friendly jest, but there was something in the eyes still that made her nervous. Ajax crept forward and sniffed at the feet of the man who held his mistress, and laid his ears back and whined softly. The man looked down.

'He thinks you're hurting me,' Nanette explained. 'Soft, Ajax, he means no harm.'

'Ajax?' He laughed. Nanette pulled herself free quite roughly, and remembered her errand.

'My mistress awaits me,' she said. 'I must hurry.'

'Of course,' he said. 'It would not do to be seen talking to me, would it?'

'I didn't mean—'

'My father was here only a few days ago, and did not ask to see me. He wishes to forget I was ever born, of course. He came to bring his grandchild to my lord of Norfolk, my master. I was sent, when it was my turn, not brought. My nephew is in the same household as me, but does not know me. I am not acknowledged—and why? For some fault? Some sin? Some disability?' He spread his arms and looked down at himself. Nanette looked too. He was tall and well-formed, a figure of a man anyone would be proud of. 'No,' he said, 'but because my father did not marry my mother.'

'I'm sure—' Nanette began uncomfortably, but he interrupted her coldly.

'You know that it is true, therefore why try to deny it? My father wishes me unborn, wishes to forget what he did to my mother. She could have been happy and respectable—yes, even *after* I was born—but he prevented it.'

'He did what he could for you,' Nanette said. 'He placed you in the way of advancement. You could not expect—'

'No, of course I could not. You are loyal to him. I hope he appreciates it. You hope to marry him, don't you? Oh yes, do not look surprised. I make it my business to know about my father—my dear, loving father.'

'I really must go—I was summoned in haste to my mistress,' Nanette said, edging away from this disturbing young man. Adrian restrained her by a hand on her wrist that looked casual, but was like an iron band around her flesh. Ajax whined again, and Nanette looked up into the dark, handsome face like one spellbound.

'Remember me, little cousin. You will see me again. And when you next see my father, tell him I will not forget what I owe him. One day I will repay him in full.'

Then he released her, and almost in panic Nanette snatched up her skirts and ran.

'Oh, Nanette, there you are at last!'

'Yes your Grace—I'm sorry, I—'

'Oh Nan, it has happened at last! The news came a little while ago, and I called you at once. A messenger from Kimbolton—Nan, she is dead. The Princess Dowager is dead.'

'What!'

'She died this morning. The messenger brought her Will and a letter for the King. I was so glad I hardly knew what to do or say. Now at last there is no doubt. I am Queen of England most truly now.'

'Does the King know?'

'Of course. The messenger went to him first. He cried when he read her letter of farewell—but he thanked God all the same that she was dead. Hal says he was almost wild with joy. He has ordered a banquet and a ball for this evening to celebrate, and we are all to wear yellow, for joy.'

'Yellow!'

'Aye, he says there shall be no gloom or darkness about this day. For propriety's sake he will wear mourning today, because she was his brother's wife, but it will only be white-mourning, and tonight he will put it off for a suit of yellow. And he has sent for Elizabeth, that he may shew her off at the ball. Oh, Nan!'

'Your Grace, I am very happy for you,' Nanette said. So this was the end of the poor, misguided Spanish woman's resistance! She had caused so much trouble and pain, so much anxiety and upheaval, all for nothing. Had she given in gracefully she could have spent the last years of her life in peace and comfort with her daughter and her friends about her, instead of dying in a cold and comfortless house in the marshes, separated from all she loved, reviled by all and mourned by none. Nanette's thoughts went then to Catharine's daughter. 'The Lady Mary—' she began, and then looked fearfully at Anne, thinking she had been tactless to mention her. But the Queen was too happy to ill-wish anyone.

'She will be very unhappy,' Anne said. 'Poor girl—aye, Nan, I do pity her, though she infuriates me. But I would not wish her pain. I will try again to make friends with her. I will invite her to Court again.'

'She will not come, you know that.'

'She may, now that her mother is dead.'

'She would think it an insult to her mother's memory to serve you.'

'I will tell her she need not carry my train—she need not shew me that much deference.'

'And she would not consent to walk behind the Princess Elizabeth.'

'I will give her precedence. She will come immediately behind me, and before Elizabeth.'

Nanette smiled. 'You are very determined to win her.'

'I am. I pity her. And I want to please Henry. And—' she laid a hand on her belly—'I have a boy in here who makes her no more a threat to me. She can do me no harm, only herself.'

'Well, I hope you succeed. I wish she may know her own best interests.'

Mary refused to accept the overtures of friendship; she refused to acknowledge Anne as Queen; refused to call her late mother Princess Dowager; refused to stop calling herself Princess of Wales. Anne gave up after that, and the King, infuriated, agreed that further attempts were useless, and ordered that Catharine be buried with the minimum of ceremony at Peterborough Cathedral; and to shew how little he was sorry at Catharine's death, he ordered a tournament to celebrate the occasion of her interment, at which he intended, despite the growing pain in his bad leg, to run several courses.

Anne did not attend the joust, but spent the day sewing in her apartments. She was large with child, and found it easier not to move around too much; also she was worried.

'You were so happy when the news of the Princess Dowager's death was brought,' Nanette said. 'Now you seem preoccupied and unhappy. What can harm you, now she is gone?'

'Word from the various ambassadors,' Anne said, putting her work down and sighing. 'It had not occurred to me before, but those who do not recognise our marriage now view Henry as a widower and therefore free to marry again.'

'But he does not regard it so, so it should not trouble you.'

Anne frowned. 'I know—but no-one, not even me, ever knows well what the King is thinking. If it should suit him for some reason to put me aside—if anything should happen—'

'What should happen?' Nanette said stoutly. She would not mention miscarriage, though she knew her mistress was thinking of it. Yet she was seven months gone, past the danger points. 'You have said you are sure you carry a son.'

'I am. But—Nan, the King is no longer young, and he will not admit it. He insists on testing himself against the younger men of the Court. Like the jousting today—not content to run one course, he must beat them all, to prove himself. And his leg has been troubling him more than he will admit. What if something were to happen to him? I would be set aside, and Elizabeth, and they would make Mary Queen.'

Nanette was silent. She knew that was true, for even those of the people who accepted the new marriage still wanted Mary as heir, she being the King's elder daughter.

'There is no reason to suppose anything will happen to the King,' she said at last. 'You may be sure he will not risk himself. Even when your son is born, he will not want to leave the kingdom with a minor to rule it. He will take care. You must not worry.'

Mary Wyatt came through from the next room to say, 'Your Grace, your uncle my lord of Norfolk is approaching.'

'Norfolk? What can he want?' Anne said, and her frown deepened. She and her uncle hated each other, and he never came to her except to annoy her in some way.

'Shall I tell him you are unable to see him?' Nanette said, beginning to rise.

'Too late,' Mary said, glancing behind her. 'He is here—he seems in a hurry for something.'

He was so much in a hurry he did not seem to have time for the usual courtesies. He pushed Mary Wyatt aside and strode into the room, not even glancing at Nanette as she stood to curtsey. Nanette looked past him and saw that his attendants who had followed him into the anteroom looked pale and anxious. Something has happened, she thought.

Anne did not rise, but looked coldly at her uncle and said, 'What does this mean, uncle? It must be something important for you to come unannounced and in this manner.'

He ignored the criticism. His face was grim.

'I come from the King's apartments,' he said. 'Brace yourself, niece—the King has had a bad fall.'

Anne's hand flew to her mouth to stifle the scream. Coming so soon after what she had said to Nanette, she had no doubt of the outcome.

'He is dead! I am undone!' she cried. Nanette rushed to her. 'Nan, what will become of us? Oh God!' and she fell to weeping hysterically.

'What, what, calm yourself, you do yourself no good,' Norfolk said, staring at her with distaste. 'He is not dead. He was knocked unconscious, and has laid so for two hours, but he is awake and sensible now, and has sent me to tell you all is well.'

Nanette looked up at him sharply.

'Could not Your Grace have broke the news more gently?' she demanded. Anne was still weeping, rocking back and forth, clutching her belly.

'He will die, he will die, and we shall be turned out,' she moaned. 'What shall I do? Everyone hates me—even my uncle.'

'I don't hate you,' Norfolk said impatiently, 'but I wish you would show more restraint and more dignity. Behave like a Queen, if you cannot behave like a gentlewoman.'

Anne jumped to her feet at that and screamed at her uncle, the veins standing out in her neck. 'Get out of here! How dare you talk to me like that! Get out! I am the Queen, and I am to bear the heir to the kingdom. You dare to speak to me as if I were one of your servants! The King shall hear of this. Oh—Nan!' She doubled over in sudden pain, and when she straightened again her rage was gone and was replaced by a deadly fear.

'What is it? Madam, what is it?' Nanette asked anxiously. Anne seized her hands with hands that were cold and clammy.

'A pain, Nan. Dear God, I think the baby is coming.'

Nanette flung a look at the Duke, and he backed off, understanding this if nothing else.

'I will leave you to your women,' he said. 'Be of good cheer, Anne. The King is not much hurt—there is no doubt of his recovery. Be calm. I will send in your women.'

And with that he turned hastily and, gathering his train as he went, he left the apartments even more quickly than he had come. Nanette barely saw him go.

'One pain may be nothing,' she said. 'Sit down, try to calm yourself. Take deep breaths and try to be calm.'

Anne sat down, but her eyes were enormous, and the sweat was beginning to break out on her forehead.

'Not just one pain,' she whispered. 'It is coming, the baby is coming, I know it. It is too early, Nan. It is too early by two months.'

'Seven month babies may live, Your Grace,' Mary Wyatt said, coming to her other side. 'One of my cousins was a seven-month baby.'

'It is too early,' Anne said again, as if she hadn't heard. Tears began to seep out from her eye-corners and run down her face. This silent weeping was harder to bear for those who loved her. 'Don't let it come! Mother of God, don't let it come now. It is too early—it will die. Don't let it come now.'

'Come, my lady, we will get you to bed,' Nanette said.

'Rest and be quiet,' Mary said. 'That is the best thing.' One either side they helped her to her feet and began to walk her to her bedchamber. Half way there she was doubled up by another savage pain, and they looked helplessly at each other across the top of her head.

Her labour was long, and her suffering terrible, but Nanette and her other ladies encouraged her with the idea that the baby had a chance of living. At last, in the shadowy gloom of the candle-lit chamber, the Queen, in anguish, forced her child into the world.

'A boy,' the midwife whispered. Nanette, clasping Anne's hand, offered a prayer and a plea. Anne had heard the words.

'I knew it was a son,' she whispered with difficulty. 'I knew—all along—it was a boy.'

'Push again, Madam,' the midwife instructed her. Anne's face was gaunt and haggard with suffering, and wet with sweat as she pushed again. A long, wrenching groan escaped her lips. Lord God, help her, Nanette prayed silently, and at last the child slithered free. Another moment, and the midwife lifted the babe clear and slapped it, but there was no sound, no heart-tearing cry to signify the presence in the chamber of a new person. Two other women turned away with the babe and busied themselves, and Anne's eyes opened and sought Nanette's.

'What's happening?' she asked feebly. 'Let me see my son.'

'Wait, wait a moment,' Nanette said. 'The midwives haven't finished yet.'

'Why does he not cry?' Anne asked, becoming aware of the unnatural silence. The midwife had returned to her side, was looking down at her with enormous compassion. Tears of weakness and defeat rolled from Anne's eyes before the woman had even spoken.

'Madam, we did all we could—'

'My son is dead.'

'He never drew breath,' the midwife said. Anne put her hands over her face and sobbed. Nanette looked across to the corner where the other women were wrapping the small, silent bundle in linen—no swathing-bands, for this Prince, but a shroud; and she saw not only the death of Anne's hopes, but the death of her own. What would happen to them now?

She was not defeated—she would not be defeated. Sooner than anyone could have expected it was she who was cheering her maids rather than vice versa.

'It's for the best,' she said. 'I shall soon be pregnant again. The baby was lost through an accident. I shall be with child again soon, and I shall have a son, a son about whose legitimacy there can be no doubt. The last one was conceived during the Princess Dowager's lifetime, and there would always have been those who would say he was a bastard. So stop your crying and condoling. We are not defeated yet.'

She would not even be perturbed by the knowledge that the King was courting dull, plain, Jane Seymour, had given her gifts and written her letters, which made it seem like something more serious than a flirtation.

'He has known her all her life,' she reasoned. 'She was Catharine's maid. He could hardly flirt with her in the usual way—it would shock her. Or she would pretend to be shocked, the puss-faced hypocrite! She's a scorpion in honey, that one. But he'll soon grow tired of her. Why, she cannot even read—what would he have to talk to her about?'

By March things appeared to be back to normal, except for the King's continued courting of the Seymour. Anne's temper sometimes frayed when faced with the 'honey-scorpion' and her complacent, stupid smile, and once, when she found her wearing a locket that was a gift from the King, Anne tore it from her throat so violently that she cut her hand on the chain. Nanette and the other maids watched anxiously. They could not believe the King meant anything serious by his pursual of Jane—she was, even to an impartial observer, stout, plain and dull, and had not even the virtue of youth, for she was only a year or two younger than Anne herself. But they could not help thinking that the Queen's temper did her no service with the King.

In April the King and Queen were seen together at mass and at dinner, and, apart from the air of restraint between them, it seemed as though her enemies had rejoiced prematurely. But at the end of April when the Court moved to Greenwich, the King held his court apart from hers, and the foreign ambassadors no longer attended her, and Anne and her ladies began to fear that the King was intending to divorce her after all.

On the first of May when Nanette came to attend the Queen, she found her already up and in a fever of excitement. Since the last miscarriage, she had been looking pale, thin and worn, and, despite her attempts at gaiety, anxious and exhausted. But this morning her cheeks were flushed, her eyes bright, and she looked more like Anne Boleyn than the failed, slighted Queen.

'Oh Nan!' she greeted her friend with open arms. 'All is not lost—I have had a messenger this morning—a messenger from the King.'

'From the King?' Nanette could not help a quickly-drawn breath of anxiety. Anne noticed it.

'No, no, chuck, it is good news. He sent to ask me to go to mass with him, and then to attend the Mayday tournament with him. You see, he cannot do without me! I told you he would tire of the Seymour creature. She has done me service—she has reminded him that there is no-one like his Anne. We shall be friends again—all will be well. It was always his favourite day of the year. We used to bring in the May together—oh, years ago, when he was still young! Well, he is not a boy any more, but he knows his Anne can make him feel young, as no-one else can. Nan, Mary, find my newest gown. It must be green, of course—the apple-green silk perhaps? Oh, I am so happy, I can hardly breathe!'

Nanette and Mary exchanged a despairing glance. Her present happiness was as immoderate as, at times, her sorrow or her rages had been. Would she never learn to behave like other people?

'Your Grace, you must be calm,' Mary said without much hope. 'It is good news indeed that the King—'

'It is wonderful news!' Anne interrupted her, taking a few dancing steps across the room to the little casement, which stood open. She leaned out to look down into the sunlit yard, and her long curling hair fell over the sill. 'It is a beautiful day—truly Maying weather. We have been gloomy too long, dear friends, too long shut up in our rooms. From now on, all will be well. Come, what shall I wear?'

It was impossible to quiet her, and all the while they were dressing her, she bubbled with good spirits, laughing and joking, singing snatches of songs, and they could not but be affected by her high spirits. This was the Anne who had enchanted the King and every man who came near her; perhaps, even now, she might enchant her husband again.

They dressed her in green, apple-green silk over a kirtle of emerald green damask, brocaded with gold. The bodice was sewn with pearls and tourmalines; the great sleeves, stiffened and slashed, were clasped with emeralds, and emeralds glittered at the base of the slender white throat and round the rim of the French hood which she resumed, girl-like, in place of the matronly five-point cap. She looked slender, breathtakingly lovely, buoyed with a brilliance, a vivacity which was more than human. She was full of witchcraft, but not the wicked sort.

Nanette and Mary accompanied her to the chapel, and when they met the King's train waiting outside for her, they saw that it was not only in their eyes that she was translated, for the eyes of every man were drawn to her as irresistibly as moths to a flame. Hal, Frank, George, Tom, all the young men of the King's chamber who had made up that special group, the inner circle, looked at her with astonished admiration, and she knew it, and glowed in their love. Nanette looked at the King. His face had been expressionless when they walked towards him, but as his eyes lighted on the Queen, a strange emotion flickered over his bearded face, and Nanette thought that there was almost as much pain in his eyes as love. Yet love there certainly was, and he looked at her for a moment as if he had never seen her before. Then he offered her his arm, and his features settled into the calm piety suitable for the King entering the chapel for mass, and together they walked in.

After mass they breakfasted, and then went to the tourney-grounds for the joust. The people cheered when the King appeared with the Queen at his side, and Nanette noted how many of the cries and cheers were for Anne. She smiled and waved and bowed her head, and took her place beside the King as if there had never been anything amiss; but Nanette, looking around her, noticed with a chill of fear that there were fewer people in the royal box than usual. Lady Worcester, Lady Oxford and Lady Berkeley were not present; neither were the two Janes, Jane Seymour and Jane Rochford. In other circumstances it might have been pleasant that Anne's enemies were so notably missing, but at present it seemed ominous.

The jousting was good, and both Hal and George were running several courses, and they seemed inspired by the Queen's unexpected presence to outshine even their normal brilliance. The King watched impassively. Once or twice Nanette noticed a flicker of that same pained expression in his face, and she wondered if he was regretting that his infirm leg seemed now to have ended his jousting days for ever. Hal ran his third course wearing Nanette's sleeve, a compliment to her as his kinswoman. He won it, of course, and he came over to the royal box, his face red with the exertion, laughing with pleasure, to return the favour. He took off his heaume, and the sunlight shone on his bright hair, and as he reached up with the green sleeve in his hand the King rose abruptly to his feet, his face set and stern.

'That is the last course,' he said. A silence fell over the crowd as if the noise had been cut by a knife. Every face turned towards the King, and Hal Norys froze, his hand still in the air, the green sleeve dangling from his stretched fingers. 'Mistress Morland, take back your sleeve. Hal, do you come with me—I ride for Westminster immediately. And you, Madam,' he turned to the Queen, and for a long moment he stared at her search-ingly. She met his gaze frankly, enquiringly, and Nanette saw his lips quiver as if he were reining in some immense emotion. When at last he spoke, his voice was quiet, but controlled. 'You shall go in to dinner. And afterwards—afterwards, there is the bull-baiting, is there not? You had better attend, as I shall not be here. Take your ladies and go. Come, Hal—'

With that he strode away, so quickly that those he passed scarcely had time to bow or curtsey before he was gone. Anne watched his departure with a puzzled frown, but then, recol-lecting herself, she turned to make the official ending to the jousting, and then withdrew with the dignity and ceremony which was expected of the Queen of England.

'What can it mean?' Nanette and Mary asked each other anxiously. The King's sudden departure troubled them; but Anne remained calm.

'He would not have asked me to attend the joust with him if I were under his displeasure,' she comforted them later as they went to the bull-baiting. 'He has much to think of. He perhaps recollected some urgent business he had forgot.'

Nanette remained unconvinced. She could not help linking that sudden departure with the absence of those various ladies of the Queen's train, but she did her best to remain cheerful and to enjoy the baiting, which was a very good one, the bull giving the dogs no easy task. But they didn't see him killed. Halfway through the entertainment, a messenger came in the King's livery, with sealed orders for the Queen to retire to her rooms and remain there. Anne received and read them impassively, but as she walked back to the palace, she was very pale, and when they reached her apartments she no longer tried to make light of the situation.

The afternoon and evening dragged by, a long summer evening which should have been filled with music and laughter. The palace was unnaturally silent, and it was impossible any longer to hide the fact that the Queen had been deserted. All her ladies-in-waiting and maids of honour had disappeared. She was attended by Nanette and Mary, Madge Wyatt and Margaret Bryan and Meg Shelton; there were a few bedchamber women and a few pages, and beyond that, no-one. Outside her rooms the palace was silent and dark, the lights not lit in the usual places; no sound of voices or movement; no comings and goings in the courtyards. Once or twice a shadowy figure was seen to cross a yard on some errand, but no-one ever looked up at the Queen's windows.

The silence made them tense, and at last Anne's attempts to amuse her women failed and they sat uneasily, avoiding each other's eyes. Anne herself sat, lost in thought, staring at the door, her fingers absently playing with the emerald ring she had put on so happily that morning. Ajax whined suddenly, upset by the atmosphere, and crawled on his belly closer to Nanette's feet, and the sound seemed to rouse Anne from her reverie.

'Come, ladies, come, we must not be so downhearted. Let us keep up our spirits. If I am no longer to be Queen, I shall at least be Marquess of Pembroke, and, if you do not desert me, I shall have all I need to lead a proper, happy life. We need music to cheer us. Nanette, will you sing to us?'

Nanette shook her head, for her throat was closed tight. 'Your Grace, forgive me, I cannot.'

'Well, never mind. Shall I send for Mark? He has such a voice as would bring a dying man back to life. He shall play and sing for us.' She looked round the circle of pale, apprehensive women, and then shook her head. 'No, better we entertain ourselves. I have no wish to send for anyone and be told they are not here. I would rather not know how few are left to me. Mary, let you sing one of Tom's songs. Let us remember here our *true* friends.'

Mary did her best, and after a while her example shamed Nanette into trying, and so the evening passed, and the short summer night. The following morning, Monday the second of May, found the same group sitting after Mass and breakfast at their sewing, trying in the face of another day of lonely apprehension, to keep up their spirits. But patience at least was not wanted of them. Nanette was standing by the window matching embroidery silks when she heard the sound of hooves, and a group of horsemen clattered into the yard.

'Your Grace—' she began, watching as their servants dismounted and ran to hold the horses' heads.

'Who is it, Nan?' the Queen asked. Nanette marvelled at the calmness of her voice, but when she glanced over her shoulder, she saw the apprehension in that white face.

'Your uncle, my lord of Norfolk, and Master Cromwell, Madam. And my lord Winchester—and—it looks like most of the Privy Council. I see Lord Oxford there—and Lord Audley—'

'Then the time has come,' Anne said, putting down her needlework. 'They cannot have come here but to see me. I shall learn at last what is to become of me.' Her lips quivered suddenly as she lost and regained control. 'It is better at least to know.'

'Oh Madam,' Mary cried, reaching out a hand. Anne caught it, and patted it comfortingly.

'I am to be set aside,' she said, forcing herself to be calm. 'I am to be divorced, even as poor Catharine was, and set aside for that Seymour bitch. And Elizabeth—' she laughed harshly. 'Ironic, is it not? My Elizabeth will be disinherited, just as Mary was. How similar is my fate to Catharine's—with this difference, that no-one will fight for me, as they did for her.'

'Oh Your Grace, don't say so! You have friends, strong friends. My lord your father—Lord Rochford—Hal and Tom—all your friends will surely speak for you,' Mary cried. Anne shook her head.

'They have no power, Mary, and well you know it. They are the King's friends, but if he will put me aside, who can gainsay him? I have no other kings, as she had, to uphold my cause, or Elizabeth's.' She sighed as she rose to her feet. 'We had better make ready to receive the Council here, ladies. Clear away the sewing.'

It was not necessary, after all. A servant came to require the Queen to attend the Council in the council chamber. Anne drew herself to her full height, quivering with outrage.

'Who orders the Queen to attend?' she demanded. 'Who has the power to summon the Queen of England?'

'Madam, the Council summons you by the King's command. His orders are that you should attend them, and not they you.'

Nanette saw Anne's hands ball into fists, and for a moment she thought the Queen would strike the servant, but after a moment she seemed to swallow down her anger, and she said in a tight voice, 'Very well then. I am the King's to command. Ladies, attend me.' And she walked out of her chambers, and followed the servant to the council chamber.

The members of the Council rose as she entered, and most of them bowed. Norfolk and Cromwell were the notable exceptions, and Cromwell cast a sharp eye round the room at the others as if in warning.

'Well, uncle,' Anne said, halting just inside the door and staring at him with her head up, proudly. 'What have you to tell me.'

'I have come, with the other members of the Privy Council, on the King's warrant, to arrest you, Madam, for high treason,' Norfolk said harshly. Nanette was standing a little to one side of her mistress, watching her anxiously, and she saw now that Anne had expected anything but that. Surprise silenced her for a moment, and then she asked in an incredulous voice, 'For treason? For *treason*? On what grounds?' It was Cromwell who answered her.

'For adultery, Madam.' He glanced at a paper in his hand—a theatrical gesture, for he knew everything contained in it by heart. 'For adultery with Henry Norys, Sir Thomas Wyatt, Sir William Brereton, Sir Francis Weston, and others still to be discovered. Your infamy is all come to light, now. There is more information arriving at every minute.'

'Such wickedness as yours could not long remain hidden,' Norfolk said now. 'I am ashamed that I have to call you niece.'

'My lord, Master Cromwell,' the Marquess of Winchester broke in, 'surely we cannot yet be sure about the evidence. It behooves us to speak gently to Her Grace, considering—'

'Considering her infamy, your objections smack of disloyalty to the King,' Norfolk snapped back. Anne had been staring from one to the other as they spoke, as if unable to understand what was being said. Now at last she spoke, and her voice was high was outraged amazement.

'Adultery? You must be mad! The King will have your heads for daring to suggest such a thing.'

'The King has signed this warrant,' Cromwell said,

unperturbed. Anne did not even glance at it. Her lip curled with disgust.

'This is some plot of yours, Cromwell, spurred on I doubt not by my gentle kinsman there. But it will not work. The King will never believe you. His own friends—his own closest friends! Are you mad?'

Norfolk shook his head and tutted at her words, but Cromwell looked graver.

'You are infatuated, Madam. The evidence has been brought before the King, and he himself has ordered your arrest and trial. I—and the other members of the council—merely act upon his orders.'

'Evidence!' Anne said scornfully. 'What evidence! There cannot be evidence of what never took place.'

'Your musician, Mark Smeaton, admitted adultery with you, and he and others of your servants have supplied the names of your other lovers. There will, no doubt, be more names forthcoming.'

Anne looked from one face to another, and Nanette saw her mounting rage. 'Mark Smeaton? You are disgusting, utterly disgusting, to suggest that I could stoop to—to associate with a servant! Uncle—my lords—Lord Winchester—you surely cannot stand by and allow this person to say such things about the Queen of England!'

'It is not for long that you will be Queen,' Norfolk said. 'And all this protest is vain. Your wickedness is uncovered. But how a kinswoman of mine could perform such unholy, such diabolical acts—' He shuddered, and then roared at her, his outrage matching hers. 'Your own brother, you vile witch! With your own brother!'

Anne's face drained of blood, and she stared from one face to another, her lips twitching in disbelieving horror. 'My brother? What—what—of my brother?'

Cromwell's unemotional voice. 'The charge is adultery and incest, Madam.'

Anne's eyes seemed to protrude with horror, and like a trapped animal she looked about her for someone to say this was not happening, for someone to shew mercy. Nanette moved a step closer, and out of the corner of her eye she saw Mary on the other side of her do the same. Cromwell went on,

'Lady Rochford came forward voluntarily to lay evidence against her husband and you on this issue.'

'You can have no doubts now,' Norfolk said. 'When a wife is driven by right Christian outrage to lay evidence against her own husband, it is a plain sign.'

'And—the King—sent you to say this?' Anne whispered at last. She closed her eyes for a moment, as if to seek respite from the horror. 'God pity me. And God pity the perjurers.' She looked now towards Nanette, and then her other ladies. 'I cannot believe that he means it,' she said, and her voice was almost conversational. 'He knows, he must know—it can only be to prove me. He wishes to test my love for him. That is all—he could not believe—his own friends, his closest friends! He must know that I love him. On whom else could I depend?' She turned abruptly to Cromwell. 'Let me see him. Let me see the King. If I can speak to him I know I can convince him that I love him. Why else—?'

'Impossible, Madam,' Cromwell said. 'You know that a person accused of treason cannot come into the King's presence until cleared of the charge. You must come with us now to the Tower, where you will await your trial.'

After a moment, she nodded. She seemed a little dazed. 'Very well. My ladies will pack some things for me.'

'No time for that,' Norfolk said roughly. 'Come as you are. You deserve no better—'

'My lord,' Winchester interrupted, 'I must protest at such language. The Queen has not been found guilty. There is no need—'

'There is no time,' Norfolk said abruptly. 'You must come now or we miss the tide. Your women can send on what you need.'

'Send on—but they come with me,' Anne said, a new fear striking her. Nanette and the others instinctively stepped nearer her, as if huddling under her lee.

'Your women do not go with you. There are four ladies waiting below in the barge who will attend you in the Tower. It is the King's orders.'

'Who are they?' Anne asked.

'Lady Boleyn, Mrs. Stonor, Mrs. Cousens, and Mrs. Sheldon,' Cromwell said. Anne nodded as if she had expected it. 'My enemies, every one,' she murmured. 'Very well, I am ready.'

She embraced them one by one, Nanette, Mary and the three Margarets, and then with great dignity turned to the door. Cromwell led the Council after her. Nanette shrank back as they passed, as if they might be carrying some plague that would strike her, but when they had passed she seized Mary's hand and followed in their wake. The procession went down the stairs and out through the river gate and there by the landing stage the great barge was waiting. Word had evidently got out, for the banks on both sides of the river were lined with people, and as the Queen passed between the guards towards the boat more than one bravely called out a blessing to her.

She looked neither to left nor right. Head high, she kept her dignity, though only the five women, watching from the gate, knew what it cost her. The Queen did not look back at them, but they knew she was aware of them, and took comfort from them, and they watched, their eyes blinded with tears, until the barge turned a bend in the river and was lost to sight.

Nineteen

THE KING REMAINED AT WESTMINSTER, AND THE QUEEN'S Household lived the next few weeks in a kind of limbo at Greenwich, waiting for news, and dreading it when it came, for it was all bad. There were further arrests—Sir Richard Page, a friend of Wyatt's, and then Madge Bryan's brother Francis. Madge was so stricken when she heard the news that she fell ill, and was permitted to return home to her parents.

James Chapham, who was in London, sent to say that he would escort Nanette home if she wished it, feeling sure that he could get permission for her to retire from Court; but she felt that, quite apart from her duty to her mistress, she could not leave the Wyatt sisters. Her presence she knew did a little to comfort them. The three of them and Meg Shelton clung together for comfort, and there was a kind of tactful pity in the way they were left alone, nothing being required of them. They were not even brought to Cromwell for questioning during those weeks when the cases against the accused people were being assembled, and that was one thing to be thankful for. They spent much of their time in the chapel praying, and the rest of the time talking quietly together about old times. By mutual consent they never mentioned the present trouble—it would have been too much to bear.

The trial of the Queen and her brother was set for the fifteenth, and of the accused lovers for the twelfth of May. In the end there were only four men brought before the jury in Westminster Hall—Hal Norys, Frank Weston, William Brereton, and the musician Mark Smeaton. It was a great relief to all the women that Tom Wyatt was not to be tried. It was a tribute to his great goodness and loving heart that no-one in all that mercenary Court could be found to swear anything against him; and perhaps, after all, the King could not bear to part with him either. He was not released, however. Such was his influence that he was to be kept in the Tower until the business was all over, for fear he should speak out on the Queen's behalf. Page and Bryan were also released, for lack of evidence, but banished to the country.

The trial was a matter of form only. The charges were read to the four men, and they were allowed to answer. The little musician, haggard and shrinking, kept the promise he had made under torture—to confess to adultery with the Queen. The other three, in clear, calm voices, denied every charge and proclaimed their innocence. They were then pronounced guilty and sentenced to death—the three gentlemen by the axe, and the musician, as a commoner, by the rope.

The following day orders arrived at Greenwich from Cromwell that the Queen's Household should be broken up and her personal belongings disposed of. Her secretary was ordered to make a list of her debts, including unpaid wages; her treasurer was required to account for all the jewel and plate, both her own and the Crown property, and the Master of Horse was required to deal with her horses and dogs. The human members of the Household were either paid off or transferred to the King's establishment. Nanette, Mary, Madge and Meg were given leave to retire to their homes, but instead they begged for an interview with Cromwell, and when this was granted they asked if they could be allowed to replace the Queen's present attendants in the Tower.

'Out of the question,' Cromwell said dismissively. 'The ladies in attendance were chosen specifically by the King.'

'We know,' Nanette answered for them. 'And we know why, too. But surely, Master, their task is done now? If Her Grace is to be tried on Sunday, you must by now have gathered all the information you require through that medium. For pity, Master Cromwell, let you ask His Grace to send us to her.' He looked thoughtful, and Nanette added quietly, 'I know you only do your job, and have no personal spite against the Queen. It will comfort her and us to be together. For pity, let you ask.'

Cromwell's face was tired. He had everything to do, everyone to oversee, a difficult master to placate, and public odium to bear for doing his duty to his master and the State; but he looked from Nanette to the other women, and his taut mouth relaxed a little.

'Very well, I will ask him,' he said. 'I think it can do no harm now. I will let you know tomorrow what he says. And now, if you please—' They took the hint, and left his small office quickly, and before they had even closed the door behind them he was already dictating another piece of business to his secretary. It was no simple matter to try a Queen for treason.

True to his word, Cromwell made the request, and late on Saturday night word came that they would be admitted to the Tower early the next morning, in time to dress their mistress for her trial. It was a grim enough duty, but as the jailer let them into the Queen's apartments, and they saw her surprise and joy at the sight of them, they felt the first happiness they had known since the Mayday joust.

The Great Hall—sometimes called the King's Hall—in the Tower was to be the scene of the most momentous trial in the history of England, the first ever trial of an anointed queen. Two thousand spectators stood in the ranks down the sides of the hall, while across the end of the hall a scaffold had been erected on which the juries were to sit: the grand jury of Kent, two petty juries of Middlesex, and the whole of the Privy Council—seventy-six people in all. The centre of the hall was empty except for one chair where the accused would sit.

The central place on the judges' scaffold was taken by the Duke of Norfolk, holding his white wand of office as Earl Marshal of England. The Chancellor, Lord Audley, sat on his right, and the King's brother-in-law Suffolk on his left. Thomas Boleyn had been excused the task of judging his own son and daughter, which would have been his duty as a member of the Privy Council. Cromwell, the Vicar-General and on this occasion the King's Advocate, stood before the scaffold, facing the chair.

This was the scene Nanette saw when the great doors at the far end of the hall were flung open by the armed yeomen, and the Lieutenant and Constable of the Tower, Sir William Kingston and Sir Edmund Walsingham, led the way in. Nanette and the three other ladies walked two-by-two behind the Queen. They had dressed her carefully that morning in a gown of russet silk over a gold-brocade kirtle, its sleeves trimmed with black fur, and a five-cornered hood of black velvet, the veil turned up and pinned, concealing her hair. She looked somberly but richly apparelled; she was pale from her long confinement, but she was calm and composed, dignified and proud—every inch a queen. Yet she and the four women who attended her could not but be aware of the final figure in that procession—the hooded headsman, carrying the axe, its blade turned away from the Queen.

When Anne had taken her seat, Nanette and the other women standing behind her chair, and the juries had been sworn in, Cromwell read the charges, his strong, beautiful voice carrying easily the length of the great chamber. Five seductions of the five accused men were given, with a date to each, and Nanette noted wryly that three of the five dates were late in the Queen's last pregnancy, when she was on progress with the King. It was said that the Queen had conspired with her lovers to kill the King, and had agreed to marry one of them when he was dead. Sworn statements of evidence were given to the juries to support the accusations, but no witnesses were brought forward—in treason trials, a sworn statement was considered sufficient.

It was then the Queen's turn to speak, and clearly, calmly, proudly she denied each accusation in turn to her silent audience. The spectators' eyes bored into her, but they were not hostile eyes, and as she spoke Nanette could feel the upsurge of sympathy that met her words. When the Queen, in answer to the charge of incest, said, 'If he has been in my chamber, surely he might do so without suspicion, being my brother?' There was a soft murmur of agreement from the listening crowd, and Anne's voice lifted to it as she added, 'I have never had any intercourse with him other than the normal, Christian and Godly intercourse that is between any brother and sister. Anything else would be as abhorrent to me as it would to you, my lords.'

She spoke well, sincerely, convincingly, and there was no doubt in the minds of any of those present that she was innocent of the charges. But the law was the law. Sworn statements of evidence in a treason trial could not be set aside, and to disbelieve them was in itself a treasonable act. When Norfolk asked the juries for their verdict, their answer was a foregone conclusion. Unanimously, they found the Queen guilty of incest, adultery, and high treason.

In the chill silence that fell then, the Queen's uncle stood and pronounced sentence: she was to die on Tower Green, either by burning or beheading, as the King's pleasure should be further known. There was an indrawn breath at that from more than one spectator, and Nanette saw Anne's hands clench. It was one thing to prepare oneself to face the swift death of the axe, quite another to contemplate the long agony of burning. Then there was a commotion in the ranks of the Privy Councillors—one of its members had collapsed or fainted, falling forwards on to the backs of the row in front of him. Always master of the situation, Cromwell called forward four yeomen to carry him out, and as he was borne past, Nanette saw the Queen turn her head for the briefest moment to look at him, and she looked too. It was hard to recognise in that thin, sickly, greying man the figure of Harry Percy whom the Queen had once loved. Perhaps he could not bear his own part in the thing that had just been done, Nanette thought; perhaps in that moment the Queen had seen in him the beginning of her doom, all those years ago.

Norfolk waited impatiently for the disturbance to end, and then addressed the Queen.

'Have you anything to say? If so, you may speak now.'

Anne looked around her for a moment before she replied. 'I am ready for death,' she said. 'I only regret those innocent gentlemen who must die for my sake. I am willing to believe you have good reason for what you have done,' she went on, looking at her uncle, 'but then it must be other than that produced in this court.' There was a murmur at that, running round the banks of spectators like wind running through the grass over a hillside. 'I am the King's true subject, and his most faithful wife.'

There was a long silence as she ceased speaking, and Nanette saw with amazement that Norfolk had begun to cry. The sight seemed to disconcert the Queen, too, and she glanced towards Cromwell as if unsure what to do next. Then she decided, curtseyed to the Council, turned, and began to walk towards the door. Nanette and the other three fell in behind her, and behind them came Kingston and Walsingham, and the headsman, the blade of his axe now turned towards the Queen. It seemed a very long way to the great doors, flung open on the sunlit, grassy courts of the Tower. Nanette felt unspeakably weary, drained of all emotion; she could only fix her eyes on that straight, rigid back in front of her, and follow it blindly. Yet it occurred to her even then how strange it was that she should be drawing strength from her mistress, and not vice-versa.

News came to them throughout Monday—that George had also, as was expected, been condemned to death, but had acquitted himself nobly in the court. The executions were set, those of Norys, Weston, Brereton and Smeaton for Tuesday, and of Anne and George for Thursday. The gentlemen were to be beheaded by axe, Smeaton was to suffer the ultimate penalty for treason of hanging, disembowelling and quartering; but for Anne, the King had ordered a headsman from Calais who was skilled with the sword. No queen of England had ever been executed before, so there was no precedent to follow, but it seemed right that something other than the common axe should be used. Anne heard the news without comment. She still could not quite believe it had all happened; the possibility of beheading seemed as remote as that of burning.

Her attitude ruled that of her ladies, and through the day they sewed, or prayed, or conversed quietly, turning their minds resolutely away from what had happened, closing their ears to the sounds of hammering and sawing which came from outside, where the carpenters were preparing the scaffold on the green for the executions tomorrow. In the afternoon Kingston brought them the news that the great Norys clan had offered the King a huge ransom for the life of Hal, virtually every penny they possessed, but it was refused.

Anne nodded. 'Of course. It is too late now. Too late for all of them.'

'Also, Madam, I must ask you to remove the jewellery you are wearing and give it to me for return to the Keeper of the Wardrobe.'

'Those jewels were gifts from the King to Her Grace personally,' Mary Wyatt said sharply. 'They are not Crown property.'

'Nevertheless, Madam,' Kingston began impassively, and Anne interrupted, 'It's all right, Mary. It is expected. I am a condemned criminal now. Here, good Master Kingston, hold out your hands.'

Nanette thought, to do him justice, he looked uncomfortable as the Queen unclasped the triple rope of pearls from around her neck and dropped it into his hands, following them up with the various rings she wore. Then she hesitated, her hands at her jewelled belt, and raised her eyes enquiringly at Kingston. He shook his head abruptly, his face reddening, and with a bow he retreated. Anne burst into laughter at his obvious discomfiture. Her laughter was the thing he had always disliked most about her.

In the evening he reappeared with an armed escort.

'Put on your cloak, Madam,' he said. 'You are to be taken to Lambeth Palace to speak to the Archbishop of Canterbury. A boat is waiting.'

'For what purpose?' Anne asked.

'The order is signed by the King's secretary. I need no other explanation,' Kingston said coldly. 'Your ladies may accompany you. You are to go at once.'

Anne shrugged, and rose, and in a few minutes the five of them were walking out under the Watergate—the Londoners called it Traitor's Gate, because it was generally by water that prisoners were taken to the Tower—to the waiting barge.

'I never thought I should leave the Tower again,' Anne said softly. 'It is good to smell the fresh air again, from outside its walls.'

'What can the Archbishop want?' Nanette asked.

'It is not what the Archbishop wants but what the King wants,' Mary said.

'Thomas knows I am innocent,' Anne said. 'He wrote to the King when I was arrested, to say that he never had better opinion of a woman than me. Mrs. Cousens told me. Perhaps—perhaps he has a plan to help me.'

Nanette and Mary exchanged glances. Was there hope? At this stage, it could not be wrong to grasp at straws. The rest of the journey up to Lambeth went in silence. It was a lovely evening, the air mild and sweet, the sun setting in bars of gold and crimson up ahead of them, so that the guard in the prow was a black silhouette carved out of the fiery horizon. On either side the banks were thick with flowers, kingcup and lady's slipper, blue brooklime and spearwort and clumps of yellow flags, and in and out of the thick rushes the ducks swam, leading their new families in exploration. Where the sun reflected on the water, clouds of late insects still hovered and danced, and the swallows were flickering back and forth across the water feeding, and filling the air with their shrill sweeting, while from further away came the evening sound of rooks cawing as they roosted in the clumps of elms.

Nanette watched the Queen as her head turned this way and that, drinking in the sights. It was a beautiful world to have to think of leaving, and hardest of all to leave it in May, when it was throbbing and bursting with new life. It was dark by the time they reached the landing at Lambeth, and Nanette was glad. It would have been cruel to have to travel back to the Tower through such a glowing world.

They were led down into the crypt, and there the Archbishop was waiting for them. Anne knelt and kissed his ring, and anxiously he raised her and stood for a moment looking at her, his eyes brimming with tears. Cranmer was no Kingston, to conceal what he felt under an impassive mask, and he loved Anne, had been her confessor since first the Boleyn family advanced him. He was now under the painful duty of having to accept that the law was just, while privately believing implicitly in her innocence.

'My child, I am commanded by the King to hear your confession in the matter of the charges against you,' he said. Anne cocked her head a little to one side.

'He hopes, then, that I will confess to the crime and make his conscience easier? But, Thomas, how will he know what I say? Does he think you will tell him?' Cranmer looked uncomfortable. 'If he does,' she went on, smiling gently, 'he does not know his Thomas as well as I know mine. Did you not tell him, dear Thomas, that you could not break the seal of the confessional?'

'I did, Your Grace, of course, tell him that.'

'And he told you to hear me anyway?'

'I said that I thought you would receive comfort from it,' the Archbishop explained.

'You are right,' Anne said. 'And I will willingly confess to you. I have nothing to fear.'

'Your Grace—' Cranmer said, and then paused, and looked about him anxiously before continuing in a low voice, 'Your Grace, I think I may be able to save your life. I have a plan—if you will consent to it.'

Even in the dim light Nanette could see that Anne had paled. To be offered life, at this stage—! 'Say on,' she said quietly.

'Your Grace, if it can be shewn that you and the King were never married—in canon law, there were two obstacles to your union, your precontract with my lord of Northumberland, and the King's relationship with your sister.'

'If I were never married—' Anne said thoughtfully.

'You would be the Marquess of Pembroke, and not the Queen, and then your supposed liaison with the gentlemen named would not be adultery, and therefore not treasonable.'

'I see. And do you think the King would accept that?'

Thomas shook his head. 'I do not know, Your Grace. But in law, you would have to be set free, since there would no longer be a charge against you. If you would swear that your marriage was unlawful—'

'And that Elizabeth is therefore a bastard?' Anne said, realising the implications.

'She will be made so anyway, Your Grace.' Anne nodded.

'Then I may be allowed to go into exile, do you think?'

'Perhaps you might enter a nunnery—you would be safe then.'

'Well, Thomas, I will do it. Have you the paper prepared? Then I will sign it. I am not so proud as Catharine. I am young, and I love life. If I can go abroad and take Elizabeth with me, I shall be content.'

She was in light spirits on the journey back to the Tower. 'There is a nunnery I know of in Antwerp. I shall go to Antwerp and live out my days there in peace. I am so tired—I do not think I could ever wish to see a Court again. A simple life—the country pleasures that Tom is always talking of, Mary—and watching my daughter grow up. I hope she may lead a better life than her mother. Perhaps Tom will join us, Mary, what think you?'

'Madam,' Mary said doubtfully, and Anne laughed.

'So cautious, dear friend! Well, perhaps not. But you will come with me, will you not? Or is exile too great a price to ask of a friend?'

'Oh Madam, how can you suggest—I would never leave you,' Mary said, almost in tears. 'To my life's end, I would never leave you.'

Anne looked around the four loved faces, and smiled. 'He will let me go. He has no wish for my blood. A Queen of England has never been executed before. It would be too shocking. The people already complain in the streets that I am unjustly condemned. No, they will let me go.'

On the morning of the seventeenth Kingston brought the news that her sacrifice had been in vain. Her marriage to the King had been annulled. She was no longer Queen; she had never been Queen; and yet she was to die for a crime she could not have committed. Worse, those men accused with her of a crime that was no crime were also to die that very morning. When she heard, she cried out. It was cruel to have hoped for life, and to have that hope snatched away. Kingston left them, and she fell to the ground and wept until there were no tears left in her.

Another glorious May day had drifted into dusk, and now the last luminescence had faded from the sky and the stars were beginning to prick its velvet blackness beyond the little window. Anne had sat there, looking out at the patch of sky she could see, until there was positively no light left, before she would allow her women to kindle the lamps. It was the last sunset she would ever see; this still and scented night the last she would ever live through; tomorrow was Thursday the nineteenth of May, and tomorrow morning she would die.

As well as the four women, her chaplain Matthew Parker was with her in the room and would stay with her until she reached the foot of the scaffold. He would not be permitted to go up with her, since she had never admitted her guilt, but Kingston, kind in his own way, had arranged for his presence thus far, and also for the presence in the small anteroom of the

Host, for the Queen's comfort. He had much to do, enough to keep him occupied all through the last night of her life, and like her, he would not sleep at all.

For Anne, there was nothing more to be done. She had chosen her dress for the morrow, written her speech, disposed of her last few possessions, confessed herself and received the Body of the Saviour, prayed until her mind could no longer encompass the thought of prayer. Now, with her companions, there was only the waiting.

'He could not have let me go,' she said. 'I did not understand why he should want my death, if he loved me—but it is because he loves me that he could not bear to be parted from me, knowing I was in the world, perhaps in another man's arms. I shall not be so far from him in death. No, no, my dear friends, don't cry, not now. I deserve to die. I am guilty—not of the acts I am accused of, but guilty of treason all the same. I failed to give the King a son, that was my crime. He had his duty, and I mine. He knew that I would understand—he saw me anointed.'

'But Madam—the others—was it necessary—?' Mary said with difficulty. 'His closest friends—Hal was with him from boyhood, and Frank, too—they were both pages with him. And Will, and George—all his friends—' She could say no more. Anne looked pityingly at her.

'I know, Mary, I know. It is hard for me, too—but think how much harder for him, to lose all those dearest to him.'

'Then—why?'

'He had to, don't you see? If I were dead, and they survived, they would have been forced to support my cause. The faction had to be destroyed. That was why he agreed to the charge. He could not have believed it. In a Court where there is never any privacy? He would have known. No, no, I cannot think he ever believed the charge. But it made it possible to remove us all.' She was silent for a while, musing. Her ladies did not speak much. It was easier to retain control in silence. After a while she smiled.

'Nanette, you were with me from the beginning—do you remember that night at Hever, before we left for Court? How little we thought then—! And yet, you know, I have thought and thought, and I cannot see where I might have turned aside from the path. There was no place where I made the decision to go on—always for me there was no choice. I could not have done any different, could I?'

Nanette shook her head, and managed to say, 'No, Your Grace. There was never anything else you could have done.'

'No,' she said, and she seemed contented with the answer. She stood restlessly and walked across to the window. 'It will be another fine day tomorrow. Another dry summer. Already there is talk of the drought. I told Kingston,' she turned with a wicked smile, 'that there would be no more rain until I was freed from the Tower. It upset him. I think he half believed the stories about my being a witch. Well, I shall be free tomorrow. What shall you do, my friends? Mary? Tom will be freed when I am dead. Shall you and Madge go back to Kent? Oh, Hever—I wish I could see Hever again. I wish,' she burst out passionately, 'that I had never left it! Oh my poor mother—'

She turned away, and her face was hidden. Nanette got up quietly and went to her, and she stretched a hand behind her for Nanette to take and hold. Her deformed finger was rough against Nanette's palm, and she remembered suddenly and cruelly all those times when she had comforted mistress Anne Boleyn for that little deformity. She had been afraid no-one would love her.

'So many have loved you,' Nanette said quietly. Anne nodded, still with her back turned. 'Life has been rich for you.'

'Yes,' she whispered. 'I have known love. I have borne a child. My Elizabeth—' Nanette thought she was crying, but when she turned a moment later, her thin cheeks were dry, and her eyes, though bright, were not wet. 'Nan, I have not done right by you. I have kept you from home, from marriage. You might have had a child of your own by now. Nan, will you forgive me?'

Nanette could not answer.

'You will go home now, won't you, and marry him? He loves you—I knew it when I saw him. You will go back to Morland Place? I know the north so little. Is it beautiful there?'

'I think so, my lady. It is wilder and barer than the south, but it has a beauty of its own.'

'Tell me.'

'I don't know how, except to say that there seems more sky there, and the sky is always moving, clouds streaming across it, racing the wind. The earth seems to move too, with the wind in the grass and the cloud-shadows running over the hills. And the colours are different—purple and brown on the upland, and dotted with white—there are sheep everywhere.'

'And now there will be lambs—it is lambing-time, is it not?'

'Yes, Madam. In May they are thick as snow on the slopes.'

'You will go back, won't you? I am glad. I can think of you when—' She broke off and walked back to her place, but her eyes turned again and again to the window, drawn by the night, the freedom, the sweet summer air, smelling of grass and trees and the river. 'I have so little time,' she said. 'I feel as though I have been blind and deaf all my life, never noticing how lovely things are.'

The night wore on, and they sat quietly, barely pretending to sew any more, waiting for dawn when they could hear mass again, waiting for the light to steal into the little chamber, waiting for the last day to break. When the sky had grown pearly outside, and there was a new smell in the air, the poignant, heart-breaking smell of morning, the Queen lifted her head wearily and said,

'Do you remember Calais? It was growing light when he came.'

Nanette said, 'He was damp with dew. His doublet was pearled with it.'

'How he loved me,' Anne murmured, smiling. 'It was all grey and still, and he came like the sun rising, a golden spark in the grey. And that was Elizabeth. I am so glad there is Elizabeth. She is our love, she will carry it on. He was always so good to me, always—'

She stopped. The hammering had begun again outside. She would not go to that window again, for it looked out on to the green where the new scaffold had been built.

Kingston came at eight o'clock to tell the Queen that there had been so much to do that it had been impossible to arrange for the execution to take place at nine, as planned.

'It has had to be postponed until noon, Madam,' he said. 'There are still things which have to be done, and by myself in person. I am sorry, but so it is.'

'I am sorry too,' the Queen said. 'I had hoped to be dead and past my pain by noon.'

'There should be no pain,' Kingston said, unexpectedly gently, for him. 'They say it is very—subtle.'

Anne tried to speak conversationally, though they could hear the strain in her voice. 'They do say that the executioner is very good. And after all, I have only a little neck.' She put her hands to her throat, encircling it, and began to laugh hysterically. Kingston looked shocked, which made her laugh all the more. Nanette and the others were in tears, and at the sight the Lieutenant beat a hasty retreat. He would never understand her.

When he was gone, her laughter stopped as abruptly as it began.

'Come ladies, you had better dress me. Madge, Mary, stop your weeping. It is not time yet for that. Come, fetch my gown. Nan, you have a light hand—do you brush my hair. I must look my best today. I must look like the Queen, this one last time.'

They dressed her with care, and with difficulty, for their hands shook and their eyes were often blinded with tears. She jollied them along, making jokes, which only added to their pain, for it is easy to be weak when someone else is strong. Her kirtle was crimson damask, her gown charcoal-grey, her coif her favourite one of black velvet, trimmed with a double row of pearls along each edge. It was the halo-shaped French coif which she had made fashionable when she brought the style back from the Court of Queen Claude all those years ago. It seemed right that she should wear it on her last day. Her hair fell loose to her waist like a girl's, as only virgins and queens might wear it. She had never known any man but one, and he was the one who had condemned her to death.

A few minutes before noon Kingston came to the door with an armed guard. 'The time is near,' he said. 'You must make ready.' Anne's face paled, and she reached a hand out to Mary to steady herself. Suddenly the time had run out. The days since her trial had seemed long, but now there were only a few minutes of life left to her in which to say and do everything she had ever wanted. Her mouth was dry, and she had to lick her lips before she could answer.

'Acquit yourself of your charge,' she said. 'I have been long ready.' She took up her prayer-book, and cast one last glance around the chamber—the Queen's Apartments, in which she had spent the night before her coronation—and then followed Kingston out of the door. Her four ladies fell in behind her. Nanette was carrying the linen cap with which to bind up her hair, and Mary the handkerchief to tie over her eyes, and the cloth to throw over her severed head.

The procession went down the stairs and out into the brilliant May sunshine. The little green beside the chapel of St Peter ad Vincula seemed crowded, but the crowd was silent. In the centre was the scaffold, and on it, two figures hard to see against the sun. Black-clad from head to foot—the executioner and his assistant.

'From Calais,' Anne murmured. Kingston bent nearer. 'Madam?' he enquired. 'I am glad he is from Calais,' she said. 'Master Kingston, you read the copy of my speech? You will not prevent me from saying it?'

'Of course not, Madam. It is your right to speak. I have here a bag of gold for you to pay the executioner—' he handed her the small leather purse. 'If you have any other instructions—any legacies that must be paid—?'

Anne shook her head. She could not speak. Her eyes, enormous in her white face, were fixed on the scaffold. She felt the grass under her feet for the last time, but the walk was so short—too short. At the steps, Kingston stood back. His duty ended there. Only her ladies could see the moment of indecision and panic, before she forced herself to lift her skirts and climb the wooden steps to the straw-covered platform. In the centre was the block—grisly object, scarred and darkened, scooped out in the centre for the victim's neck. The executioner came forward and knelt and said, 'Madam, I crave Your Majesty's pardon, for I am ordered to do my duty.'

Anne looked startled, having in those few minutes forgotten that he was French. Collecting herself, she said, 'Willingly,' and put the purse in his hand. But where was the sword? She looked round, and saw the sun glinting from it in the hands of the assistant.

Then she walked forward to the rail to make her speech to the sea of upturned faces below her. It made it easier to die when there was an audience, when it could still matter how she appeared, how she acquitted herself. She spoke clearly, in a calm cheerful voice.

'Good Christian people, I am come here to die, for according to the law and by the law I am judged to die, and therefore I will speak nothing against it. I come here to accuse no man, nor to say anything of the matter for which I am condemned to die. But I pray God to save the King and send him long reign over you, for a gentler nor a more merciful prince was there never, and to me he was always a good and gentle sovereign lord. And if any man will meddle with my cause, I require them to judge of the best. And therefore I take my leave of the world and of you all and desire you heartily all to pray for me.'

So it was done; there was nothing more to do in this life. Many of the spectators were weeping by now. The Queen turned to her ladies, and they were all blinded by tears, so much so that she had to take off her coif herself. Her dark hair gleamed in the sunshine as she held out the pearly cap to Nanette, and Nanette, her hand shaking, took it and gave her the linen cap to put on, and helped her tuck the long hair up into it, so that it would be out of the way of the sword. Her long neck looked very fragile, very naked.

'Mary,' she said, and Mary went forward, and Anne kissed her and gave her the prayer-book she carried. 'Give it to Thomas, with my love. Tell him—tell him my dearest thoughts were of our childhood in the gardens of Hever. Go home to Kent, Mary, my dear.'

Mary, weeping hopelessly, could not answer. The Queen kissed Madge and Meg and said a few words of comfort to each, and then turned to Nanette.

'Dear Nan,' she said, and their eyes met, and there was nothing else to say. 'Tie on the handkerchief for me, and then I will not need you anymore. You will be free to go.'

They embraced, and Nanette's tears wet Anne's thin cheek. Nanette took the handkerchief from Mary, and saw as she did so that the Queen was looking over her shoulder towards the gate, as if she yet wondered where freedom lay. Nanette stepped behind her and tied the handkerchief, and the bright dark eyes were hidden for ever from view. Then the terror came over Anne again. Alone in the dark, she could not move. The executioner prompted her, bidding her kneel and say her prayers, and then with a brisk nod at Nanette and Mary he indicated that they should guide her to the block. They took her by the arms, and they felt a second's resistance before she obeyed them and allowed herself to be guided to the block and knelt.

She began to speak, quickly as if afraid her words would be cut off. 'To Jesus Christ I commit my soul. Oh Lord have mercy on me. To Christ I commend my soul. Jesu, receive my soul!'

The executioner stepped forward. Nanette bit her lips, but the only thing she could now do for her mistress was to watch to the end, and she forced herself not to close her eyes. A flash of metal in the sun, a hissing sound, and then her breath was jerked out of her convulsively as the sword thudded through flesh and bone and Anne's head fell on to the straw, her body jumping with the force of the blow, spouting blood from her severed neck. With a despairing cry, Mary stepped forward to fling the white cloth over the head, but not soon enough to prevent Nanette seeing that it was face up, and the lips seemed still to be moving, as if in prayer.

The air was shaken by a cannon-shot—just the one, the pre-arranged signal. The executioner picked up a handful of straw to wipe the blade of his sword, and the four women turned away, and made their way down the steps. The crowd was beginning to drift away too, and Kingston and Walsingham were waiting impatiently to take the executioner and his assistant to their quarters where they must be entertained before being sent on their way back to France. Nanette, Mary, Madge and Meg went back to the Queen's apartments to collect their belongings, but it was long before they were able to do anything but weep.

The shadows lengthened in the courtyard, and on the scaffold the grey-clad figure still leaned against the block, arms outstretched, the raw exposed neck black with flies, while the once-white cloth stuck in patches to the object it concealed in the straw. It was not until late that afternoon that Kingston realised that in the confusion of all he had had to attend to, he had forgotten to have the Queen measured for her coffin. 'Find a box of some sort,' he told the yeomen on duty, 'and take the Queen's remains to the chapel.'

They found a long, narrow elm chest that had been used for storing arrows but was now empty and into that they put the body and head, and carried it to St Peter ad Vincula. George Rochford's body was buried under the altar there, so it seemed fitting that they should prise up the stones and slide the arrow-chest down beside the other coffin.

Not long afterwards the four ladies left the Tower, stopping on their way at Kingston's office to ask what had been done with the Queen's remains.

'It is what she would have wanted,' Mary said. 'They will be together in death.'

'If you are going up to Whitehall, ladies,' Kingston said, 'I have a boat waiting now to take a letter of mine to Master Cromwell. You may travel with my messenger if you wish. Yeoman—escort the ladies to the boat.'

When it did not conflict with his duties, he was a kind man. They thanked him wearily, and followed the yeoman through the fading light towards the riverside postern.

Twenty

$\mathscr{A}$ FEW DAYS LATER NANETTE SAID GOODBYE TO HER THREE friends and, in the company of James Chapham, who again offered his services, and four servants, set off for York. Though she felt weary to the bone, she insisted on riding: the idea of being jolted mile after slow mile in a stuffy litter made her sick, so a little palfrey was hired for her. Her maid, Audrey, rode pillion behind one of the menservants, and another carried Ajax before his saddle.

She saw nothing of the first part of the journey, but as they left London further behind, she began to feel a lightening of her spirits. When they stopped for the first night at an inn, she was feeling cheerful enough to choose her own dinner, and to chide Audrey for turning up her nose at the accommodation offered.

'You are grown too nice,' she said. 'What need have we of feather-pillows? Hop-harlots are good enough for uncrowned heads, and they say they bring good dreams.'

'There is much to be said for peaceful sleep in a crude bed,' James said, looking at her with sympathy. She smiled bleakly.

'You are right. More than one has discovered that there is too high a price to pay for soft beds.'

'But now you are going home. Home will heal you, in time. You see how already you are more cheerful than when we set off.'

'I am a northerner at heart,' Nanette admitted. 'We are never quite happy away from it.'

'You need never leave it again,' James said, and then paused, looking at her with difficulty as if unsure whether to proceed. She did not notice, being at that moment intent on cutting a piece of gristle from her meat and giving it to Ajax, who was at her feet under the table. 'Nanette,' he said at length, and she looked up, her cheeks a little flushed from bending. He thought how beautiful she was, and how black velvet shewed off her white skin and her vividly blue eyes.

'Yes, cousin?' she asked.

'I, too, have had my disappointments,' he went on. She nodded.

'I have not forgotten. Margaret was a sad loss. And yet I have wondered why you do not marry again. It is almost five years since she died, and you must want an heir.'

'I have thought about it,' he said, playing with his knife-case to avoid her eyes. 'I have thought about it very much recently, though it is not so much for the want of an heir but—' He paused for a very long time, and Nanette waited sympathetically, thinking he brooded on Margaret. She was a little surprised, not having thought he loved his wife so much. At last he looked up, and said, 'I wonder—perhaps you already know—have guessed what I want to say? You are going home, and of course Morland Place will always be home for you as long as you need it. But do you not want an establishment of your own? Have you not thought of marrying? Nanette, in simple words, I wish to marry you.' She was silent with aston-ishment, and he hurried on, looking down again with some embarrassment, 'It is not a sudden thing. I have long thought of you. I know you have no dowry, but I am wealthy enough not to need to care about that. I will make you a generous portion, have no fear. You will be mistress of a good house and as many servants as you wish.'

'James—' she began, not knowing how to answer him. He reached across the table and took her hand and said, 'I have loved you for a long time, but I have not spoken before, knowing how you did not wish to leave your mistress. But now—forgive me if I hurt you, but she does not need you now, and you must think to your own future.'

'James, cousin, I am grateful, and very honoured—'

'You must not be grateful. You are a woman any man would want for a wife. I can see you are about to refuse me, but please, think for a while about it. Don't say anything. I do not expect you to be able to answer at this time, when your sadness is so much upon you. I only wanted you to know that an establishment is waiting for you, when you are ready to come to it. Think about it, and give me your answer in a few months' time, when you are ready. And now we will talk of something else,' he said, determinedly cheerfully. He changed the subject so firmly that she had neither will nor desire enough to re-open it in order to tell him that his proposal was vain. There was no opportunity that evening, and the next day they were upon the road so early that there was no chance then, either. She decided to wait until they reached Morland Place, when everything would become plain to him. But she was grateful that he had thought of her in that way. She was more loved than she felt she deserved.

As they travelled through the country there was much evidence to be seen of the drought, and the consequent poverty and hunger that had been afflicting the people. They were warned again and again by inn-keepers not to travel after dark, for fear of the bands of beggars, their numbers increased by want, but the days were long enough in mid-May for it not to be necessary. Absorbed in her grief and her longing to be home, Nanette noticed little of it; her eye was open only to the delights of nature.

Then at last they were on familiar ground, and she saw up ahead a group of footmen waiting at the crossroads and wearing the black-and-white Morland livery.

'God bless you, Mistress,' they called, and, 'Welcome home. Master sent us to meet you.'

So escorted in style they rode the last two miles home. They were on Morland land now; these sheep were Morland sheep, bearing the family fortune on their backs; and there, as they topped the rise, was Morland Place at last, its rosy bricks glowing in the afternoon light, its windows flashing gold, its moat glinting in the sun, its tall chimneys cut out against the deep, summer-blue sky, its gardens bright with flowers, its clumps of park trees growing to maturity in the green peace that is the heart of England.

Tears were on Nanette's face as she rode towards the gates, but she was smiling too. Grief and mourning would have their day, but there was happiness to be found too. They crossed the moat-bridge, clattered in under the arch, and halted in the yard to a chorus of greeting. The steward was coming forward to receive them officially; the servants were clustered around the yard or hanging out of the windows; and the family was all there at the door to greet them. There was Amyas, looking younger than his years despite his spoiled looks and his discontented expression, and young Robert and Edward, fine, well-grown boys of sixteen and fourteen. John Butts and Lucy were there, and Young John with Catherine in floods of happy tears, and a nurse holding young Samson by the hand and carrying baby Joseph in her arms. There, too, was Ezekiel, and dear Arabella Neville, all smiles, and their son Hezekiah, a happy, chubby three-year-old, apparently untroubled by the weight of his name; and with them, too, was Eleanor, grown tall and thin at thirteen, pinched-faced and pale and shrinking close to Arabella as if in her lay her only safety.

But best of all, there in the midst, overtopping all, was the tall, broad figure of Paul. He was sixty years old now, his hair under his feathered bonnet was grey and his cleanshaven face lined; but he was firm and upright and manly, and as he smiled in his great pleasure and Nanette met the bright gaze of his brown eyes, she could feel only that he had lost nothing of his handsomeness; it was wonderful and astonishing that he loved her.

She took the loving-cup from the steward and drank and spoke the formal words, but as she gave the cup back it was Paul who was beside her horse ready to lift her down. She put herself trustingly into his strong arms, and he lowered her to the ground gently, but he did not at once release her; holding her, he looked down into her face enquiringly, and her candid look told him all he wanted to know.

'Welcome home,' he said.

'I am glad to be home,' she replied, and he kissed her, and old Alexander came to thrust his wet nose into her palm in greeting. She was released then, and greeted and kissed the rest of the family, and then on Paul's arm went into the house. As she crossed the threshold she turned her head to look back at James, following the rest of the family in, and she saw in his face that there would be no need of further explanations to him: he knew, and understood.

A lavish supper of twenty dishes was served in the great hall to an entertainment of singing, for the chapel at Morland Place still kept eight boys, to be schooled by the chaplain, Father Fenelon. Nanette sat on Paul's right as guest of honour. Soon, she reflected, she would occupy the empty place on his left; she would be mistress of Morland Place. The keys of the buttery and pantry and cellar would be given into her care; she would have sway over the kitchen, the bakehouse, brewhouse, bolting-house, and store-rooms; she would govern the laundry, the woodshed, the dairy, the henhouse, the pigsties, the fish-ponds and the grainstore; she would command the servants, order their meals, make their clothes, doctor their ills, supervise their births, deaths and marriages; she would feed the poor at the gates and visit the sick in the villages, and perform all the other thousands of tasks that fell to the duty of the mistress of a great house.

And she would have her lord to love, cherish and obey. She glanced sideways at him, and felt a shiver of love as his eye slewed sideways at the same moment to catch hers, and his beautifully-sculpted lips curved into a smile that was for her only. Why had she wasted so much time? She prayed God would send them a long life together. Would she bear him children? She was twenty-eight, but, sure, that was not too late. Anne had been over thirty when the King had married her for the sake of the son she might bear him; and Jane Seymour was thirty and more, whose pregnancy had hurried Anne to her grave. Under a fold of the nap, she felt her hand sought, and gave it to his strong, lean-fingered grip. She knew what answer he would give if she asked him: he had no need of more children; if God sent them, he would be glad, but if not, it did not matter.

After supper the servants cleared away and the family settled down to an evening of domestic pleasure in the hall, of games and singing and reading-aloud and handwork, until it was time for household prayers in the chapel, and bed. Paul and Nanette had no moment alone together, and all that needed to be communicated between them had to be done by looks or held back for another time, but he had his own way of assuring her that his love was unchanged. When Audrey lit her up to the guest-chamber, the first thing she saw on entering was the tapestry of the maid and the unicorn, which he had had hung there for her homecoming.

She lay awake long after Audrey was snoring softly beside her, listening to the night-sounds from outside the shutters, so different from the sounds she had been used to in London, and her thoughts were tumbled and confused, of Anne and Paul, of London and York, of grief and happiness; and as she drifted at last into sleep, she thought of shining dark eyes, and love and loss seemed one, and all part of the same pattern, a pattern it was not for her to try to work out. Lord Jesu, she whispered in her mind, forgive my pride: I trust you, I give my life to you, to order as you will; everything I am is yours. And at the very last, as sleep claimed her, the old prayer from her childhood came back to her: forgive me—give me grace.

Nanette was awake early the next morning, called from her sleep by the bright sun and a riot of birdsong, and with a heart filled with gratitude she dressed herself and went down to the chapel to await the five o'clock mass. As Father Fenelon entered and she rose to her feet, she was joined by Paul, who took his place beside her with a quiet smile, and then, most properly, turned his attention entirely to his devotions until the mass was over and they could rise and walk together out of the chapel. In the passage outside he turned to her.

'I thought you would be here. Will you ride out with me? God knows when we will be able to be alone together again. Will you come?'

'Willingly,' she said.

'Is your maid awake? Go and wake her, then. We must take a maid and a man for propriety's sake, but if I take Matthew, he will keep your girl's attention occupied. Go then—I will meet you in the stable-yard. And hurry—I do not wish to waste any moment of this time.'

Smiling, Nanette hurried away to prize her unwilling girl from the arms of sleep and get them both suitably dressed. Such was her eagerness that with all the yawning and eye-rubbing Audrey could do, it was not more than half an hour later that they were pattering down the west stairs and out into the yard, with Ajax running in front of them, waving his plumy tail and nobly restraining himself from barking.

Paul was waiting for them, with his young serving-man Matthew holding the four horses, and Alexander and his other tall hounds ran forward as they appeared to greet them and to sniff over little Ajax.

'The mare is for you,' Paul said, indicating a milk-white palfrey with gentle eyes. 'She is one of our own, bred here. Her name is Puss.' It was a local word for a hare. 'And the bay jennet is for your maid.'

'God 'a mercy, Master, but I have never ridden, except in a park,' Audrey said, eyeing the placid jennet as if it were a saddled tiger. Matthew grinned broadly.

'Don't worry, lass, I'll teach you all you need to know,' he said. Audrey sniffed at the idea, but Paul smiled and said, 'That's right, trust yourself to Matthew. He will help you mount. Come, Nan, are you ready? Let me help you up.' Nanette placed a foot in his hand and he sprang her on to the little white horse. 'What about your dog?' he asked.

'It's all right, he can keep up,' she said, smiling down at the laughing spaniel. 'He is small, but very enduring.'

'Good. Then we go.' And he swung himself on to his horse, and they rode out of the yard side by side, the servants following and the dogs running ahead. It was a warm morning, and the dew was already off the grass, but the fresh smell of dawn was not yet killed by the heat. They rode in silence, and Paul set a good pace, wanting to get away from the house and up on to the higher ground as quickly as possible. They rode through the in-fields, the broad, neat strips where already some of the peasants were at work, the orchards and pastures; through the out-fields and scrublands, where village children tended pigs, goats and geese at their grazing; then began to climb through the higher grazings where the great flocks of sheep ran with their young families, watched over by the shepherds who were so gnarled and hardened with the weathers that they looked like blasted tree-stumps.

Then they were out on to the moors, and the sheep grew scarcer, and the horses were picking their way upwards through heather and bracken and great outcrops of granite, gilded with moss and lichen, and the dogs ran this way and that, nose-down to the strange wild spoors of small creatures. The ground grew steeper, in places boggy, in others treacherous with scree, and then at last they were on the very tops, where the grass was thin and bitter and a cool wind blew even on the hottest day, and here at last they stopped and dismounted. Matthew took the horses away and hobbled them at a little distance, and seating Audrey on his jerkin with their backs to their master and mistress, set about entertaining her. Paul and Nanette walked to where the ground fell away, and looked.

Down below in the valley a burn glittered as it ran over its rocky bed and from it the spurs of green climbed the rough hillsides where the sheep grazed, almost hidden in the bracken. On either side the moorland spread away, grey and purple, already hazy in the heat, below the great blue bowl of the sky, veined with the running silver of the wind. Here and there the fragile flowers of the uplands bowed to the wind, faint harebells, celandines, rockroses, pink thyme, yellow toadflax, the blue flames of gentians and the crimson tongues of the vipers bugloss. Nothing moved but a kestrel, cruising high up on the wind; no sound but the faint cry of a curlew, and the distant roar of a torrent far below, feeding the burn.

'I have known this all my life,' Paul said at last, 'but I can never tire of looking; just looking.'

'I used to dream of this, in the south,' Nanette said. 'Of the wind and the wildness.' Paul glanced at her, and then reached for her hand.

'Your hand is cold,' he said. 'We had better sit down, out of the wind.' He began to take off his doublet, but Nanette, less fastidious than her maid, forestalled him and sat down in the heather, her back to a sun-warmed rock.

'Would it shock you,' she asked presently, 'if I took off my head-dress? I would love to feel the wind in my hair once more.' Paul smiled and shook his head.

'Can I help you?' he asked.

'I can manage,' she said. She was wearing a velvet bonnet over a starched linen cap, and they were easy enough to deal with; then the pins were drawn out, and her mass of dark hair tumbled free, the light fronds around her brows catching the wind at once and whipping across her face so that she laughed and caught them back in protest. Paul watched her with a spike of pain in his heart, remembering Ursula who had loved to lose her silvery hair to the wind. He had sat up on the moors with her in this way, too, so long ago. He remembered Uncle Richard saying that it was her he was looking for in Nanette. Was that true? Was this disloyalty to Ursula? Or was it disloyalty to Nanette? The woman beside him turned to look at him, frowning, puzzled by his expression. Dark eyes—no, no, blue eyes! Dark blue eyes! He shuddered, forcing himself to grasp reality.

'What is it?' Nanette asked him softly. 'You look troubled. Do you want to talk?'

'I am haunted,' he said. 'Forgive me.'

'Adrian's mother?' Nanette asked. 'I can understand that. Sometimes—things seem to be more than one thing at a time.'

He was surprised by her acuteness. 'You understand,' he said. 'Oh, Nanette, I've waited so long for you to come home I hardly know how to be glad that you are here. You *are* here, aren't you?'

'I believe so,' she said. She held out her hand. 'Does this seem real to you?' He took it, and warmth started up between their cold palms. He smiled, the shadows passing from his eyes.

'Do you still come home to me? Don't be afraid to tell me the truth. You know that whatever you want I will do. I am an old man—I have no right to the love of a young woman.'

'That is a strange thing to say. I am not young any more, Paul. And you are not old—you are strong and vigorous. I have come home to you, to marry you if you still want me.'

For answer Paul kissed her hand. 'You must say when you are ready.'

Nanette shook her head. 'I have been your wife these many years, if you remember. What should we wait for? God knows, I have made you wait long enough.'

'Nevertheless—'

'I love you, Paul. It seems to be time I knew myself.'

The sound of Audrey laughing drew their eyes away from each other. The servants were at a distance, their backs turned, and Matthew was evidently shocking and delighting Audrey to the extent that she probably would not have noticed the world ending just behind her. It constituted as much privacy as they were likely to have. Paul took her into his arms and with a shiver she reached up for his beautiful mouth, feeling the old savage sweetness rising up in her. Surely it could not be wrong? Not all human kind were designed for the celibate life. The warmth and hardness of his body drew her as the sun draws growing things, and she pressed herself against him, longing to be one with him again, to experience again that strange translation of flesh and spirit that she could never forget. He drew her down to lie against him on the grass, and a flood of happiness caught her up like driftwood. Daughter, know thyself, a voice whispered in her mind. She answered: forgive me—give me grace.

The Church in England's having left Rome made things easier for Paul and Nanette, for it meant that their dispensation had to be obtained from the Archbishop, who was much more accessible than the Pope. For them, indeed, it was unexpectedly easy, for Paul was able to make use of the patronage of the Duke of Norfolk to have his application considered ahead of the usual queue; and Thomas Cranmer of course knew Nanette as Anne's friend, and hurried the matter through as an act of friendship, in memory of the dead Queen whom he had loved. And thus it was that only four weeks after her arrival home, Nanette was married to Paul very early one morning in the chapel at Morland Place, with only their servants for witness.

It was the way they both wanted it. 'No ceremony,' Paul had said. 'We have no need of it. And the settlements can be arranged later. Let us simply be wed, and have done with it.'

So when they went in to breakfast that morning, they went in as man and wife, to make the announcement to the rest of the family. No-one but Amyas was much surprised, and even he had no real objections. It seemed to him shocking that his father should marry his own niece without proper dispensation (for to him only the Pope had the power to permit the marriage) but then to judge from the way they looked at each other they were already lovers, and it was better that the situation should be regularised as far as possible than that he should keep his niece as his mistress. So while he could not actually congratulate them, he did not say anything against them either, which was as well for the family's peace.

For Nanette, the summer passed in a dream of happiness. It was only by examining her present contentment that she realised the distress she had been in ever since she committed that sinful act with Paul all those years ago at Hampton. In sinning thus, she had put herself outside the Church; she had been carrying a load of guilt that she had no way of lightening; but now it seemed that with their marriage not only was the sin expiated, it was translated into no sin at all. Nightly in the scant privacy of the bedcurtains they loved without sin. She worshipped him with her body, as the marriage vow had bid her, and he shewed her an ecstasy she would not have believed could be experienced on this side of the grave.

Paul wanted to give her things, heap presents upon her, fill her lap with flowers. The tapestry was already hers, and it now hung in their bedchamber, on the wall opposite the great Butts bed where they slept. Paul gave her the little silver-oak chest for her clothes, the chest that had belonged to his great-grandmother, and also her leather-bound missal with the running hare embossed upon the cover. The missal had been given to Margaret, but had returned to the family on her death.

Puss, the white palfrey, was hers, and Paul had a new saddle and bridle made for her, of soft crimson leather tooled with gold, the bridle hung with gold swags and little bells. Hardly a day passed without his bringing Nanette some little gift to delight her: a set of knives like his own in a blue leather case; a pair of leather hawking gloves embroidered with silver wires; a cedar drinking-horn with a silver rim, carved with scenes of the chase, for her to take hunting next winter; a set of ivory pins for her hair; new silk ribbons for her lute. Her portrait hung on the wall in the winter parlour to one side of the fireplace, and Paul sat for his own portrait to hang on the other side.

But one of the best gifts he gave her was one she knew nothing about: he contrived to keep from her the news of the outside world, which was all bad news. The honey-scorpion had a miscarriage; Anne's death had been in vain. The King, despairing, it seemed, of getting a son, had an Act passed through Parliament to say that from now on the monarch could will the Crown to anyone he pleased, just as if it were his own property. It was thought he meant to make his bastard son Richmond his heir, but if that was his plan, Fate forestalled him, for the boy wasted away and died of a consumption only days after the Act was passed. After that, there seemed no surety for the future of England, no alternative to civil strife when the King should die. The common people, who hated Cromwell and blamed him for all their troubles, ludicrously feared the King would make him his heir; the gentry, more realistically, thought he would leave the Crown to his sister Margaret's son, the King of Scotland, which in its way was worse. Already there was talk of resisting the Scottish succession: it could not be valid, the people said, because the King of Scotland was not born a subject of the laws of England.

All was unease and unrest. The commissioners were out again all that summer investigating religious houses and closing them down; other commissioners were out attempting to collect the latest tax, imposed by the King of course, but blamed by the people on Cromwell, for the 'subsidy', as it was called, was his idea. Amyas was still wildly against the suppression of the monasteries as he was against the split with Rome, and it was all Paul could do to moderate his language within the house and to prevent him praying openly for the Pope in the chapel.

The mass celebrated in the chapel was unchanged except for the omission of the Pope's name and the prayer for the King as Supreme Head, but Amyas talked about it as if it were a heretic communion-service, and only attended it because it was less 'heretical' than the service in the village church.

Paul himself was more worried about the taxation, for it seemed that this King was developing a habit of taxing in peace-time as well as in time of war, which was unprecedented. The King seemed to feel that the excellence of his rule was worth paying for by the people, and if this were the case there might be no end to the taxes demanded in the future. He also had a personal worry to cope with: word came from Micah that Adrian had disappeared, leaving no word to say where he had gone. Micah thought he had run away, perhaps abroad as a mercenary; but Paul was afraid he had met with an accident, and was dead, for surely he would have told someone where he was going if he had left of his own will.

But these things he managed to keep from Nanette during that summer, and it was a time of delight for them both. They were perfectly in accord, and everything they did together seemed enriched by each other's company. Together they rode out, sometimes hawking—though Paul would never carry a bird, but would only watch while Nanette flew her merlin—or at other times just galloping over the moors for the delight of the fresh air. Together they tended the gardens, for they both loved flowers, and Paul planted a new rose bush for her, even though it was the wrong time of year, and, marvellously, it flourished, and bloomed the white roses Yorkshiremen love.

Together they rode about the estate, supervising and directing the work; together they interviewed the cook and wrote lists of the things needed to be got from York or from London; together they went to mass, three times a day, more on holy days, and to church in York on Sundays. In the evenings they played and sang, talked and worked together. They walked together in the Corpus Christi procession, danced together at the St John's Eve celebrations in the sheep-fold in their own in-fields. But best of all were those moments when, alone at last behind the drawn curtains of the bed, they wrapped their arms around each other and were as much one flesh as human kind can be.

It was impossible to keep out the world for ever. The summer was another dry one, and soon the talk of the drought and the poor harvest salted the other complaints. It was seen as a sign of displeasure from Heaven—the ungodly ways of the English were being punished. On a cool day in August Nanette woke from her dream with a cruel abruptness. Audrey was chattering as she dressed her mistress, and Nanette was agreeing with her absently, without having the slightest idea what she was talking about. She had, in self defence, long ago ceased to listen to her maid's chatter, but the air coming in through the window from the pale grey, dewy morning was cool enough for her to shiver and close the casement, and she found herself listening instead of dreaming.

'They say the new law will mean no-one will be allowed to eat white bread, or goose, or capon, without paying a tax to the King,' Audrey was saying. Nanette stared at her in amazement.

'Nonsense,' she said. 'Who says such a thing?'

'Why everyone, Madam. The talk is everywhere. The King is looking for new things to tax all the time, and they say all horned cattle are to be taxed, which puts the village folk in a fright for their goats and the milch cows. And the commissioners that are looking at the churches, they are to tax all the births and deaths and marriages, so that folks who can't pay will have to go without benefit of the Church at all. And the jewels and plate that are in the churches are to be taken away and made into money for the King—they are going to start on that when they have done away with all the monasteries. Oh Madam, it will be a terrible ungodly world we live in when they are done.'

'I don't believe a word of it,' Nanette said, perplexed. Had the world gone mad while she dreamed?

'But it's true, Madam,' Audrey said earnestly. 'The commissioners are in our shire this very minute, making reports on the holy houses. They have already sent a notice to Holy Trinity Priory, to say it is to be shut down, but Father Prior paid it no heed and said he would not leave, and everyone fears they will be dragged out and put to the sword, now that the King has said there is to be no more sanctuary. Lord, I don't know what the times are coming to. And they say that every man in the country is to make a report of his possessions down to the least cooking pot, and if he gets one thing wrong, they will take everything away and give it to the King. It is Lord Cromwell's doing, Madam, so they say.'

'Now, Audrey, you know better than that. You are not an ignorant country girl. You have lived at the Court. How can you say such things? It is all nonsense. You have seen Master Cromwell yourself. You know that he is the King's servant—'

'Oh Madam, hereabouts they say he is someone else's servant—the Dark Gentleman's. They say he leads the King astray, and that it was all his doing that the heretics have been allowed to take us away from the Pope. It's no good me telling them different,' she added righteously, 'for they won't listen.'

'And do you tell them differently?' Nanette asked, narrowing her eyes.

'Oh yes, Madam, all the time. But it's whistling in the wind as far as they are concerned.'

Nanette did not believe a word of it. Audrey was as ignorant and credulous as the rest, and Nanette knew she would drink in the grossest nonsense provided it were shocking or scandalous enough.

'Well, enough of it now, girl,' she said. 'It is time for Mass. Give me my missal and my beads.'

'Oh Madam, there is a new law they say to prevent anyone carrying beads, like the churches have stopped telling them and praying for the Pope and giving out the saints' days and—'

'I said enough, Audrey. We still bid the beads in our chapel, and that is all you have to know. Now frame your mind to a proper state for mass, and come with me.'

After Mass they went in to breakfast, and when grace had been said Nanette said to Paul, 'What is happening to the world, husband? My maid has been chattering this morning about all kinds of alarms, to do with taxes and heresy, and I feel as if I had been sleeping a hundred years. Have you been keeping me in a state of blessed ignorance?'

'I have tried,' Paul said, smiling ruefully, 'but it seems I did not muzzle your dogs tight enough. There is a great deal of unrest and I'm afraid it is building up into something worse.'

'But why did you not tell me? Why keep it from me?'

'You have had so much grief to bear. I did not want to impair your happiness too soon. And you did seem so happy.'

'I am happy,' Nanette said, touching his hand. 'But I feel guilty that I have been heedlessly enjoying myself. What is this that Audrey was saying about not giving out saints' days?'

'Ah yes—that is one of the newer troubles. Another of the "reforms" of the Church. Saints are no longer to intervene for us, and the saints' days are not to be announced or celebrated by the priests. It is, indeed, as was feared—that once the Church is laid open to question, there is no end to the changes that will be made. It is like a breach in a perfect defence—once made, the whole wall crumbles, and heresy rushes in. I was glad of the break with Rome. I never felt that it was good that our affairs should be governed by an outside power, or that the fruits of our labour should be paid to a prelate who never set foot in the country. But it seems few are willing to go thus far and no further—not even the King himself.'

'But Paul—the King is a true Catholic. No-one could be more devoted than him. He hates heresy. He is a true son of the Church.'

'Is he?' Paul gave a wry smile. 'Perhaps he wants to be. But perhaps he has discovered that once you ask the first question, you can no longer be sure what the truth is.'

They looked at each other consideringly, each knowing this to be true. After a moment Paul went on, 'The man who invites the wolf in over his threshold is no longer in a position to ask him to leave. That is a truth it were better none of us ever had to learn.'

BOOK THREE

THE ROSE AND THE CHERRY

Her lusty ruby ruddes
Resemble the rose buddes;
Her lippes soft and merry
Enbloomed like the cherry:
It were an heavenly bliss
Her sugared mouth to kiss.

John Skelton
'Philip Sparrow'

Twenty-one

$\mathcal{A}$LL THROUGH THE SUMMER THE TALK WAS OF DISCONTENT and rebellion, and in October, when the meagre harvests were in, the risings began—in Lincolnshire on the third, a week later in South Yorkshire, a week later still further north as the climate dictated, for until the crops were gathered in, folk had no leisure for politics. The commons of the City of York declared rebellion on the tenth of October, and held to it even though two days later news came that the Lincoln rebellion had collapsed on hearing of the arrival at Stamford of the royal army under the Duke of Suffolk.

The following day, on the thirteenth, a deputation of tenants came to Morland Place to speak to Paul. There were about twenty of them, and as they seemed quiet enough, they were admitted to the great hall, but Nanette was nervous and begged Paul not to see them.

'Send them away,' she pleaded.

'Without asking them what they want?' Paul said with a smile. 'That is no way for a master to treat his tenants. I have always said that they should have access to me at all times.'

Amyas snorted at this idea. 'I sometimes wonder, Father,' he said, 'whether you know who is master, them or you?'

'Oh yes,' Paul said. 'I know. Consider, my son, how you

ride a horse. The horse is bigger, heavier, stronger than you. The only reason you can master him at all, is because he does not realise he is stronger.'

'All the more reason to *shew* them,' Amyas interrupted. 'Shew them your strength.'

'You are a fool. One man is not stronger than twenty. No man rules but by consent of the ruled. If consent is withdrawn and it comes to a trial of strength—I will see them. Amyas, you will come with me—but keep your mouth shut, do you understand?'

'Yes father,' he said sulkily.

'Paul, let me come too,' Nanette begged. He considered for a moment, and then nodded.

They made their entrance at the dais end of the hall, to find the deputation standing huddled in small groups, talking in low voices, while various members of the household lounged nearby, longing to hear what was going on, but not willing to make themselves part of the group. As Paul stepped up on to the dais the rumbling of talk died away, and the tenants moved forward, doffing their caps, and looking up with an uncertain eagerness at their master.

'You wished to see me,' he said. There was some delay while the chosen speaker was nudged and jostled forward.

'Maister,' he said at last, 'we have come to speak to you—it's about the rebels. We want to declare for the rebels, like the commons of York have. We have talked about it amongst ourselves, and it was decided that we here should come and speak to you. We speak for all, Maister—don't we lads?' There was a rumble of agreement. Paul's face was impassive.

'You want to declare for the rebels? Rebellion against the Crown? That is a treasonable offence, don't you know that?'

'Nay, Maister, nay, we have nothing against the King—we are King's men, all of us. God bless him, we say.'

'Aye,' and 'God bless him,' the others agreed.

'It is not against the King we are rising, maister, but against the lord Cromwell and the heretics.'

'Cromwell is the King's servant. He does what the King bids,' Paul said, watching them closely.

'The King has bad advisers, Maister, and one of 'em is lord Cromwell. It is his doing that we are in the case we are, losing our religion to the wicked heretics, our monasteries being shut down, the saints abolished. There will be terrible punishment come to all if we do not go back to the true religion. That's why we are rising, Maister. We want our monasteries left alone, and those that have been put down restored again.'

There was a yell of agreement at this. The house servants were creeping nearer, sympathy in their faces. When the noise died down a little, Paul spoke.

'And what is it you want of me?' he asked. He knew, of course, but it had to be said.

'We want you to lead us, Maister. The King will pay us more heed if the gentle-folk are with us. The folk of the East Riding and Marshland are on their way to York this moment, and it's said the North Riding is up too. We want to join the rest in the city, but we want you to lead us.'

Their faces were tilted towards Paul, confident of their success. They knew their cause was just, and they knew their master was a good man. How could he refuse them?

'And if I refuse? What then?'

They looked at each other, confused.

'Why, Maister, I suppose we must go without you,' the leader said, puzzled. 'But—'

'I will not lend my name to this,' Paul said abruptly. 'Whatever you may tell yourselves, this is rebellion against the King. I will not have the Morland name linked with treachery.'

'But—but Maister, you think like us about the religion, we made sure. Why, you keep the old mass in the chapel here—'

'My religion is a matter between myself and God, but an armed rising is a breach of the law of the land,' Paul said. He did not think his tenants would understand the distinction, and they did not.

'Why, Maister, we have nothing against the law. Nor against the King, neither. We only want our religion restored, as is our right. Won't you lead us?'

'No,' Paul said. 'I won't.'

Puzzled but orderly, the tenants trailed out, talking in low voices amongst themselves. Paul dismissed the wistful house servants, and went back to the solar with Nanette and Amyas. The latter was bursting to speak, and waited only until they were in the solar and the door was shut behind them.

'Father, surely—'

'Amyas, stop. Before you speak, consider what I said. The law is the law.'

'Not if it is a bad law,' Amyas said excitedly. 'If the law has not competence, as it has not to change our religion, then how can we be bound to obey it? If everyone makes a stand against the destruction of the monasteries and the influx of heresy—'

'It does not make it any less wrong for the individual,' Paul said.

'But you heard them—the East Riding is up and marching for York. Sir Thomas Percy is leading them, and the whole Percy clan is behind them. The Percy's father, the most powerful family in the north!'

'Amyas, Amyas, you don't think they are marching for the sake of the Church, do you? Northumberland himself is cringing in terror of the King, because of the troubles he has made for himself, and hopes a rising may displace the King and free him from his worries. And Sir Thomas is angry because the King would not accept him as Northumberland's heir. As for the rest of the gentry—taxation is their grudge, and power their aim. The commoners may be marching for Christ's sake, but do not delude yourself that their masters help them for the same reason.'

The argument went on at intervals through the next three days, but neither could ever hope to change the mind of the other. Nanette's fears were more practical. The army closing on York was said to number ten thousand at least, and the presence of ten thousand angry peasants was likely to give rise to trouble, looting, burning, stealing, drunkenness—and Morland Place was too close to the city for that to be a pleasant prospect. The house itself was stout, but the servants—could they be relied upon? Would their loyalty to the family be strong enough to overcome their hatred of Cromwell and the new order?

Her first fears were unfounded, for when the army marched into the city on the sixteenth, it was quiet and orderly. Their leader, a gentleman named Robert Aske, was an honest, peaceable, upright man, whose religious convictions had led him to talk about the rebellion as a pilgrimage, and already the rebels were referring to themselves as pilgrims. Aske was so revered by his followers that he had no difficulty in ensuring their good behaviour. There was no disorder, no looting; no arms were allowed to be carried within the walls, and all goods obtained had to be paid for. The first proclamation he made declared the aims of the pilgrimage to be the preservation of the Church, the realm, and the King, and to petition the King for reformations of what was amiss in the realm.

All this strengthened Amyas's arguments, and weakened Paul's. The northern contingent was drawing near, and the ranks of the gentry known to be supporting the rising were thick with Percies, Mortimers, Staffords, and all the great Neville clan and their connections. The main body of their army entered York on the eighteenth, and in the afternoon of that day there were unexpected visitors at Morland Place: Lord and Lady Latimer came to seek hospitality of their friends, and shelter for Lady Latimer when the rebels moved on.

It was the first meeting for many years between Nanette and her old friend, and it was not without awkwardness at first, until their mutual regard thawed them. Nanette found Katherine virtually unchanged, except that she was a little plumper. Small, neat and sweet-faced she was still; her clothes were elegant and very rich, but not quite in the first fashion. Whether Katherine found *her* changed or not Nanette did not know; Nanette certainly felt very different from the passionate, unformed girl she had been when she had left the shelter of the Parr household. During the latter years they had been unable to keep up their friendship because the Latimers were supporters of the Princess Dowager and Katherine herself was an intimate friend of the Lady Mary, and spent much time visiting her.

Now, however, while Latimer walked about the room talking to Paul, Katherine and Nanette sat together in the window seat and felt their way cautiously towards their former intimacy.

'So here we are, both wearing matron's hoods,' Katherine said at last. 'We doubted when we were children, did we not, that it should be so.'

'You never doubted you would be wed,' Nanette reminded her. 'But I—without a dowry, how could I expect to marry?'

'One can never foresee how God will dispose,' Katherine said. 'And we are both married to older men. I remember, Nan, how you did not much like the idea when I was first given to Lord Borough. Tell me—dear friend, are you happy?'

'Oh yes!' Nanette exclaimed, and her face was enough to dispel any doubts Katherine might have had. 'I love him so very much, Kate, I sometimes wonder how I could have been so blind in the past! And you—are you happy?'

'Yes,' Katherine said, but more sedately. Her passions had never been aroused, her knowledge of happiness and unhappiness were more placid than Nanette's. 'I am happy. John is kind to me, and he is a good man, a true Catholic.'

Nanette glanced towards the two men as Katherine spoke and wondered at the contrast they made. John Neville was not much older than Paul, but he was grey and dry like a dead stick, while Paul seemed beside him so full of life, and passion, that he appeared almost flamboyant. She compared also her own marriage and her love for Paul with Katherine's—as she imagined it—with John Neville, and wondered that two such different states of affairs could both bear the same name.

'But do you love him, Kate?' she asked. Katherine looked at her, it seemed, a little wistfully.

'Of course I love him,' was her reply. 'He is my husband, and a good man.' There was a wealth that was not said, that perhaps did not need to be said. Nanette changed the subject tactfully.

'And do you get on with your children?' she asked. Katherine's face softened with affection.

'They are my best friends,' she said. 'It took me some time to get used to being called "my lady mother" by men and women older than myself, but now it hardly seems strange, and they are my greatest support in affliction. For *you* know how difficult things have been.'

Their eyes met in sympathy. Nanette said in a quiet voice, 'The Lady Mary—is she well?'

'Not as well as we would wish her, but not as ill as she has been. She suffers dreadfully with her teeth, and there are few pains so distressing. But she keeps wonderfully merry. She's such a high-spirited young woman, despite all her troubles. She loves to sing and dance, loves pretty clothes and play-acting. It is quite dreadful that she has been shut up in solitary poverty for so long.'

'Kate, you know that I never—that we—'

'Hush, Nan, I know. Sometimes situations make us do things we would rather not. I could not love your mistress, but she has paid dearly for whatever her sins were. The new Queen tries hard to be good to Mary, though, poor soul, one cannot say how long it will be in her power. She has not conceived again, you know.' They were silent for a moment. It was a sobering thought. Nanette could not love the scorpion-in-honey, just as Katherine could not love Anne; but there could be no doubt about Jane Seymour's marriage being valid, since both former Queens were dead at the time. If she could not be divorced, and she did not conceive, there was only one way the King could be rid of her. Nanette shivered. Jane Seymour had had one miscarriage already, and she had never been crowned; her tenure of her position looked fragile indeed.

'And Princess—I mean, Lady Elizabeth?' Nanette asked at length. 'How is she?'

'The King neglects her more even than he neglected Mary, but she is a strong, robust, forward child. With her better health, I think she will always suffer less from her position, though it be more precarious than Mary's. Mary pities her, and tries to help her. She is a saint in the making, you know. Everyone loves her.'

Nanette nodded, but turned her head away for a moment, for all this was painful to her. Her eyes fell again on their husbands, pacing up and down. She said, 'Kate, what are you doing here? Why has your husband joined the rebels?'

Katherine shook her head. 'We had no choice. Here in York things are much quieter, the people seem gentler. The further north you go, the stronger the passions boil up. The rebels have been recruiting all the way down, and those that would not join for asking were threatened until they did join. John feels strongly about the issues involved, but I think he would not have joined with the rebels if it weren't for their threats. They said they would fire the house and kill all the household one by one.'

Nanette stared. 'That is terrible. No wonder—but is that why *you* came?'

Kate nodded. 'John did not think it safe to leave me at home. I could have gone to my relatives, but they are all in much the same position. Then I thought of you. So close to the city, I felt it would be safer. And when we sent out a servant to enquire, we found your husband had not joined. But, Nan, you must warn him. If the Earl of Poverty should come here—'

'The Earl of what?'

'That's what he calls himself—the Earl of Poverty. He is one of their leaders. No-one knows who he is. He looks and speaks like a gentleman, but he dresses in peasant's clothes. He was the one who threatened us. He was a terrible figure—a young man, very handsome, tall and dark, dark-haired and dark-eyed, but somehow frightening. There seemed a darkness inside him, as if he was marked by evil. And yet he marches under the banners of the saints.' She shook her head, puzzled. 'If he comes here and threatens, your husband will yield, I am sure.'

'I hope not,' Nanette said. 'I should not like him to be forced against his will to join the pilgrimage. Besides—I am afraid, I confess it, that he will be hurt. If it should come to battle—'

'I do not think it can. The rebel army is forty-thousand strong, the King's forces little more than four thousand. All of the north, everything north of the Don, is behind Robert Aske now. How could there be a battle? As long as everyone stands firm, our cause must prevail.'

It seemed that way. Pontefract Castle fell to the pilgrims without any blow being struck, and there they set up their headquarters. The Duke of Norfolk had been given the task of dealing with the Yorkshire rebellion, and he was stationed at Doncaster, and from there requested the rebels to send four of their number to treat with him. Aske had no wish to fight—a show of force was all he wanted—and he overcame the more bellicose elements and eventually sent four envoys to Doncaster on the twenty-seventh.

Paul was again favourably impressed by this. 'It seems this Aske really means what he says. He does not want any violence—only restoration of the old religion. Almost I honour him.'

'Honest he may be,' Nanette said, 'But is he wise?' She looked up at him across their game of nine-men's-morris with which they were occupying the evening. Katherine was there too, sewing shirts in company with her maid, while Amyas was going over an accounts book in his corner of the solar.

'Surely it must be wise to want to avoid bloodshed,' Katherine said.

'But the pilgrims are thirty-thousand strong, and a well-disciplined army. Norfolk has at most eight thousand men. He would not pitch battle,' Nanette said.

'Then what do you think they should do?' Paul asked.

'March south. No-one would resist them. If they want to get their way, that is what they should do.'

'I agree with you,' Amyas said hotly. 'Why waste time treating with Norfolk?'

'Because they think he can use his influence at Court to persuade the King to their demands,' Paul said.

'Then they are fools,' Nanette said, 'for the King sent Norfolk to put them down, and he will do it one way or another.'

'Norfolk, the hero of the north, the victor of Flodden?' Paul said with some irony.

'Norfolk, the King's servant,' Nanette countered. They knew each other's minds very well by now. 'He will promise whatever it takes to disperse the forces, and once the men are all gone home, the danger to the King will be past and there will be no need to honour any of the promises.'

'Do you really think that is the way it will be?' Katherine asked, laying down her needle.

'Can you doubt it?' Nanette said. 'You have been at Court. You know the King.'

'Perhaps not as well as you do, but—I must agree it sounds very likely.'

'Then the pilgrims should be warned, they should march at once,' Amyas said eagerly.

'Those who felt so were outnumbered or outvoted by those who would treat,' Paul pointed out.

'I think I should like to write to my husband all the same,' Katherine said.

'You cannot want them to march and fight? You cannot wish for bloodshed?' Paul said, surprised.

'I do not wish for bloodshed, but I do wish for my husband to succeed in the business he has undertaken, albeit against his will. I agree with Nanette—I do not believe there would be resistance.'

'If they are fooled into dispersing,' Nanette added quietly, 'it will be easy to round up the leaders afterwards and execute them.' There was a silence at this, and then Amyas turned to his father and cried passionately, 'Father, let me go to Pontefract! Let me take everyone we can find and go to Pontefract and warn them! I can speak to Lord Latimer, he and I together can persuade the leaders we have the key. We must act, Father, surely you see that?'

'No,' Paul said. Amyas raised his hands in frustration, but Paul went on, 'It is not yet time to act. We must wait and see what the result of the talks will be. We know that the King will not agree to all the articles, but he may agree to some. He must be aware of the threat. We must wait and see what happens.'

'But Father—'

'My child, when it is time to act, I will act.'

After the meeting with Norfolk at Doncaster it was decided that two of the leaders should take the petition to the King at Windsor, and they duly set off on their journey south, while the pilgrims waited at Pontefract. October turned into November, and the pilgrims grew restless and suspicious, for the two envoys did not return and there was a renewed desire to march on London. At last, however, on the eighteenth of December the two gentlemen reached Shipton and there gave the King's reply to the rebel leaders.

It said nothing. It made no reply to the pilgrims' petitions. It emphasised the King's good rule, impartial administration of justice, and his right to govern as he thought fit and to choose whatever ministers he felt suitable. It commanded the pilgrims to go home, and declared that through the compassion of his princely heart he would forgive them all, except ten of the ringleaders, of whom an example must be made.

The peasants were infuriated; moreover there were rumours of royal troops approaching from the south and plots to assassinate Aske; the situation was growing dangerous, and now Paul decided it was time to act.

'I must pitch my small weight into the balance,' Paul said to his family on the evening that the news arrived. 'Aske will find it hard to hold his mob. At all events, things must be held together.'

'What will you do?' Nanette asked. She was pale, a dread over her. The rising seemed to have taken on again the disturbing element that had first aroused her to fear.

'Will you let me go to them now, Father?' Amyas asked eagerly. Paul faced him wearily.

'No,' he said.

'But *Father*—!'

'I am going myself. It is for me to do what little there can be done. You must stay here and protect the household.'

'But why can't I go, and you stay?'

'You can less well be spared, if anything should happen. Besides, it is a matter for a calm mind and a clear head. You are too easily swayed by your emotions. I will take a few men and join the pilgrims, and do what I can to persuade them to stand firm and avoid bloodshed.'

On the twentieth he left for Pontefract, but on the following day he was back in York, for the council of the pilgrims met in York on the twenty-first to discuss what they should do. Aske's personality and the strength of his following won the day, and it was agreed to treat again with Norfolk, and to draw up a manifesto of demands. It was hoped that Norfolk's influence would counteract Cromwell's at Court, and someone read a letter from Cromwell to one of the commanders of the royal army in which he said that the rebellion would be put down and a fearful example made of the rebels. In vain Paul and others like him pointed out that Cromwell and Norfolk were members of the same Council, servants of the same King.

The manifesto that was drawn up was a mixture of the commoners' demands and the gentry's demands. The commoners wanted the restoration of the papal supremacy, all elements of the old worship, and those monasteries that had been dissolved; heretical works banned, heretical bishops tried and punished; Cromwell and Rich punished as subversive influences. The gentry wanted a separate parliament for the north, the succession restored to Lady Mary and the Act allowing the King to dispose of the Crown by Will repealed; reform of the treason laws and the common law; restoration of the church liberties; and reform of the tenant laws.

Many of these articles were dear to Paul's heart, and he found himself more in sympathy with the rebellion than he had expected. He liked Aske, too, on sight, and, his influence not being negligible, he was asked by Aske to be one of the representatives who took the manifesto to Norfolk at Doncaster.

'You know His Grace,' Aske pointed out. 'He has long been your patron. You will be able to talk to him on a more friendly basis, and perhaps find out how far he is empowered to grant what we ask.'

On the fifth of December, in company with the other chosen envoys, Paul came down from his quarters in Pontefract Castle into the courtyard to mount up for the journey to Doncaster. The yard was crowded with pilgrims, the common folk whose voice was never heard, whose only means of expression was rebellion, and a great cheer went up when they appeared. There were banners being held aloft all over the yard, mostly decorated with religious symbols, the Five Wounds, the emblems of St Cuthbert and St Wilfred, the Blessed Virgin, St Clement; some shewed family or regional devices—the canting-arms of Horncastle, the white rose of York, for instance, and a crude representation of the Morland hare-and-heather was raised in one place, where Paul's own tenants called out a blessing on him.

He looked towards them, to smile and wave a hand in acknowledgement, but his eye was arrested by a figure in the front of the crowd, a tall young man in ragged peasant clothes whose eyes were fixed on him in a burning gaze. Paul's mouth dried. The young man's companions were holding aloft a banner bearing the device Paul had heard described before, the device of the peasant's mysterious leader they called the Earl of Poverty.

As Paul halted, the young man stepped forward.

'Take me with you, Father,' he said. 'Let me be your lieutenant.'

'You are the Earl of Poverty?' he asked. He still felt dazed. There was not time yet for bitterness. 'So that is why I was not coerced like Latimer and the others.'

'Take me with you,' Adrian said again, urgently. His dark eyes glittered with emotion.

'It is not for me to decide,' Paul said. Adrian's mouth curved in a bitter smile.

'Even if it was, you would not take me, would you.' Paul shook his head. 'Why not? Because I am a bastard?'

'Yes, because you are my bastard son. But not in the way you think,' Paul said. In his mind he saw Amyas's face. It would be betrayal of Amyas to take Adrian. There was no time for more—the others were mounting. Hurriedly he said, 'I will speak to you when I return,' and turned away.

Norfolk made fair promises, but Paul sensed that they were hollow. There was an air of haste and perfunctoriness which suggested that he would have agreed to almost anything to get rid of them. He greeted Paul kindly, like a kinsman, but the wise dark eyes in the hatchet face warned him not to meddle in matters out of his power. Aske seemed satisfied with the promises, and when the Lancaster Herald brought forward the King's pardon to all the rebels, there seemed nothing more to do. They returned to Pontefract, Aske assured the pilgrims their terms would be met, the pardon was read publicly, and the great army of the north began to disperse homewards.

Adrian sought out Paul in his quarters where he was preparing for the journey home, and at once fell on his knees and held out to him a white rose.

'A sign of peace,' he said. There were quantities of white rose bushes in the castle grounds, for it had been the home of the Duke of York before it became crown property. 'I found it growing in a corner of the courtyard. It's sheltered there, and I suppose the winter sun made it bloom. It was the only one. Will you wear it, Father, as a token you have forgiven me?'

'Forgiven you?' Paul said, puzzled. The soft dark curls of the naked bent head tempted his fingers. 'For what?'

'For leaving my lord's household,' he said after a perceptible hesitation.

'Ah, yes,' Paul said. 'Why did you?'

Another pause. Paul reached out, took the offered rose, and then gripped the hand that had held it and pulled the boy to his feet.

'Adrian,' he said. 'My son—for once, tell me the truth. For once, speak what is in your heart without wondering whether it is wise or not. Let me *know* you.'

For a moment he thought it had worked, and the wide dark eyes as full of uncomprehending pain as a stricken deer's gazed into his; then a shutter flicked down, and the tense control spread again across the handsome face.

'Know me? It is too late for that, Father. You let pass the chances you had for that. Nevertheless, I will, just once, tell you what is in my mind—but not now. It is not yet time.'

'Very well,' Paul said coldly, and turned away.

'May I ride with you?' Adrian asked. Paul glanced over his shoulder wearily.

'If you wish. Where are you going?'

Adrian shrugged. 'Wherever chance takes me. I have a notion that the King will want scapegoats for this escapade, and I have no desire to be one. I shall go north—one respects the lion more at a distance.'

'Is that why you came here anonymously as the "Earl of Poverty"?'

'A shrewd guess, Father—yes, I took care no-one should know who I was.'

'But why did you come at all?'

Adrian looked at him for a moment with the bright, calculating gaze of a bird. He seemed for the first time not quite at ease, as if truth were about to break through the perfect carapace. 'I thought—I felt—the cause seemed good. The people needed a leader.'

'Needed a leader. And—a leader becomes beloved, is that it?' Paul asked quite gently. The carapace hardened again.

'Necessarily. Adulation is a pleasant diet.'

Paul nodded. He felt he understood a little more about his son than before. No-one in particular in the Norfolk household, he had left to become someone very important to an army of peasant rebels. Love in some form was an essential.

'Ride with me,' he said abruptly. 'I must leave now—come.'

Adrian dropped his head dutifully, and they walked out together. In the thin winter sunshine, Paul paused to unclasp his cloak-brooch, and pinned the white rose on with it. Then he ordered the lightest of his attendants to ride pillion with another and give his horse to Adrian. The young man mounted with a lithe grace that reminded Paul painfully of himself at that age; despite his ragged clothes, Adrian was a figure it was impossible to ignore, tall, hard and handsome. Paul beckoned his son to ride beside him, and the small cavalcade clattered out of the yard and on to the road north.

As they travelled they left the sunshine behind them and rode towards a horizon increasingly lowering. It grew colder, too, and Paul observed his son shivering from time to time in his inadequate rags, but he had nothing besides his own clothes to give him. His damaged arm ached: there would be snow later—it looked like a considerable storm of snow. Often when the first snow is delayed in winter it heralds a long bitter spell. Paul was longing to be home. He thought of the torchlit rooms, the great blazing log fires and braziers, hot food, mulled wine, the warm pressure of his hound lying against his legs as he sat in his chair in the winter parlour talking to his family. Most of all, he thought of Nanette, her slender beauty burning like birch flames, thought of her quick intelligence, her sensitive understanding, thought of her miraculous body leaning against his and her slender limbs twined round him as they made love in the stuffy darkness of their bed. He rode faster, setting a steady quick pace, and wasted no time or energy on talk.

It was when they reached the hill overlooking Morland Place that he drew rein, wondering belatedly about Adrian, he glanced towards his son, and saw his eyes fixed on the house below with an intense expression that was either great desire or great hatred. Adrian looked towards him then, and said urgently,

'Father, I must speak to you.'

'Speak then.'

'No—alone. Father, send on your servants, and let me speak to you for a moment—only a moment.'

Paul hesitated for a moment and then nodded. 'Ride on down,' he told his attendants. 'Tell your mistress to make ready for me. I shall follow you shortly.'

The servants bowed and rode on, and when they had gone a little way, Adrian shivered and said, 'Let us ride back into the shelter of the trees. It is too exposed here for comfort.'

The two horses were turned and moved gratefully into the edge of the coppice, the hounds following. Adrian did not stop there, however, but led the way deeper into the trees until the sound of the wind was lost except high up in the top branches. Then he stopped and swung himself down to the ground, and he held Paul's rein, silently inviting him to do likewise. Paul dismounted, Adrian hitched both horses to a bush, and then came back to stand before his father. Paul had shrunk a little with age, and the boy overtopped him by an inch, but otherwise there was little to choose between them as they stood at opposite ends of vigorous manhood.

'Well, you wanted to speak to me.'

'Yes, Father. I told you why I ran away from my lord's house—'

'Did you? Did you tell me the true reason?'

'I heard that the north was in ferment. The cause seemed good to me, and I wanted to help it. But more than that— Father, can you understand? *Will* you understand?'

'I will try,' Paul said awkwardly. The boy was serious now, he saw.

'Then listen, and try. Father, I am a man of twenty-eight years, and in all that time, since my mother died, no man has loved me or wanted me, and why? Because I am a bastard. Because my father and my mother were not married. That's all. I am despised and set aside for something I could not control or alter. But I am no different from other men. I want to be loved and esteemed, just as other men do. So I ran away, and went north, to find something in which I could make a place for myself.'

'And did it answer?' Paul asked quietly.

'At first. They loved me, almost worshipped me. I can't tell you what it was like after so long. But yesterday, when they had their answer and there was no more to be done, they turned away from me, they walked past me as if I were invisible. They wanted to go home—they all wanted to be in their homes again, just as you do now. I have watched your face as you rode. They wanted to go home, and had no more time for me. But where can I go? I have no home. Father, let me come home with you. Let me come home to Morland Place.'

'I cannot.'

'Father, don't refuse me! Don't!'

'Listen to me, Adrian, and try to understand—aye, in your turn, try. I have a duty to my other son. Once I beat my wife, was ready to kill her, because I had a duty to your mother. But now I have a duty to my son, and if it means that I must turn you away, or even kill you, I will do it. Yes, mistake me not, I will do it.'

'Though you don't love him?' Adrian said with unexpected insight. Paul stared, and his mouth twisted wryly.

'Yes, though I have never loved him, and though I love you; though I loved your mother, and never loved his; but still I must do my duty. You must go, whither you will. I will help you if I can. But I cannot give you a home at Morland Place.'

Adrian stepped forward, his eyes burning. 'Don't send me away, Father. I warn you—'

'Warn me?' Adrian's hands balled into fists as all the old frustration welled up in him.

'Yes,' he cried fiercely. 'I am driven to desperation. If you turn me away I will have nothing to live for. I will kill you. Don't doubt me—I came prepared to kill you. See!' He drew out from under his doublet a long knife, and it glittered dully in the heavy, unnatural light. Paul looked at it, and then at his son's face, with pity.

'Yes, I see. You are a fool, and I never thought you a fool, if you think you can buy love with threats.'

'Love—yes, your love is what I want, what I have always wanted. Love me, Father!'

'You can't blackmail me, Adrian. You are not a child now. You are a man. Love can't be got by blackmail, only by earning it.'

'But I cannot earn it! I am a bastard!' Adrian cried bitterly.

'Perhaps you cannot,' Paul said calmly. He felt no fear, only a vague sorrow mingled with contempt. The boy stepped closer again, so that their faces were hardly apart.

'Father, don't look at me like that. Don't make me kill you. Don't make me, Father.' Tears began to run from his eyes, and he turned his head slightly, baring his teeth, half enraged, half anguished. 'Love me, Father, love me.'

But the pity and contempt in Paul's eyes did not change. Adrian cried out, a cry of fear and hate and surrender and defiance such as a hunted and cornered fox makes at the very last, just before the dogs fall on him, and with a convulsive, desperate movement he jerked the knife into Paul's chest.

Paul hardly knew he was struck, was aware not of pain but only surprise. He and Adrian were pressed together as if embracing, but when the boy let him go, reeling backwards, sobbing, Paul fell, like a felled tree. The branches above him whirled away and back, and darkness ebbed and flowed on the edge of his vision and he became aware at last of a cold burning in his chest, but he still knew only surprise. He heard Adrian's hopeless weeping, heard him stumble away to the horses, heard the dogs barking as the horse crashed away through the trees.

Then the dogs came nosing and whining about him, licking his face, and he knew he should get up. His hand turned palm downwards, pressed against the cold crumbly earth, he pushed himself up, and then gasped in agony as it seemed his body gaped in dissolution. The shock that had numbed him passed from him: he knew himself mortally hurt, and as he fell back on the earth a turmoil of emotions rushed through him, anger and fear and regret and above all longing, longing for home. Tears began to run weakly from the outer corners of his eyes. He pushed the dogs away, commanding them to go home, but they whimpered and pressed closer. At last, a long time later it seemed, they wandered away, and he heard them moving about in the undergrowth, and then he heard them no more.

Nanette heard the horses return, and from the quality of the noises below knew enough to relax. He was home and safe, thank God, oh thank God! Lord Latimer had sent word he would be back tomorrow; things had passed off better than she had feared. She waited, eagerly, for the sound of her husband's footsteps, knowing that he would come straight up to her, but when after ten minutes, then fifteen minutes, he had not come, she grew restless and went down into the hall. She called to a servant, who fetched one of the attendants.

'Where is your master?' she asked.

'I was just coming up to you, Madam,' he said. 'The master sent us on ahead and bid us tell you be ready. He is back in the shawe, talking to the young man.'

'What young man?' Nanette asked with a puzzled frown.

'The one that rode back with us from Pomfret, Madam.' He looked away from her a little awkwardly, and then back, and said in a low voice, 'He calls the master "father", Madam.'

Nanette drew a sharp breath. Adrian! It was not only surprise, it was fear too. Why should the mention of his name fill her with apprehension? And yet she remembered the meeting with him, the sense of darkness that came from him. 'You left him alone with this man?' she asked sharply.

'He gave us orders, Madam,' the attendant said resentfully. What else could he do but obey?

'Go saddle me a horse at once,' she said. 'I must go and meet him.'

'Madam, is it wise? It begins to snow—it is growing dark.'

'You obeyed your master's orders readily enough—now obey mine. I will fetch my cloak and I want the horse ready by the time I come down.'

'Who will ride with you?' he asked, anxious now.

'Send some men after me. I will go on ahead. Hurry.'

The air was so cold it took her breath away, the hard, improbable cold that exists only for the short while before snow: already the first thin flakes were wandering down. It was darkling, but her anger and anxiety prevented fear. She pushed Puss into a hand canter, riding up the track towards the copse—shawe was the local word for it—and she had just crested the rise when the two great hounds flew out of the gloom towards her. It was only by their barking that she knew they were not wolves, and the lurch of her heart that their appearance gave her made her regret for the first time that she had come alone. But Paul must be coming—they had run ahead of him, she thought. She halted Puss and waited, but there was no sound, no crackle through the wood of an approaching horse. The hounds stood close, looking up at her hopefully, their tails swinging, their amber eyes glowing in the weird snow-light. She called Paul's name, and her voice fell flatly across the empty gloom.

Now fear entered her. Something had happened to him—why else were they not with him? She pressed her heels into Puss's flanks and rode forward, cautiously. The track did not penetrate the wood, but there was only one obvious way forward where use had subdued the undergrowth and opened a passage. The hounds ran past her, frisked ahead of her, barking. She pressed Puss into a trot, and burst abruptly into a clearing, hearing Paul's horse whicker and in the same instant seeing his supine figure.

She flung herself from her horse, not stopping even to hitch it, and thrusting away Alexander's enquiring muzzle she knelt beside the indistinct shape of her husband. His face was white and still in the murky light, and her heart closed, thinking he was dead. She touched his face—it warmed under her fingers—his eyes opened. Relief broke from her lips.

'Oh Paul, what happened? Are you hurt? Where is Adrian?' But already her other hand had found the wet stickiness all across the front of his clothes. His eyes wandered and found hers. He said, 'He has gone. He has killed me. Nan—'

'No!' she cried out. 'No, I will get you home. You will be all right. Where are you hurt? Was it a knife?'

'Nan—peace, listen to me—' Paul said with difficulty. 'If you move me, I will die. I wanted to see you again. Thank God you came.'

'Let me get help,' she cried, beginning to stand. His voice rose, cracking with anxiety.

'No, don't leave me!' He struggled to reach her, coughed blood, and fell back, his eyes sinking in his head. Nanette knelt down beside him, and he clutched her as if she could hold him back from death.

'Stay with me, Nan,' he said. 'It won't be long.'

A flake of snow fell on Paul's cheek, and then another, and she brushed them away.

'It was not his fault,' he said. His eyes had wandered from hers. 'I never loved him enough. It was always that way, all my life. Amyas and Jack and Ursula—I loved them too little, or too late.'

She could think of nothing to say. Her hands pressed against his wound were slippery with blood. He moved his head restlessly.

'I'm cold.'

Nanette lay down and stretched herself against him, trying to cover his body with hers, and she put her arms round him and rested her cheek again his, finding again the familiar smell of his skin and his hair. She closed her eyes against the welling agony. The snow was falling faster, and she tried to shield him with her body. For a time he was silent, and when he spoke again his voice was weaker, as if he were drifting out of reach.

'Richard was wrong,' he said. 'It was you. She was only the forerunner.'

'Who, dearest?' she asked. He did not answer. He began to yawn as men bleeding to death will do, and she pressed against him, trying to give him her warmth. Would help never come?

'You must marry again,' he said sleepily. 'Promise me.'

His cold skin was wet with her tears. She could only nod. She thought of the wasted years, and of the empty years to come, and knew already the depth of bitterness. After a while he spoke again, faintly and drowsily.

'So cold. Nan. Dark. Hold me—'

His voice stopped and her tears stopped and for a long time there was silence. The wind grew in the upper branches, but there was quietness in their shelter, and the snow fell peacefully, lightly covering the man and the woman, crusting the coats of the quiet hounds who lay at a little distance, watching. Darkness coalesced round them. After a long while Paul yawned again, easily like a tired child, and settled his cheek against Nanette's more heavily.

'I love you,' she whispered against his ear.

She did not feel him go. He seemed only to grow more and more heavy, until at last she had to know that it was not a warm, living weight. Even then she did not move. Let me die here, she prayed.

When the servants found them, the scene in the clearing was unchanged, the horses nose-to-tail drowsing, easing one hind leg and then the other; the hounds lying chin on paw, their amber eyes half closed but watchful; the man and the woman stretched out as if sleeping, the woman's hand resting on the white rose, its petals now crusted dark with the flowering blood.

Twenty-two

~~~~~~~

$\mathcal{S}$EARCH AND ENQUIRY DISCOVERED NOTHING, AND RUMOUR provided only a hint that the murderer had gone north. It seemed not unlikely—once over the border into Scotland it would be easy enough to take ship for France and oblivion.

Paul was buried at Morland Place, and his old hound, Alexander, was buried with him, having outlived his master by only a few hours. The funeral was on the eighteenth, and the chapel was crowded with servants, tenants and villagers who were genuinely stricken by the loss of the master of Morland Place; and not a few cast anxious eyes at the new master, wondering how things would be under him. He was known to have been wild in his youth and had a reputation for being impatient with the commoners; but on the other hand he was strong for the Old Faith, so perhaps he would turn out for the good.

The family spent the Christmas season in deep mourning, and in February on Paul's month-mind a mass of remembrance was held for him. It had been intended for it to be held in Holy Trinity Church, but the Ten Articles issued last year forbad prayers for the dead, and as it was thought this view would soon be enforced by law, the priest of Holy Trinity was unwilling to take the risk. So the service was held in the chapel at Morland

Place: Father Fenelon, as he had grown older, had grown more and more orthodox, and was now as staunch a Papist as even Amyas could have wanted. While Paul was master, he had framed his words and actions to his master's views, but now there was nothing to stop him, with Amyas's help, turning Morland Place into an outpost of the Roman Church.

Despite the uncertain religious climate, the month-mind was well attended. Thomas Boleyn, looking old and sick after the downfall of his hopes and plans and the death of the brightest of his children, was there to honour his old friend. The Latimers came, and Sir Edward Neville, and Sir Thomas Percy represented his brother who was too sick to travel, and Geoffrey Pole, the youngest of the remaining heirs of the House of York came to honour the family who had spent so much blood in its name.

Luke Morland and Alice made the journey up from Dorset, bringing with them the eleven-year-old twins, Elizabeth and Ruth; the Buttses were there, and the Bible Morlands, and Micah brought young Paul from Framlingham, where the Norfolks had spent Christmas. The family was almost complete again, and the presence of so many people did something to raise Nanette's spirits. She found comfort in the presence of her old friend Katherine, and from talking to Micah, and young Paul whom she found sensitive and intelligent, and more like his grandfather than Amyas was.

Luke Morland's little girls seemed to feel at a loss at first. Robert and Edward were too grown-up to make them feel at ease, and Eleanor too quiet and listless; it was young Paul who played the host to the twins. Though he was only rising twelve, his life at Court had given him an early maturity and a strong feeling for what ought to be done, and he was unable to see his young cousins lonely unhappy or bored without taking it upon himself to relieve their suffering. Nanette noticed it, and honoured his gentle heart.

'He has absorbed better principles than one could have hoped for him,' she observed to Micah. 'Going from a confused home to a corrupt court one would not have expected him to turn out so well. I am sure you have had a hand in it.'

Micah smiled and shook his head. 'I believe he had a natural virtue which resisted bad example. And my lord's household is strictly run. You know of his political ambition, but his domestic life is very orthodox. The Howards are a strong Catholic family, and things in Norfolk and Suffolk are always quieter than you know them. It is a backwater out of the main stream of life.'

'Whatever the cause, I am glad that he has turned out so well. Robert and Edward, too, I am proud of. I wonder a little about Eleanor. She is so quiet—one scarcely hears her talk from one day to the next—and she seems to learn very little. Arabella says she was the same when she was younger. I wonder what will come of her.'

'Her father will find her a match,' Micah said with a shake of his head, 'if she lives so long. I do not like to think of a child like that being married off, but it will happen. Amyas is ambitious.'

'Do you think so?' Nanette asked in surprise. 'I thought that he was too interested in the restoration of the Old Faith to be ambitious.'

'That is his ambition,' Micah said.

'Then—do you not think the Morland marriage will come off—Robert and Elizabeth?'

'I don't know. I would expect Amyas to look for a connection with an old family, but with Amyas one must always expect the unexpected. But you, cousin what will you do?'

Nanette shrugged—that little foreign gesture she had caught from Anne Boleyn and never lost—and said, 'I suppose I will stay here.'

'You will marry, surely?'

Nanette remembered her promise to Paul. One could not go against the promise made to the dying. 'One day, perhaps. But for the time being, I would like to see my young kinsfolk growing up. I had hoped Elizabeth and Ruth would come to live here, as Paul planned. They would be so good for Eleanor—and I hope I would be good for them. Later, if I have any offers of marriage—for I find myself in the position I was in most of my youth, you know, cousin. I have no dowry.'

Micah raised an eyebrow. 'But surely—your marriage portion—you must have inherited it as a widow?'

'Paul was so eager to be married, he did not wait for the legal matters to be arranged. So in law I have no portion.'

'Well, that will not signify,' Micah said, patting her arm. 'Amyas will make the settlement in his father's name. Even if the amount of the proposed settlement were not known, he would deal fairly with you.'

Nanette let him think her comforted, but privately she wondered whether Amyas would be willing to let any of his new inheritance go, especially to someone he disapproved of. He had nothing definite against Nanette, but she had been handmaid to The Concubine, and minds like his knew that sin was contagious. It might be that she would remain at Morland Place for the rest of her life, a dependent widow—but there were worse fates. She would be glad to stay here, in her child-hood home, in the place where she had know a bliss so intense, though so shortlived.

Luke Morland, who had reformist tendencies, had come to Morland Place with some doubts as to the wisdom of leaving his daughters in the household of a man known to be an outspoken Papist, but there were many influences brought to bear on him during his stay to counteract the doubts. Alice wanted it—she would be glad for her daughters to be sent away to a place where an aunt's affectionate eye would be on them; the connection with the York Morlands was a desirable one; Nanette's refined mind and elegant manners would be good for the little girls, one of whom was growing rough and boyish and the other of whom was growing clumsy and inarticulate from their country retirement.

The deciding factor, however, as far as Luke was concerned, was the presence at the feast of Geoffrey Pole. Through his wife Luke was connected with the Courtnay branch of the House of York, and he was as fanatically Yorkist as Amyas was Papist. In fact, the two men were more alike in their characters then either would have liked to think, and in their support of the old line they found a common ground. When Luke and Alice finally set off for Dorset again, Elizabeth and Ruth remained at Morland Place.

Spring came, and still the north was unsettled. Small rebellions broke out again here and there, and once more Norfolk was sent north to deal with the trouble. He declared martial law, and rebels were hanged at Carlisle and in Cumberland; and as Nanette had predicted the ringleaders of the Pilgrimage of Grace were quietly rounded up and sent to London for trial. It was a frightening time for the Morlands. Their friend and patron Sir Thomas Percy was one of those executed; his brother, Harry Percy, sick and frightened, warded off execution by making over all his lands and property to the Crown; and Amyas for some time feared for his life, and only the patronage of the Duke of Norfolk himself saved him from suffering for his father's involvement in the Pilgrimage.

This made him less sympathetic towards Nanette, and in vain did she try to point out that Amyas himself would have gone on the Pilgrimage had Paul not prevented him. In all probability, Amyas would have involved himself so deeply that even my lord of Norfolk could not have saved him. Amyas was not a person it was possible to argue logically with, and in the end he lost his temper.

'You would do well to remember, Madam, that you are a dependant in this house—aye, and kept here only by my charity!' he shouted at her.

'I am your father's widow,' Nanette said with quiet dignity. 'You owe me at least the respect of a son.'

'I owe you nothing!' he said. 'Your marriage to my father was not valid, since you did not bother to wait for a dispensation—oh yes, I know you obtained one from the Archbishop, but even if he were not a damned heretic, he would not have the power to allow your marriage to your own uncle. You are not his widow—you were never his wife. You were his concubine, and were you not also my cousin I would throw you out.'

'You insult your father's memory when you insult me,' Nanette said passionately. 'Do you not remember the fifth Commandment?'

'I remember it, Madam. I do not need *you* to teach me my faith. But think you, my father also knew he was not wed to you—why else did he delay in making a settlement on you? You were wise to hold your tongue and remember your place. You are not mistress here any more.'

'Do you intend to cast me out?' Nanette asked in cold fury. Amyas looked at her with a pitying smile.

'No, I will keep you from common charity—I am a Christian after all. But when I marry again—and I shall shortly be looking for a wife—you might be wise to think of retiring to a convent, and finishing your life in mending your soul.'

It was only after he had gone that Nanette allowed herself to weep. Gladly she would have retired to a convent if she had only herself to think about; but there were the little girls—how could she abandon them to a womanless household? And then there was her promise to Paul—if she entered a convent it would be impossible to fulfill. So for the time being she must set her teeth and endure. Perhaps in time Amyas might mellow.

Life, however, was full and not unhappy for Nanette. Despite his words, Amyas had done nothing to remove the duties of mistress of the house from her. Habit had made authority sit more easily on her, and she directed the affairs of the great house with the ease of skill, though Amyas complicated the day-to-day running to an unexpected degree when he decided that the family would no longer dine in the hall, but take all its meals in the winter parlour, except for on the greater feast days. This meant that Nanette had always to order two meals, one for the family in the winter parlour, and one for the rest of the household in the hall.

It was not only for this reason, nor even in memory of Paul's feelings on the subject, that Nanette deprecated the change: it seemed to her altogether a bad thing that the servants should be denied the example of their masters' behaviour, and should be kept separate as if they were not human beings or Christians but some lower form of animal. On a purely practical level, Nanette did not feel the steward, whose duty it was to supervise in the hall when the master was not there, was capable of keeping proper order amongst the lower servants. Their moral welfare was ultimately her responsibility, and it troubled her that they might be tempted into light behaviour or ungodly talk at the table.

A great deal of her time that was not devoted to running the household was given to the upbringing of the little girls, and this was something she enjoyed so much she scarcely felt it to be a duty. She found Elizabeth and Ruth had good qualities, despite their unpolished manners. Elizabeth was rather boyish, and conversation with her revealed that she had been in the habit at home at Hare Warren of slipping away from her attendants and running wild with the stable boy and the shepherd's son. She was an excellent horsewoman, and knew a great deal about hunting and hawking. Nanette took her out and let her handle her merlin, and found her so good she promised her a bird of her own next autumn.

Ruth was quieter, obviously used to following Elizabeth's example in everything. She was not naturally graceful, but her clumsiness concealed a sweetness, and she had a lovely voice that Nanette was glad to encourage her in—there had not been enough music at Morland Place of late. Both the girls seemed quick-witted, though they were untaught; they made a sad contrast to Eleanor, whose manners and deportment were excellent, thanks to Arabella, but whose mind was shuttered like a winter house so that it seemed no light would ever penetrate there.

Nanette was anxious that they should learn other things besides needlework and the correct way to attend a lady, but Philippe Fenelon had too much to do in supervising and teaching the boys to give them instruction, and Nanette's time would stretch no further, so after careful enquiry in the city she found, and with Amyas's permission engaged, a respectable, educated women, a Mrs. Stokes, to be their governess. Mrs. Stokes had in her youth been attendant on a gentlewoman of York, and had later been governess to her children. Now her mistress was dead and her former charges grown up, she was living comfortably on her pension, but was very happy to leave her retired life for Morland Place.

'I am comfortable enough, Madam,' she told Nanette, 'but I have passed most of my life in a large household, and cannot like the quietness, or the lack of doing.'

Nanette liked her at once, and found her ideas sound and her morals unexceptionable. The little girls, after an initial period of reserve, thawed to her and treated her with a respectful affection which was just what Nanette would have hoped for. Mrs. Stokes taught them French and Italian and Latin, read with them, improved their writing, supervised their needlework and oversaw their devotions. Nanette taught them etiquette, music, singing and dancing; and Elizabeth, who was the most intelligent of the three, joined the boys for Father Fenelon's Greek lessons, where her facility with that language soon put them on their metal.

Life was busy, but it was also full of pleasant pastimes. Nanette visited, and received visits from Arabella and Lucy and took much pleasure from their company. A visit to the city always meant either dinner or supper at the Butts house, and she often met James there, for he and John Butts did a lot of business together. She hunted and hawked frequently, attended by Elizabeth, who was a satisfying companion, and the unwilling Audrey, and sometimes accompanied by Arabella, sometimes by Philippe and the boys. But much of her unoccupied time she spent in the chapel, and when she had finished her prayers and devotions she would just sit, her hands in her lap folded over the missal Paul had given her with the running hare on the cover. Here where he had spent so much time he did not seem so far away, and she did not think God or the Saints would blame her for thinking of him in that place. In bed, in the crowded bedchamber, she would fall asleep as soon as her head touched the pillow, but here in the empty quietness of the holy place she could close her eyes and drift outwards to a place where he waited for her, dark eyes and rich smiling mouth, to be with him.

All through the summer of 1537 religious houses continued to be closed down, although those in Yorkshire were spared, at least for the time being, probably because of the unrest that still prevailed. The monks whose establishments were removed were given the choice of being transferred to another house, or leaving their order with a pension, and many of both sorts came north to Yorkshire. Those who transferred were frequently transferred to Yorkshire houses, which had a reputation for piety and propriety, and those who left the orders often took secular posts in the north. Philippe Fenelon liked to talk to them and repeat their views to Amyas and the rest of the family, and he had reluctantly to admit that there was little to be complained of in the way the ex-monks were treated.

'The pensions are small, but there seems no doubt they will be paid,' he said, 'and the closures seem not to be attended by any unseemliness or violence.'

'The very act of closure is a violence,' Amyas retorted roughly. 'You seem to forget of what we are talking.'

'I do not forget,' Philippe replied with dignity. 'I am not in any way excusing the fact—I only report that it is done in as seemly a manner as such a thing could be done. And, in justice to your late father's views, there is little resistance from those in orders. Many houses indeed have surrendered voluntarily even before the commissioners send the order.'

'You speak like a heretic,' Amyas said in disgust.

'Sir, you forget yourself,' Nanette said in horror. 'You speak to an ordained priest.'

Amyas had the grace to look ashamed, and Philippe went on, 'The greatest evil seems to fall on the nuns—they have no great wealth, and of course no opportunity to take on secular posts. Their pensions are too small for them to live in respectability; the best one could hope for them would be a decent marriage, but the King has forbidden them to relinquish their vow of chastity, so even that is impossible for them.'

Amyas said, 'Marriage could hardly be classed as a decent way for a nun to spend her life.'

'Better, at least, than whoredom,' Philippe replied quietly, and there the subject was abandoned.

Despite the continued conflict on the religious front, the year was quieter than the one before, for there was no drought, and the harvest was good at last, and men and women who are busy in the fields have little time for rebellion. There were one or two small outbreaks, but on the whole men talked rather than acted. There was good news from London to sweeten the year, too, for Jane Seymour's second pregnancy was going better than her first, and in October the news flew up the country like a forest fire that she had laid-in of a son, a healthy son, born on St Edward's Eve, and named for that reason, Edward.

The news was cause for rejoicing for every man, for the worst thing any Englishman had to fear was an uncertain succession and its accompanying civil war, and for a time factions were forgotten in joy. The news was followed to Morland Place by a letter from Katherine Neville to Nanette giving more particulars.

'The labour was dreadful, and the Queen suffered terribly,' the letter said, 'and at one time the midwives thought that one or other must die, but both survived the ordeal. The long-awaited Prince is a large and healthy child and already very beautiful. He was born on Friday, the twelfth of October, and yesterday, on Monday, the christening took place in the chapel here at Hampton Court. The Queen was brought in on a litter, wrapped in crimson velvet and ermine, and my dear Lady Mary carried the infant Prince to the font. I attended her, and my sister Anne attended the Lady Elizabeth, who was carried through most of the service by the Queen's brother Edward. The King sat by the Queen's pallet through the service, which took above three hours and was not over before midnight. Then there was a torchlit procession to the Queen's apartments where she was required to give the child her blessing. Lady Mary took her sister's hand through this part of the ceremonial, and when we finally retired, Elizabeth was too tired to walk any longer, and it was Mary who carried her back to the apartments they share. She must be as glad as anyone in the realm that the succession is at last assured.'

The letter reached Nanette on the twenty-second of October; a week later came the news that the Queen was dead. Early in November Lady Latimer travelled north to spend the Christmas season at home, and she stopped for a short visit at Morland Place to tell Nanette more.

'There was talk of poison, of course, but then there always is,' Katherine said as they walked about the solar together. 'There is no substance in it. The Queen died of a fever. Some think she caught a chill being carried to the chapel for the christening, but I have seen women die in childbed before, without ever having moved from their beds. I think it was her dreadful suffering that caused it.'

Nanette nodded. 'It is strange how Queens seem to suffer more at those times than other women.'

'Perhaps God ordains it so. What is worth having is worth suffering for,' Katherine said. She and Nanette exchanged a long glance. 'It is strange, is it not,' she went on, 'that here we are, middle-aged women, and neither of us has ever born a child.'

'I think perhaps neither of us ever will,' Nanette said. 'I am a widow now—'

'And I have twice been wed to an old man, though both were good, gentle husbands—' They were silent, thinking about it. Nanette roused herself to ask, 'Is the King very grieved?'

'The people talk of it,' Katherine said, 'but I saw him, and it is my belief he is so overjoyed at the birth of a son that he does not much regard the loss of the mother. He would not even stay to keep vigil over her as he should. He left Hampton immediately she was dead, and Mary had to do what was proper in his stead. And,' she lowered her voice, 'I have heard since that he has already spoken to Cromwell about getting another wife.'

'Another?' Nanette was startled.

'One infant son is a slender thread to depend upon for a King no longer young. We must all pray that the King lives long enough for the Prince to reach a man's years, or the trouble we have all feared will come to us none the less. A minority would be almost as bad as a contested succession—and the King is not entirely healthy.'

'I will pray for him,' Nanette said. 'I will pray for him and the Prince at every mass. There is trouble enough in the realm—'

'And here, for you?' Katherine asked quietly. Nanette's head, in her neat widow's hood, was turned away from her friend to hide a pang of sadness. 'Servants talk, you know, Nan. I want you to know that if you should wish to leave Morland Place, I would be very happy to offer you a home. Don't you remember how we talked as children, and you said that if you were not wed when you grew up you would come and live with me? Think about it, dearest Nan.'

'Thank you,' Nanette said, much moved. 'For the moment, I must stay—I have the little girls to think of. But I thank you with all my heart, Kate, and if things grow worse, I will come to you.'

Katherine nodded, satisfied. 'There are troubles ahead, and I should be glad for us to be together when they come. And now, dear friend, shall we talk of more cheerful things? Tell me how your young charges are getting along.'

So they sat in the window-seat together as they had done so often in their lives, the two pretty young matrons, and talked of their childhood in Kendal, and their present domestic affairs. In between, their lives had taken such strange courses that there were few subjects they could touch on without pain to either.

Twenty-three

*I*N 1538 JOHN BUTTS DIED. HE WAS FIFTY, AND APART from Micah he was the oldest of the family and the last survivor of his generation. He left a world much changed and full of unrest, new ideas and old rubbing shoulders uneasily with each other. At Lucy's request he was buried at Morland Place instead of at Holy Trinity, for with a private burial the old form of mass could be said without any fear of Reformist objections. The normal sadness of any funeral was increased for the Morlands because the troubles of that summer had caused a rounding-up of all the last representatives of the House of York. The Duke of Clarence's daughter, Margaret Lady Salisbury had been sent to the Tower, along with her son Lord Montague, and his wife and baby son, and her youngest son Geoffrey Pole. Her other son, Reynold, Cardinal Pole, was abroad, and it was the threat of an invasion in his favour that had sent his relatives to the Tower.

Also imprisoned was the grandson of King Edward IV, Henry Courteney, Marquess of Exeter, and his wife and young son. Exeter and Montague were under sentence of death; no-one doubted that the deaths of the others would follow.

'The King will do away with anyone whose blood is more royal than his,' Lucy said bitterly when the family was gathered on the day after the funeral at the house on the Lendal. 'To be near the throne is crime enough these days.'

'It was always so,' young John said. 'Kings must make their thrones safe—it is the way of things. And the King has an infant son now to provide for.'

'I say it was Cromwell's doing,' Amyas said and they all looked at him in surprise.

'What threat were they to him?' John asked. Nanette understood—it was said that Geoffrey Pole had bargained for his life by implicating the others, and Amyas could not bear the thought of the guilt of his friend. To avoid a confrontation she said, 'Cromwell is only the King's instrument. The sword is not to blame, but the hand that holds it.'

Amyas, unable to decide whether Nanette was arguing on his side or not, said roughly, 'Have we come to this, where women teach us philosophy?' and Nanette blushed with anger and looked at the floor. Her sister Catherine, with unexpected tact, changed the subject.

'Is it known when Jane and Bartholomew are coming back?' Lucy picked up the threads.

'They are to come over on the *Mary Flower* when she makes her next trip, and that will probably be early in January. I wish it was not a winter crossing, for the sake of the children, but they would come home.'

'I wish they had been in time to say goodbye to Father,' John said.

'Ezekiel, too, will be sad to have been away at this time,' Nanette said. 'He was very fond of John.' Ezekiel was on the *Mary Eleanor* in the Levant, trading for silk, perfumes and carpets.

'Perhaps when Jane comes she will bring us some new fashions. They say the French Court is very elegant,' Catherine said. 'Ours is so dull, now we have no queen. I don't suppose we will have another, either, until the Prince of Wales grows up.'

'The King will marry again,' James Chapham said abruptly. He was standing by the shuttered window, more of an onlooker than an outsider, and if anyone had been observing him they might have noted that his eyes were often fixed on one particular person who sat on a cushion on the floor by the fire: a person slender of form, dressed in black velvet and a peaked widow's hood, whose hands rested in her lap, folded over a small leather-covered missal. 'He has already been negotiating,' James went on, 'and he delays only to be sure he chooses the most valuable match. Now he had a son, he can afford to marry for reasons of policy—but marry he will.'

'For more children?' Lucy asked. 'That I could understand, for one son after so long is not enough for a King to be easy with.'

'Not so much for that reason,' James said, 'though he must want a Duke of York, but because a King's marriage is too valuable to be left unused.'

'And have you any idea of whom he might marry?' Nanette asked. 'You are our only contact with Court now—is there rumour as to the likely match?'

'Plenty of rumour, cousin,' James said. 'Cromwell and Cranmer of course are eager for a union with the Protestant countries, while Norfolk's party favours a French match. But it's my belief that the Protestant interest will win, because the Protestant countries need the alliance more. There has already been talk about the King's suit being refused by two princesses, though it is not safe to say so in London. My belief is that the next queen will be Princess Ana, the daughter of the Duke of Cleves. The Duke is almost penniless, and squeezed between two great Catholic powers—he will be willing to overlook the King's age and his treatment of his former wives.'

There was much to be thought about in what James had said, but Amyas burst in immediately with his own reaction. 'A fine thing that will be for England—a heretic queen! Better the Scottish succession than that!'

'Your words are treasonable, cousin,' John said quietly. 'You should keep your voice down.'

'Why, cannot you trust your servants?' Amyas asked scornfully. 'Perhaps you keep them too close to you. Keep them at a distance, cousin, then they cannot betray you.' There was an awkward silence as the family avoided each others' eyes. Amyas had become more and more impossible over the years, to a point where no-one really knew any more how to react to his outbursts. Nanette, feeling in some sort responsible for him, tried to change the subject again.

'It will be interesting to see Jane and Bartholomew's children, won't it, Lucy? And what strange names they have given them—Faith, Hope and Charity. Though there have been strange names in our family before, of course—'

'Protestant names,' Amyas said. 'It would seem that our cousins have been keeping bad company.'

'Perhaps Jane will let them come to me at Morland Place,' Nanette went on doggedly. 'I like to have fresh young faces around me.' It was a wrong thing to have said. Amyas looked at her sneeringly, and said, 'You are very free with your invitations, Madam, considering the weakness of your position. You might do well to reflect that there is only one person entitled to invite people to Morland Place, and that is the person who keeps *you* there out of charity.'

It was too much for Nanette. She could not stay and keep her temper, and so she stood up and without a word walked quickly from the room, and ran down to the gardens to cool her cheeks by walking about the fragrant alleys. A few moments later she turned at the end of one path and saw James coming towards her. He was still a very good-looking man, she reflected; in common with most other courtiers he had grown his beard, and it made him look younger, even though it was flecked with grey; and the broad-shouldered, padded clothes that were the present fashion suited his height and figure.

For a while he did not speak, but falling in beside her walked with her in sympathetic silence. Then at last he said, 'It is growing too much for you now, isn't it? I think you are finding it harder to hold your tongue.'

'Not so much for myself—the insults to me I can bear with very well,' Nanette said reluctantly. 'But I cannot bear to see him changing and destroying all the things that Paul built up. You know that he no longer holds the manor court? And he has commuted almost all the labour for money-payments, and he is taking back strips when their lease falls in so that he can enclose the land as pastures. Some of the tenants have offered him three and four years' rent as gressing, but he has refused it. They mutter and grumble amongst themselves, and talk of the old master—' Nanette stopped abruptly. James saw his opportunity.

'Nan, my dear, is it not time you left Morland Place? You are not happy there, and things are likely to get worse rather than better.'

'I cannot leave.'

'You can. You know what I mean. I want you to marry me.'

'Oh James—'

'You have been widowed two years, Nan. It is time you married again—no-one could say you hurried into it. I have waited for you without a word, because I know that you loved Paul, and I would not hurry you, but now—'

'It is still too soon,' Nanette cried anxiously. 'I don't want to marry again yet. It is too soon.'

'Nanette, I told you I have waited for you, but now I must tell you that I have to have your decision now. I want a wife, I want children, and though I would rather have you than any woman in the world, if you will not marry me now I must take another.'

'You have someone in mind?' Nanette asked. She was surprised to find that she minded the idea of his marrying someone else.

'Yes, I have,' he said. They stopped walking, and James turned to face her, and taking both her hands in his he said gently, 'I have been talking to Amyas. He has offered a very satisfactory dowry with Eleanor.'

'Eleanor! But she's only a child!'

'She is fifteen,' James said. Nanette realised this was true. Eleanor always seemed so much younger than her years, it was hard to realise she was grown up. James went on, 'If you will not marry me, I will take Eleanor. So you see I must press you for your answer.'

Little Eleanor, to marry James! Nanette thought. But it would be a very good establishment for her, and James would be kind to her, which a stranger might not be. If there was any hope of happiness for the child, it must lie with James. It was a good reason to refuse his hand. Nanette was attracted to him, knew it would be a good match for her—better even than for Eleanor, for Eleanor had a dowry. She might never get another offer, and she had promised Paul she would marry again—but it was too soon. She did not yet want to give to another man that which she had given with such deep emotion to Paul. She longed to get away from Amyas and from her position as unwelcome dependant—but on the other hand, to do it this way would be to do it at the expense of her niece. The struggle in her mind was hard, but short. With some regret she said,

'Cousin James, I am very grateful to you, and I will always love and esteem you, but I must say no. I cannot marry you—not now.'

James stared at her for a long moment, as if imprinting her image on his brain, and then he sighed, and lifted her hand, and kissed it. 'I am sorry,' he said. 'Well, I wish you luck, Cousin Nan. If ever there is anything I can do for you—'

'Thank you. I will remember,' Nanette said. He hesitated for a moment longer, and she thought that he was going to kiss her, but with a small smile he turned away, saying only, 'God bless you.' Nanette watched him until he entered the house, and then resumed her walking, with Ajax pattering along behind her. She wondered even then if she had done the right thing, and longed for the solace and comfort of prayer. She wished she was in the chapel, where it was quiet and one could hear the whispers of one's own heart. She longed to be home—but how long could she call it home?

What heart did not feel a surge of happiness at the arrival of spring? It was the end of winter endured—it meant fresh meat and vegetables after months of nothing but salt meat and dried beans; fresh air after months in closed rooms which, while never thoroughly warm, were always stuffy; mild and gentle air to benison flayed faces, and hands and feet swollen and raw with chilblains; freedom to move about and enjoy the land after months of plodding through mud, battling with snow, or being isolated indoors. The first new growth of grass, the budding of the trees, the first and bravest of the flowers, daffodils and snowdrops, heralded as the season strengthened under thin blue skies the stunning beauty of a world renewed, and here in Yorkshire, above all, the lambs like a snowfall on the hillsides.

Nanette found herself happier than she had expected to be again. That spring of 1541 saw her thirty-third birthday past and her life settled into a pattern which there seemed no reason to expect ever to change. She was sitting near the window of the solar enjoying the sweet air as she embroidered an altar cloth for the chapel which she hoped to have ready for Easter. Easter was her favourite of all the Church festivals, and the cloth which she had designed herself combined the elements she loved most, the sacred mystery of death and resurrection and the rebirth of nature. The liturgical colours of Easter—gold, purple and white—reminded her of crocuses, the flowers of Easter.

Beside her sat her youngest sister, Jane, now a matron of twenty-eight, impossible though it seemed. She was plump and fair and pretty, and her clothes were very elegant. She had a great knack of making over old dresses into new, so she always seemed to be dressing in something one had not seen before. She was working at one end of a wall-hanging, while the twins, Elizabeth and Ruth, worked at the other. The hanging was intended for the chamber Elizabeth would share with Robert when she was married next winter. The twins had just turned fifteen, and the manners and minds of both had undergone much improvement since they came to Morland Place, but they still had little aptitude for needlework. Nanette watched them for a moment with a smile as they worked at the tapestry. Ruth had a minute patience which would always find out the way to do a thing, given enough time, but Elizabeth struggled grimly and uncomprehendingly with needle and wool as if they were alive and had minds of their own. If Jane had not come most days to help them with it, Nanette doubted whether the hanging would have been even half done by the wedding-day.

Mrs. Stokes, on the other side of the room, cast an agonized glance across at them from time to time, evidently longing to take the work over herself, but Nanette had decreed that it must be the twins' own work, so she could only glance in the intervals of supervising the work of her new charges. These were Jane's daughters, Faith, a tall, thin child of almost eight, Hope, who was six, and four-year-old Charity, who was plump and pretty with golden curls and already able to get her own way in everything. They needed little enough supervision—Faith had been well-taught by the nuns in Calais, and Hope and Charity had been in Mrs. Stokes's own charge from the beginning.

'You are not setting us a good example, sister,' Jane said, smiling across at Nanette. 'You haven't made a stitch for the quarter of an hour, you have been so lost in thought. What preoccupies you?'

Nanette smiled and hastily lifted her needle again. 'Oh, many things, none of them important. I was thinking how wonderful it is to have spring weather again. Now the roads are open at last we shall have news—how the new Queen is faring, for instance. I wonder a lot about her—she is Queen Anne's cousin, you know, and I wonder if the King saw a likeness to Anne in her.'

'Did you know her in your days at Court?' Jane asked, and the twins looked up with interest at the question. Nanette said, 'She wasn't at Court in those days, of course, but I did once see her, when Queen Anne visited the house at Lambeth. I must say I can't remember her very well—there were so many of them. The Edmund Howards are numerous and very poor, and Catherine is only one amongst so many Howard cousins. It is impossible to think of her being Queen—she's only a child.'

'Old enough to attract the King,' Jane said, with a hint of disapproval.

'The marriage with the Princess of Cleves was never consummated, Jane,' Nanette said. 'The annulment was perfectly in order.'

'That is to say, it suited both of them,' Jane said. 'And the Norfolk clan were quick to encourage the King's preference.'

Nanette nodded, and thought suddenly of Anne, in her

last hours, saying 'There was never a choice. There was never anything else I could have done.'

'*She* would have had no choice, poor child,' she said. 'I wonder what she thought of it all. The sudden rise to fame, the jewels, the courtiers fawning on her—but she's only a child, hardly more than our Eleanor.'

'But you must at least be happy about Eleanor's match,' Jane said. 'She is very happy, is she not?'

Nanette glanced at Jane swiftly, not wishing it to be thought she had any reason to disapprove of the match. 'Oh yes,' she said hastily. 'I believe it was the best thing that could have happened to her. James is kind and patient with her, as perhaps no stranger could have been.' Jane put down her needle.

'Nan, is it true you refused him? Catherine said you did, and that was why he married Eleanor. Why did you? It would seem to me to have been an excellent thing for you.'

Nanette shrugged. 'At the time, it seemed wrong. I had nothing to guide me but my prayers, but it seemed to me I was reserved for some other fate. Now sometimes I wonder—I have lost that sense of purpose, of waiting for something to happen. Perhaps it will come back. But it was very strong then.'

'And now? Do you regret it?' She gave a significant glance towards the door, as if to indicate Amyas, who was below in the steward's room with a number of visitors. 'Life is not always easy for you, I suspect.'

'I have found a pattern, a routine that is rarely disturbed nowadays,' Nanette said. 'We get along together in our way.'

'Who are all those people?' Jane said, her curiosity overcoming her discretion. 'What are they meeting for? They have been talking in there for hours, it seems to me.'

'I don't know many of them. Sir John Neville is there, I know, and Thomas Davison, from Lord Percy's household, and Hugh Smithson, but the others I know not, and as to what they are talking about—another wild scheme I suppose.' Aware that she was talking indiscreetly, Nanette changed the subject abruptly. 'I wonder what the *Mary Flower* will bring us back in the way of new fashions this year. James says that the Medici collars are becoming very popular at Court. I wonder what we shall have next.'

As the days passed and the comings and goings at Morland Place grew more frequent and numerous, Nanette began to worry that this time Amyas had plotted something really dangerous. His air of preoccupation was tinged with a self-satisfaction bordering on glee which did nothing to calm her, and Audrey soon began to drop pieces of servant gossip which hinted at some political involvement, even—the word was used—rebellion. Nanette told her sharply to hold her tongue. If Amyas was involved in a plot to rebel, the more people who talked about it the more dangerous it would be for him.

In the end, however, she knew a great deal about the plot by the time Amyas came to tell her that he was riding out on the morrow for Pontefract.

'It is time you knew, Madam,' he said as they sat down to supper in the winter-parlour, 'that by this time tomorrow the whole of the north should be in our hands.'

'Our hands? To whom do you refer?' Nanette asked.

'A group of friends of like mind with myself. We are to march on Pontefract tomorrow, there to capture the head of the Council of the North. Once we have him, we will take over the Council and hold it until money and men arrive from Scotland. Then, when we have a strong enough base, we shall invite Reynold Pole to lead us on London. We shall capture the city, execute the heretic ministers, depose the Tudor, who is already excommunicated, and crown Reynold king and marry him to the Princess Mary.'

Nanette stared, almost open-mouthed. It was as lunatic a plan as she had ever heard, and impossible of success without very extensive backing.

'How many men have you behind you?' she asked.

'Oh, several thousand, I should think,' Amyas said vaguely. 'But that does not matter at this stage. We need very few men to capture the President of the Council. Robert and Edward and I and a handful of men will be enough—the others will be more for a show of force—'

'Robert and Edward?' Nanette said, aghast. 'Amyas, you don't mean to take them with you?'

'Of course. Why should I not?' Amyas said, surprised.

'Amyas, consider, reflect. This plan of yours cannot work. Don't you remember how the Pilgrimage of Grace failed, though they had forty thousand men—how can you succeed with so few? If you must go, go alone—don't involve your sons. Don't bring total ruin on our House. Don't you know that the servants have been talking about this for days—there can be few people in Yorkshire who do not know what you plan. If they know, the King's men will also know. It cannot succeed.'

'You speak of things you do not understand, cousin,' Amyas said coldly. 'And if the servants have been gossiping, you should have told me. It is your business to control the household staff.'

How many times had he told her she was not mistress of Morland Place, but a mere pensioner? Pointless to argue with him—yet for her nephews' sakes she tried to dissuade him. It was in vain. He only grew angry, and eventually refused to listen to her. In the grey light of the hour before dawn Amyas and his two sons rode out of the courtyard with a handful of followers to join up with the main force on the great south road. Nanette watched them go in anguish: Amyas, a child of forty-one, the light of crusading zeal in his eyes, leading the way on his big bay horse; Robert and Edward, youths of twenty and nineteen with all their lives before them, tense with excitement at the adventure they thought was ahead. All that lay ahead for them was failure, and failure meant summary death, or conviction and execution for treason.

And what then would become of the rest of them? She gathered her charges together in the solar and set them tasks to do, and put on a brave face for the sake of Elizabeth and Ruth whose betrothed husbands had ridden away that morning and who were old enough to fear that they would not come back. She talked cheerfully, but inside she was cold and still, waiting for the inevitable ill tidings.

They had not long to wait. It lacked still an hour to dinner time when a servant came rushing into the solar, white-faced and terrified.

'Men coming, mistress, armed men on horses. Coming down from the road—not our own men.'

'What livery?' Nanette asked. He shook his head, panting and rolling his eyes with fear as a dog does.

'I knawt, Mistress, none that we ken. More like a rabble, but gentlemen in front.'

'How many? Can you tell?' He only gaped at her, and in exasperation she seized his shoulders and shook him. 'How many?'

'I think—fifty—happen more. What shall we do?'

'They don't come in friendship, that will be sure enough. Run down and tell them to shut the gates, and bar them, and shutter the windows. No, peace, I'll do it. Come with me. Mrs. Stokes, get the children's cloaks and go down to the west gate. I'll get as many men as I can to go with you, and you'll take them over the fields to Shawes. You'll be safe there.'

Though terrified, Mrs. Stokes nodded, making no fuss. Nanette was already at the door, and found Elizabeth there beside her.

'I stay with you,' she said.

'No—you and Ruth must go with the children.'

'Ruth shall go—I stay with you,' Elizabeth said firmly. Nanette did not waste more time arguing. She ran down the stairs with Elizabeth and the servant behind her, and began to give her orders. 'Who do you think they are?' Elizabeth asked her.

'I don't know. I suspect they'll be King's men, reformists, come to take revenge. Anyone with a grudge against us will join them. No doubt they'll have the King's warrant, but they won't stick to it—they'll burn the place down if we don't stop them.' She turned abruptly to Elizabeth, and the girl's eyes bulged suddenly as she realised the danger she was in. 'You must go with the children,' Nanette said again.

Elizabeth swallowed, and shook her head. 'I cannot leave you. If I am to be Robert's wife and mistress here one day, I must stay now and defend the house.' Neither of them said aloud that already her betrothed might be dead but both knew it. 'If I am to die, I had sooner die here than running away,' she said. Audrey, standing near them, began to wail.

'Oh Madam, they'll kill us all, maybe worse. Oh Madam, let us go now—we can get away across the fields. Please, Madam—'

'Hush, Audrey, or I shall hit you,' Nanette said angrily. Elizabeth glanced at the maid.

'Let her go with the children,' she said. 'She'll be no use here. Let her help Mrs. Stokes with the children.'

Audrey seized at the idea, gibbering with relief, and Nanette ordered her abruptly away. 'Don't leave the children, whatever happens,' she said fiercely. 'If I hear you've left them for a moment, I'll cut out your liver with my own hand.'

'No Madam, no, I won't, I promise you, by the Rood!'

Audrey stammered, and a few minutes later Nanette saw the women and children out by the side postern with a couple of menservants. 'Holy Mother, bring them safe home,' she said as she shut the gate and barred it again.

They left only just in time. Nanette had barely regained the hall when the noise of the horsemen's arrival battered their ears, and she ran up the tiny narrow staircase to the little chamber over the gate, and looked down from the slit window. It was a motley mob, gentlemen on horseback in the vanguard, one of them the Justice of the Peace, one of Cromwell's men and a Reformist, Amyas's bitterest enemy—no doubt glad that at last Amyas had put himself outside the protection of Norfolk's patronage.

Behind him a rabble of ruffians, some perhaps the gentlemen's followers, others commoners with a grudge against Amyas, others still probably unemployed vagabonds out for spoil. The worst kind of mob to deal with. There was a thundering on the outer gate, and one of the gentlemen called out, 'Open up, in the name of the King! We have a warrant here, under the King's seal! No harbouring of traitors! Open the gates and give up the traitors and no harm will come to you!'

Quite properly, no-one answered. The battering on the gate resumed. Though moated, Morland Place was not built to withstand direct attack by such a force, and it would be only a matter of time before the outer gate was broken in, and the men would surge into the courtyard. Her hope was that help would come from Shawes or from their own tenants before that stage was reached. She went down the stairs again, and herded the servants into the chapel where Philippe Fenelon was already about his business. Lookouts were posted at upper windows on each side of the house; Nanette herself could not settle, but went back and forth between them, wondering whether she had done all she should, or if there was anything she had forgotten.

While Philippe kept everyone occupied with prayers, Nanette took the steward aside.

'I think the best thing is to stay here,' she said. 'They will hardly violate the chapel, and a few of us armed might keep the door. What do you think?'

The steward looked doubtful. 'Some of them look very vagabonds, Madam. I would not trust to the sanctity of the chapel.'

'What do you suggest then?'

'When they break though—we might keep the cellar. Or perhaps it would be better just to run.'

Nanette shook her head. 'Well for those who can—but the old and the children—what of them? And it would leave the house undefended.'

'We cannot defend the house in any case, Madam,' the steward said gently. 'Let the infirm get to the cellar, and the fit run for it.'

A rending crash from without told the end of the outer gate. Nanette said grimly, 'It is only a matter of time. Choose a few men to help you remove the old servants to the cellar. I will speak to Father Fenelon.'

But suddenly there was no time left. The attackers, with more organisation than the defenders, immediately discovered the whereabouts of the household, and with a shocking crash they stove in the chapel windows and moments later flung in burning rags and torches.

The servants leapt up shrieking and ran panicking to the door. Philippe sprang to beat out the flames that were already licking up from the altar cloth and running up the hangings, but Nanette called him back.

'No Philippe, it's too late. Look to your children!' she cried. The boys of the chapel choir who were his special charge were likely to get trampled underfoot if he did not take care of them. As he turned away towards them, a servant trying to battle his way in against the fleeing crowd caught Nanette's attention—he was one of the lookouts.

'There's another band of men coming towards the house from Shawes side,' he called to her over their heads.

'Shawes men?'

'Don't know—may be. But they look rough to me.'

It ended the possibility of flight, then. A second band, perhaps of beggars hearing a chance of easy spoil, coming up from the other side meant they were hemmed in.

'To the cellar, everyone,' she cried out. 'We can hold the cellar until help comes.'

But it was already too late. The steward, not knowing about the second band, had sent a man to fling open the north postern, and those servants who had not reached the cellar door found themselves caught between the two groups. The yard door was open, and the first attackers were pouring in. Shrieking like demented souls, the servants ran and scrambled towards the cellar, the steadier ones snatching up children as they ran. The steward and his chosen men tried bravely to hold the flanks, and after a moment the pressure on them eased for it was pillage the vagabonds were eager for rather than murder, and once in the house they scattered.

Nanette and Elizabeth and one or two others, however, were driven back to the chapel by the press of men. Elizabeth's eyes were wide with terror, and she clung speechless to Nanette's arm. The chapel was full of smoke, and Nanette seized Elizabeth round the waist and hurried her into it, hoping to escape in the smoke and get out through the vestry door through which Philippe had gone with the chapel children. Already there were vandals in the chapel—as with streaming eyes and smarting throat Nanette pulled her young charge forward, she could hear the sounds of destruction, and once heard a man's rough voice shouting 'Smash the Papist idols!' The smoke now was too thick to see anything, and Nanette did not know which way she was facing. Elizabeth tripped over something and fell, and was jerked out of Nanette's grip and Nanette at once lost her. Stumbling forward, she found the familiar shape of the altar, and, reorientated, she went down on to her hands and knees where the air was a little clearer to look for Elizabeth.

Behind the altar two young women servants crouched, so terrified that they neither moved nor spoke as Nanette reached them. She doubted if they even saw her. Then she heard Elizabeth screaming.

'Elizabeth! Where are you?' Nanette cried out desperately. The screaming went on, the full-blooded shrieking of a young woman in anguish. Nanette's hands closed on one of the great gold candlesticks from the altar, presumably swept off it by one of the raiders and lost in the darkness of the smoke. Clutching it awkwardly to her chest Nanette got to her feet again and staggered in the direction of the screaming. She could hear her own hoarse breathing labouring in her ears; she was dizzy and nauseated by the smoke. The screaming fell away in a sob and stopped, and then it seemed that the smoke was clearing. Instinctively Nanette followed the clearer air—perhaps towards the windows—and then abruptly she could see. Elizabeth was lying on the floor of the chapel, blood on her face, her gown ripped, and a man in ragged clothes was crouching over her in the act of getting up.

Nanette had no doubt as to what had happened. Laboriously, almost it seemed in slow motion, she dragged the candlestick up to lift it over her head, and in the same moment the man heard her and began to turn his head to look at her. For what seemed like aeons the two actions continued to a point of equilibrium where the candlestick was poised to descend, and the man's head was turned fully to look up at Nanette's face.

The beard was unfamiliar; the face, black with dirt and

smoke, was older, horribly older, lined and scarred with age and bitterness; but the eyes—she could never have mistaken the eyes. Dark pools, strangely familiar, but at their depths not the living warmth she had loved but an emptiness so desolate it was as if the doors of death had opened and the cold air of eternal darkness blew from them. For a long moment they looked at each other as all of time was suspended, and then as his arm began to move upwards to defend himself Nanette brought the candlestick smashing down on his skull.

It was not a matter of decision: the end of the movement was implicit in its beginning. The weight of the candlestick did the work, without effort from the woman who merely held it, and the man's skull was crushed like a blown egg. He fell backwards and sideways; but for an instant before he fell it seemed to Nanette that his expression changed, and that in the eyes that looked into hers there was understanding, and a strange relief, as if he had reached the end of a long and terrible journey.

Twenty-four

AMYAS AND HIS TWO SONS NEVER EVEN REACHED PONTEFRACT. They were waylaid on the road only a few miles from York and killed by the same band that afterwards marched to Morland Place and broke in. It was the work of one Robert Tanner, the local Justice of the Peace and an ardent reformist who, being charged with arresting Amyas had seen his chance to rid the world of a Papist and destroy a Roman temple. The chapel had been his target at Morland Place. Other damage and looting had been in the main carried out by the vagabonds and beggars who had joined in the attack on the house for that very purpose.

The news of the deaths was brought to Morland Place where Nanette and Arabella were struggling to restore some kind of order.

'The price of folly,' Nanette said bitterly. 'I wonder if even he would have thought it worth all this—' and she waved her hand around the great hall where they had gathered together all the survivors and were treating the wounded and giving orders for clearing up. 'Well, the bodies had better be brought back here. They can lie in the chapel—what's left of it—with the others.'

'They are already on their way, Mistress,' the messenger said. When he had gone, Nanette said to Arabella, 'Perhaps it is for the best. Had they been arrested and tried they would surely have been executed, and then more harm would have come to the family. Perhaps since they have been murdered without a trial no further action will be taken against us.'

Arabella looked at Nanette sadly.

'So hard, Nanette? Is there no grief in you for them?'

'Too much to speak of, cousin. My concern is for the living. We must send a message to young Paul in London to bring him home as soon as possible. A terrible homecoming for him—pray God there be no reprisals against him for his father's fault.'

With the Morland Place men back, and with the help of servants lent by Shawes, things were soon orderly enough for the damage to be assessed. The inside of the chapel was burnt out, half the roof gone, and the outer wall partly destroyed, and the gold and silver altar vessels had been stolen. Throughout the house windows had been broken—those glass windows for which Morland Place was famed throughout South Yorkshire—and the outer and inner doors had been smashed, and furniture and valuables had been destroyed or stolen. But the worst damage had been to the inmates: Mrs. Stokes and Ruth and Audrey had got the little girls safe away, and Philippe had managed to escape unscathed with his charges, but amongst the rest of them there were a number of injuries—burns, cuts, broken limbs and the like—of varying degrees of seriousness; and when the bodies were brought back from the ambush, there was a total of twelve dead.

When she had finished tending the wounded Nanette went to the ruined chapel where the bodies had been laid out on the floor. Vigil would be kept over them until the next day when they would be buried here at Morland Place, Fenelon Philippe presiding over a joint funeral mass. In grief and anger Nanette walked along the line, pausing by each one to make a prayer for the soul of the departed who had died for his master's pride and folly: young men cut down alongside him, old people who had served the Morlands all their lives, members of the household mortally wounded in its defence, a child trampled in the panic. Here were the two sons, Robert and Edward, fine young men just beginning manhood's adventure. Edward, downy-cheeked still, lay as if asleep, a long rent down his side from which life had escaped as grain will run out of a sack slit open; but Robert's eyes were open, he looked surprised as if death were not anything like his imaginings. He had taken a wound in the chest, and his hands were against it as if he had tried to stop the opening with his fingers.

Nanette pulled her skirt back and knelt beside him and tried to press his eyes closed but the lids felt springy against her fingers and would not roll shut. There was one more body in the row and as she knelt beside her nephew its dead arm was against her leg. She looked down. One side of the face was warped and bloodied from the blow that had killed him, but the other was strangely untouched, looking young and innocent in the relaxation of death. It was as if two people lay dead there, the villain, soul twisted into evil by unhappy events, and the man he might have been, his beauty stillborn.

What had brought him back here? Driven by the torment of love turned to hate, had he come back to finish the destruction he had begun? If she had not stopped him, how much more would he have destroyed?

'It was your fate,' Nanette said aloud. 'All of it. And mine, and his—all linked. We could not escape it. You to be his death, and I to be yours. Forgive me my part of it, as I forgive you yours.'

And then she thought of the young woman upstairs. Was the pattern then not yet worked out? What was her part in it? Nanette got to her feet and walked away towards the doorway. Strong wine and poppy had at last brought Elizabeth sleep, but until it released her she had wept and shrieked in Nanette's arms as if her reason were departing. Only time would shew whether sleep and quiet would heal her wounded mind, but what prayer would do, Nanette would try. She was weary to the bone, but rest was still a long way from her. She walked slowly up the stairs towards the bedchamber where her young cousin lay.

It was a sad homecoming for Paul. He had been studying law at the Inner Temple in London, for younger sons needed a career, and the law was not only a profession in which he could make his own independent fortune, but was a useful calling for one of the family to follow in those litigious days. He had not lived at Morland Place for six years and in that time he had seen very little of his family. He was resigned to spending his life in London and practising the law, when at the age of sixteen he found himself master of Morland Place and all the Morland estates and fortune. The messenger who brought him the news accompanied him home.

He was shocked at the desecration of the chapel, the damage and loss to the house, the numbers of the dead, and the pitiful condition of his cousin Elizabeth. He was master now, and it was for him to take over from his Aunt Anne, who clearly expected him to take responsibility, but it was a whole day before he could even begin to comprehend what had happened, and a week before he could give an order that had not been suggested to him by Nanette.

By that time the news of the abortive rebellion reached them—the other ringleaders had been rounded up and taken to London for trial. It was beyond doubt that they would be found guilty and executed, and it became something to be thankful for that Amyas and Robert and Edward had at least escaped that fate. Sir John Neville was kept back and executed in York as an example to the north, and for a long time the Morlands lived in trembling. But the King was not naturally revengeful, and Paul escaped with nothing more than a heavy cash fine for being the son and heir of a rebel.

There were other consequences, however. In May Margaret, Lady Salisbury, the grand-daughter of Richard of York, the niece of King Edward IV, was beheaded on Tower Green for the crime of being the mother of that Reynold Pole whom the rebels wanted to make king. The old lady—she was almost sixty-eight—was the last of the Plantagenets, and she died like one, fighting to the end. The shocking story ran quickly all over the country. On the scaffold she had declared that she had committed no crime and did not deserve to die, and she would not therefore submit herself to the axe. If they wanted her head, let them take it, she cried, and there followed a grisly spectacle in which she ran round and round the scaffold while the executioners pursued her, hacking at her with the axe until they had wounded her enough to bring her down so that they could strike off her grey head.

In May also was confirmed the suspicion already entertained that Elizabeth was pregnant. Her distress was terrible, and for a while Nanette and Mrs. Stokes were afraid that she would lose her reason, or take her own life. They watched her closely, never allowing her to be alone until the worst of the shock had passed, and at last she resigned herself to her fate. Nanette kept the secret of the attacker's identity to herself, for only she had seen him. In the confusion and terror of the moment, and the darkness of the smoke-filled chapel, Elizabeth herself had no clear idea of what he looked like; and though one or two of the servants had recognised the late master's son in that battered corpse, no-one had any reason to think it was he that had raped

Elizabeth. For all anyone knew, the attacker had run away with the rest, unharmed, and Nanette had no desire for it to be any other way.

In the summer the King made a progress north with his new wife, plump, pretty little Catherine Howard, Anne Boleyn's cousin, and for the first time in his reign he came as far north as the city of York. It was a magnificent progress, intended to impress the people with his power and richness, and it was intended that he should be met in York by the King of Scots, his sister Margaret's son. But the King of Scots had no desire to risk his person south of the border, and he did not come. Instead there was a ceremony held during which all the gentry and nobles who had had anything to do with the rebellion came forward to make tributes of money to the King and ask his pardon on their knees. Paul had to do it in his turn, and the tribute and the fine he had already paid put the family into some financial difficulties. Wool was commanding a high price at the moment, and there was an increasing demand for cloth, and so it would be no more than a matter of time before the family's fortune was restored; but it prevented, as indeed did prudence, the rebuilding of the chapel.

Father Fenelon stayed on as family tutor and confessor, though he no longer had a chapel of which to be chaplain, and the family had to go to the village church at St Nicholas for their daily masses; but the chapel-children had to be sent home. Nanette also reconsidered her future, and spoke to Paul about it one evening in the solar after supper.

'Long ago Lady Latimer offered me a home with her,' she said. 'She has asked me since, more than once, to live with her as her companion, and I think the time has come for me to accept her offer.'

Paul was taken aback. Since he had come home, his aunt had been his mainstay, and he relied very strongly on her advice.

'But Aunt, why?' he asked now. 'You don't really want to leave Morland Place, do you?'

'I have known much happiness here,' she said, 'and also much grief. But you have troubles enough now, Paul, and I am an expensive item in your accounts. It is better that I should remove myself and relieve you of the expense of my maintenance.'

'You mustn't think about that, really you mustn't,' Paul said, distressed. 'By rights you should be mistress here—I know that my father deprived you of your portion. You should not think of living on charity.'

'All the same, my dear, I will go. You will have a wife of your own one day—one day soon, if you are wise—and there cannot be two mistresses.'

'But—you won't go yet? Please, Aunt, don't think of leaving yet. We need you. My cousin needs you: you cannot think of leaving Elizabeth?'

'No, indeed. I will stay until Elizabeth is safely delivered, and I myself will arrange the disposal of the child, if it survives. It is better that I should do it. But then I will go. For Elizabeth's sake, if for no other, it is better for me to go. I would bring too many unhappy things to mind for her.'

Paul argued with her, but she was adamant, and she wrote the next day to Katherine Neville, who was at home at Snape Hall. The answer came, kind and glad to have her, and Nanette became eager to have the business done with and go away. She observed a growing affection between Paul and Elizabeth, and had hopes that when the unfortunate business was over, they might marry; if they did, she must not be there to remind them of the horrible thing that had made their union possible.

The baby was born at the beginning of February, and was a boy. The labour was straightforward, and Nanette had good hopes of a quick recovery for poor Elizabeth, who had borne the burden with increasing distress. Nanette was present in the birth chamber, and it was she who took away the baby even before Elizabeth had a chance to see it. It was better that way, everyone had agreed. She had made her arrangements beforehand, and so that no-one but herself should know where the bairn was taken, she rode herself, and alone, with the little creature inside her cloak, through the snow to the cottage of the peasant couple who would bring the child up.

Dick the smith and his wife Mary were waiting for them. Mary had had a babe of her own two weeks before, and would feed both infants at her breast. They were gentle, quiet people, living in the small, single-storey cottage attached to the smithy, with their small holding of land behind where Mary kept a cow and a pig and a few hens and grew vegetables and white roses. As Nanette dismounted before their door it was opened by a small, tow-headed, solemn child of two who stared at her in silent wonder. Dick appeared behind him and cried out, 'Come in, Mistress, come in and welcome; I guessed it was you, at this hour. You have brought the bairn? You should not have ridden alone—it isn't proper.'

'How else could I be sure the secret was kept?' Nanette asked. 'Here is the child—Mary will know what to do with him, I imagine.'

She ducked under the low lintel into the tiny cottage. It was dim with smoke, for it had no chimney, and the smoke from the raised hearth drifted upwards to find its way out through the thatch in its own time. What light there was came from rushes dipped in animal fat, and they gave out with their small light a great deal of stinking smoke. But the room—the single room in which they lived and slept, Dick and Mary and their two small sons—was scrupulously clean and neat, the pewter and wooden dishes scoured and stacked on the wooden cup-board, the hard-packed earth floor covered in clean dried rushes, which kept it warm and dry, their few clothes and belongings stored away in a stout chest which they now offered to Nanette as a seat.

She accepted it, and the offer of ale from Dick, for it would not have been polite to refuse, and while she drank she looked around and wondered at the difference in the way these people lived. Yet they were not in want. There were dried meats and smoked fish hung up on the walls, and bunches of herbs, and ropes of onions, three different sorts, and in the half-attic above one end of the room she knew there would be grain stored along with the turnips and carrots and beans, and perhaps a bucket of salt fish and another of pickled eggs. On a loom at the far end of the room a new piece of cloth was being woven, strong woollen cloth to keep out the weather, and the bed in which they all slept had woollen blankets, dyed bright colours in stripes, and hop-harlots for their heads.

It would be a good home for the child. The money she provided for its upkeep would provide them all with small luxuries to make their lives more pleasant. The child would not want, and would be brought up in a decent Christian household, and would be loved. She saw that already, as Mary crooned over the infant and offered it her breast.

'He's a bonny bairn, Mistress, and lusty and healthy too. He'll grow up a big, bonny man. There, there, hinny, don't you cry. That's right—Lord, see him suck! He's a knowing child, is this little lad.'

Dick and Nanette watched in silence for a while, and then Nanette gave Dick the purse of money which was the first of the payments for the child's upbringing.

'You must have him learn to read as soon as he is old enough,' Nanette instructed. 'And when he can read, buy him a missal. I will send you the money for that.'

'Yes, Mistress, I will see to it,' Dick said. 'And shall I have him baptised, Mistress, or has it been done?'

'No—that must be done, of course, and as soon as possible,' Nanette said. 'Can I leave you to see to it, Dick?'

'Aye, Mistress—but what shall his name be?'

Nanette was startled. 'I—I had not thought,' she said. Mary and Dick exchanged a smiling glance, and then Mary said, 'Here, Mistress, take him a while and look at him—maybe it will come to you.' She eased the baby from her breast where he was beginning to sleep and Nanette took him and laid him in the crook of her arm, and drew the blanket back from his face. She was sitting by the fire, and the flickering light chased across the face, wrinkled and sweet like a store-apple. She had not thought about him before this moment as a person, only as a problem, but now, feeling the slight weight of him, looking at his small clenched fists and red face, she realised that here a new life was beginning, a new world had been founded with this child at its centre.

He was no different from any other baby in essence: Nanette remembered the last infant she had held, the infant Princess Elizabeth, remembered how the nurse and the mother had thought her beautiful. He opened his eyes—eyes as unfocused as a new kitten's, but already dark, a very dark blue. Surely they would be brown like Adrian's—like Paul, Adrian's father—like Ursula, Adrian's mother, whom Paul had called Little Bear. A strange heritage, this child had, the Bear Cub. The eyes wandered loosely across Nanette's face, and suddenly love jerked at her belly like a gripe. She had never born a child, probably never would. If she and Paul had had a child, it would perhaps have looked like this, and she wanted to press it to her heart, feed it at her breast, hold it and keep it for ever.

'Have him baptised John, after my father,' she said. Dick and Mary nodded in approval.

'A good Catholic name, Mistress,' Dick said. 'John it shall be.'

'I had a little brother, too, called John, only we called him Jackie,' Nanette said. 'He died of the Sweat.'

Nanette gave the babe back to Mary and stood up. 'You must not go back alone,' Dick said. 'I will ride with you as far as the long track. I'll take care no-one sees me. And have no fear for the boy, Mistress. He'll be safe enough here. Mary and me are quiet folks, we see few people. No-one will know where he comes from.'

'Thank you,' Nanette said. 'God bless you both.'

'Will you come and see him again before you go?' Mary asked as Nanette reached the door. She shook her head.

'I shall leave in two or three days' time. I shall not come here again before that.' She took one last look at the baby which had so strongly moved her, but it was a mere blanket-bundle in Mary's arm now, and with a shrug she pulled her cloak round her and ducked out into the cold night.

'He has changed so, Nan,' Katherine said, putting down a finished shirt and taking up another from the pile between them. 'Last Christmas-tide the Court was so lively, he was so happy, almost like a young man again. His daughters were given new dresses, and when Lady Mary knelt to the little Howard Queen, she pulled her to her feet and kissed her, and said it should be the other way round, that *she* should kneel to Mary.'

'Perhaps she knew herself there,' Nanette said. Katherine looked at her with distress.

'Oh Nan, she was such a pretty little thing, she looked more like a child than a woman, although she was eighteen. But she had a merry, snub-nosed, childish face. She had no great wit, but she was the kindest-hearted little creature in the world. She gave away practically everything the King gave her. She made sure the princesses had new clothes and were invited to the

Palace parties. She was the greatest of friends with her predecessor, Princess Ana. Why, she even sent Lady Salisbury a suit of warm clothes when she was in the Tower awaiting execution, though her ladies warned her it might upset the King.'

'And did it?'

'No—he tried to explain that the Countess was an enemy of the State, and Catherine said that as far as she was concerned Lady Salisbury was a venerable old lady and ought not to be allowed to starve of cold for want of a few clothes. There was no arguing with her. He simply took her on his knee and cuddled her.'

'And this—little girl—he put to death?' Nanette said slowly.

'The Council discovered she had been unchaste before her marriage, and told him so, thinking he would put her away. But they had reckoned without his feelings for her. He was so infatuated that he forgave her and ordered them to forget it. So then they brought an accusation of adultery against her. The King was so grieved he wept and screamed. They say he called for a sword to go and kill her with his own hand. And when they arrested her, she was so frightened she escaped her guards and ran down the private stairs to the chapel, screaming for the King as a child will run screaming to its father.' She shuddered. 'We heard her in the chapel. We heard her screams for him as they dragged her away. The King just sat there, staring ahead, but the tears ran down his face as if they would never stop.'

'Katherine—do you believe the accusation?' Nanette said. 'The accusation of adultery?'

'I don't know,' Katherine began, and Nanette interrupted.

'Kate, you who know the Court, you know how impossible it is for anything to be done in secret. Consider, Queen Anne was accused of the same thing, falsely as we know—'

'Do we?'

'*I* know. Kate, I was her personal attendant. She had no secrets from me. *Two* queens, both committing adultery in a Court where privacy does not exist?'

'No,' Katherine sighed. 'It doesn't seem likely. I cannot believe that that child, however silly she was, would have done what they say she did. I think the Council brought up the charges for their own purposes. And the King killed her in a jealous rage, as surely as if he had taken a sword when he called for it and run her through.' She shook her head bitterly. 'She was condemned to death without a trial, and executed before her Act of Attainder was passed by Parliament. What manner of King have we, who could do such a thing? And he loved her, Nan, to distraction. I've never seen a man so infatuated with a woman. And Christmas this year was so different. No laughter, no merry-making. The King sits and broods like a great grey eagle. He looks old, and ill. His leg pains him terribly, and his temper grows short with the pain.'

'You talk about him as if he were an old man,' Nanette said.

'He is an old man.'

Nanette shook her head. 'A King is never that. I knew him when he was a young man, and he was not just a young man. A king is a king.'

Katherine smiled sourly. 'He knows that, Nan, as surely as you do. The Court calls him "Your Majesty" now, like the French King—on his orders.'

'*Your Majesty?* Your Grace was good enough for kings until now. Kate, I begin to think I do not want to visit this Court of yours.'

'Not "of mine". I go for the children's sake—and I know you will love them too. We need do no more than pay our respects to the King. And John wants me to go south when my lord of Norfolk invades Scotland. We are too close to Carlisle here. You will come, won't you, Nan?'

'Come? Of course I will come, foolish,' Nanette laughed. 'Only I do not promise to like it—it will bring back sad memories for me, I am sure.'

'Well, there are enough of them in life, dearest,' Katherine sighed. 'There's no escaping them, wherever we go. Now who is this?' she added as footsteps approached the door. A moment later her woman, Annie, came in.

'A chapman, Madam, from the town,' Annie announced, curtseying. 'He says he has something you may like to buy.'

'Not now, Annie,' Katherine said. 'It is very nearly time for mass, and then it will be dinner time, and you know his lordship will not be kept waiting for dinner.'

The woman nodded and turned away, but paused to add with a sly smile, 'I believe it was a pair of shoes he brought, my lady.' Katherine hesitated, and was lost.

'Very well, send him up,' she said weakly. 'But tell him to be quick. I will give him only until the chapel bell rings.'

Annie curtseyed and went out, and Katherine turned to Nanette, who was smiling with amusement. 'Another pair of shoes, Kate? How many does that make?'

'Now, Nan, don't censure me,' Katherine said defensively. 'We all have our little weaknesses. And I do love to be well-shod.'

'Yes, I know. You have pretty feet, and a great deal of money. Why should not the two be put together?'

'Another word, and I shall send the chapman away.'

'Oh, I would not put you to that pain, my love,' Nanette laughed, putting aside her work. 'I know you will have to do penance for your vanity later. Enjoy your shoes while you may. And if I had feet and legs as pretty as yours, I dare say I would buy them as many shoes and stockings as you do.'

It was great pleasure and great pain to be at Hampton Court again. Here above all ghosts walked: Nanette had been young here; here Anne Boleyn had had her triumphs; here Nanette had walked and talked and sung and laughed with her, and with her bright satellites—George Boleyn, Hal Norys, little Frank Weston, beloved Tom Wyatt. All were dead now—Thomas Wyatt, the last of them, had died only that summer, at home in Kent, a lonely and bitter man, who had loved all his life and received in return only pain.

Nanette was apprehensive, too, about meeting with the Lady Mary, who, she feared, would have no cause to love her. Katherine and Nanette met her in an anteroom, and at once curtseyed very deeply—while there was no Queen, Mary was the second lady of the land, immediately after the Princess Ana—and heard her deep, rather husky voice bidding them rise.

'How are you, my dear Lady Latimer?' Mary said with real affection, embracing her warmly. Nanette, standing a pace back, noted sadly the change in the King's daughter, brought about by years of bitterness and neglect. She had been such a pretty girl: now at twenty-six Mary looked older than her years. Her red-gold hair had faded to sandy, her face was lined with pain and her skin unhealthy, and she had got into the habit of screwing up her eyes, partly because she was short-sighted, and partly as a reaction to pain, for she suffered dreadfully with her teeth, and frequently had ear-ache too, and devastating headaches.

Yet for all that hers was not an unpleasant, nor a naturally bad-tempered face. Neglected and tormented, she had always retained a love of fun, of dancing and music, of flowers and pretty clothes, of jokes and innocent horseplay. It was well known that her fool was the highest paid member of her small household. And now, when she smiled at her friend—keeping her lips closed to hide her blackened and rotting teeth—her genuine pleasure lit her face, and restored to her plain features something of her former prettiness.

'Your Grace, may I present my dear friend and companion, Anne Morland?' Katherine was saying now. Mary peered at Nanette, the smile disappearing, and Nanette nervously went down in another curtsey.

'Rise, Mistress Morland, please rise. Yes, I remember you, of course, though it was some years ago that I last saw you. But you have hardly changed, though I believe you have been married?'

'Yes, Your Grace. I am a widow now,' Nanette said.

'Well, I am sorry for that. Yet you must have been glad to have been married at all. For myself, I have been promised to so many men, none of whom I have ever met, that I feel I must be the most oft-married maid in Christendom.'

'Your Grace—' Nanette began awkwardly, not knowing what to say. Mary smiled suddenly.

'I was but jesting. Peace, Mistress Morland. I am, if nothing else, just. One cannot be held accountable for one's master's faults—nor yet one's mistresses. You are welcome here.'

'Thank you, Your Grace,' Nanette said, gratefully. Mary turned again to her friend.

'And now, shall we go to the nursery? I have brought some presents for the children—'

'And I too,' Katherine said. 'Nanette and I have made some stockings for Lady Elizabeth and Lady Jane, and we have brought a toy soldier for the Prince.'

'I'm glad of that—he should have some merry-making as well as much study. He works hard, as he should, but sometimes I think his tutors are too strict with him. If it weren't for Elizabeth, there would be no laughter at all in the nursery— Jane is too timid even to smile unless the prince does first.'

The royal nursery was well-guarded, both against human invaders, and invading diseases, but with Lady Latimer and Lady

Mary, the King's daughter, there was no difficulty in passing the guards. Etiquette was firmly observed, and the three women approached the five-year-old boy as if he were a king, curtseying once at the door, once in the middle of the room, and once at his feet, where they must wait for him to bid them rise. The child observed them solemnly, for he was the most noble, the right glorious the Prince Edward, Prince of Wales and Duke of Cornwall, heir to the thrones of England and Ireland, but when the proprieties had been observed and he had bid them rise, his face broke into a great grin, and he cried, 'I am so glad to see you Aunt Mary, Aunt Kate. What have you brought me this time?'

'All in good time,' Mary said, returning his hug. 'First, let me present to you a friend—Mistress Anne Morland.'

Instantly the formal mask was resumed. Nanette found it oddly touching that this child could twitch formality on and off so easily. He was tall for his age, and stout and healthy, and the image of his mother, with the same pale, heavy face and thin mouse-fair hair. In repose his mouth was sullen, and Nanette thought that he would not have a tractable temper. Probably when he became King he would be heavier-handed than his father, and without his charm. Nanette curtseyed and was received without enthusiasm, but she was content to remain an observer. There was too much to disturb her here.

The other occupants of the nursery arrived a little while afterwards—the Lady Jane Grey, eldest grand-daughter of the King's sister Mary who had been Queen of France before she married my lord of Suffolk, had been born on the same day as the Prince, and was being brought up with him, sharing his lessons and his plays. She was slight and pretty, as pretty as her grand-dam had been, with the Tudor red-gold hair and dark blue eyes. She and the Prince were great friends, and it was already popularly supposed that they would marry when they reached adulthood.

The other person who entered with Jane Grey was a young woman of nine, dressed in a green gown which she wore with an air of mature feminine judgement. Nanette looked at her, and caught her breath. She had her father's long, flat Welsh nose and bright copper hair, parted neat and glossy and puffed at the sides in front of her low French hood, but the rest of her face was her mother's. She was not really pretty, but her face had a breath-taking quality that drew all eyes to it, an alien, magic charm. Her eyes were huge and dark, set on the tilt like those of a wild animal, a fawn perhaps, above high cheekbones; her mother's curious, subtle mouth, deep rather than full, curled with her mother's strange smile; the little chin and long slender neck and the haughty carriage of the head completed the likeness.

Nanette looked at Anne Boleyn's daughter, and felt her legs tremble. Presented to the Lady Elizabeth, Nanette curtseyed and was received with an automatic and insincere charm, but when she looked into the small proud face, Nanette saw that Elizabeth knew who she was. The great dark eyes were troubled; Nanette must say something to let her know that it was all right. Quietly, that they might not be overheard, Nanette said, 'Your Grace, I had the honour to be the first person to hold you, aside from the midwife, at your birth.'

'You have the advantage of me, Madam. I cannot remember the occasion.' The words were spoken coldly, but the eyes were warm. It was not possible, not permitted, ever to mention the former Queen Anne, and emphatically not in the presence of her daughter; but Elizabeth's heart was a shrine to her all the same, and Nanette had found a way to lay an offering at that shrine. They looked at each other with love and goodwill, and the tacit promise that one day it would be possible to talk. But not now—now the proprieties must be observed. The Prince of Wales was demanding attention, presents and games. That he might be born, Elizabeth's mother and five innocent men had been condemned to death; that Elizabeth might be born, Mary's mother had been cast out to a lonely and miserable end in a house in the marshes; but the two former princesses paid their attentions to the Prince without resentment. It was the way of things. They were all bound by the same rules, and if those rules often caused them pain, yet it was only those rules that held a chaotic world in check.

Twenty-five

ETIQUETTE DEMANDED THAT KATHERINE AND NANETTE PRESENT themselves to the King as soon as possible, and so they left the nurseries in time to be at the afternoon audience. They left Lady Mary at her own apartments, for when they asked her if she attended the audience too, she shook her head and said, 'I go to the King when I am sent for, which is not often. He likes to know where I am, but he does not like to see me. Where do you sup tonight?'

'At Richmond,' Katherine said, 'With the Princess Ana.'

'Then I shall not see you. Will you sup with me tomorrow? Margaret Douglas and Mary Richmond come to play at cards with me.'

'Gladly, Your Grace,' Katherine answered. Mary nodded kindly to Nanette.

'I hope to see you too, Mistress Morland,' she said.

'That was kind of her,' Nanette said when they had passed on. Katherine smiled.

'You will think it kinder, when she has lost her petticoat to you. Mary is a reckless gambler, and an unlucky. Last summer she lost her breakfast to Margaret Douglas three days running, playing at bowls. But come—we must not be late.'

The audience was attended by much more grandeur than Nanette had remembered from the past, when there had been a kind of elaborate informality surrounding the King. There was nothing of that now. The monarch who had himself styled 'Majesty' had nothing of informality about him any more. Nanette's palms were damp with apprehension as she advanced across the floor, eyes down, making her three curtseys. At the King's feet she remained down, and kept her eyes bent upon the toes of the broad velvet shoes. She remained down for some time, long enough to notice the unpleasant, sickly smell that hung about the thick roll of bandage that swaddled the royal leg under the yellow silk stockings, and for her wits to grow so addled that Katherine had to kick her covertly to get her to rise.

'Your Majesty, may I present—' Katherine had begun, but the King's voice interrupted her. It was the voice Nanette remembered, but rougher with age, and without the resonant boom it had had in his younger days.

'Yes, yes, I know who it is. Come, Mistress Nan Morland, did you think I would not know you?'

It seemed a question fraught with difficulties, and Nanette considered carefully before framing her answer.

'I had not looked for the honour of being remembered by the King, Your Gr—Your Majesty,' she said at last, remembering only just in time the new honorific. It seemed to be acceptable.

The King chuckled and said, 'Quite right, quite right, Mistress, but the King never forgets a face or a name. And he especially remembers modest, virtuous ladies. You are a friend of Lady Latimer's?'

'We were brought up together, Your Majesty,' Nanette said.

'Were you now? Come, yes, I remember Maud Parr had three little girls in her schoolroom, besides Kate here—you were one of them?'

'Yes, Your Majesty,' Nanette said, and did not attempt to conceal in her voice her wonder at the King's memory for detail. He really did know everyone, as it was said of him. He heard her admiration, and chuckled again.

'Ah, yes, Mistress Nan, we remember. You have been married, I believe, and widowed since we last saw you?'

'Yes, Your Majesty, to my uncle, Paul Morland,' Nanette said, and now at last she dared to lift her eyes and look at the King. It was a terrible shock. This grey-bearded old man with the cropped grey hair and the face lined with pain seemed at first nothing like the King she remembered.

He was huge, certainly, bigger than any mortal man had a right to be—bigger even than Paul, who had been tall and broad—but those great muscles, like the muscles of a war-horse, had turned to fat, for the athlete was tied by the leg to his chair, crippled by the wound he had got to his hip in that fall so long ago in the tiltyard. It had never healed, and had run into ulcers all down the leg. At best he could walk with the help of a stick or a shoulder. At worst he had to be pushed in a wheeled chair from place to place.

But still he was the King. It was not only his magnificent clothes, heavy with gold thread and jewels, brilliant with colour, rich with textures of velvet and satin; there was a magnificence about the man, too, even though he was trapped in a failing body. As she looked, Nanette saw his hands grip tighter at the arms of his chair as he endured a blade of savage pain; but worse was the helplessness he had to endure—he who had been the finest athlete in Christendom, the most tireless rider, the spriteliest dancer. Inside the mountainous, helpless body, the King was the same man he had always been, and he endured the terrible change in his circumstances with a grim and monumental stillness. It was not possible to pity a King: but if it had been, Nanette would have pitied Henry Tudor.

'You are welcome here at Court,' he was saying now. 'We value the example of virtuous matrons for our young people, and both for the sake of our friend Lady Latimer, and for your own sake, we shall be glad to see you here often.'

'Thank you, Your Majesty,' Nanette said, and curtseyed again, and moved aside, aware that there were a great many people waiting for the King's attention, and not wishing to lengthen unnecessarily what must already be a long session to endure.

Katherine and Nanette moved away to a quiet corner where they could converse, but they had hardly gained it when they were accosted by a tall, heavy-built man with a loud voice.

'Ah, Lady Latimer, there you are! I believe you have been visiting my nephew today? If I had known, I would have arranged my own visit for the same time, but I am going there now instead.'

With this hint Nanette recognised him: it was one of the younger brothers of the late Jane Seymour—Thomas, she fancied his name was. Yes, Thomas—there had been two of them, Thomas and Edward, around the Court that last Christmas, the Christmas of 1535. Edward was a thin, dark, small man, intelligent and pleasant-mannered enough. Thomas, the younger of the two, had been more boisterous, given to flirting with servants and drinking too much. Nanette had not liked him, and thought him not improved now.

He was handsome enough, certainly, and had filled out in the intervening years and had grown his beard, a thick, long, curling affair, slightly darker than his long chestnut hair. His skin was tanned from healthy exercise, his eyes bright blue, and he was dressed in black velvet with sapphires sewn everywhere to make the most of his colouring. But to Nanette there was something coarse about him. His voice was loud and grating, and she felt sure that he would swear a lot and probably pinch her bottom if she left it within range.

Katherine was greeting him, however, pleasantly and politely, and was now making the introduction between him and Nanette.

'Master Seymour, may I present you to Mistress Anne Morland, my close friend from childhood.'

'God's day to you, Mistress,' Seymour said, bowing low. He did not recognise her, Nanette saw, and she did not enlighten him, but as she made her curtsey he looked down her bosom, and as she straightened up his rather bulging eyes made an automatic and practised inventory of her body. He quickly returned his attentions to Katherine, however, and Nanette saw how it was, and wondered that Katherine could endure his near-insolent manner to her. But he smiled a great deal, showing his big white teeth, and pulled at his long silky beard, and laughed with a loud, outdoor, sportsman's laugh, and Nanette supposed it possible that Katherine found him attractive. He was certainly a complete contrast to Lord Latimer, or Lord Borough for that matter.

When he had gone and the two women were on their way to their apartments, Katherine asked Nanette how she liked Thomas Seymour.

'His voice is too loud for enclosed spaces,' she said cautiously.

'Yes—his natural place seems to be out of doors. He is a magnificent rider, and plays tennis better than anyone,' Katherine said. 'I think the King likes him for that—it reminds him of himself in his youth. The Prince adores him, of course. He is always talking of uncle Thomas—and it is always his purse the Prince dips into when he is short of money for his little toys.'

'The Prince is fortunate in so generous an uncle,' Nanette said ironically, but a glance at Katherine told her she had taken it literally. Nanette observed the heightened colour of Lady

Latimer's cheeks, and said no more; but she hoped they would not see too much of Thomas Seymour, or she feared her friend might be led into error.

The Duke of Norfolk, that aged warhorse, led the army into Scotland in October and on the twenty-third he beat the Scots army resoundingly just outside Carlisle. Three weeks later the Scottish King turned his face to the wall and died, it was said of despair, leaving as his sole heir a week-old baby girl who had been christened Mary. Now at last it seemed there might be an end of the time-long troubles between the English and the Scots, and the equally long-standing threat of the Scottish-French alliance. The infant Queen of Scotland was to be betrothed to Prince Edward, and they were to rule the two countries jointly after King Henry's death. Meanwhile the infant Queen was to be brought to England to be raised with the Prince in the royal nursery, and Henry was to be Regent in Scotland for his lifetime.

It was a magnificent plan, a perfect solution to the Scottish problem, and the English people, especially in the north, rejoiced. King Henry's grandchildren would be Kings of England, Scotland and Ireland; the border would no longer be stained with blood and scorched with fire; the French would no longer press against England's back door like wolves in famine-time. In Yorkshire, at Morland Place, Paul brought the news to his cousin Elizabeth as he had brought so many other small gifts, for he longed to please her. She was not within the house, but he had not far to search for her, for he knew her places by now.

She was sitting on the lowest part of the broken wall of the ruined chapel, looking outwards, her hands in her lap, her posture dejected. Her position was invidious, he knew—she had been betrothed, and her betrothed was dead; almost a wife, and not quite a widow; she had born a child, but was not a mother. Her sister Ruth had returned home to Dorset, and as a matter of honour Paul had found money enough to supply her portion just as if she had married his brother, and now she was married to a young man from her own country. Paul had offered the same kind of settlement to Elizabeth, though praying inwardly that she would not accept it. She had refused, and had not even seemed to care when her sister went home, leaving her alone at Morland Place.

The fines he had had to pay, together with the settlement on Ruth, had left Paul with too little money to do anything about rebuilding the chapel. The roof and the interior had been gutted by fire, all the windows smashed, the valuables stolen, and part of the outer wall destroyed, along with all the memorials which had been on that wall. Amongst them was the plaque to the memory of Robert and Eleanor, the common ancestors of Paul and Elizabeth, which Paul had vowed to replace as soon as he could get the money together to repair the chapel. The lovely old wooden statue of the Holy Virgin had survived, though it was damaged at the bottom and all the paint had been burned off, and he had sworn to Her that he would have Her repainted with plenty of gold leaf the very first thing. He had a particular reason for wanting to please the Queen of Heaven, she who had been a mother but no wife. He wanted Her help in winning Elizabeth.

Elizabeth often came to the ruined chapel, drawn to it by a mixture of horror, and delight in its tranquility. Already here and there grasses had sewn themselves in the cracks between the paving stones, and creeping green things, mosses and lichens, softened the harshness of the burned roof-beans and the fallen stones of the wall. It soothed her to see that the buoyant force of life could so soon overcome the sterility of death. She had loved the beauty of the chapel before, but now it seemed more personal to her.

She accepted Paul's presence without comment, and accepted his gift of news as vaguely as she received all his presents. She scarcely noticed him. She lived in a kind of dream on which he scarcely impinged, a dream of The Man who blocked out the light with his height and size. He was a figure of terror, and yet strangely compelling. He fascinated her. She had no real memory of the actual flesh-and-blood person—her mind had wiped it out with shock—and so she had created for herself a fantasy figure on whom she had dwelt for so long that she felt more at ease with him, in spite of his frightfulness, than she did with real men.

Of the child she never thought at all. It was like a strange illness she had been through, a fever from which she had recovered. She had never seen the child, and so it was nothing to her. Through the long days of her pregnancy, Nanette had been her mainstay and comfort, and yet she was not sorry when Nanette went away. There was something terrible about Nanette, a grimness, a strength of purpose. She had loved Nanette, but never wanted to see her again.

She did not know what would become of her; that was the main cause of her listlessness. She was afraid of the future, afraid of what she might have to face up to, afraid that she would be forced to marry, afraid that she would never be able to marry at all; so she took refuge in vagueness, clinging to the illness which protected her from any need to acknowledge the future.

Most of all she was afraid of Paul. He was the one from whom she had most to fear, for he was the master of Morland Place, and he might turn her away whenever he had a mind, send her home, or merely put her out of doors like an unwanted kitten. She tried to escape from him, but he would not leave her alone, and so she retreated further from him into the vagueness, accepting his offerings and putting them aside without looking at them. If she looked at them, if she admitted him, she was lost; but it was becoming harder and harder to remain in her dream. Life, that same force of life that relentlessly covered over the fire-scars, healed her too, and filled her with restlessness and a longing to be doing, seeing, feeling again. Desperately she turned her head away from Paul and fixed her eyes on the pale November sky.

For a while Paul stood near her in silence, respecting her absent mood and longing more than ever for her attention. She was so beautiful with her pale skin and long dark hair, and her eyes that were a darker blue than the sky ever was, the dark, intense blue of gentian flowers. He remembered when she had first come to Morland Place, and he had spent his time putting her and her sister at their ease. There had been in her a delightful yielding, a growing dependence on him which he remembered now with longing. He wanted to please her, to have her smile at him and look for him to come when he was absent, to depend on him for her pleasure and be never completely happy when he was away.

Paul had been brought up in a strict household, and had learnt to take great pains with anything he undertook, and to be patient of the vagaries of his elders and betters. He had broken his own colt, too, when he was first old enough to own one, and a fiery, wilful creature it had been. Patiently, gently, he had dealt with its rages and its refusal to understand what was required of it, pursuing it with love relentlessly until at last it had turned to him and put its muzzle into his hands, giving in to him completely, worn down by his persistence. He had sensed all the stages of the colt's gradual yielding from the first moment he had seen its ear and eye flick back to him as it trotted defiantly away from his hand. And now as he stood near Elizabeth, looking at her resolutely averted profile, he saw her glance at him once, quickly, from the corner of her eye.

'I have to ride over to Twelvetrees on some business,' Paul said after a while. 'Would you like to come with me?' She did not answer, but she listened.

'I kennel the big hounds there, as you know,' he went on, feeling his way carefully. 'One of the bitches had a litter yesterday. She's a brindled wolfhound, but the sire was the biggest of the mastiffs—Herakles, we call him. I think the pups will be very valuable. It's an interesting cross, don't you think?'

She had always been interested in dogs. Almost she spoke. He went on as if he had not noticed.

'They'll be big, anyway, that's for sure. Perhaps the biggest dogs in Yorkshire. That will be something to see when they grow up. I shall sell them, but I'll pick the best of the litter to keep. Of course, it takes a good eye to know which one will be the best.'

Elizabeth turned her head and looked at him. Carefully, non-committally he said, 'Come with me and help me choose. The weather is mild—it will be a good ride. Come. Come then.'

Gently he coaxed her to her feet and through the chapel into the house. All the time he was afraid she would bolt, like a wild animal drawn too near the houses of men, but she followed him, slowly and unwillingly. She was sixteen, and at sixteen it is not easy to shut out life.

The winter weather ended the Scottish campaign at the end of November, and John Neville came south to London to join his wife at their house in Charterhouse for Christmas. Katherine greeted him with placid affection, as always, and Nanette was very glad to see him, for she had felt her friend to be in some danger from the attentions of Thomas Seymour, whom they met almost every day either in the royal nursery or 'by accident' in and around the Court. Her relief was short-lived, however. Lord Latimer went to bed early on the night of his arrival, complaining that he felt tired from the journey, and in the morning he could not be woken. He had died quietly in his sleep.

Katherine mourned him sincerely, though more as a father than a husband. He was her cousin, known to her from childhood, and had always been kind to her, and she had loved and esteemed him as a good man and a benevolent relative. Her conduct was seemly, sober and restrained, and she ordered her mourning-clothes with a sad face; but it would have been too much for anyone to expect her to be grief stricken, or to weep and tear her hair, or to pay less attention than usual to the cut and style and quality of her gowns just because they were black.

She was thirty years old, and now twice a widow, but in many ways she was much younger than her years, for she had been wed only to elderly men, and had never born a child, so there was an innocence about her that made her seem almost like a girl. She was also very, very rich. She had not only the inheritance left her by her own family, but the considerable estates left her by her first husband, and now the greater fortune left her by John Neville. Lord Latimer was buried in St Paul's, and they spent Christmas very quietly, seeing no-one, but as soon as the new year of 1543 was in, Thomas Seymour lost no time in paying Katherine a visit.

This time Nanette did not hide her disapproval.

'It isn't seemly, Kate,' she said sternly. 'Your husband scarcely buried—his Will not even proved yet—and you are accepting the attentions of that man.'

Katherine laughed. 'Oh Nan, how disapproving you sound when you say *that man* and purse your mouth like that!'

'I am disapproving. He has a bad reputation.'

'Reputation for what?'

'You know what I mean.'

'Yes, I know, and I am surprised that you listen to malicious gossip. Men say those things about him because they are jealous,, because he is handsomer and bolder and more charming than any of them, and beats them all at tennis.'

'Dearest Kate, it is only you I am worried about. I am afraid you are in love with him.'

'I am, but it is nothing to be afraid of,' Kate said happily. 'I know it is soon after John's death, but I can't help it. Nan, you have been in love—you know how impossible it is to deny your feelings. Oh, I shall be sober and sad in public, but to you, surely to you I do not need to dissemble? I love him, Nan. I am in love for the first time in my life, and it is wonderful.'

Nanette stared at her in dismay. 'Oh Kate, do be careful. Be careful of him.'

'Nan, he means me no harm, believe it.' Katherine took her friend's hands and gazed at her earnestly. 'His attentions to me are all honourable. He wants to marry me as soon as a decent period of mourning has passed. So you see, there is nothing to fear.'

Nanette shrugged, and then, unwilling to hurt her friend's feelings, smiled and kissed her.

'Well, I wish you happiness of it, Kate. If he really loves you as much as you deserve, you will be happy indeed.' Not for anything now would she speak of the unpleasant rumours that surrounded Seymour, that he had been paying court to the Lady Elizabeth in the hopes of marrying her when the King died, and had been warned off by the King himself. If the rumours were true, then it must be Katherine's money and position that attracted Seymour, and not the overwhelming love she thought it was. But where Seymour was concerned, Katherine seemed to be blind, and Nanette could only hope that it would turn out for the best. Certainly he behaved in a very loving way towards her, but Nanette had seen the looks he cast on other women too. It seemed to her that for Thomas Seymour flirting with women came as naturally and automatically as breathing.

Twenty-six

*S*PRING CAME, LORD LATIMER'S WILL WAS PROVED, AND Katherine's three-month retirement came to an end. The Court was again at Hampton, and when Katherine and Nanette had paid their first visit there to see the royal children, a warrant came granting Lady Latimer lodging at Court for herself and her friend Mistress Morland and a suitable number of servants.

'How kind,' Katherine said, flushing with pleasure. 'Someone has spoken up for me to the King. Lodged at Court, I can see the children and Mary more often.'

Nanette smiled. 'Of course, it is the desire to be near the children that brings that colour to your cheeks, is it not, Kate?'

Katherine turned her innocent face to Nanette. She had very fine, arched eyebrows, which gave her a perpetually surprised and wondering look, and she could make very good use of what nature had given her. 'But of course,' she said. 'What other motive could I have?'

'I suppose there is nothing more for you to wait for, is there?' Nanette went on. 'When shall you be wed, you and your sailor Tom?'

'In June, I suppose,' Katherine said. 'It would hardly be decent to marry earlier than six months from my widowhood, though Tom is more than willing to flout the conventions.' Nanette frowned at that. A man who did not care for conventions might well be equally careless over moral and religious matters.

'At any rate, we shall move back to Court, shall we?' Nanette asked.

'Of course—one does not ignore the invitation of a King—it has all the force of a command,' Katherine smiled.

'And then, in due course, I must look for another home,' Nanette said lightly. Katherine's smile dropped.

'But why, Nan? You cannot suppose that I would not want you to stay with me after my marriage?'

'I don't think you would ask me to leave, but you will be too preoccupied with your charming new husband to want me there, always in the way. You'd be stumbling over me in every alcove. No, Kate, it wouldn't do. When you marry your Tom, I shall take myself off somewhere, very quietly, and you will not even notice I'm gone.'

Katherine's eyes filled with tears. 'You don't like him, do you?' she said.

'It is nothing to the purpose whether I like him or not,' Nanette said.

'But you don't, do you?' she persisted. Nanette looked at her in affectionate exasperation. There was no possible way she could make this infatuated young widow see how impossible it would be for the three of them to share a home. Even apart from her own disapproval of Seymour's character, how long would it be before he flirted with Nanette openly enough for Katherine to notice it? Already his bulging eyes stripped her naked every time she came into the room. But she could not tell Katherine that.

'No,' she said at last. 'I don't like him, and he doesn't like me. I'm sorry Kate, but there's nothing I can do about it.'

'I see,' Katherine said stiffly. For a moment she was angry, and Nanette thought she was going to ask her to leave at once, but her better sense prevailed. 'Well, there is no help for it, I see,' she said at last. 'Come kiss me, Nan. We have been friends for a long time, and this shall not part us. Though we cannot share a home when I am Lady Seymour, we shall still see each other, shall we not? If you wish it?'

'With all my heart,' Nanette said.

It was strange to be living at Hampton again. So much had changed, and so much was the same. Young Surrey was the Court poet now, and his verses were styled very much after the fashion of Wyatt, who was his god; but Surrey was no Wyatt either in his person or in his skills. Bold, bad Tom Seymour hung on the King's shoulder much as Suffolk had once done, and like Suffolk was a big, burly, loud-voiced man. Suffolk was mortally ill now and could not leave his country house; and Tom Seymour was no Suffolk. Suffolk had been the King's childhood companion, was a simple, bluff, good-hearted man, but Seymour was a selfish, ambitious schemer.

Norfolk was still there, Norfolk the indestructible, balancing the disadvantage of being Catherine Howard's uncle with the advantage of being the only able soldier in the realm, but the rest of the ministers seemed a poor bunch to Nanette, chattering, unstable climbers without an ounce of ability between them, like a cage full of political monkeys. They had achieved Cromwell's death between them, but not all of them together could replace him. The King, Nanette felt, must notice the difference as much as she did, for while relying on the permanent Household staff to keep things running smoothly, he played off one set in the Council against the other, favouring first one, then the other. In the same way he kept religious impartiality, executing Papists and Protestants alike. Papists he had beheaded for treason, while Protestants he had burned for heresy.

But it must be lonely for him, she reflected, watching him one day leaving the presence chamber on the shoulder of one of his pages. Of all his old friends, only two were left—Thomas Cranmer, still the primate, whose life he had saved from the Council by simply refusing to let them have it; and his fool, Will Somers. Will had been banished from the Court in the days of Queen Anne because of his implacable hatred of her, but after her death he had crept back to his master's feet, and now was hardly ever apart from him. Those two men alone remained to him to love him. The rest of the Court feared him, flattered him, fawned on him, begged favours from him.

Once or twice Nanette caught his eye, and once when he passed her in a corridor she thought he was going to stop and speak to her, but he only nodded and passed on. Yet she must remind him, perhaps painfully, of the old days. She had gone back to Cranmer as her confessor, and he had welcomed her with tears in his eyes, and had spoken guardedly of things past and of old friendships. If it was so for Cranmer, how much more so must it be for the King. Since he had sent Anne to her death, no-one had ever called him by his Christian name, and now he was too high for anyone ever to do so again.

But though Nanette recognised that the King must be lonely, it did not occur to her that he would seek a remedy. He often met Katherine in the nurseries, often had her to sit beside him after dinner and talk to him, but there was nothing strange in that, for he had known her all her life, she was the daughter of an old friend and the friend of his daughter. June had begun, and Katherine was increasingly absorbed in the contemplation of her forthcoming marriage to Tom Seymour, and Nanette increasingly sought the cool peace of the yew-walk in which to puzzle out what she should do when the marriage took place.

Then one day when Nanette was returning to the apartment she shared with Katherine from the gardens she met the King coming away from it.

Nanette sank to the ground in confusion, and the King paused a moment and looked down at her. He seemed very agitated, and leaned so heavily on the shoulder of his boy that the child's knees buckled visibly.

'Mistress Morland,' he said, and paused, evidently having something to say.

'Your Majesty?' Nanette said, looking at his feet, for she had not been bidden to rise. Other feet were behind him, the feet of the various attendants without whom the King could never stir from his bedchamber.

'Mistress Morland, yes,' the King said again, seeming confused, and then, 'Yes, Nan, you will be pleased for us, I know.'

'Your Majesty?'

'Go to her—yes, yes, rise woman, rise—and go to her, Nan. She will need you, I doubt not.'

And with that he moved on, limping more swiftly than usual, as if much agitated. Nanette stared after him in astonishment. He had spoken more kindly to her than ever before. The last pair of feet to pass her stopped, and glancing up Nanette saw Thomas Seymour, who paused only for long enough to give her an agonised, pleading look, before hurrying after his master. Nanette rose to her feet and ran the last few yards to the door of their chambers, her heart in her mouth.

Inside, Katherine stood by the window, looking out onto the courtyard. She turned as Nanette came in, and her face was white and shocked, and her eyes wide and tragic.

'Kate, what is it?' Nanette cried. 'The King has been here? What is it? Not—something about Thomas?'

Katherine tried to speak and could not. She began to tremble, and Nanette hurried to her side and helped her to a seat, and then knelt beside her and chafed her hands. 'Kate, what's happened? Tell me? What's wrong?'

Katherine licked her dry lips. 'The King—' she began.

'Yes, yes,' Nanette prompted her.

'He asked me to marry him,' Katherine said.

'What?' Nanette was horrified.

'It's true!' Katherine cried, and then she burst into a storm of weeping. Nanette knelt up and put her arms round her friend, drawing her head onto her shoulder to let her weep in comfort. Poor soul, she thought, poor soul. 'God help us,' she murmured aloud, and Katherine wept the more violently.

The storm of weeping had subsided. The two women sat together in the growing dusk and talked quietly. Katherine's eyes were swollen and red with weeping, but she was calm now.

'What did you say?' Nanette asked.

'What could I say? I said I was unworthy—I pointed out my age and the fact that I had been twice widowed. But I could not refuse, nor even appear unwilling beyond that.'

'People say that now the law has been passed that no unchaste woman may accept the King's hand, his choice will have to fall on a widow,' Nanette said. Katherine shuddered.

'Don't jest, Nan. Oh God, that I had gone back to Yorkshire when John died! But I could not go away from Thomas. Oh Nan, why didn't we get married at once!'

'And have people shake their heads at you for slighting your husband's memory?'

'What would that matter? If we had married, the King could not have thought of me. Nan, I am afraid for Thomas. He is so rash, I am afraid he will say something about our love— challenge the King for me perhaps.'

Nanette hardly knew what to say. She thought of Seymour's face as he passed her—well, no doubt he did love Katherine, but he was not a man to put his head on the block.

'Seymour can take care of himself, Katherine.'

Katherine put her hands over her face. 'It's like a nightmare. What will become of me?'

'You will become Queen, Kate, that's what will become of you,' Nanette said, trying to hearten her.

'Aye, he will make me Queen, and his ministers will make me a corpse,' she said bitterly.

'You will give them no cause.'

'When have they needed cause?'

'Katherine, be brave. There is no help for it, and so you must make the best of it. Think of the good you can do, and the people you can help.'

At that moment the door of the chamber opened and Audrey came in, her eyes almost out of her head with curiosity.

'Yes, Audrey, what is it?' Nanette asked sharply.

'Oh—I—I thought you sent for me, Madam.'

'I did not. You may go.'

Audrey writhed. 'Madam—they say—it's all over the Palace—such stories—'

Nanette took pity on her.

'Yes, Audrey, it's true, if that's what you came to find out.'

'Lord!' Audrey breathed, gaping.

'Now leave us.'

When they were alone, Katherine suddenly began laughing.

'What is it?' Nanette asked. Katherine stroked her friend's hand.

'I was just thinking, Nan—what you said about the King marrying a widow.'

'Yes?'

'It might just as easily have been you.'

Nanette thought of that over the next few days. If her father had been a knight instead of merely a gentleman, perhaps it would have been, and how would she have liked that? To be Queen? Well, an honour, of course, and a sign that one was chosen by God. To be anointed—crowned—as Anne was—but such a high and perilous position to climb to, and such a long fall down.

Katherine after that first night resigned herself to her fate, and soon grew more cheerful, eased as she was by the news that Thomas Seymour had been sent abroad for a long turn of duty in Flanders. No doubt the King knew that Seymour had wanted to marry Katherine, and had put him out of harm's way. A tiny scrap of a note, prudently unsigned, worked its way back to Katherine via a trusted servant.

'It will not be for ever,' the note said. 'I will wait for you—my heart is yours as I believe yours is mine.'

Katherine was joyful, Nanette shocked.

'It is treasonable,' she said. 'You must burn it at once. If anyone came to hear of this—'

'Peace, Nan. It is not signed nor addressed. It could have been from anyone to anyone. But I will burn it—you are right. I must be above reproach from now on. I am to be Queen of England.'

'Has the King decided on a date?'

'The twelfth of July. He says there is nothing for us to wait for. Nan, he calls me his second wife. On the address to Parliament, it refers to me as his second wife. He acknowledges only Jane Seymour before me.'

'Well, all the others he had annulled. Did you expect him to forget that?'

'No, but it seems so—strange—' She thought for a moment. 'I am not to be crowned, you know. I am to be his wife, and

Queen by courtesy, but not crowned. He has not crowned a wife since Anne Boleyn.'

Nanette nodded. It raised echoes in her mind of what she had thought before, that now he was so high, no-one could reach the same plane as him. Katherine would never call him Henry, and she would never be crowned. The King was very different from the King she had known.

'But one thing I am glad of—I will be able to do something for Mary and Elizabeth. I shall enjoy being their mother—and mother to the Prince. It seems to be my lot in life, to be mother to other women's children. I shall try and persuade the King to reinstate his daughters.'

'Have a care, Kate.'

'I will, dearest. At the very least, I shall see to it that they have more money, and some new clothes, even if they have to come out of my own income. We shall—' She stopped abruptly, and looked at Nanette.

'What's the matter?'

'I have just remembered—you said that you would seek another home when I married.'

'When you married Seymour.'

'Nan, you won't leave me, will you? Please say you'll stay. I shall need you more than ever now.'

'Of course I will stay, Kate, if you want me to.'

'I do want you to. Promise me you won't leave me.'

'I promise,' Nanette said, and she had to turn her head away to hide the tears, for she could not help remembering the other Queen to whom she had made that promise. She had promised Anne that she would stay until she no longer needed her, and that promise had been redeemed only by Anne's death. Please God it would not be so with Katherine! Perhaps the King, being old and unwell, would be contented with this wife—and yet, the Queen would have enemies, whoever she was. Ministers had removed Catherine Howard as easily as they had removed Cromwell, and the King had loved both of them. Yet he had saved Cranmer. All was confusion in Nanette's mind, of hope and fear, but again and again she found herself remembering Anne's question—'What choice did I have?' Like Anne, Katherine had no choice. There was never anywhere she could have turned aside from the path.

The wedding was held on the twelfth of July in the Queen's closet at Hampton Court and was attended by a large number of ladies and gentlemen. Gardiner performed the ceremony, and the Lady Mary and Lady Elizabeth were both present in new gowns of crimson damask over white cloth-of-gold. Their presence was a compliment to the new Queen, for they had not been present at any of the other weddings, as was the presence of the King's niece the Lady Margaret Douglas. This consideration comforted Katherine almost as much as the presence of her friends—Katherine Willoughby, now Duchess of Suffolk, who was a friend both of Katherine's and the Lady Mary's; her stepdaughter Margaret Neville; her sister Anne Herbert; and Nanette.

Nanette observed Katherine closely. She looked pale, but that was to be expected, given the solemnity of the occasion. Otherwise she looked well. The gown of cloth-of-gold suited her colouring, and the low French hood, trimmed with rubies, became her more than a widow's hood. She looked much younger than her years and very conscious of the honour that was being paid her. It seemed that now she had made up her mind to accept her fate, she was able to do justice to her position.

And the King? Nanette turned her eyes on him, but could glean very little. He was, after all, the King, and no-one ever knew what he was thinking. He too was dressed in gold, gold cloth and white satin, glittering with rubies and diamonds, and his massive figure dominated the room like a more than human presence. He was smiling, and he looked well, as a man should who was marrying for love—and that was one thing Katherine could contemplate with satisfaction, that the King could not have chosen her for any other reason than love.

The ring was placed on the Queen's finger, the mass taken, and the ceremony was closed. The King turned to his attendants to claim their congratulations, and the Queen to her ladies to kiss and hug them. There were gifts to be given, too. Nanette saw Katherine give lady Mary two gold bracelets and a purse of money; she herself received a pearl cross for her bodice; and then the Queen must receive the congratulations of the King's attendants—Anthony Denny and Anthony Browne and the rest—while the King came to kiss and chaff the ladies. Nanette made her curtsey to him, and found herself to her surprise raised to her feet by the King's very hand.

'Well, Mistress Nan, you are pleased I hope?' he said.

'I wish you every blessing, Your Majesty, and pray you find great happiness in each other,' she said nervously, for he still had hold of her hand. She looked up into his face as he towered over her, and suddenly forgot the occasion and the other people around them; he was smiling at her, a smile of extraordinary charm and newly-minted for her alone and more precious than gold. She had forgotten his power to charm, but now it came to her again.

'She is lovely, is she not?' he asked softly. Nanette assented warmly. 'I know how to appreciate her, Nan. I have known her since she was a girl. She is a fine, virtuous woman. And you, Nan—you are a good friend to her, I know. You are faithful to those you love, are you not, Nan? Believe me, I know how to value that, too. God bless you, Nan Morland.'

She curtseyed again as he left her and moved on to the next woman. She was shaken. Foolish of her to have forgotten how he could charm. Suddenly she remembered Calais, the smell of rain and fresh air clinging to him as the beads of mist clung to the fur of his coat, and the torment of love in his face. He remembered it too, she knew. He had said, 'You are faithful to those you love'. He remembered Anne. He was telling her that he, too, was faithful, but the King's way was not Nan Morland's way. Trust him and love him, for he is the King.

Afterwards the royal couple went separately to their own rooms to rest for a few minutes before the feast, the King attended by his gentlemen and the Queen by her ladies. In the Queen's anteroom, Katherine turned to her friends, and, mindful of etiquette, all curtseyed and stayed down.

'No, no,' Katherine cried, tears on her cheeks, 'none of that between us, my dearest friends. In private, we are still as we were. Margaret—Anne—Kate—Nan—come kiss me and wish me joy.'

'We do, Your Majesty,' lady Suffolk said, coming forward to embrace her. Katherine stared for a moment, and then understood. The Queen must be the Queen—it was not for her to choose. They could not call her Kate any more—only the King could do that. Nanette saw her draw herself up a little as, inwardly, she had to draw herself away. When she in turn came to embrace the Queen, she held her a moment longer than was etiquette, pressed her cheek against Katherine's very hard for a moment. It was her way of saying goodbye. The Queen's distance from the world is governed by the King's. Nanette could never be as close to Queen Katherine as she had been to Queen Anne.

※

The spring of 1544 was an exceptionally fine one, the good weather beginning in April and building up to that brilliantly clear heat that is special to the north country. Every day broke fresh and dewy and cool under skies of cloudless milky blue. As the day advanced the sky would deepen to cornflower and the larks, madly carrolling, flew higher and higher until they were the merest black flecks in the zenith. The green stain of spring crept rapidly up the hillsides, and the spring-flowering heather bloomed a dusky rose-purple. Over the high ground, broken here and there by the vivid sparks of gorse and broom in flower, the bracken spread its new and tender growth, and the sheep browsed contentedly in it like white birds in a green sea, growing their long rich fleeces over their skinny bodies to maintain the Morland fortune.

Shearing time came early too, because of the weather, and Elizabeth, already feeling the surge of spring in her blood, could not help becoming involved in the preparations for shearing. The sheep-shearing was always a great festival, and was joined in with gusto by everyone from the highest to the lowest. Life was hard and work was harder, but the feasts and games and holidays, the laughing and drinking and dancing and loving, were as much a part of ordinary life as pain, discomfort, want and death; and while trouble was to be endured without complaint, pleasure was to be enjoyed to the full with as much noise and fuss as possible.

Jane and Arabella came to Morland Place in the absence of a mistress to make preparations, and for weeks before the chosen date they were making lists of food, examining the store-rooms, opening boxes and bins, inspecting stores, pursing their lips over quantities, and ordering more of everything, 'just in case of need'. Great quantities of good things had to be ordered and fetched from the city, and the cook and his boys were working themselves up into a frenzy days before they needed to.

Bullock-carts trundled into York, and returned laden like treasure-ships with sugar of three qualities, currants and raisins, sacks of sweet wrinkled prunes and dates and apricots, nutmegs, ginger, mace, and cinnamon, saffron from East Anglia brought round the coast by ship, a barrel of treacle and oranges and lemons and figs from farther afield, pipes of wine and kegs of ale to augment the ale, cider and perry brewed at home at Morland Place.

All the folk from the surrounding villages would be coming in, as well as all the Morland people, for shearing was done communally, as were so many of the big jobs in sheep country, and when the shearing was done, the feasting would begin. On the chosen day the activity started before dawn. The men and boys went out with their dogs and little hairy ponies to bring in the sheep, the women and the cooks began the preparations for the feast, and the young girls went out to gather green boughs for decoration, and flowers to make garlands. Elizabeth joined with her young cousins Faith, Hope and Charity in making the twenty-four garlands for the shearers, who were the kings of the feast, and Eleanor, who had come with James for the day, was made an honorary maiden for the occasion, and given the task of making the crown for the ram.

'Keep her with you,' Jane whispered to Elizabeth, 'and let her be busy. She is no use to me and gets under the cooks' feet.'

Elizabeth, who had not seen Eleanor since Christmas, thought she was looking paler and thinner than usual. She had never been a robust young woman, and now she seemed troubled by a cough. She passed it off as dust in the throat, but Elizabeth noticed the red flush on her cheeks when the coughing fit had passed, and wondered, crossing herself discreetly. Eleanor had been married five years now, and there was no sign of a child, not even a pregnancy. It made Elizabeth feel almost embarrassed by her own rude health, and she did her best to be kind to Eleanor, and praised the wreath she so laboriously made. It was hard work, however, for Eleanor never showed any signs of pleasure, any more than displeasure. She was pale and quiet and shy, and that was all.

Then it was time to meet the flock at the washing-place, a part of the river which ran close to Twelvetrees, where there was a stretch that ran suddenly deep with a gravelly bed. One bank was steep, a short sudden drop into the river; the other bank sloped gently in a little curving gravel beach. Here Elizabeth and the other girls found everyone waiting, and amongst them her cousin Paul, the Master, ready to direct operations when the sheep arrived.

Paul greeted his cousins happily, and admired the spray of yellow fumitory Elizabeth had pinned against her dark hair. He was directing the work of putting up the hurdles to make a bottle-neck to the river-bank where they wanted the sheep to jump in, and the weaving of branches to form a barrier across the river down-stream of the place, in case any sheep should try to swim out that way.

'It's a perfect place for the washing,' Elizabeth said. 'You would think it was designed for it.'

'Well, and so it was,' Paul said. 'God does nothing without a purpose, little cousin. Who has the garlands—I can hear the flock coming.'

The noise of the sheep grew as they came down the hill, the huge flock like a sea of cream pouring towards the narrowing funnel of willow-hurdles. The chosen men waded into the river to make two lines to guide the sheep between them, and others who came down with the flock hurried across to receive them on the other side. The onlookers began cheering, and the two priests stepped forward to bless the flock and start the singing of the hymn for the washing. The sheep reached the bank and paused there, the old ram and the bell-wether teetering on the brink, weighing the choice between the water and the dogs. Then with a splash that sent drops of water sparkling in the sun, the old fellow jumped in, a cheer rose, and the flock followed.

The sheep swam across the river, guided by the washers, who gripped them by the fleece and helped them on until they reached the gravel beach and could scramble out. On the other side the shepherds grabbed the ram and the wether, his bell clonking hollowly, and Elizabeth and the other girls came forward, and Eleanor knelt before the ram and twisted his garland round his ridged yellow horns. It was a pretty thing, a rope of yellow and white flowers plaited with blue ribbons, and when she had fastened it, she put her arms round his neck and kissed his nose. Elizabeth looked on with alarm. The ram was firmly held by brawny shepherds, but he had long yellow teeth and a nasty temper, and she would not have risked such a gesture.

The ram took it calmly, however, and when released only shook himself and trotted a few steps forward, his head held high as if he were proud of his crown of flowers. Now Eleanor put the other wreath round the bell-wether's neck, and Elizabeth took her arm and pulled her out of the way of the shepherds who would now drive the flock to the shearing pens where the kingly shearers waited with their blades sharpened and shining.

The white sea trotted past, fleeces jouncing, the dogs running low on either side, and the crowd followed. Elizabeth saw amongst them a family of gypsies whom she knew were professional wool-winders, and who travelled the country from one shearing to another. The winding came after the shearing, and for weeks at a time the winders would settle down and camp amid the mountains of wool to tease it and comb it and clean it of grit so that it could be packed by the Morland

packers into great canvas sarplers. Packing had to be supervised by Morland men, for wool was sold by weight and the winders were paid by weight, and it was not beyond credence that a winder might pack a few rocks in amongst the wool if he were not watched.

Now the main business of the day began. In the growing heat the shearers worked, one shearer and a boy to each sheep, the boy to hold and the shearer to cut, and there was work for everyone in bringing the sheep up and driving them off and dragging the masses of fleece away to the barns. The din was deafening as the sheep bleated in protest, the ram yelled defiance, and the workers shouted instructions and cursed the sheep that evaded their grasp. It was thirsty work, and dusty work, and smelly work, and even the women, running to and fro with pitchers of water, thin ale, and buttermilk, took on a film of sheep-yolk to which the dust stuck tenaciously.

Inside the barns the wool rose to the rafters and as the spring darkness came, flaring smoky torches were lit in the pens to light the last of the work. Then all was done, and it was time for feasting. The dusty workers washed in the yard troughs, the bonfires were lit, the trestles carried out, and the food and drink laid out in delicious array. The prettiest of the young girls came forward with garlands and nosegays of flowers for the twenty-four shearers, and were kissed for their trouble, to the delight of the onlookers.

No-one had eaten since before dawn, and so at first there was no leisure for anything other than satisfying the pangs of hunger. There was plenty of roast meat—pork and mutton—and fowls, heaps of good wheaten and barley bread, oatcake and rye plaits; and then there was fruit—oranges and lemons and figs and dates and sweet little wrinkled store apples, the last of the crop saved for this occasion; and then there were the delicious sweetmeats, saffron cakes and puddings and delicious spicy pastries stuffed with fruit and brown sugar, ginger cakes, cakes flavoured with cinnamon and nutmeg, honey wafers, custard tarts and jugs of creamy syllabub.

When the eating had slowed down a little, the drinking began, and then it was time for singing. The Morland musicians were augmented by others from the villages, bourdon and bagpipes and silver whistles, and as well as a choir of boys, under the direction of Master Philippe, ten of the shearers had got themselves together in a three-part chorus. They sang all manner of songs—holy songs, sweet sad love songs, ancient shearing songs as old as the hills the sheep grazed and full of words no-one any longer remembered the meaning of, modern popular songs from the south, and jolly pagan country songs that they all knew and loved.

And when the food had gone down a little, the young folk began the dancing round a bonfire in a square marked out by flares. There was morrissing, too, and the Horse and the Clown made their appearance to shrieks of merriment and chased the young village girls into the bushes, and ribbons were stolen and probably many a precious possession lost in the scintillating spring night. Elizabeth loved every minute of it, ate and drank and sang and danced, laughed at the antics of the morris clowns, cheered on the quintain-riders and the wrestlers, one of whom fell in the fire and laughed as loudly as anyone when he found the seat of his britches burned away.

Then at last when the stars were almost out came the last dance of all. The old folk were nodding by then, and the children already sleeping, tumbled in corners, sticky-mouthed and happy, or curling their granddam's laps. The last dance was the sheep-dance, the traditional ending to the feast, where the young people split into two teams, the girls dancing the ewes and the boys the rams, making concentric circles round the fire; the boys danced clockwise round the outside, and the girls, holding hands tightly, reeled widdershins round the fire, facing outwards, going faster and faster until they were drunk with the speed and shrieking with laughter. It was hard to keep your feet dancing backwards, and they went on and on, faster and faster, until finally someone tripped or fell or just became too dizzy to keep going. That was the moment for the boys to dash in and choose their partner, and all broke up into couples.

When finally the circle broke and the girls all tumbled breathless to the floor, it was Paul who sprang to Elizabeth's side, and grabbing her hands pulled her to her feet.

'We'll be the first,' he shouted exultantly. Elizabeth went with him, laughing wildly. She was dishevelled and dusty, drunk with spring and dancing. She had lost her cap, and her hair flew like a wild mare's mane over her shoulders, and her chemise had come undone at the neck so that her tender white throat shewed. Desire for her flamed through Paul's blood. The last spoor of the fire was dying down. The couples were still waltzing round, but in a moment the lads and girls would run in and leap the fire. It was traditional that a couple who wished to marry would jump the last embers, and if they cleared them, they were assured of many children.

The greatest luck and pride was to the couple who jumped first.

'We'll be the first—Elizabeth—jump with me!' Their whirling ceased abruptly and they looked into each other's faces, suddenly sober, wondering. 'Will you?' Paul asked her, and he opened his hands and spread them to her, in a gesture offering her himself and everything that was his. 'Will you, Elizabeth?'

'With all my heart,' she said, and then with a wild whoop she seized his hand and ran towards the bonfire. There were still one or two flames licking up at its heart, and the other dancers scattered out of their way and took up the lusty cheer, driving them on with ferocious cries of glee. Paul ran, feeling his heart pounding inside him, Elizabeth's thin hand gripped so tightly round his he thought their fingers must snap. A log broke, a spurt of flame jumped up, and with a shriek, wild as a maenad, Elizabeth leapt right over the heart of the fire, clearing it like a deer, with Paul beside her. As the other couples followed their lead, Paul took her in his arms and kissed her, there in front of everyone, and the old folk cried out, 'God bless the young mistress! God bless the master!' And so it was done.

Twenty-seven

HE WEDDING WAS IN JUNE, A LUCKY MONTH, AND PAUL was determined to have as big and lavish a celebration as could be contrived, firstly because it was an important event, the marriage of the master of Morland Place, and the tenants and servants would expect it, and secondly, 'Because the times are so dark and uncertain it will do us all good to make merry.' The darkness he was referring to was the continuing religious strife within the country, and the coming war with France. Scotland had rejected the proposal to marry their infant princess to Prince Edward, and had turned to France for help, while Spain had solicited English help in their campaign to capture Paris, and so an army was to be despatched to France that summer. It had meant, of course, new taxations to raise the money, and the King, lacking clever ministers, had had to resort to other methods as well, to raise the necessary funds. He had called in the 'Benevolences' made illegal by the late King Richard, and had begun to sell off the lands taken to the Crown from the religious houses. Worst of all he had debased the coinage—adulterated the gold with base metals to make it stretch further.

'It will affect our trade,' John Butts had said to Paul of this last contrivance. 'When the dealers in Antwerp start to look askance at a piece of English gold, they will put the price up again.'

'That can be good for us,' Paul pointed out.

'Aye, cousin, but what happens when the gold is so abased they will not take it at all?'

'Surely it won't come to that,' Paul said. John smiled grimly.

'You think not? I wonder. Here we have a King who needs money, and who has learned a trick to double his money on the instant. And when the King is gone, what then? A gaggle of ministers who have watched him perform the trick.'

'The King may live for many years yet,' Paul said. John nodded.

'You had better hope that he does. I pray for it every day, that he may live until the Prince is a man.'

The wedding itself was to take place at Morland Place, and Philippe was to perform it, for there was no church nearby where the family felt safe enough from dissenters and reformists. So the winter parlour was decked out with flowers and green boughs, the rushes strewn with sweet-smelling herbs, rosemary and camomile and sweet mallow, and a table set up before the fireplace for an altar. Over the fireplace was the panel painted with the Morland arms, crest and motto: it seemed a suitable thing for the couple to observe during the ceremony. To either side of it were the two portraits, to the right that of Paul's grandfather, the elder Paul, and to the left that of Nanette.

Nanette came home for the wedding, and at Elizabeth's request she helped Arabella dress the bride. Nanette was surprised and pleased to be chosen—she had known that Elizabeth was not sorry she had gone away—and was not surprised that Elizabeth was very quiet while they helped her into her wedding clothes. They were very rich—the kirtle was of white silk figured in gold with a design of heather-sprigs, the sleeves wired and slashed, the gown was of heavy gold-coloured damask with the broad sleeves turned back to shew the sarcenet lining, the head-dress a French hood of white velvet trimmed top and bottom with bands of gold sewn with pearls. From under it Elizabeth's dark hair flowed loose. She was not virgin, but it was traditional, and besides, she had not fallen from virtue. What had happened was none of her fault.

'You look beautiful,' Nanette said, stepping back to admire her. Arabella was giving her hair a final polish with a piece of silk.

'She does indeed,' she said. 'Now, Bess, all we need is your pearl necklace that Paul gave you, and you will be ready.'

'It is in my little box,' Elizabeth said, almost the first words that had passed her lips. 'I'll get it—'

'No, I'll get it, I know where it is,' Arabella said, and whisked away to fetch it. While she was out of the room, Nanette took the opportunity to do something she had planned on as soon as she had heard that Paul and Elizabeth were to be married.

'Elizabeth,' she said, 'I have something for you.' She pulled at the chain at her waist and drew up the missal that hung at the end of it. 'You see this? This was a gift from the elder Paul to me on our wedding-day, and I have worn it ever since. It belonged to his great-grandmother, Eleanor Courteney—you see, here, the white hare embossed on the cover, the Courteney device that she brought into the family—we shew it on our shield. It is said the great Duke of York, father of King Edward and King Richard, gave it to her, though I don't know if that is true or not.'

'You are giving it to me?' Elizabeth asked, raising her eyes to Nanette's face. 'It seems too precious to give away.'

'I want you to have it,' Nanette said. 'If Paul and I had had children, it would have gone to them, but we did not. It is a thing that should stay in the family. Eleanor Courteney was your great-grandmother too—it is right that it should come to you, and you in turn will give it to some future daughter-in-law, and that way it won't be lost to the family. Take it, my dear, and fasten it to your belt, and take my blessing with it.'

Elizabeth reached out and folded her hands gently round the little book, as if afraid of breaking it.

'Thank you,' she said. 'I will treasure it as you wish me to. And—cousin Nan—I'm sorry.'

She did not say what she was sorry for, and Nanette did not need to ask. Tears came to her eyes. 'There is nothing to be sorry for,' she said, and kissed her. 'What has to be done, has to be done. But this is a time for rejoicing. Be happy, Elizabeth. God bless you.'

The family crowded into the winter-parlour for the ceremony. The bride was attended by three maids, her cousins Faith, Hope and Charity, dressed in miniature versions of her own wedding clothes, while the groom's pages were John and Catherine's sons, Samson and Joseph, ten and nine years old respectively, and Arabella's sole child Hezekiah, who at eleven already overtopped his mother and promised to be a giant like the elder Paul when he was full-grown. As it was, it could be seen when he stood behind the bridegroom that he was not much shorter than him.

All the Morlands were there: Elizabeth's parents, Luke and Alice, had travelled up from Dorset with the twins Mary and Jane, who were now sixteen and both betrothed, Mary to a local man, Tom Bennet, and Jane to a gentleman's son who was apprenticed to a goldsmith in London. Luke and Alice had lost their only son, Stephen, when he was six, and it was likely that Mary and Tom Bennett's children would inherit Hare Warren, and the notion made Mary preen herself at her sister's expense.

Elizabeth's twin, Ruth, was absent, being at that time too great with child to travel.

George Courteney and his wife had also made the journey, for a happy reunion with Lucy Butts, who was now looking very much a handsome and prosperous widow. Ezekiel and Arabella, John and Catherine, Jane and Bartholomew all crowded in, and Nanette began to feel conspicuously single. On the other side of her were James Chapham and Eleanor. The latter looked better than she had for some time. There was a little colour in her cheeks, she looked less frail, and did not cough so much, but there was still no sign of a child, and Nanette thought with pity that James had been unlucky in his choice of wife. Besides his own fortune, he now had the estates his wives had brought him, and no-one to leave them to. Eleanor's dowry had been the Watermill House estate, the lands Paul the elder meant to settle on Nanette, which Amyas had withheld from her and eventually given to his daughter. If James and Eleanor both died childless, it would come back to the Morland heir, which, Nanette thought, would be appropriate.

Philippe entered, and the ceremony began. Nanette's eyes were on the young couple, particularly on Elizabeth, and she wondered what the girl was thinking. It was a strange ending to it all, but a good one. Paul was evidently much in love with her. She should have been mistress of Morland Place as Robert's bride; she had suffered for the House; and the House was now hers. On her belt hung the missal which the mistresses of Morland Place had worn for a hundred years: that too had returned to its proper place, and Nanette was glad she had had a hand in it.

Paul was quiet and steady—the Morlands should do well under his guidance, and if Elizabeth fulfilled her part and produced a healthy crop of children, all would be well. Nanette, looking at the back of Elizabeth's head, could not help remembering her own wedding to a Paul, this Paul's grandfather. But that had been in the chapel, next door, and the chapel now stood in ruins. The June sunshine poured into it unimpeded by roof or wall. Moss grew over the stone flags of the floor and grasses and flowers had rooted themselves in the cracks and crevices between the stones. One day, when fortune was full, it would be rebuilt. The wheel turns, Nanette thought, and God is not mocked. He sees us, He knows what must be.

The feast afterwards was lavish and very merry, with much entertainment, food and drink and song, a play performed by the villagers, and a troupe of tumblers hired for the occasion. Nanette was glad to find herself seated next to James, for she enjoyed talking to him. He had not been at Court that year, having had business in York to attend to, and their conversation naturally reverted to Court matters again and again.

'So the King will go to France, I hear?' he said to her. 'I wonder he can consider it—the reports of his health are no better than they were.'

'Some days he is better, some days he is worse,' Nanette said. 'On his good days he can walk with help, but on his bad days he has to be wheeled in his chair. He conceived the idea of going to France to lead his own men on one of his good days, and no-one dares dissuade him.'

'And he leaves the Queen as Regent in his absence? That is a compliment to her, is it not?'

Nanette nodded, pleased. 'It is. He thinks highly of her judgement, and I think his choice of her as Regent was deliberately to shew those factions in Court who are against her that he values her as much as he did the first Catharine. He left her as Regent once, too, you remember. It is like him—those he values he protects. He will let their enemies advance only so far.'

'The Queen has enemies, then?' James asked carefully. Nanette glanced out of habit over her shoulder, and caught herself doing it, and laughed. All the same, she lowered her voice.

'Intrigue and plotting are the air we breathe at Court. If the courtiers did not gather into factions and plot against each other they would have nothing to do. The Queen is interested in the New Learning, and that makes her a natural target for the Old Catholic party. Gardiner and Wriothesley have tried several times to remove her, but the King lets them get only so far, just as he did with Cranmer.'

James nodded. 'Yes, I remember—they planned a tribunal to question his orthodoxy, and the King permitted it, but then made Cranmer head of the tribunal at the last moment.'

Nanette laughed. 'You should have seen their fury at being thwarted like that!'

'It seems, then, that the King favours the new learning, if he permits the Queen to dabble in it, and protects Cranmer from the Catholics.'

'I don't think he favours one side or the other,' Nanette said. 'He is as orthodox in his worship as any of the old Catholics, but he has an inquiring mind, and can't help wondering about things. I think he likes that in the Queen. He encouraged her to supervise the royal children's education, and that speaks for itself.'

'It does. But what will happen—afterwards? Even when I was last at Court the rival parties were flexing their muscles. Shall we have civil war, do you think?'

'I don't think it will come to that. God only knows what will happen—I dread to think of it. I greatly fear that the reformist party will gain power, and then we shall have no more religion in the land.'

'You do not favour the New Learning, I conclude.'

'I am interested in new ideas, of course, but I see the danger of questioning the old rules. There has to be discipline in religion, and one set of rules for everyone. But once it is seen that the rules can be questioned and changed, there is no more authority, and every man decides for himself.'

'Is that so very bad?' James asked gently. Nanette looked at him in surprise.

'It is chaos,' she said. 'You, I suppose, may be able to make out a case for chaos, but I have witnessed too much of its effects to think it a desirable state.'

'Peace, cousin, I do not wish to wrangle with you,' James said. 'No, I don't like the idea of chaos. It's just that some-times—I wonder—' Nanette softened, and lowered her voice again. 'Everyone wonders from time to time, James. What we all chiefly wonder at the moment is whether the King will come safely home or not. If he should die abroad, it would be a terrible thing. And the Queen is terrified that something will happen to the Prince while the King is away, and that she will be blamed.'

'Is his health giving cause for concern?' James asked.

'Oh no—he is a stout, healthy boy. But a child's life is always uncertain, and London in the summer can mean plague and pest. I think she should move them all out to the country—but it is her decision, of course.'

'You are still close friends?' James asked.

'As close as one can be to a Queen. Don't mistake me—she has not grown too high. Quite the reverse. When she signs her name, she signs "Kateryn the Queen" and then "KP" at the end, KP for Katherine Parr, to remind herself and everyone else of who she is. But a Queen must keep state, and she must keep as much state as the King's position demands. I cannot be as close to Katherine the Queen as I could to Anne the Queen.'

'But you are not unhappy?'

'No, no indeed. I enjoy Court life, for all its hazards.'

'You look well,' James said, smiling at her. 'Your clothes—the height of fashion. That bonnet, for instance—very becoming. Are hoods going out of fashion? A cap is much more suitable for hunting. Will you come hunting with me while you are here? I have heard there are red deer on the edge of Shawes.'

Nanette looked into his eyes, and felt herself blushing. There was no mistaking his interest in her. The blood surged through her veins with excitement at the thought of the chase. The sedate life of London, the long sitting and sewing, the lack of sport—for the King did not hunt any longer—made her restless. She lowered her eyes, aware that her behaviour was not seemly.

'I should dearly love to go hunting while I am here. We see little sport now at Court.'

'Then I shall arrange it,' James said jubilantly. 'Ezekiel will like us to rid him of a stag or two, for they bark his fruit trees and eat his ripe corn. And the young couple will come out with us too. I dare say Paul will be glad of some venison to replenish his stores after this feast.'

On the day after the wedding there was a fair, and on the day after that the promised hunt took place, so it was not until the third day that Nanette had the leisure to pay a visit to Dick the smith and Mary. She did not go empty handed—she had gifts for the couple as well as for the Bear-cub and his foster-brothers, and she took with her a man-servant leading a horse on to which all the gifts were packed. Audrey, in whose discretion she had no faith, she sent off beforehand on an errand to Shawes, so that the maid might not know she had gone. The man was Matthew, who had served the elder Paul, and was trustworthy.

The little cot looked no different from the outside, but inside there were little evidences here and there of greater affluence which were the result of the money Nanette sent them. Mary greeted Nanette affectionately. She had another baby at her breast, a girl-child of a year's age, whose hair was bleached almost white by the sun.

'Dick is not far away,' Mary told her. 'He expected you would come, so he is working nearby, at the brake just beyond the river. I will send my Robin for him—he will fetch him presently.'

Robin was now a sturdy child of four, and trotted off with his message with an air of importance.

'And where are the others?' Nanette asked when the child had gone.

'Playing out at the back,' Mary said. 'Jan grows at such a pace you will hardly know him. He is to start to school after the harvest with the priest down in the village, just as you said.'

'Jan?' Nanette queried.

'We call him that to distinguish him. Our little boy is John too. Shall I call them in, or will it please you to go out?'

'I'll go out,' Nanette said, and followed Mary outside and round the back of the house. There on the sunny side of the house the two small boys were playing in the dust of the strip of bare earth that was beaten all round the house. They were playing at five-stones with some small smooth pebbles, and they stood up as the women appeared, and at the sight of Nanette in her rich clothing they first gawped and then, at an impatient signal from Mary, bowed.

There was no doubt as to which was the Bear-cub, for he overtopped his companion by a handspan. They were of an age, of course, two years and a half old. John, Dick's son, was a stocky, fresh-faced boy with barley-fair hair bleached by the sun like his young sister's; but the Bear-cub, Jan, was already growing taller and more wiry in frame. His hair was lustrous, black and curling, his skin brown, his features fine, promising good looks when he grew up, and his eyes were blue, dark, dark blue like the blue flames of gentians. He smiled shyly when Nanette approached him, and answered her questions hesitantly but with good will.

'Do you know who I am?' she asked him. He shook his head, looking up into her face with the innocent curiosity of a very young child.

'Shame, for shame, Jan, you do know! Didn't I tell you? It is your benefactress come to see you. Say that you remember, for shame!' Mary cried.

'Yes,' Jan said, still staring at Nanette wonderingly.

'Madam,' Mary prompted sharply. 'You must call her Madam.'

'Yes, Madam,' Jan said.

'I have brought you presents,' Nanette said, and then smiled at the other child. 'And for you too, don't fear. Shall you come and look at them? Come, then. Come, Jan. Will you take my hand?'

She had a pleasant hour playing with the children and talking to them, and to Mary and Dick, who came hurrying in from the woods with the older boy. There were presents for all—a bolt of fine cloth for Mary, a drinking-cup for Dick, a poupee for the girl-child, who put it straight to her mouth and began sucking the paint off the head directly, and toys for the little boys. The gift that caused the greatest delight to the children was the carved bear she had brought for Jan. It had movable legs which had sticks attached to them, so that when you moved the sticks up and down the bear danced.

'Take it outside and play,' Nanette said at last, and the three children ran gratefully out into the sunshine with their booty.

'He looks well,' Nanette said to Dick and Mary when they had gone.

'He is, thank God,' Mary said. 'He is a strong and healthy boy.'

'And clever too, I doubt not, Madam,' Dick said. 'He is to start lessons after the harvest, down in the village.'

'Mary told me,' Nanette said.

'He is to go there just in the mornings, and our Robin will take him and learn to read and write too, thanks to your bounty, Madam,' Dick went on. 'And in the afternoons I will teach him what I can, until he is old enough to go to the grammar school. He'll learn to shoot straight, and track a deer at any rate.'

'Good things for a man to know,' Nanette said. 'He is in good hands with you, I am sure. Has anyone asked about him? Has there been any awkwardness?'

Dick smiled broadly. 'Nay, Mistress, who should care if Dick the smith has two bairns or three or a dozen or none? There's nowt to wonder at and no-one to wonder it. He's safe, Mistress, never fear.'

'I must go now,' Nanette said. 'I will come again, perhaps, before I leave. You will hear from me, in any case, in the usual way.'

'Shall you say goodbye to the bairns before you go?' Mary asked. Nanette thought of the dark-haired little boy with the sea-blue eyes and smiled. His fascination was understandable, but too potent.

'No,' she said. 'Let them play in peace.'

The period of Katherine's Regency passed without mishap, and the King came back from France pleased enough with his capture of Boulogne and glad to be home, glad to see his wife and children again. Christmas that year was a merry one, a family one. Queen Katherine ordered a new suit of clothes in rich red velvet for the Prince, and saw to it that the King's daughters were brought to Court to dance in their new dresses.

The Lady Mary was to be restored to her place in the succession, after the Prince and any children that the King might yet have; but the Lady Elizabeth was still bastardised and ignored. Nanette spent much time with her and liked her sharp mind and quick wit, which reminded her of the girl's mother. The Lady Elizabeth idolised her father, and wanted more than anything to be reconciled with him, and she looked to her stepmother and Nanette between them to intercede for her. But though the King often looked wistfully at her when he thought no-one was looking, he would not have her restored, and treated her distantly when she was in his presence.

In March 1545 the King became ill with a severe fever and the ulcers on his legs grew sharply worse. The Queen, in defiance of all custom and etiquette, had her bed moved into the King's dressing room and slept there so that she could nurse him more easily. She was coming to know a great deal about salves and lotions as well as the other medicines he required. His inability to exercise made him costive and gave him indigestion, and she kept a store of olive-oil suppositories and liquorice pastilles to hand, along with the plasters and sponges, fomentations and bandages with which she dressed his diseased legs three times a day. The Lady Mary's health had always been bad, and she took great quantities of mastick pills and Elsham ginger. One of the subjects upon which she and her father could talk for hours without disagreement was the fascinating one of medicines, treatments and cures.

It was a very different Court from the one Nanette remembered back in the twenties and thirties, less frivolous and more serious. The Queen liked to have learned men about her, and loved to read serious books and discuss the new ideas in them. She was a follower of Erasmus, and she gathered round her the enquiring Erasmian minds of scholarly men. The King liked to listen to their talk and join in with them, and he allowed the Queen to appoint the best of them as tutors to his young son. The Prince had his own Household at Ashridge in Hertfordshire, but he often came to Court, and when he was not at Court the King and Queen often went down to visit him. The Lady Mary had her own small Household at Enfield, but was often at Court; the Lady Elizabeth lived in the Queen's Household.

The Queen's Household was very devout, hearing Mass three times a day, and since the Queen's piety was unquestioned and her interest in the New Learning intellectual rather than dogmatic, neither Nanette nor the Lady Mary found it difficult to live there. It was not all seriousness—there were dances and entertainments, too, and the Lady Mary was able to indulge her passion for gambling at the Queen's card tables. The late Catherine Howard had left an enormous wardrobe of fabulous jewelled dresses, presents from the King, and Nanette and the Queen's other ladies spent much time making them over into new dresses for the Queen and her stepdaughters.

Shoes were a different matter. Katherine had always had a passion for shoes, and she had a new pair almost every week, and always sat with her feet shewing under her gown so that she could glance down with satisfaction every now and then at her latest acquisition. She loved flowers, too, and every day fresh cut flowers were brought to all the rooms the Queen might be in during the day. One of Nanette's small tasks was to arrange the flowers for the Queen's bedchamber. Another thing that Katherine could indulge her fancy for was pets. She had a number of greyhounds, and as Anne had given Nanette a spaniel like her own—little Ajax, dead years since and buried— Katherine gave her a greyhound which Nanette called Urian. Katherine also had two monkeys, with which the Prince loved to play when he came to visit. Nanette kept well away from them. She hated monkeys as much as a horse does.

News from Morland Place was good—Elizabeth had born a large and healthy baby boy whom they had called John. The wool crop was a good one, and the soaring prices which followed another debasement of the coinage benefited the Morlands more than it penalised them, so that, even allowing for the heavy taxes which were still being levied to pay for the inconclusive war with France, which was ended that year in yet another peace treaty, Paul hoped he would be able to start rebuilding the chapel in a year's time.

In the new year Thomas Seymour returned to Court, and as his coming brought new strength to the reformist party, the Catholic party stirred themselves to try to persuade the King to suppress heresy more firmly. They clamoured for fires, but the King wanted balance between the factions, and gave them little of what they wanted. One victim was claimed, however—a childhood friend of the Queen's who had come to Court the year before, and who was a fanatical Protestant.

The Queen's leniency to new ideas had attracted many whose views were more extreme and even repugnant to her. Nanette had noted this, as had others of her friends, with alarm, and none had raised her hackles more than Anne Askew, known as the Fanatic. Nanette hated her heretical outpourings, and she hated her carelessness of herself and of others. The Queen treated her with kindness—she repaid it by putting the Queen in danger. Nanette at one time went so far as to point this out to the Fanatic, suggesting that she leave the Court and find some other refuge, so that she might not bring the Queen to the same fall as her predecessor. But the Fanatic merely glared at her with her wild, mad eyes and told her that the martyr's death was a glorious one, and that her reward would be in heaven.

It was no surprise to anyone when Anne Askew was arrested that summer and taken to the Tower. What followed was more shocking. The Catholic party under Gardiner and Wriothesley wanted to implicate the Queen in the heresy in order to have her removed and replaced with a puppet of their own—perhaps the widowed Duchess of Richmond, the King's daughter-in-law—and they tortured Anne Askew to try to make her give information against the Queen. She would say nothing, and in their rage they turned the wheels of the rack themselves until the woman was almost dead from the agony and the Lieutenant of the Tower was so alarmed that he rode hotfoot to Westminster to beg forgiveness from the King and excuse himself from any part in it. Racking a woman—and a gentlewoman at that—was something not even the street mob could countenance. The King reprimanded but did not punish, and the Fanatic was burned at the stake.

Encouraged by this ambiguous attitude, Gardiner and Wriothesley tried again, and brought a Bill of accusation against the Queen, which the King signed, giving his consent for her to be questioned about her religious orthodoxy. Nanette had seen the trick done before—letting them go so far and no further—but it was not the less terrifying for that. Katherine, who saw the signed warrant by accident, was frightened into hysterics and screamed and sobbed so loudly that in the end the King had himself carried to her bedside in his chair to comfort her. When Wriothesley came the next day to arrest her, the King sent him away with a tongue-lashing that made it clear to him that while the King lived he would protect his Queen as he protected his beloved Primate.

But when the King dies, Nanette thought, what then? The King himself had no doubts—Nanette saw him once drop his arm across Cranmer's shoulder and say, 'Poor Tom, when I am dead they will rend thee to pieces.'

Cranmer shuddered, knowing it to be true. For such a

notoriously flexible man, Cranmer could be surprisingly tenacious about some things.

The King went on progress again that summer, the summer of 1546, and once again the Queen's Household lived out of trunks, moving from place to place in a well-ordered confusion of waggons and baggage-beasts, linen and portable furniture, lists and inventories and requisitions and lost articles. It was intended to visit the north, and Nanette looked forward to seeing her own country again, if only briefly, but the progress proved too much for the King's health, and when he reached Windsor he was too ill to go further. He recovered enough to do a little hunting there, at the favourite of his country palaces, and when he was not hunting he was occupied still for up to twelve hours a day in business, closeted with his clerks, receiving envoys, reading and writing, his spectacles in their gold frames pinching his long thin nose. The Court stayed at Windsor until November, and then returned to Whitehall for the King to take his medicinal baths.

On Christmas Eve the King suffered a seizure which prostrated him, and though he recovered, it was plain to everyone that the end was near. An air of tension ran through the Court, a subterranean tremor of excitement and fear undermined the superficial quiet, and people were seen in the wrong places at the wrong times, and were missing from their accustomed places at other times. Messages passed back and forth in the hands of messengers who walked hurriedly and glanced over their shoulders from time to time, and the silence of night was broken by the distant sound of footsteps or fragments of whispered conversation.

It reminded Nanette depressingly of the terrible day when she had waited with Queen Anne in her rooms, the day she had been arrested. She longed to go home, to go back to

Yorkshire, but of course it was impossible. Even if she could have brought herself to leave, it was certain that Katherine would not want her to go. At a time like this she needed her friends around her.

Twenty-eight

A SILENCE SETTLED OVER THE COUNTRY AS THE MONTH OF January dragged on. Soon after the new year the King suffered another seizure and took to his bed, and the Queen's Household moved to her apartments on the advice of the doctors. The King rallied enough to receive a foreign embassy on the fourteenth and to order the execution of the Earl of Surrey on the nineteenth, but it was evident to all that he was dying. The Seymour party was quietly confident. The fall of Surrey, which they had engineered on the grounds that he displayed the leopards of England on his arms, took the Duke of Norfolk to the Tower for misprision of treason. If only they could persuade the King to sign the death warrant before he died, it would be a crippling blow to the Catholic Party.

But the King grew weaker, and though he clung to life he was no longer able to write or to take part in business. He lay helpless, imprisoned in his mountain of dying flesh, only his eyes moving, calling occasionally for drink to quench his feverish thirst. Sir Anthony Denny, a councillor who had become close to the King in the last few months, came daily to give a bulletin to the Queen and her ladies—otherwise they were forgotten. Early in the morning of the twenty-seventh he came to tell the Queen that the King had suffered another seizure.

'It is only a matter of time now, Madam,' he said. 'I felt it necessary to inform His Majesty that his doctors advised him to make ready for the end, and I asked him if he wished to see any of his divines. He said he would see none but Cranmer, and even him not yet.'

'Do not wait, Denny,' Katherine said. 'Send for Cranmer at once—on my authority if you wish. The King will change his mind when he sees him.'

'Madam, Master Cranmer is not in London. He is at Croydon, so I thought it best to send a messenger for him at once.'

Katherine gave him her hand. 'Good Denny, good friend. Is anyone with him—with the King—apart from the Council? Any of his friends?'

The distinction was made a little bitterly. Denny pressed her hand very slightly. 'Will Somers is there, Madam. He sits on the floor at the bedside, where the King can see him only by turning his head. They talk together sometimes, but Will is crying so hard he can scarcely be understood.'

'Poor Will,' Katherine said. 'Does the King ask for me, Denny? Am I to see him?'

'No, Madam, he has not asked for you.'

'Has he spoken of me? Did he mention my name?'

Denny shook his head. 'It is my belief,' he said gently, 'that he does not know where he is, or what year it is. Those words I can distinguish seem to bear on the past.'

'I see,' Katherine said dully. 'Well, Denny, you had better go back to him. Thank you for telling me. You will let me know at once if—if anything happens? Or if the King asks to see me.'

'I will, Madam, be assured,' Denny said, and withdrew. Katherine sat for a long time in silence, and then raised her eyes towards her women who were sitting near. Her sister and stepdaughter were there, but it was Nanette she addressed.

'I am glad at least Will is there. And if Thomas can be with him, too...'

'He will not be alone,' Nanette said.

'Only those two, out of so many. He has outlived all his friends.'

Nanette bit back the comment that sprang to her lips, that he killed so many of them it was small wonder. She thought for a moment, bitterly, of Anne, of George, of Hal Norys and Frank Weston, of Tom Wyatt, of young Surrey who had been the best friend of the King's son Fitzroy. It was the price of Kingship, the necessity of sacrificing your friends to the greater good; and in truth, her heart too was moved to pity at the thought of the great King laid low, of that powerful, glittering, shrewd and subtle emperor trapped helpless and dying by the frailty of human flesh. He was the anointed King, he stood for his people before God, answered for them, took their sins upon himself because they were too weak to bear them themselves. And when he died, his death was for them, as his life was. Anne had come to understand that, at the end. She had been anointed Queen—the last of his queens to be so—and she had understood the dedication of the life, and the sacrifice. Katherine did not understand that. She saw the King, and she saw the man, but she did not see the blending of the two which was more than either, more than both.

He had been loved and he had been feared, but above all else he had been the King, and there was none to come after him, none but a small boy and a pack of ravening dogs. Hertford was the best of them—the Prince's elder uncle—but Hertford was not strong. The King, in dying now, was abandoning his people to the dog-pack, and he above all must know that as he lay struggling to live. He was leaving them masterless, and like the hound who loses the master who both beats and feeds him, the people would mourn him, and fear.

The Queen's companions did not sleep all through the night of the twenty-seventh, and in the early hours of the twenty-eighth, before the grey January dawn had begun to grow outside the windows, Denny came, hollow-eyed and with the marks of tears on his cheeks, to tell them that their lord was dead.

'He died just before two o'clock, without speaking,' he said. 'Cranmer was there. The king could no longer speak, but when Cranmer asked him if he begged forgiveness for his sins, he squeezed his hand as a sign. He died as true a Catholic as he lived.'

'God receive his soul,' Katherine said, crossing herself. She alone of those present was dry-eyed. 'Who is with him now?'

'Cranmer and Will Somers are there still, with the rest of the bishops. My lord Hertford has gone to the Prince with the rest of the Council—as I must too,' he added grimly. The race was on, and the laggard would take no prizes.

When he had gone, Margaret Neville asked, 'What will you do now, Madam?'

Katherine shook her head to clear it. 'I hardly know. It seems there is nothing for me to do here. They will bring Edward here, I suppose, and then I can see him. He will need me, in his grief. And then—I shall go to Chelsea, as we planned.'

The Dower Palace was already prepared for her, the pleasant little Palace on the river close by the chain-walk at Chelsea. Her widows weeds were all ready for her to assume, the arrangements made for the dispersal of her Household. The King's Will had been drawn up, the succession decided, preparations made for the funeral, for the dissolution of Parliament, for the interim government. All these things had been done as soon as it was known that the King was dying. Why then did his death catch them all so unprepared?

He had been there all their lives, the great, glittering, all-powerful figure of the King, directing and controlling, governing and guiding. He had ordered their lives for as long as they could remember, and the closer to Court a person had been, the greater had been his influence. It was impossible, therefore, to think of him dead, impossible to accept that he was no longer there, at the centre of the web that fastened them each to each, and all to him. Those who had something to do were the lucky ones. The rest wandered aimlessly, waiting for something to happen, weeping for their lord.

Nanette woke abruptly, and lay in the muffled darkness of the bedcurtains wondering what had woken her. Beside her Audrey snored softly and the warm weight of Urian was against her feet. All was as it should be—ah, there it was again, the faintest gleam of light passing across the curtains. Nanette slid to the edge of the bed and got out without waking her companion. Outside the curtains it was marginally less black, there being a very little starlight from the window, enough to be able to make out the shapes of the few furnishings. Nanette went to the window and looked down into the courtyard and after a moment was just able to make out the shape of horses, a more solid core of darkness in the dark. Then a muted cough—there was a man there too—and the clink of a bit-ring came to her, clear in the silence.

Men and horses to a northerner always spelt alarm, especially at night, but there was no air of menace, only furtiveness, and Nanette was puzzled rather than frightened. She did not even jump when something cold and wet touched her hand—Urian had crept from the bed after her. She looked down at him, and saw him cock his ears and turn his head towards the door, and a moment later heard footfalls and the quiet swish of cloth against the wall outside in the next room. Whoever it was would have to come through this room to proceed further, for like most houses Chelsea Palace was built with all the rooms letting one into the next. Quickly Nanette moved into a corner and concealed herself with a fold of the arras, and stooping placed her hand round Urian's muzzle to keep him quiet.

The door opened and two figures came through, a woman and a man, the woman carrying a candle which, by the smell of hot wax, had only just been snuffed. It must have been that which woke her. The figures passed her hiding place, and Nanette saw that the woman was the Queen's maid, Annie. The man was tall, heavily built, bearded; as his profile came against the thin grey light from the window, a straight-nosed, high cheekboned profile, Nanette recognised him, and realised at the same moment that there was only one person it could have been—Tom Seymour.

They passed through the next door, and Nanette came out from her hiding place and released the dog. Anger rose inside her. What did he mean by it, visiting in this way, at night, secretly, and the King not a month dead? Of course, he wanted to marry the Queen Dowager, and meant to get his bid in first. He was an ambitious man, Tom Seymour, though not a particularly intelligent one. The Queen Dowager, to her own and everyone else's surprise, had not been named as one of the boy King's guardians, was excluded from the Council and from any political role in the protectorship; but the young King was very fond of her, loved and respected her, and had been brought up by tutors who owed their position to her influence.

Also she was without question the richest woman in the kingdom, having dowers from all three of her husbands as well as a generous pension settled on her under the terms of King Henry's Will. She was, in addition, still young enough to be attractive, though Nanette doubted whether that counted for much with Thomas Seymour. His brother, Edward, Lord

Hertford, had been chosen by the Council from amongst their number as Lord Protector, though it was no more than assenting to a *fait accompli*, since Hertford had moved quickly in securing the young King's person immediately on the old King's death, and had kept the news of the latter secret until he was assured of his position. The Protestant party was well in the ascendant, but even within its ranks there were rivalries. Dudley had a faction of his own, and was hungry for power. Thomas might be trying to consolidate his brother's position by this liaison with Katherine, but Nanette thought it more likely that he hoped, by marrying the King's stepmother, to take over supreme power himself.

Katherine's heart might be broken by this adventurer. If he made a bid for power and failed, her life might be forfeit. But there was worse than that to be feared: under the terms of the King's Will, any children she might have by him were next in line for the succession after Edward, standing above the Lady Mary even if they were girls. If the Queen Dowager should prove pregnant now, and it became known that Seymour had visited her secretly at night, the consequences would be dire.

She was angry with Seymour for risking these things, but she was angrier with Katherine, who ought to know better. She would have to speak to her in the morning, however difficult it might be. Nanette shivered—it was only February, and though not bitter, unpleasantly cold. She got back into bed, thinking she would never sleep with so much on her mind, but she did not hear Seymour's return journey, and did not wake until Audrey got out of bed the next morning.

Her chance to speak to the Queen came after second Mass, when they were returning to the Queen's chambers to prepare for dinner Katherine was smiling to herself, looking younger and prettier than she had for years, and when she smiled at Nanette and the smile was not returned, she drew her aside and said anxiously, 'Nan, what is wrong? You seem very distracted this morning.'

'May I have a word in private with Your Grace?' Nanette said. Katherine looked puzzled.

'Of course you may. Come into my bedchamber.' She motioned the others to wait in the anteroom. In the bedroom, Nanette felt her anger rising again—it was here, perhaps, that the smiling prettiness of the Queen this morning had had its origins. Katherine turned towards her, and Nanette began without preamble.

'I know who was here last night. I was disturbed in my sleep by his passage.'

Katherine cocked an eyebrow in an attempt at standing on her dignity.

'Well, so you know who was here. What then?'

'Katherine, are you mad?'

'You forget who you speak to, Madam.'

'I don't forget—Katherine, Kate, I speak to you as a friend. We have known each other since girlhood, we have not had need of formality. I speak to you from my heart—Kate, you must not do this. You must not receive him.'

'I shall receive anyone I please,' Katherine said, her face reddening. 'How dare you—'

'Not like this!' Nanette cried. 'You have not considered—what if you should prove with child? What then?'

'You must think I have taken leave of my senses, if you think that—'

'You have a great deal of sense, Kate, about most things,' Nanette said more quietly.

'But not about him?' Katherine said.

'No. Not about him.'

Katherine walked up and down the room a few paces before speaking, and her hands were clenched together with urgency, though she kept her voice calm.

'Nan, I know you have never liked him, and only because I love you could I have permitted such a heresy.' She smiled tightly, but it was hardly a joke. 'But you are wrong about him, and wrong about me. Do you really think I would have so little sense as to take him to my bed at this time? No, no, dear friend, I assure you that being Queen for four years would have taught me better sense if my mother had not already taught me better values.'

Nanette was a little ashamed, and said, 'Even the very fact of his presence here, Katherine—'

'No-one knows, no-one will know. Annie is safe, and I do not believe you would speak against me. But I shall not meet him again at night, if that is what troubles you. He will come here by day, but secretly. Annie will stay within sight of us, though not within earshot.'

'Oh Katherine, take care,' Nanette said anxiously. 'Don't give him your heart too easily.'

'What are you telling me? Nan, you are wrong about him. See how he has waited for me since the King married me. He could have had anyone, but he waited for me. He loves me, and me alone.'

Nanette regarded her sadly. She did not know, then, that he had made a bid for the hand of the King's daughter, the Lady Elizabeth, and when that had failed, for the hand of the Lady Jane Grey, the King's great-niece. Nanette could not bring herself to say it. Both these young girls—Jane Grey was rising ten, the Lady Elizabeth rising fourteen—were under the Queen Dowager's care, living in her Household. The position was very sensitive.

'I cannot judge of that, Kate. I can only say, think of your position, think of the scandal. You are guardian not only of your own honour but of that of the King's kinswomen. Do not receive him, Katherine, not yet. Not until the three months is up, at the very least.'

Katherine softened, and crossed the room to embrace her friend.

'Dear Nan, I can't promise that. You see, I love him. I have never loved a man before, and I never will again. I have married three times for duty or to please other people. Now I will marry to please myself. I cannot marry him yet—you see, I am not so foolish as to think it—but as soon as I can marry, I will, and until then—I have to see him, at least see him. I cannot live without him. He is the breath of life to me. But I will be discreet. I promise you that.'

You are not, thought Nanette, in a position to know when you are being indiscreet. But she said nothing, only bowed her head in assent. There was nothing more she could do. The Queen was as wildly in love as any woman ever had been, and she would have her own way.

Katherine married her Thomas in May, the earliest safe date. She had known, of course, that she was not pregnant by the King for she had not shared his bed since some time before Christmas, but the public could not know that. Having married, both of them applied to Edward for his approval, Thomas in person, and Katherine, who had not yet been granted access to the King's person, by letter. Katherine had a very kind and touching reply, and the King promised to make it all right with the Council. Seymour in the meantime had written to the Lady Mary, asking her support in pressing his suit with the Queen Dowager as if marriage was only contemplated, and not accomplished. Mary's reply was characteristically dry and straightforward. She said that there was nothing she could do to influence the Queen, and that as she knew nothing of matters of wooing, she could not help him. It was the best they could expect. Mary had always been a stickler for etiquette, and was not likely to approve a marriage which took place within the accustomed mourning period, especially when the slighted dead was her father, and the King to boot.

Seymour joined the Chelsea Household, and things settled down again. Nanette had to admit that she liked having men around the place, liked the comfortable sound and smell of men and men's concerns. The female servants did not bicker so much when they were working side by side with male servants. Audrey kept herself cleaner than Nanette's nagging could achieve when there were handsome young footmen to impress. And there was no doubt that Katherine was blissfully happy with her new-wedded lord, who in his turn treated her with the affectionate care a man in love should shew towards his bride. But still Nanette could not like or trust him, and it made her restless and dissatisfied.

She wondered whether it would be a good idea to go home to Morland Place. She knew that Paul would be glad to give her a home, and Elizabeth was settled enough now not to resent her. She thought longingly of the north-country. The news from home was mixed: Elizabeth was pregnant again, and her first-born, John, who was rising two, was a bonny, healthy child and everyone's pet; Lucy Butts had finally decided to go back to Dorset to live out the rest of her life with her brother and sister, and the parting had upset John Butts, who was very attached to his mother; and Eleanor was plainly dying of the wasting disease, and had come home to Morland Place, much to Paul's distress, for he had always been tender towards women and had known his sister better than his brothers.

Nanette could not decide whether to request permission to go home or not, and so things drifted on, and the days passed, some good, some bad, bringing Nanette to the end of her thirty-ninth year. That August, the August of 1547, another attack was made on the Scots. The Lord Protector, Lord Hertford, who had now created himself Duke of Somerset, took his role very seriously, and though Nanette did not like him personally, she judged of him as an honest man, a conscientious man, and, provided he could hold on to the power he had seized, the best man in the circumstances to hold the reins of the country until the boy King reached a man's years. The attack on the Scots succeeded, and drove them back in defeat at the Battle of Pinkie, but the quarry escaped them all the same. The child Queen of Scotland was hurried abroad, and taken to France to be brought up in the French Court and eventually, it was assumed, married to the Dauphin. The union of France and Scotland seemed assured. It was not a happy prospect for England.

There was domestic trouble, too, as the year wore on, for the Duke of Somerset's wife, Ann Stanhope, hated Katherine and brewed trouble for her. It was the Duchess's contention that as wife of the Lord Protector she took precedence over all women in the land. The late King's Act had provided that the Princess Ana of Cleves should take precedence over everyone except the reigning Queen and the King's daughters, and so Katherine's position was clear enough, but the Duchess would not accept it, and frequently jostled or pushed the Queen Dowager out of the way. The Duchess had been even more incensed than Somerset himself when Thomas Seymour had married Katherine, and she said frequently and loudly that it was not right that she should be preceded by the wife of her husband's younger brother, and that though Katherine had been Queen, it was only because the King had married her in his dotage, when he had sunk so low through vice that no decent woman would have him. Somerset had to restrain her from repeating such remarks, but they had been spoken, and were carried round by gossiping servants all the same.

More practically, the Duchess had instigated the withholding of the Queen's jewels from her by the Council. It was given as a reason that they were Crown property, but the line had always been very firmly drawn between the Crown jewels worn by the Queen, and those given to her as her personal property by the King, and Katherine was furious, and complained bitterly. But it did no good. The jewels were not returned to her, and to add insult to injury, one or two of the most notable of them were later seen adorning the person of the Lord Protector's wife.

It was in the autumn that Nanette became aware of another kind of trouble which threatened the Queen Dowager's peace, and it came from the most critical source—Thomas Seymour, Lord Admiral of England, her husband and the man she loved. Nanette, in common with most people other than Katherine herself, was aware that the Admiral had made a bid for the hand of the Lady Elizabeth once Katherine had been removed from his reach by marriage to the King. The Lady Elizabeth was now fourteen, and nubile, and of a passionate nature, and it seemed that the temptation of her was not solely her position as third heir to the Crown. Nanette soon began to see significant glances passing between the Admiral and his royal guest.

Nanette at first dismissed it from her mind. Elizabeth was forward for her age, and, though not beautiful nor even pretty had a great deal of her mother's fascination, much of her father's charm, and a great opinion of herself which made her seek attention and admiration. The Admiral was one of those men who could not pass any woman between the ages of thirteen and sixty without flirting with her—he had pinched Nanette often enough for her to understand that. But there came a time when the attentions he was paying the young princess seemed to be more decided than that.

The first time Nanette noticed the change in their attitudes was on a fine morning in November, one of those autumn days which are still and sunny enough to be mistaken for summer.

Nanette had been to the Queen's room, and discovered her still abed, feeling tired and a little indisposed.

'I shall stay here a while, Nan,' she said. 'I will get up for dinner. Don't be alarmed—it is nothing but overtiredness.'

Nanette eyed her curiously. It had been Katherine's dearest wish since she married for the fourth time to bear a child. Her previous marriages had all been barren, but since each of her previous husbands had been elderly, there was good reason to suppose it was their fault and not hers that she was childless. So it was natural to Nanette to wonder if this indisposition might be the first sign of pregnancy. Katherine smiled, reading her friend's mind without difficulty.

'Who knows, Nan?' she said lightly. 'But do not speak of it—it's unlucky. Would you take my dogs out for me and walk them in the gardens a little? I don't like to send them with a servant—they are so nervous.'

'Willingly,' Nanette said, and Katherine's maid found the leashes of the two shivering white dogs, and Nanette led them away. It was as she was about to descend the stairs that she heard the noise coming from the floor above, a good deal of banging and shrieking, and a woman's voice upraised in protest of some kind. Nanette turned about and mounted quickly. The end room on the floor above was that of the Lady Elizabeth, and as Nanette reached the top of the stairs the door of it opened and the Admiral came out. He was laughing to himself, looking well pleased and a little red in the face, as if from exertion. He was wearing his bed-gown, and Nanette did not know if he had anything else on besides, for he held it close around him.

Instinctively Nanette drew back, and still laughing, the Admiral turned in the other direction without having seen her and went through the next door which led to the long gallery, from which there was another stair down to the next floor. When he had closed the door behind him, Nanette went to the Princess's door and knocked and entered. Several of the serving-women were in the anteroom in some agitation, although there were some broad grins to be seen which Nanette would have liked to remove. The chief amongst the women there was the Lady Elizabeth's governess, Katherine Champernowne, and it was she who came to Nanette and curtseyed and said, 'Madame, did you want something?'

'I heard the noise, and came to see what was happening. Kat, the Admiral was here.'

Kat Champernowne glanced about her uneasily and lowered her voice. 'He came to bid my young lady good morning, Madam, that is all.'

'In his bed-gown?' Nanette asked in surprise. 'And where is your young lady?'

'Why, Madam,' Kat said uneasily, 'she is still abed.'

Nanette stared at her, and the woman's eyes pleaded. 'The Admiral came in his bedgown to visit the Lady Elizabeth in her bed. Why, Kat, what were you thinking of to let him in?'

'I could not keep him out, Madam. And he is, after all, my lady's stepfather.'

'The husband of her stepmother, rather. Kat, this must not happen again. It is unseemly. Look at these women—do you think this story won't be repeated?'

'It won't happen again, Madam, you may be sure of that.'

But it did happen again, and the Admiral, perhaps foreseeing the objections that might be made, enlisted Katherine's help, and in her company frequently went in the morning to wake up the Princess, often sitting on her bed, claiming a father's kisses from her, slapping and tickling her familiarly. In the end, Nanette felt she must remonstrate with Katherine.

'Why, Nan, it's only fun,' Katherine said, smiling. 'You are as bad as Kat—she has been to me to bid me tell the Admiral he must not say good morning to his stepdaughter any more.'

'But it is not seemly,' Nanette persevered. 'She is no child any longer—'

'Don't be silly, Nan. She is only a girl, and if I am there, what can be unseemly about it?'

It was hard after that to say anything. Katherine, in love with her husband, could not see, and would not comprehend, that she added only another spice to the game which the other two were playing to rules of their own. Where Thomas was concerned, the Queen was blind—and due to be blinder yet. At Christmas she thought herself to be pregnant; in the new year of 1548, she was sure that she was, and her happiness reached a pitch of blindness where she was willing to hold the Princess down while her husband romped all over the bed tickling her until she called for mercy.

In February they moved from Chelsea to Hanworth while the former was sweetened, and the Admiral's visits to the Princess did not cease on that account. The Queen, contented in her pregnancy and viewing everything through a rosy cloud of happiness, laughed at their antics. The three of them were walking in the garden one morning, with Kat and some of the other women at a distance. The Lady Elizabeth was wearing a new gown of black velvet which she thought very sophisticated and Nanette, who was indoors busy arranging flowers, a task she had continued to perform wherever the Household was, was shocked and amazed to see Elizabeth come running in from the gardens dressed in nothing but her underclothes and kirtle, with no more than a few shreds of black gown hanging from her shoulders. Nanette jumped to her feet in alarm, but the Princess ran past her and up the stairs, her cheeks red and her eyes bright with laughter. Kat came hurrying in after her, and Nanette caught her arm as she passed and said,

'Kat, in God's name what is going on?'

Kat's eyes sparkled with fury. 'He goes too far this time,' she said without preamble. 'And the Queen is blind to it all, blind! I do not know what to do. It is a monstrous game, and will lead to evil, but they will not listen to me.'

'What happened to her dress?'

'The Admiral cut it off her with his dagger.'

'What!' Nanette was shocked.

'Aye, it is so indeed! She was shewing it off to the Queen, and the Admiral said how it was too grown up a dress for such a child. The Princess cried that she was a child no longer, and the Admiral said she was indeed, and the dress should be took off her for unsuitable. She clutched it about her, so he took out his dagger and cut it to shreds from off her body.' Kat was trembling at the memory of the outrage. 'The King's daughter! Her body handled so, by a commoner!'

'And the Queen?' Nanette asked, feeling breathless herself at the very thought of it. 'The Queen stood by and let it happen?'

'The Queen,' Kat said bitterly, 'held my lady's arms behind her while he did it, laughing as if it were a joke.'

The two women stared at each other.

'Something has to be done,' Nanette said.

'Aye, but what? I cannot speak to any of them. They will not see sense.'

'How if I speak to your mistress?' Nanette said unwillingly. 'Perhaps if she were not to encourage him—'

Kat shook her head. 'You can try, Madam, but she's as wilful as—as her royal father, and I believe half in love with the Admiral herself.'

'Kat!'

'Well, we all are, one way or another,' Kat said unrepentant. 'But do you try to speak to her, Madam—only give me time to get her dressed again.'

The Princess received Nanette in her chamber, unwillingly, but to please Kat, of whom she was very fond. She was dressed decently again in a green velvet gown, but it did not hide the bruises on her shoulders. Nanette was shocked anew at the sight of them, but she held her tongue and curtseyed, aware both that it was proper, and that it would please the Lady Elizabeth, who liked such formalities to be observed.

'Well, Mistress Morland, what did you want to see me about?' the imperious young woman asked. Nanette eyed her warily.

'Your Grace, I saw you come past me into the house just now.'

'Well?'

'Your Grace must be aware that it is very unseemly for you to be seen in such a state of undress.'

Elizabeth look sulky.

'If you are come to rate me like Kat, you had better go. I won't be talked to so.'

'You *must* be told—forgive me, Your Grace, but you must not allow the Admiral such familiarities. It is very wrong, both on account of your own rank, and because he is the husband of your stepmother, your royal father's widow, in whose care you are.'

'My stepmother, you forget, was present the whole time—indeed, it was she who held me so that I might not struggle. I cried out to the Admiral to desist, but if she allows it, what can I do?'

'You know quite well that he would not do such things if you did not permit him to. Come, don't look at me like that—you have enough fire in your eyes when you wish, to burn even Thomas Seymour. If you told him to stop and meant it, he would stop.'

Elizabeth's face was red enough now to clash with the flaming colour of her hair. Her dark eyes glittered with a mixture of emotions, and she drew herself up to her full slender height.

'How dare you speak to me in such a way? How dare you

suggest such things? By what right do you, Mistress Morland, presume to tell the King's daughter what to do?'

'By the right of caring about you, my lady,' Nanette said, unflinchingly. She lowered her voice, instinctively stepping nearer. 'I served with your mother at Court, child. I was her friend and her companion. My father was the friend of her father. My cousin played and hunted with your mother's brother.' No-one ever mentioned her maternal kin to Elizabeth, on pain of rousing her wildest temper. Her face turned from red to white now, but her great dark eyes stared at Nanette with something that was not fury, something lost and lonely and longing. Nanette went on. 'Elizabeth, I was with your mother when you were born, I took you from the midwife's arms. I loved your mother dearly, and that is why I dare to speak to you. I cannot stand by and see her daughter dishonour herself without speaking.'

'Dishonour?' Elizabeth said in a low voice. Nanette looked grave.

'Yes, Your Grace. Search in your heart for the truth. It never lies to you, for God has set that guardian inside us which, however others deceive us, and however we deceive others, is not deceived itself. You know that what you are doing is wrong.'

Elizabeth's eyes met hers steadily. She would never lack for courage, this young woman, the finer courage which can admit of its own faults.

'Will you speak to the Queen?' she asked at last.

'Do you wish me to?'

'No. I will repel him if he makes such advances. I do not want the Queen to be troubled.'

'Very well, Your Grace. I think you are right—the Queen is best left unenlightened.'

'Thank you. You may go now.' The last was an attempt to

resume dignity, and Nanette played up to it, curtseying low and withdrawing. Outside she nodded to Kat.

'She has promised to rebuff him. She asks that nothing be said to the Queen.'

'God grant it is over then,' Kat said.

'It would be better if she could go away, but how can one suggest it to the Queen?' Nanette said.

In the event, it was not necessary to suggest it. The truth had seemed to be shielded from the Queen's eyes, but that was destined to change. In early March, the Queen, attended by Nanette and some others of her ladies, went to pay a visit on the Lady Elizabeth in her chamber, and on walking through from the anteroom found the young woman and the Admiral together. The Queen backed out and shut the door quickly, saying, 'Why, she is not here. I wonder where she may be?' but Nanette, who was at her shoulder, had seen, though the others had not. The Admiral had his arms round the Princess, and she was looking up urgently into his face. It was not the look a daughter gives a father; and the Admiral's look was that of a hungry man. The Queen took her ladies back to her room. Later, when she and Nanette were alone, she looked at her friend and read the truth.

'Have you known all along?' she asked.

'As much as you have known,' Nanette said cautiously. Katherine made an angry gesture.

'I would have expected honesty at least from my friend,' she said.

'He is guilty of nothing more than treating her as he treats all women,' Nanette said. 'I do not think it is important with him. And she has mistaken herself, as you have. She thought it harmless, too. Don't blame her, Kate.'

'I blame myself for being blind,' Katherine said bitterly. 'I have encouraged this. Why did you not speak to me before?'

'How could I? As you said, you were blind to it. How could

I suggest it was not as harmless as it seemed? But she has sworn to put him off, and perhaps no harm has been done.'

'Did that look like putting him off?' Katherine said.

'We saw only that she looked at him seriously. She may have been telling him to go away.'

'In his arms?'

'He is a strong man.'

'No, Nan, no. I have been blind, but I am not a fool. She is young and inexperienced. I do not blame her. And he—he cannot help his nature. It is myself I blame. But what is to be done, now? What can I do?'

Nanette was silent, for the solution would suggest itself to the Queen without her help.

'I must put her out of harm's way, at least,' Katherine said after a moment's thought. 'It must not appear to be punitive in any way. She shall be sent on a visit.'

'Perhaps to Denny's house?'

'At Cheshunt? Yes, that is a good idea. Good Denny, faithful Denny. And she likes Lady Denny. She will be happy there. I will send for her now.'

'Kate—don't be bitter,' Nanette said, reaching a hand out to her.

'I have said, I don't blame her.'

'Don't blame anyone. I think it was meant only for fun, just as you thought it was. But sometimes things take hold of themself, and there are no guilty ones, only victims.'

Katherine sighed, placing her hands over her belly. 'I am tired, Nan, tired to death. Don't talk to me any more, I don't want to hear it. I have been a fool—let me at least have my folly to myself. Send for Elizabeth.'

The Princess came, subdued and anxious, and her eyes, after one nervous flicker towards Nanette, were fixed on her stepmother in earnest plea.

'Elizabeth, I have decided to send you away for a holiday. I think you need a change of air. Would you like to pay a visit to Sir Anthony Denny at Cheshunt?'

'Oh Your Grace—Madam—please don't be angry.'

'I am not angry, Elizabeth.'

'I was telling him, truly I was,' she cried, and this was half to Nanette. 'I was telling him that it was unseemly—he meant no harm. I meant no harm. It was all in fun. Don't send me away—please, Mother.'

Katherine winced at the last word, but she said calmly, 'I know, Elizabeth, and I believe you. I am sending you away for your own good, because I feel it would be wise for you to be removed from each other's company for a while. I am not angry with you, child. Go now. I will tell you when the arrangements have been made. You too, Nanette—leave me. I want to be alone. I am tired.'

Outside the princess turned her tragic eyes on Nanette.

'It was true—what I said,' she cried.

'I know,' Nanette said. Then, 'She will get over it.'

'I hope so. I pray so,' Elizabeth said. 'I would not hurt her for all the world. She is like a mother to me.'

Nanette felt great pity for the Princess, so proud and so vulnerable, trapped in her way even as her mother was trapped. What future was there ahead for a bastard princess? No foreign prince would take her, and she would not be permitted to marry an Englishman, for fear of civil war. She was both too important, and not important enough, to be happy. Nanette longed to take her in her arms, but one could not even offer to do that to the Lady Elizabeth even though there was that in her eyes that cried out for it. After a moment's hesitation, Nanette curtseyed to her, and with a nod the girl donned her dignity again and walked away.

Twenty-nine

*I*N JUNE THE QUEEN DOWAGER, HER HUSBAND AND HOUSEHOLD retired to Sudeley Castle where the Queen would await her lying-in. The Lady Elizabeth and her train had been almost two months resident at Cheshunt, under the kindly eyes of Sir Anthony Denny and his wife. Edward Seymour's wife was also pregnant, due to lie-in at the same time as the Queen, as if even in this way she could not resist the temptation to vie with her rival.

The Seymour party was well in control, the power of the Catholics broken. Wriothesley had been dismissed from the Council, Gardiner was in the Tower, and though the King's death had saved the Duke of Norfolk from the block, he was still in retirement, and like to stay there. Parliament had repealed the heresy laws, giving free rein to Protestant reformists and cranks alike, and setting the scene for a sweeping-away of the old religion. It had also repealed the treason laws, a very necessary step, for they had become so repressive in the last years of the old king's reign that a man hardly dare speak for fear of being reported by professional informers.

It was at Sudeley Castle that the news reached Nanette of Eleanor's death, and she asked permission then to pay a visit home, for Paul had expressed a wish in his letter to see her.

The Queen was not due to lie-in until late August or early September, and there was plenty of time for Nanette to go home and come back. But Katherine, who had been growing more and more morose as the weeks passed, told her that she need not hurry back.

'If you find you wish to stay longer, do not let my condition trouble you,' she said. 'You leave me in good hands—you see I have Jane to sit with me. Jane will not leave my side.'

Lady Jane Grey, now almost eleven, was mature for her age, quiet and scholarly and devoted to the Queen. She was never far from the Queen's side, and raised her eyes now at the sound of her name, and quickly looked down again.

'Your Grace, I assure you—' Nanette began. 'If you wish it, I will stay—there is no need—'

But Katherine shook her head irritably. 'Tush, Nan, go if you will. It makes no difference to me.'

In that she spoke no more than the truth. Since her discovery of the Admiral's perfidy, she had drawn in on herself, grown moody and irritable. Nanette trusted it was partly the strain of pregnancy and that she would recover her usual spirits once the baby was born. For the time being, however, the worst thing was to argue with her. Nanette curtseyed and left her.

She travelled home through Kenilworth and Coventry and Leicester and Nottingham, her spirits rising at every mile she travelled further north, for though she had spent so many years of her life in the south, she was still a northerner at heart, and reaching Morland Place was most truly coming home. The house was quiet, its occupants still in mourning for Eleanor whose short life—she was only twenty-five—had been such a quiet backwater. She was buried at Holy Trinity, the chapel at Morland Place being still in ruins.

'I do not know when I shall be able to begin rebuilding it,' Paul told Nanette. 'Since the repealing of the heresy laws, the reformists have been growing bolder. We have to be careful what we do and say.'

Nanette was surprised. 'I should have thought that you were safe enough here,' she said. 'One expects the north to be more conservative than the south, and the Queen still holds mass twice a day. I don't believe the Protector cares for Protestantism.'

'No—I think you are right, and I trust Hertford,' Paul said, forgetting the Protector's new title. 'But how long will he hold back those wolves of his? Dudley, now—there's an ambitious man. And the merchant folk are behind him. I've heard John Butts talk—it is always the merchants who bring in the new ideas, and once you have let the wolf in over your doorstep, you cannot keep his muzzle out of your dish.'

'The wolf in this case being the Protestants?' Nanette said. 'Well, you may be right at that. Paul—your grandfather—said much the same. But why should Dudley, even if he gains power, favour the reformists?'

'For the simple reason, dear aunt, that a discontented group confers power on the man who offers to redress their ills. Dudley cannot expect the people who are contented with Hertford to help him take over as Protector.'

Nanette saw the force of this. 'Well,' she said comfortingly, 'the Seymours are a strong clan. Perhaps they will not fall.'

Paul shook his head. 'Dudley will find a crack in their armour, and if I am not mistaken, the crack will be that Admiral of yours. There's a rash man, for you, and a foolish one. Is it true, what we hear about him and the Lady Elizabeth?'

'I don't know what you hear,' Nanette said stiffly, 'but I would think it is no more than idle gossip.'

Paul smiled. 'She defends her cub. Much flirting, some indecorous behaviour—I set aside the wilder rumours, that the Princess is with child by the Admiral.'

'For shame!' Nanette cried.

'I said, I set them aside. But there must be some substance in it.'

'It was harmless play, that's all,' Nanette said. 'A little morrissing that might happen in any home between father and daughter. The Queen was present—she knew all about it. I wish you would not let scandal be repeated in your hearing.'

'I shall quash it whenever I hear it,' Paul said. 'But I fear, all the same, that the Admiral will be the downfall of his brother. And then—then we shall have rapine indeed. Dudley comes of an attainted line—his hunger for power will be the more voracious for having so much ground to make up. No, aunt, I think the chapel will not be restored just yet. We must wait for kinder times. What think you of my wife? Does she not grow more fair with every year that passes?'

'She looks very well indeed,' Nanette agreed. 'Pregnancy seems to suit her.'

'She has a fair belly,' Paul said proudly. 'And have you seen the boy? There never was such a child, for size or health or intelligence.'

'I think he will take after his great-grandfather, if he continues to grow at such a pace,' Nanette said. 'He stood at six feet and a handspan more, you know.'

'I know it,' Paul said ruefully, looking down at himself. He was a foot smaller than his grandsire's fabled length. 'He does not take after me, it seems.'

'You are a good height for a man,' Nanette said soothingly. 'Too many giants in one family would be uncomfortable.'

Paul smiled and took Nanette's hand and kissed it. 'It is good to have you here again,' he said. 'I wish you would come home for good, make your home here with us.'

'Perhaps I may, one day soon,' Nanette said. 'I am weary of Court life, I admit.'

'I would like you here for your own sake as well as mine,' Paul said. 'I fear trouble from the south. When the King died—we all knew how it would be. For the moment it is quiet, but quiet cannot last long with a boy-king, and two female heirs. If he should die—which God forfend—what then? Aunt, come home and be safe, I beg you.'

'You speak like a northerner,' Nanette said lightly, 'who thinks all bad things come out of the south. You may be right, however. But would you want me here? I would add greatly to the cost of your Household, you know.'

'You would be of more value than cost,' Paul said. 'Elizabeth—does not find it comes easily to her, to manage the house.' It was difficult for him to speak without criticising his wife, which he had no wish to do. Nanette nodded quickly.

'It is a hard task for one not used to it,' she said. 'It was part of my upbringing, to observe how things were done, especially at Kendal. Maud Parr was an example to all womankind of the proper ordering of a household. Well, if that is how you see it, perhaps I will come home. At the end of the year it should be possible.'

'Why not stay now? Do you have to go back at all?'

Nanette thought of Katherine's dismissal of her. The form of the words freed her, she need never go back if she were to regard them. But there was more than a form of words to be considered. If she did not go back, she would be guilty of unfaithfulness to her friend and mistress. And besides, she would want to be there when Katherine's time came.

'Yes, I have to go back,' she said. 'But by the end of the year, I should be free.'

'You know your own circumstances better that I can,' Paul said. 'I take your word for it. But know that you will be welcome whenever you want to return home.'

It was a pleasant stay. The weather was fine, and she had some good hunting, and renewed her relations with her cousins of both generations. The young heir of Morland Place was a fine, bonny child, and had he not been possessed of a sweet nature and gentle temper, it was likely he would have been spoiled by too much petting, for his mother and nurses idolised him, and his cousins were for ever in the nursery playing with him, more as if he were a poupee than a live creature. Faith and Hope, at least, were subjects of his charm. Charity declared herself to prefer dogs, and was hardly ever to be torn away from the kennels. She got under the kennelman's feet, but knew more about the breeding, lineage, properties and diet of Paul's famous hounds than anyone except the kennelman and Paul himself.

Nanette saw little of James while she was in Yorkshire, for he was in deep mourning still, and was not able to join the various parties until Nanette's visit was almost finished. He looked older and greyer, and Nanette felt pity for him, that once again he had lost a young wife who had left him childless. It seemed that he was doomed to leave no heir. He had not married Eleanor for love, but he had been kind to her, and it was plain from his demeanour that he had grown to love her, perhaps drawn to her in some sort by her illness, for he was a man who would be gentle with sick creatures. They hunted once or twice together before Nanette went back to Gloucestershire, and Nanette did her best to amuse him and draw him from his sadness.

She did not forget while she was at home to pay a visit to the smith's house, and in fact once having paid the first visit was there very often, for the child was growing up in a very satisfactory way. The Bear-cub was now six-and-a-half, tall for his age, a wiry, brown-skinned boy, very lively and supple, with a shock of black curly hair and those astonishing dark blue eyes. He was doing well at his lessons, Nanette was told, and when she questioned him she found she had a quick and reten-tive mind. He was beginning to learn Latin, Greek and Spanish at school now, and already had a fair grasp of French. He had outstripped his foster-brothers, and it was evident that he felt himself to be different from them.

'We have not told him the truth of his birth, Madam,' Mary said, 'as you requested. He knows, of course, that he is not our son. You, we have told him, are his benefactress, but it's my belief he begins to suspect you are his real mother. He has a quick mind, and is bound to wonder about things, you know.'

'Has he asked you such a question? Or said anything to make you suppose his fancy tends that way?' Nanette asked her.

'Nothing I could be definite about, Madam, but since you have been here I have seen him watching you in a way that—well, I don't know how to describe it, but his eyes follow you. He has asked about you, who you are and so on, but I have not told him anything. But after all, he does look quite a lot like you, Madam—the family resemblance, I suppose, but really, if I did not know better, I could suppose him your own child.'

Nanette had never considered that before, but his resemblance to his mother made him superficially like herself. Paul had remarked on the similarity of looks between Nanette and Elizabeth, and Nanette had noted with pain how like Paul Adrian had been. If the child, therefore, looked like his parents, he would also look very much like a child of Nanette and Paul. Had they had a son, he might have been very like Jan. The idea, once planted in her brain, took root, and was one of the reasons she went more often to the cottage than she had intended. Matthew, the only servant she trusted to accompany her, must have wondered something along the same lines, but he was too well-trained to wonder aloud. Nanette, gaining the child's affection quickly and easily, took him out riding once or twice, liking to talk to him, glad to see that he had a natural seat on a horse, managed the animal like a gentleman, and had his grandfather's sensitive hands. A friendship grew up between

Nanette and Jan that she knew she would find it hard to break off. Another reason, then, for coming home.

He asked her one day about himself, one day when they had drawn rein at the top of a hill and were looking down over the valley below. Nanette had been pointing out to him the extent of the Morland lands and the divisions between various properties.

'Are any of them yours, Madam?' he asked her. Nanette smiled and shook her head.

'No, I own no land. One of the estates should have been mine, but it was withheld from me by an accident.'

'What accident?'

'I think you are too young to understand it,' Nanette said judiciously. He accepted this, and asked eagerly, 'Which estate was it? Can you see it from here?'

Nanette looked. 'Some of it. You can see the house, at any rate. You see down there, the lake with the willows round it?'

'Yes, I see.'

'Well, behind the willows you can just see the chimneys of the house. That is Watermill House. The land spreads to the south-east. You cannot see it from here.'

'Who lives there now? Is it a nice place?' Jan asked, his eyes fixed on it.

'It is a small house, but comfortable. Warm, and with a pleasant aspect. From the solar you can look over the lake, where the swans swim.'

Jan smiled up at her. 'It sounds a good place. I should like to see it.'

'Perhaps you will some day,' Nanette said, and she thought that it might be possible one day to re-introduce the child to society. Perhaps Paul would help—but no, how could he, without injuring Elizabeth? Her face must have reflected her sadness, for Jan said,

'Does it make you sad that you do not have the house?'

'No—not really. Well, yes, in a way, I suppose it does, but it was not that I was thinking of.'

'What makes you sad, then, Madam? Is it something to do with me?'

She looked down at him sharply. Was that merely a guess, or did this child with the far-seeing eyes have some power nearer the mother's side?

'Yes, it was to do with you,' she said. His face grew very still, as if he was afraid of disturbing something rare and important, and he spoke almost in a whisper.

'Are you my mother?'

Tenderness surged through her. 'No, child, I am not your mother.'

'But you know.'

'Yes, I know.'

'Will you not tell me?'

'Not now,' Nanette said. 'Perhaps never. I don't know. If it is ever possible, if it is ever necessary—if, even, when you reach a man's years it will do you no harm to know, I will tell you. But not now. Do not ask me again.'

Jan turned his head away from her, but not before she had seen the shine of tears in his eyes. He looked out over the land, towards the distant lake with its willow-trees, and Nanette did not speak, allowing him his dignity. Then, when she judged he had recovered himself, she said, 'Come, Bear-cub, we must go back.'

He turned his horse obediently and followed her. In a moment he said, 'Why do you call me Bear-cub?'

Nanette smiled. 'That also I may tell you one day.'

'But not now,' he finished for her, and sighed. 'I wish I were a man. There are so many things I want to know.'

'Time passes quickly enough,' Nanette said. 'Don't wish your life away. One day you may wish these years back.'

But Jan looked unconvinced.

Nanette was back at Sudeley Castle by the beginning of August, and found the Queen Dowager in better spirits, with her husband in attendance and shewing her great affection, talking of the son she was to have and all the wealth and fortune that would attend his life. The Admiral had had his fortune told recently, and had been promised 'a great sort of sons', and the prophesy pleased both him and his wife.

The lying-in chambers had been fitted out with as much splendour and luxury as if it was the King's child she was to bear, and not the Admiral's. The walls were hung with costly tapestries, the beds hung with scarlet silk and taffeta, the ewers and basins all of gold, the chairs covered with cloth-of-gold, and a splendid collection of furniture and plate set aside for the expected infant. Because of her high station, the Queen was to be attended by a doctor, Robert Huick, as well as the midwives, and her chaplain, John Parkhurst, was to be close at hand for the spiritual refreshment of the Queen.

Katherine went into labour at last on the thirtieth of August, a week past the time the babe was expected. Nanette was in the chamber with her, and remembered the last time she had attended a Queen in childbirth. Though Katherine's labour was not as hard or as long as Queen Anne's had been, the occasion had its similarities: the long-awaited, confidently expected child was a girl, born late in the evening.

Katherine, on learning the sex of her child, did not seem much troubled. She was exhausted by her labour, a hard thing for a woman of her age, and turned her head away from the baby without interest. It was a beautiful child, however, and the Admiral, when the baby was placed in his arms, cried out that she was the prettiest babe he had ever seen, and he would not exchange her for a hundred sons. He despatched a bragging message to his brother at Sion House immediately, and called the chaplain in to baptise the child, though she seemed in perfect health and like to live. The name chosen was Mary.

Katherine seemed much recovered the next day, was able to sit up in bed and take nourishment, and talk to her husband, who sat beside her most of the day holding her hand and predicting a wonderful future for little Mary Seymour.

'Who should be good enough to marry her, except a prince?' was the theme of much of his talk. She would be a very rich young woman, even allowing for the multitude of brothers she was to acquire. Her exceptional beauty, her parentage, and her wealth, would make her a fit consort for a prince. He did not mention King Edward, but the thought was evidently in his mind, for he said at one point, 'Eleven years—he could well wait. Eleven years between them is not much.'

On the following day, the Admiral continued to bear his wife company, and in the intervals of amusing her he walked about the room with his daughter in his arms, in a way that reminded Nanette inevitably of the late King. He was tall and heavy-built and bluff, as the King had been, and the King had walked up and down with Princess Elizabeth in just that way. It made Nanette shiver, and pray for better fortune for this youngling. But her dislike of the Admiral softened somewhat, for it was a goodly thing in a man, to love his daughter so much, and he was truly attentive and affectionate towards his wife.

On the second of September the reply came from Thomas's brother, a postscript added to a letter already written, congratulating him and the Queen on the birth of their daughter, and perhaps a little wryly on the expected birth of the 'great sort' of good sons in the future. Thomas read it to his wife jubilantly. She smiled, but distractedly. She was a little feverish and restless, and after a while Lady Tyrwhitt, the senior lady of the bedchamber, drove him away saying that the Queen needed to rest. On the following day the Queen's temperature was much raised, and it seemed sure that she had a fever. Nanette went to John Parkhurst and prayed with him most urgently that the fever might be nothing serious, and not the terrible childbed-fever which carried off so many mothers.

On the fourth of September the Queen was worse, feverish and delirious, and towards the evening Huick shook his head and pronounced her to be weakening.

'I do not think she can live,' he told Lady Tyrwhitt. 'It would be wise for her to be prepared for the worst.'

Nanette heard the words only half comprehendingly. It had happened so suddenly, she could not properly believe it. Lady Tyrwhitt, too, seemed unable to accept the doctor's word.

'Not yet,' she said. 'Let her sleep tonight. Tomorrow she may wake well. It was a hard labour for her—she is only tired.'

But she did not wake refreshed, and the next day seemed much weaker. The Admiral came in in the morning and sat with her for some time, holding her hand and talking to her soothingly, until Lady Tyrwhitt drove him out so that the doctor and chaplain could speak to her and apprise her of her serious condition. She was too weak to make her Will, and so Nanette wrote it down to her dictation, and the doctor and chaplain witnessed that it was the Queen's nuncupative Will that she left everything to her husband, from the depths of her love.

'She does not mention the child,' Nanette said to Lady Tyrwhitt in a whisper. Lady Tyrwhitt shook her grey head.

'It is often so,' she replied softly. 'I have seen women before in the grip of the childbed-fever. It seems God blots out from them the knowledge of what has caused their condition. Perhaps it is to make it easier for them to leave life, for it they remembered the child, they would be grieved.'

'But should she not be reminded?' Nanette asked. The other lady shook her head.

'The Admiral will care for the child, never fear. Parkhurst, do you take care of the document. And now, if you will, bid the Admiral to come back. I think Her Grace would take comfort from him.'

As the day wore on, the Queen grew more restless and at times fell into delirium, crying out that she was ill-used, and had been neglected. The Admiral did not leave her side, but soothed and petted her, though at times she muttered and raved against him and tried to push him away. It was terrible to see Katherine brought so low, to hear her hoarse, angry voice, to see her at other times twist her head from side to side on the pillow, seeking hopelessly to escape the pain that filled her body.

Lady Jane Grey, Lady Tyrwhitt, and Nanette between them kept watch in the chamber, one of them always being present, frequently more. The Queen lingered two days more, growing weaker and feebler in her mind, long periods of unconsciousness succeeding fits of restless babbling, and towards sunrise on the seventh of September she died. Even though they had been prepared for the event, her women were stunned and grief-stricken, and it was a long time before they were able to rouse themselves to perform their appointed tasks. The Admiral shewed all the instability of his character in a paroxysm of grief, and was unable to attend the funeral, which took place the next day in the chapel. Jane Grey took his place as chief mourner; in her way, she had regarded Katherine as a mother, and indeed the Queen had been more motherly towards her than her natural mother, the Marchioness of Dorset, had ever been.

For two days the household was gripped in a silence of grief that was like death; and then the lord Admiral stirred himself, began to write letters, and emerged from his chamber for long enough to announce he was breaking up the Queen's Household.

'Those of you who have homes to go to—Mistress Neville, you, for instance, and Mistress Morland—may go as soon as you like. I shall send you home, Jane, as soon as your father will have you fetched. Lady Tyrwhitt, you will stay and look after the bairn, I suppose. For the rest—I shall find you places. The Queen left no bequests, but I shall see you placed.'

And abruptly he turned and went back to his private rooms. Tearfully the women prepared for the leavetaking.

'Don't go just yet,' Lady Tyrwhitt said to Nanette. 'I shall have need of ladies for the child's establishment. And he may change his mind. Stay a little.'

But Nanette had nothing to stay for. 'I always meant to ask her for leave to go home,' she said. 'I came back for the birth of the child, but after that I meant to go. I am weary for home—can you understand that?'

'Of course I can,' said the other. 'You are fortunate to have a home to go to, and I wish you good fortune in it. It is a sad business, but we cannot question God's will. She was a righteous woman, and He will want her by Him.'

'I have known her all my life,' Nanette said. 'We grew up together. I can't believe she is dead. Hers was such a strange life—I wish I could comprehend—but you are right. God's ways are mysterious, but we cannot question them. I shall be glad to go home, at any rate.'

'You will not look for another place? You have been at Court, I think, a long time.'

'There is no place at Court for me,' Nanette said.

'The Lady Mary would be glad to have you, I imagine. And there are other places—'

'No, I thank you. For me there is only one place now,' Nanette smiled. Lady Tyrwhitt cocked her head like a wise bird.

'I have a feeling, Mistress Nan, that you will grow tired of doing nothing. And if that day should come, and I can be of any help to you—'

'I will remember,' Nanette said.

Thirty

ANETTE OFTEN THOUGHT OF LADY TYRWHITT'S WORDS IN the months that followed, thought of them at first with a wry amusement, for as soon as she arrived at Morland Place Elizabeth gave over the running of the household to her with a sigh of relief. There was an excuse for it, for she was very near her time, but after the birth of her child—a daughter whom they named Lettice—she did not resume the reins of management, but left them in Nanette's hands.

There was enough to do then, even in the quiet season of winter, and it was fortunate that Nanette had the experience behind her from the years when she acted as housekeeper to Amyas. Her days were busy and her nights quiet, and yet as the spring of 1549 arrived to release them from the prison of the house and the salt-meat diet, she began to feel restless and unfulfilled, even—Lady Tyrwhitt was right—bored.

The boredom stemmed from a lack of purpose, of direction. Her occupations were leading nowhere. She had thought that she would be glad to settle into old age, would relish the quiet and uneventful life away from Court, but instead she longed for news from the south, and found excuses a-plenty to go into the city to the house on the Lendal where the news came first. She became a familiar sight, picking her way through the

Mickle Lith on her bay palfrey, accompanied by Audrey and Matthew, and followed by the three white greyhounds—for she had taken charge of the late Queen's two dogs, Shem and Japeth, out of pity for them, when it became plain that no-one else would care for them.

She made a pretty enough sight in her fashionable clothes, cut in the Italian style, with the high Medici collar and huge puffed sleeves. She wore black, mostly, or dark blue, velvet trimmed with fur, and she had taken to wearing soft velvet bonnets with long trailing feathers, rather than the old-fashioned head-dresses which were so heavy and uncomfortable. The guards on the gate all knew her, and greeted her with smiles, remarking in audible voices on her prettiness when she had passed. The beggars too called out blessings, for she rarely passed without something to drop into their cups.

Audrey and Matthew were always happy to go into the city, Matthew because he liked to gossip with the Butts servants, who always had some spicy titbit to relate, and Audrey because she was in love with one of the Butts footmen, and was hoping to bring him to the point of marriage. Nanette's sisters always made her welcome, and after exchanging greetings and news of the health of the various members of the family, there would be a slight pause before Nanette asked with an air of suppressed eagerness, 'Well? What news?'

The main news during the winter months concerned her old master. The lord Admiral had changed his mind about breaking up the Queen's household only a week or two after Nanette had left. He had written to my lord of Dorset asking for Jane Grey to be left in his charge, and had confirmed the appointments of all the members of the household who had not left. It had been supposed at first that he did this to provide a retinue for his infant daughter, but before the year ended there were rumours of a more serious nature—that he was intending to marry the Lady Elizabeth, with or without the Council's approval, and that the establishment was for her.

In mid-January Dudley, glad to have the means of striking at his rival Somerset, had Thomas arrested and sent to the Tower for plotting to seize the throne for the Lady Elizabeth, with whom he intended to rule as her husband. It was a ridiculous notion, but the Admiral's reputation as a wild man made it just credible. Elizabeth was placed under house arrest and her servants—particularly Kat Champernowne—were questioned. Bit by bit over the next few weeks the story came out of the romps the Admiral had had with Elizabeth under the protective eye of the late Queen. Elizabeth, faced with the confession of her servants, admitted the truth of the stories, but denied she had ever intended to marry Seymour, or seize the throne.

There was no evidence against her, and so nothing more was done than to place her under a gentlemanly restraint that amounted to imprisonment in her house at Hatfield. Thomas Seymour was less lucky and on March the twentieth paid the price of his folly with his head.

All Seymour's goods and estates were seized by the Council on his execution, and thus it was that Mary Seymour, who was known as 'the Queen's child', lost before she was a year old both her parents and all her inheritance. She should have been the richest heiress in the land, but instead she was sent with a small household and a little plate and furniture first to her uncle Somerset at Sion, and then to the charge of her mother's old friend Katherine Willoughby, the dowager Duchess of Suffolk.

Lady Suffolk received the charge unwillingly, and before the child had been with her a month was complaining of the expense of keeping her, and had dismissed all the baby's servants but two. Nanette heard all these stories with great sadness, and could be glad only that Katherine had died before she had to discover the true worthlessness of her husband, and that she did not witness the fate of her longed-for child.

Other news from the south was worrying. Somerset was pressing on with his religious reforms, and Cranmer's English prayer-book was established by law, and was the only one which might be used in Churches. The form of the church service was also laid down, and though it was closer to the Catholic service of King Henry than the Protestant service, it alarmed the people of the north.

'It is but the first stage,' Nanette said to her sisters.

'I thought that you said my lord Somerset is a moderate man, and dislikes Protestants,' Catherine said.

'He does—but there are those who will push him, and he will yield little by little.'

'Though it is said he has permitted the Lady Mary to have the old form of Mass said in her household,' Jane added. 'Perhaps he will be contented to leave well alone, when it comes to private houses.'

Nanette smiled. 'If you are thinking we may yet have the mass at Morland Place as we did before, you will be disappointed, dear sister. The Lady Mary is heir to the throne until the King marries and has a child. Somerset is wise not to antagonise her. The King may die young—though he is a strong healthy boy, life is always uncertain—and then the Protector who treated the Lady Mary with respect may find himself in a high position on her Council, despite his reformist leanings.'

Catherine looked puzzled.

'But if that is the way he thinks, then surely he won't force the country to accept too many changes in the mass?'

'*He* would not,' Nanette said, 'but he will not long keep power. He is too gentle, too scrupulous. He is, I believe, a good man, and the times do not favour good men. No, Dudley has removed one Seymour, and he will remove the other before long. And then—'

'Remove the King's uncle?' Jane said.

'The King is little more than a prisoner, Jane. He will not be able to protect Somerset when the time comes. King Edward is no King Henry—and even King Henry had to throw a scrap to his pack every now and then. Look how he gave them Cromwell, whom he loved.'

There was a silence while they thought of this. Nanette sighed.

'I'm afraid there are bad times to come. We must hold fast, and pray, and trust in God. Our best hope is the Lady Mary. Perhaps Amyas was not so wrong when he wanted to seize the north.'

As the summer wore on, Nanette's pessimistic views were born out by events. Prices were again rising steeply, the coinage had been devalued again, foreign traders were becoming wary of accepting English gold for anything, and the number of the unemployed was rising to a level where they began to roam the countryside in bands, getting a living by robbery. The poor laws provided for indigents who came within the towns to be provided with work, food and lodgings, to pay for which a rate was levied from the town residents, but out in the country there was no control, and workmen who had been turned off because their masters could no longer afford to pay their wages might wander without ever coming within the scope of the law.

In September, at the same time as Elizabeth, who had conceived again immediately, gave birth to her third child, a daughter they named Jane, a rebellion broke out in Norfolk. Like the Pilgrimage of Grace it was an uneasy union of workers and gentry, the gentry complaining about taxes and the farm workers about enclosures which had put them out of work. It was ruthlessly crushed by Dudley, who, while he still had the army at his heels, then made his bid for power. Somerset fled with his nephew the King to Windsor, but Dudley pursued him there, captured him, and sent him to the Tower, while he escorted the King back to Hampton Court. And so by the ninth of October, Dudley was in sole charge, King in all but name.

The news was still fresh enough to be discussed when Elizabeth came down from the birth-chamber for the first time and the family had a celebration dinner for the occasion. Even Ezekiel was there, and it was the first time that Nanette had seen him in many years, for he had always been away when she paid her visits home; all the Butts family were there; and Nanette found herself sitting next to James, to her pleasure, for she found him very conversable.

'So you were right, sister,' Jane said when the first course was on the table. 'Dudley has taken over, even as you said he would.'

'I assure you it gives me no pleasure to be right. But one only had to know the man—'

'One only had to know his father,' Ezekiel said. 'They are a pushing family, to rise from attainder to power in one generation.'

'And now you think we shall have more Protestant legislation,' Catherine said.

'There cannot be any doubt of it,' Paul answered for Nanette, and she went on, 'What worries me most now is the threat to the Lady Mary. She was forced to accept her father's religion, and with Queen Katherine's teaching she came to love it. But she will not accept the Protestant dogma, the denial of the sacrifice of the mass, and that will give Dudley just the weapon he needs against her.'

'Against her?'

'She is his most dangerous enemy,' Paul said quietly. 'Though she would never harm him of her own will, yet all those who hate Dudley must look to her as their leader.'

'All who hate Dudley may not be Catholics,' Jane pointed out.

'It does not need that,' Paul said.

'I understand you,' James came in. 'You mean that the alternative to Dudley, ruling as jailor of the King, is Mary as Queen, ruling in her own right.'

'Exactly so.' Paul looked around the faces at his table. 'He will kill her if he can.'

'He cannot kill the Lady Mary, the King's daughter!' Catherine cried, shocked.

'He can,' Paul said, and they knew it was true.

'It would be best, perhaps, if she could get out of the country—go to Spain, to her relatives. And then, in time—' James began, but Nanette shook her head and said quickly,

'No, no, she must not go. Once she leaves the country, she will never come back. She would lose the love of the people if she came back as a conqueror with Spanish troops at her heels.'

'But if she stays—' Catherine said.

'I don't know,' Nanette said. 'I don't know what she can do. We can only hope and pray—pray that God guides her through this difficult time. It cannot last for ever. No tyrant ever does. Dudley is as mortal as the rest of us.'

'Aye, mortal he may be, but while he lives—' Paul did not need to finish the sentence. They could all imagine the consequences. Elizabeth shivered suddenly. She had taken no part in the conversation, and now she said,

'This is gloomy talk for my rising. Let us talk of other things. After all, we are a long way from London. The Morlands will survive, come what will. Let us have some music, or the tumblers. I do not like this kind of talk.'

'You are right, Elizabeth,' Paul said, always eager to please his wife. 'We'll have the tumblers in, to make us laugh.'

And he gave a sign to his steward, and the man sent to fetch in the troupe who had been hired for the occasion. They were not gypsies, as was usual, but a family who lived in the city permanently and got their living by tumbling at every feast and fair in York and the surrounding villages. Everyone had seen their act a hundred times, but no celebration would have seemed complete without them.

When the meal was over, the nap had been drawn, and the broken meats taken out to the gates for the poor and the beggars, the family settled down in the great hall for singing and music, and after a while Nanette, feeling the need for a breath of air, got up and slipped quietly out into the herb garden, into what was sometimes called Eleanor's Walk, and wandered there, smelling the sweet pungent odour of the herbs and the cool, grassy smell of the air. She had walked here sometimes with Paul during the few happy months of their marriage, and it gave her a sense of peace. The three dogs pattered after her, sniffing at the evening smells and snapping after moths that alighted on the grass borders, and after taking a few turns she sat down on the stone bench at the centre and looked up at the darkling sky.

It had been a warm, sunny day, and the sky was clear. It would cool quickly after sundown, and there would be a frost probably, the first of the winter. The year was dying, and soon the prison doors of winter would close behind them. Another year gone, and Nanette was forty-one years old, and she wondered what the next year would bring, what she had to look forward to. The restlessness had not abated. There was an emptiness inside her, a place that needed to be filled, and yet she did not know how to fill it, what to do to ease the ache of her limbs. She tried to think of Paul, but he seemed far away: it was thirteen years since he had died, and it seemed like a lifetime ago.

She was roused from her reverie after she did not know how long to find James standing before her, blocking out the sky. She rubbed her hands over her eyes, bewildered—she had been so far away, she might have been asleep.

'Did you speak?' she asked. 'I'm sorry—I was in a dream.'

'So it seemed. No, I didn't speak. I wondered why you had been so long away, so I came to find you. The hall is dull without you.'

She smiled, and quoted, 'Elyng is the hall, there the lord and lady liketh nought to sit.' It was a line from Piers the Plowman.

'Laugh if you will, but it's true. May I sit with you a while?'

'With all my heart,' Nanette said, and made room for him on the bench. He sat beside her, and she looked at him with admiration, thinking how handsome he was and how elegant. He, like her, took great pride in dressing with the fashion. As if he had read her thought, he said, 'We make a fine couple, don't we, cousin Nan? A gentleman and a lady of fashion.'

'That we do.'

'So much so, that I could wish we might be a couple all the time.' He was not looking at her, but up at the sky, and she turned her face away too. After a moment he said, 'You give me no answer?'

'I did not know you had asked me a question, cousin.'

'You did, Nan, you did. I asked it long ago, and more than once, and each time you gave me only half an answer. Well, I'll ask you once more, for I do not know of any reason why you should not say yes. Mistress Anne Morland, I offer you my hand and my heart and my home. More than that now, I offer you that which should have been yours long ago, together with that which has been yours for longer than you know.'

'You speak in riddles, cousin,' Nanette said. She did not know what to answer, not having been prepared for this. 'I thought the last time, when you wed my niece—I thought then—'

'Whatever you thought then, think now afresh, Nan. Will you have me? I can offer you an establishment of your own, where you may be mistress in name as well as in deed. I can offer you the condition of life you deserve, as a gentleman's daughter. What do you say, Nan?'

'James, cousin, have you considered?—I am over forty, it is not likely that I can have children, and you have no son. Have you considered that?'

His face had been turned towards her eagerly, and now it grew serious, and he stood up and paced up and down the path in front of her, so that she had to turn her head this way then that to follow him.

'I have thought of it. When I asked you the last time, I told you that I could not wait, that I must marry and have a son. So I married Eleanor, God rest her poor soul, and though I grew to love her in time, yet she was never a wife to me, more a child, a sickly child that I must nurse; and God sent me no son, no child at all. I have been lonely, Nan, lonely, and I have grown to value other things more than sons.'

He stopped, and feeling he wished to be prompted she said, 'What things?'

He turned towards her and stood still, looking down into her upturned face as a man in reflective mood looks into a still pool, seeing and unseeing.

'Nan,' he said, 'do you remember the first time we ever met? No, I don't suppose you do—there was nothing for you to remember about it.'

'I do remember,' she said. He went on as if she hadn't spoken.

'But I remember. I had come to Morland Place to wed your cousin Margaret, and you came down from upstairs to be introduced. You came up to me to give your curtsey and you looked up at me without interest as a child looks at an adult, as if to say "There is nothing here that I need attend to". But there your eyes stopped, and you stared at me with such an expression, Nan, of wonder and surprise, as if you had recognised me from long, long ago; a frank, and puzzled, and innocent stare. And I loved you at that moment. I had recognised you, too, in some way I did not understand. I loved you from that moment onwards, though I married your cousin and then your niece, with all my heart. And I still do.'

Nanette stared at him, her mouth dry. 'But—James—you know that I loved Paul—'

She got no further. He hunkered down in front of her and took up her hand from her lap and held it in both his, against his chest.

'Love is not a closed circle, Nan, to be gone over and over, never to be broken. That you loved Paul only means that you know how to love. You were formed for loving, to love and be loved. You knew me once, before you turned your eyes away from me. You knew me then, that first day, as a person you could love—that was what you recognised, and if you look into your heart you will know me again. Nan, say yes, say you will marry me.'

She stared at him, troubled, wondering how to answer, how to be worth what he offered her, how not to punish him either by her refusal or, worse, by her acceptance; and then it came to her in a great light, everything falling into place in her mind with such an inevitability that she wondered how she could not have noticed before that the pieces fitted so exactly.

'James,' she said, 'there is a child—a child I am responsible for. I pay for his upbringing, and though I am not his mother, I love him like a mother. He is a fine, good boy, well grown and forward, of great beauty and intelligence. If we adopted him, you would have the son you longed for, to bear your name, and inherit your estate. And though he would not be of your blood—'

'If you want it so, Nan, then let it be so. But say, first, that you will have me.'

'I will marry you, James, and right gladly.'

'Oh my darling—God bless you.' He pressed his lips to her hand, and then as her eyes met his and gave him his answer, he drew her gently to him, and placed his mouth over hers. It was long, long since she had kissed a man, but it did not seem strange. *He* was not strange to her; the taste of him was familiar, and her body trembled as to a touch it knew and acknowledged. After a long time he lifted his head from hers and looked down at her tenderly.

'It will be all right,' he said.

'Yes,' Nanette said. 'It will all be all right.'

The next day they went to the smith's cottage to see the boy and to tell him the news. Jan greeted Nanette with both respect and affection, and though he looked curiously at the gentleman of fashion who accompanied her, he minded his manners and said nothing.

'Jan, will you walk with us up to the top of the rise? I have something to say to you.'

'Of course, Madam,' Jan said. When they reached the seclusion of the hill crest, they stopped, and Nanette turned to face Jan.

'Do you remember, Bear-cub, when I pointed out to you the house by the lake?'

'Yes, Madam—of course. But—'

Nanette's cautioned him to listen in silence. 'This gentleman is the owner of it. Watermill House and its estates belong to him. He is James Chapham, and he is a merchant of the city of York.'

'Your servant, sir,' Jan said, bowing as his dancing-master had taught him. James bowed in return, his long, mobile face concealing a smile.

'Master Chapham has asked me to marry him, Jan, and I have accepted.'

There was a silence. Jan looked at her, the cool autumn wind lifting the crest of curls over his forehead, and his dark blue eyes were doubtful, as he wondered whether this would make any difference to him. At last Nanette said, 'Is there nothing you would say?'

'I—of course Madam—I—I wish you every good fortune—and you, sir—but—'

'But what, Bear-cub?'

At seven he was too young to be subtle, or to hide his true concern.

'Does it mean I shall not see you any more?' he blurted out. Nanette felt a pang of pity that his happiness should be so little secure, and he so young.

'No, Jan, no, quite the opposite, for if you would like it, we wish you to come and live with us at Watermill House.'

'If I like it?' Jan said, his astonished eyes going from one to the other. James no longer tried to conceal the smile.

'It is your choice, child,' Nan said, 'and if you would rather stay with Dick and Mary—'

'Oh—Madam—' he could not readily speak. James now spoke for the first time.

'Also, if you wish it, we would like to adopt you under the law as our son, so that you would inherit everything as if you were my son of my own flesh.'

Jan stared at him, and Nanette could see that he was not really taking it in. At last he said to her, 'Would it mean that I could call you Mother?'

Nanette's eyes filled with tears, and she put out her arms, and he ran to them, and she hugged him hard against her. 'Oh my darling, I should like nothing better,' she said. And when she released him, he turned to James, and after a moment's cautious survey of his face, he went and knelt to him, for his blessing, and over his bent head Nanette met James's eyes and they smiled their assent to each other.

Afterwards, when they were riding away, James said to her, 'Watermill should have been yours. I am glad it comes back to you, and glad that there will be someone to inherit it, though it be not a child of your body. He is a fine boy.'

'Yes, a fine boy,' Nanette said thoughtfully. James looked across at her abstracted face, and smiled to himself.

'If you had had a child, he might have inherited a great deal more—all of Morland Place, perhaps. Well, there is no questioning God's ways. And there is a kind of rightness, too, about this particular boy's inheriting, if not Morland Place, at least a part of it.'

Nanette's head jerked up. 'You know whose child he is?'

'I know whose child he is. Come, Nan, it was not hard to guess. But don't be afraid—nothing shall be said, and when he is ours, no-one will be able to take him from us, nor point the finger at him. He looks like you, you know. I don't know that I could like even a blood son of mine better.'

'You are a good man, James,' Nanette said gratefully. 'God will reward you.'

'He has rewarded me already,' James said.

The marriage was to take place at Morland Place on St Katherine's day, in the winter parlour just as Elizabeth's had done. The preparations were not in any way so extensive, for Nanette was a relatively unimportant member of the family, and the nuptials of a widow and widower were never as wildly celebrated as those of a young couple; but there was enough to do for Nanette to be glad to slip away from the bustle on the eve of the wedding to seek the solitude for a few moment's quiet reflection.

She headed first of all for the herb garden, but voices told her in time that there were others there before her—probably the cook and his assistant plucking those herbs that had to be gathered after dark, for tomorrow's feast. So she turned about and, after a moment's thought, walked along the passage to the scarred door of the chapel, and went inside. There was no moon, but there was enough starlight for her to pick her way towards the front of the chapel, and sit down on a fallen beam, with her back to the wall.

The sky was clear, and overhead was a canopy of stars instead of the roof, more stars than a man could count, crusted over the blackness of the night like sugar on the wet rim of a glass, giving a faint, blue-grey light that made everything seem strange, uncanny. As she tilted her head back to look up, she could see here and there jagged bites of darkness where the remaining roof-beams were silhouetted against the sky, and above the broken outer wall the lines of seeding yarrow and willowherb where the wild was pioneering the ruin. The sounds of the night came to her—rustlings and movements, sometimes the half-heard shriek of some small death, a distant dog barking. In the winter sometimes one heard wolves; in the summer the swallows would go on sweeting long after dark while the warm air was full of insects; now Nanette heard an owl cry, far off, and then nearer, and she shivered and crossed herself. Owls were unchancy things. The common folk thought they were harbingers of death, or else the dead themselves who would not sleep.

She pressed herself against the wall, and her hand, as it hung down by her side, caressed the smooth wall, and found with its finger tips the little carving of a bear which had always been there, ever since she remembered. She ran her fingers over it, and thought of Paul and of Jan, the Bear-cub. Paul had always been easier to find here, in the chapel, than elsewhere, and with the image of Jan in her mind she could visualise Paul more easily, forming him slowly out of the darkness, his height and breadth, his slow, dark eyes, his proud face, the curving, beautiful, sensuous lips. How true an image was it? She could not tell. Perhaps it was Jan she saw, a Jan projected into the future when he would have reached a man's years. Or perhaps it was Adrian. Or a mixture of all three.

But it comforted her, wherever it came from, that image. She had loved, and the love was not wasted. Paul's death was not wasted, nor his life, and he was as near as sleep to her, now and always, there in the dark world behind the eyelids. He had loved before, and could still love her; so she that had loved him could love James without betrayal. And there would be Jan—that was the best of it.

The pattern was worked out. She had a feeling both of finish and renewal, like coming home, a sense of completeness. The wheel had turned, the sin was expiated, the debt paid, and the pattern worked out which had begun so long ago with the woman she had never known, whose child's child Nanette would nurture and love. Paul lived again in this child, as love lived again in her and James. Nothing was wasted.

She sighed and stretched, knowing she must go back. There were things to be done, tomorrow and all the tomorrows to be taken care of, but she was loath to leave this place, a small piece of quiet peopled with the past. Hard times were coming, that was sure—but Elizabeth was right, the Morlands would survive, because of love, and because of faith: *Fidelitas*—the strength of the White Hare.

About the Author

Cynthia Harrod-Eagles won the Young Writers' Award with her first novel, *The Waiting Game*, and in 1992 won the Romantic Novel of the Year Award. She has written over fifty books, including twenty-eight volumes of the Morland Dynasty—a series she will be taking up to the present day. She is also creator of the acclaimed mystery series featuring Inspector Bill Slider.

She and her husband live in London and have three children. Apart from writing, her passions are music, wine, horses, architecture and the English countryside.

Visit the author's website http://www.cynthiaharrodeagles.com.

READING GROUP GUIDE

1. Paul repeatedly chooses Amyas, his firstborn and legal heir, over Adrian, his beloved son out of wedlock. Despite his love for him, Paul rejects Adrian again and again, telling him that it would not be fair to Amyas to house his son born of a mistress. To Paul, the dignity and integrity of the Morland name is more important than his love for his son. Do you think this devotion to protecting the family name is still prevalent in today's society? How would you handle Paul's situation?

2. Paul constantly cheats on his wife and treats her terribly. As a result, she accuses his mistress of witchcraft. Was she vengeful toward Ursula, or do you think she just wanted to hurt Paul? Do you think she was trying to save her marriage?

3. There is an implication of witchcraft floating around Ursula and her son Adrian. In addition to the obvious accusation made by Anne, there are several instances of conversation between Paul and Ursula in which a strange power is alluded to. In addition, the strange intensity of Adrian's eyes is mentioned. What role do you think witchcraft plays in this novel, if any?

4. When the Sweat descends upon England, Paul loses almost his entire family in a matter of weeks. How would you cope with such loss? Paul mourns especially for his half-brother Jack, shortly thereafter falling in love with Jack's daughter, Nanette. Does Paul and Nanette's mutual grieving bring them together, or do you think Paul's love for Nanette is tied to his love for Jack—that by loving Nanette, he can hold on to Jack?

5. After Ursula dies, Adrian is left in the care of Paul. However, since Paul already has a family, Adrian is brushed aside. He is stuck as a bastard child; he will never be able to escape the circumstances of his birth. He repeatedly asks for Paul's love and favor, but Paul repeatedly denies him. This rejection hardens his heart and he becomes a murderer and a rapist. Do you empathize for him at all, or do you think his wicked actions make him unworthy of such empathy?

6. Paul and Nanette fall in love despite the fact that she is his niece. Both of them try to resist their desire for one another, but eventually they succumb to it. Do you approve of this relationship? Does the fact that Nanette grew up apart from Paul make the relationship less inappropriate?

7. Tom Seymour flirts with his young niece and stepdaughter, Elizabeth. He behaves inappropriately with her and she responds to his advances. How is their relationship different from the relationship of Paul and Nanette?

8. Katherine Parr repeatedly joins in on Tom's pranks on Elizabeth, but it is not until she sees Tom trying to kiss Elizabeth that Katherine realizes Tom's true intentions.

Do you think Katherine had suspicions all along that Tom wanted Elizabeth, or was she in denial? Did she join in on the pranks to keep an eye on Tom, or do you think she hoped her involvement would deter his behavior? How would you react in her situation?

9. Anne Boleyn is represented as an angry, selfish, vengeful woman. She has a violent temper, resulting in two miscarriages and a stillborn child, and she demands more and more time of Nanette, refusing to release her even after she knows Nanette wants to go home and marry Paul. Do you feel sorry for Anne, or do you think she deserves her fate?

10. After witnessing Adrian rape her cousin, Nanette kills him by striking his head with a candlestick. When the resulting child of the rape is born, Nanette takes responsibility for finding him a home and providing for him. Years later, she adopts little Jan and remarks that he reminds her of Paul, being his grandson. Do you think it was important to Nanette that this child was a part of Paul, or do you think she would have taken the child even if he wasn't a direct heir?

11. The Morland chapel is a major focal point of the story. It is where Paul grieves for Adrian's mother, where Paul refuses Adrian's pleas to love him, where Adrian promises to kill Paul, where Adrian commits the rape. What about this chapel do you think makes it so central to the relationship between Paul and Adrian?

12. Several of the female characters wait several years to wed the men they love. Katherine Parr has to live through three

marriages with elderly men before she can finally marry her sweetheart, Tom Seymour; Anne Boleyn has to wait for Henry's divorce to be finalized before she can marry him; even Nanette, who has no Court-related bonds holding her back, longs for Paul for many years before she finally agrees to marry him. What do you make of these characters' patience? Do you respect them for it or do you think they should have been more assertive in their wants?

13. Amyas plans rebellion after rebellion, hoping each time to disable the Crown and reinstate the old ways of life. When he leaves with his two sons to carry out his final rebellion, a mob attacks Morland Place. Amyas's family and household, most of whom do not like or even respect him, are punished for his actions. How would it feel to live in a time when your family members' thoughts and actions bear so directly upon you? Does any semblance of this family blame still exist today? Have you ever experienced it?

14. By the time James marries Nanette, he has already lost two young wives, neither one of which bore him children. He knows that Nanette will not be able to bear him any children because of her age, but he marries her nonetheless, having waited several years for her. Paul also waited several years for Nanette, refusing to marry another. What qualities does Nanette possess that make her so worthy of these men's desire and patience? Are these the same qualities that are valued in women today?

15. The Morlands own land and run a successful business, yet both heads of household, Paul and Amyas, are discontented for the majority of the novel. Paul's happiness is confined to the few short months he spends as Nanette's husband, and

Amyas's happiness is shattered with the death of his wife. On the other side of town, the peasant family to whom Jan is sent seems happy with their lot, despite their modest income and humble dwelling. What is this novel trying to say about the pursuit of wealth, love, and happiness?

16. Uncle Richard makes a long journey to Morland Place in the dead of winter in order to die in his family home. Being close to his family in death is so important to him that he risks his feeble life to get it. Does Richard have an ulterior motive? Do you think he knew that Paul was struggling and needed his love and care?